CONTENTS

Copyright

In Time

Dedication

Prologue   1

Chapter one   3

Chapter two   22

Chapter Three   48

Chapter Four   59

Chapter Five   85

Chapter six   96

Chapter Seven   115

Chapter Eight   127

Chapter Nine   153

Chapter Ten   168

Chapter Eleven   183

Chapter Twelve   195

Chapter Thirteen   210

Chapter Fourteen   231

Chapter Fifteen   246

Chapter Sixteen   256

Chapter Seventeen   269

Chapter Eighteen	281
Chapter Nineteen	290
Chapter Twenty	303
Chapter Twenty One	313
Chapter Twenty Two	323
Chapter Twenty Three	334
Chapter Twenty Four	345
Chapter Twenty Five	356
Chapter Twenty Six	367
Chapter Twenty Seven	377
Chapter Twenty Eight	385
Chapter Twenty Nine	392
Chapter Thirty	405
Chapter Thirty One	418
Chapter Thirty Two	429
Chapter Thirty Three	437
Chapter Thirty Four	450
Chapter Thirty Five	464
Chapter Thirty Six	479
Chapter Thirty Seven	494
Chapter Thirty Eight	508
Chapter Thirty Nine	519
Chapter Forty	528
Epilogue	546
Acknowledgements	550
About the author	553

IN TIME

A Novel

By En Bee

For those of you who have loved and lost but still hold onto the hope of finding love again.

PROLOGUE

Christmas Eve, a few years ago

S he couldn't believe her eyes. Tom was kneeling in front of her on one knee, a black velvet ring box extended towards her in his right hand. The ring was beautiful, an emerald cut diamond flanked by two smaller diamonds in a platinum setting.

She looked into the depth of his eyes where anxiety and hope bloomed. As if standing on the millennium bridge in the frosty winter evening with the backdrops of the historic St Paul's cathedral on one side of the river Thames and the iconic Tate Modern art gallery on the other wasn't breathtaking enough, he'd pulled out this surprise.

She never would have seen this coming. She knew Tom loved her, he told her often and expressed it openly and passionately. But marriage? He always avoided that topic when their friends teased them about how they had been together so long they were like a married couple. That was the reason she never brought it up. He seemed so uncomfortable about it all. Talk about being sucker punched.

She was brought out of her shock seeing his sudden drop onto one knee on the frosty bridge and by the realisation that a crowd had started to gather around. They had attracted London's curious and hopeful bystanders.

"Alexa De Luca, will you do me the greatest honour and share your heart, your home and, most importantly, your bed with me for the rest of your life by consenting to being my wife?"

She looked down into those beautiful light brown eyes she knew so well, the brown hair lightly falling over one eye. A single tear of joy rolled down her cheek as she nodded and said the words he and everyone gathered there wanted to hear.

"Hell yes!" She squealed when he jumped up and grabbed her in a hug and whirled her around, both of them laughing as people cheered and whooped, some whistling as he kissed her winter chilled lips.

Gathering their wits about them, they thanked the well wishers and Tom placed the ring onto her ring finger. She pulled him close to her, placing her arms around his neck and whispered seductively.

"So, you want me to share my heart, my home and my bed huh?"

"Mmmhmm. Especially the bed..." He smiled sexily down at her.

"Well, I agree. As long as it's my bed that you share exclusively, no straying mister," she smiled, kissing the corner of his mouth.

"Baby, it's always going to be you, exclusively."

"Otherwise I'm going after your balls," she threatened, trying to hide the humour and look serious. He laughed and cupped her face in his hands.

"I bet baby. You have every right but it won't happen, I only want you. Always."

She smiled and spoke just as his lips covered hers.

"Always."

CHAPTER ONE

A moment of clarity

I could just see it, they were all going to laugh at me. Typical English girl wanting in on the American dream.

I scoffed at myself as I looked in the mirror in the hallway, hanging up my coat on the peg next to it. My light brown hair needed a cut, it was way too wild, hanging down to waist length. I tucked a loose strand behind my ears, nervous. My hazel eyes showed panic as I stared at my reflection. Today they were more green than brown, which was a sure sign of my anxiety. I seemed to have lost one of my ear studs. Again. I decided to untuck the strands from behind my ears so that it framed my face to hide the missing stud. My hands were so dry, I realised in that moment that I needed to take better care of myself. Later, maybe.

I was wearing casual clothes having just come back from work. My blue jeans and white shirt with the top two buttons open were acceptable enough for a sales assistant at Trinity. We had to wear a uniform when we got to work anyway.

You are pathetic, you are not going to last a minute in there if you can't even look confident about your decision!

It had taken a lot of thought and soul searching for me to reach this point. *I can do this*, I thought, trying to psych myself up.

Alexa De Luca, you are a coward. I took deep breath and employed a tactic that had gotten me through my early years in secondary school and imagined that I was in a giant impenetrable bubble. Yes, thats right. I. Had. A. Bubble. Not as crazy as having an imaginary friend yet not quite normal. I was aware that if i ever told anyone about my bubble I could find myself being sectioned under the mental health act. Which was why I was the sole bearer of this particular secret.

In my bubble, I was Super Alexa, Master of calm and devourer of all things chocolate. In my bubble I could allow myself to pick and choose my conversations and who I would allow to briefly step into my bubble with me to have my whole undivided attention. I could also block out annoying people and breathe without feeling like my chest was being stomped on by an elephant. My Bubble allowed me space to step away from situations and think. Luckily I had never been carted off in an ambulance for it...yet.

Bubble having been deployed and stepped into, today I was in army stealth mode.

Take position soldier. Target at twelve o'clock! Your mission is to find Captain Granna then relay the message in clear instructive manner to the civilians and return to base without injury Must avoid all signs of waterworks and confrontation as these can be explosive. God Speed soldier.

I turned the handle of the living room door as if I was anticipating a monster jumping out at me. I was not entirely wrong.

Aunt Audrey was the first person I laid eyes on and she was in a foul mood. I knew better than to engage her in any sort of communication when she was suffering from such afflictions. She was sitting to my left on the chesterfield single seater beside the table on which my mother kept the cordless phone and a vase of tulips, her fingers running through her red shoulder length salon blow dried hair.

She was very attractive for a woman in her fifties and had

always taken care of her appearance. Her long lashes were coated with expensive mascara and her perfect pouting lips were pursed in anger. French manicured nails weaved in and out flame red hair. I was scared that her hazel eyed venom might make the flowers wilt. Luckily Bubble could not be penetrated by dirty looks. Just about.

The living room was cosy. The wall between what used to be two reception rooms was knocked down before my family moved in many years ago to make a through lounge. The floor was fitted with dark wood flooring, the walls painted in the lightest shade of purple. In one corner of what was essentially the first room was a floral motif painted in black, my work of art that I was immensely proud of. The windows were big and the light voile netting allowed enough light into the room so we didn't get swallowed up by the dark floor. There was a large oat coloured L-shaped sofa by the corner wall where the windows were and on which my poor uncle Jack was seated next to his heavily pregnant wife Cassandra who looked very uncomfortable. They both smiled hello. Uncle jack is my mothers youngest sibling and still in his mid thirties. His messy dark blonde hair and electric blue eyes made him look even younger.

Cassandra on the other hand had Mediterranean dark brown hair pulled back in a ponytail and light brown eyes. She is a real Spanish beauty and a teacher just like Jack.

The chesterfield plus one grumpy aunt Audrey was opposite them. Uncle Jack looked up at me with a silent plea in his electric eyes to rescue him from both his sister and wife, indicating with gentle nods of his head toward the two of them . I wickedly smiled at him and shrugged my shoulders with my hands up in surrender, receiving a exasperated sigh from him in return. His twin six year old boys came running in from the garden, wild unruly dark hair and blue eyes full of excitement and mischief, pulling him onto his feet. The relief on his face was so obvious that his wife scowled at him.

5

"Thanks boys," he whispered to them as soon as they were out of earshot and passing me by. He stuck his tongue out at me in a "thanks a bunch" kind of way. So mature uncle Jack. I rolled my eyes in reply, equally adolescent.

The second part of the room was where our television was, floor cushions scattered against the wall and a small comfy dusty grey couch diagonally opposite where my half sister Megan was sitting with our cousin Tara discussing some model reality show. My sister is nothing like me, she gets her jet black hair and dark brown eyes from my step dad Ed. She's taller than me, slender and fashion conscious. Her darker Mediterranean complexion makes her very attractive. She's also ten years younger than me aged 16 and I practically brought her up, which she hates being reminded about. Tara is a year older than Megan and is aunt Audrey's daughter. She has the same hazel eyes as her mother but dark blonde hair and a very pixie like face with delicate features. She's very pretty and she knows it and just as raucous as my sister.

I returned their waves hello, not wanting to engage in conversation.

The chimney opposite the grey couch had a faux log fire running on gas. At the end of the room were bi-folding doors opening out to the kitchen extension. There were two raspberry and black floral print rugs in each room that felt soft under my feet. I relished the fluffiness, rubbing my feet on the fibres in an attempt to comfort myself and calm the nerves before the big reveal.

I walked through the bi folding doors into the kitchen, Bubble squeezing through with me. This would be where I needed it the most.

It was a decent sized kitchen, to my right the kitchen was fitted with wood cabinets stained light walnut. The tops were granite and in the middle of the kitchen was a breakfast bar. The floor was black and white checkered tile.

The dining table was on my left is set out with salads and burger buns, condiments, plates, cutlery and drinks. I grabbed a Coke and headed out onto the raised patio where the barbecue was set out alongside the wrought iron furniture and forest green umbrella. A short brick wall signified the end of the patio and an opening, below which were three steps leading onto the grass. To the left were mums prized Victorian roses, ten varieties all in all. They looked beautiful in their pinks, reds, whites and yellows. They smelt heavenly in the early June afternoon.

Uncle Jack and the boys were kicking around a football and the boys were giggling at their fathers attempts at retrieving the football every time they kicked it nto a bush. I had started to think they were doing it intentionally and my suspicions were confirmed when I caught a mischievous twinkle in my young cousins' eyes.

At the end of the garden was the old swing our parents set up years ago and the small wooden garden shed. Still going strong. So many memories in this house. I sighed inwardly and was brought back to reality with sounds of my family out by the barbecue.

You can do it, just keep calm. Just the usual faces of my wonderfully intrusive extended family. Some may say I was overreacting and making a bigger deal of everything before anything had even happened. They would be wrong. I loved my family, really loved them. I mean, who doesn't love their family? But my issue was that my family was really close, including my extended family on my mothers side. And they cared too much. My mother and aunts freaked out when I told them I wanted to get married at age 22 and although I understood I was young, they didn't accept it until after I got married. They made it a point to voice their concerns every single day. It got to a point where I was being bribed to wait a bit longer with an all expenses pain trip to Majorca. Yeah. They were that kind of crazy.

It was the annual family barbecue at my parents house, consisting 99% of family members on my maternal side, and there was too much going on all at once. My stepfather, also known as dad, was flipping burgers on the grill wearing mums frilly apron. He looked ridiculous and I decided on teasing him about it later, to get him back for all the times he'd embarrassed me. He looked up at me with concerned eyes when he saw me fidgeting with the ring pull on the coke can. I smiled reassuringly to ward off the worry.

My mother and aunt Grace were marinating the chicken and lamb chops for the barbecue and gossiping at the same time. Aunt grace and my mum look a lot alike. Both have the same light brown hair, although mum's is shoulder length and wavy and aunt Grace wears hers in a bob and they both have blue grey eyes. Same soft features, not harsh like aunt Audrey's. I guess aunt Audrey had always felt like the black sheep of the family, as well as being the eldest sibling. The thought never occurred to me before now. Explained a lot.

My cousins Brian and Hannah, Aunt Grace's children, were sitting on the wall deep in conversation. Uncle Nick, their father, was putting some drinks in the ice box. He's a tall but cuddly man with a very warm smile and sparkling green eyes. His salt and pepper beard and hair made him look like a wise old giant. He stopped and smiled at me, walking over to give me a fatherly hug. After a squeeze and a kiss on the cheek he set me down and held me by my shoulders, concern in his eyes.

"How have you been darling?"

He was of course referring to my recent divorce. Actually, my marriage had really ended a year and a half ago but everything had finally been sorted out in terms of property and paperwork this past month. Yesterday I had to clear the last boxes of my possessions from the house we shared, my dream house, so that we could sell it and go our separate ways for good.

To be honest, I tried every day not to think about it but my lovely over concerned family couldn't help but remind me about the situation. There were only a certain number of times they could tell me how strong I was and how I was much better off without him. Him, meaning Tom. He was the love of my life.

I stopped my train of thought abruptly, sealing that crack in my Bubble that allowed his memory in and realised I would have to answer uncle Nick now with the usual bull crap that came out of my mouth as an answer to mask the rawness of the pain I actually felt.

"I'm good uncle Nick, I am glad that I've sorted out my affairs and now can move forward."

He gave me a sad smile. I knew that he was very fond of me and his worry for me was genuine, but I didn't want to cry in the back garden where every member of my family had been enjoying the summer evening. *No more sympathy please, lets just get through this day without thinking about Tom and the slut.*

Smiling back at uncle Nick, I moved towards Brian and Hannah who saw me coming and shuffled apart to make space between them on the wall for me to sit.

"Hey Lexi," Brian smiled and leant over for a hug, his familiar blue eyes sparkling and floppy light blonde hair needing a cut. Hannah gave me a kiss on each cheek. She has the same blue eyes as her brother but darker blonde hair, looking more like our uncle Jack's, which was cut short to her shoulder length and tucked behind her ears. They are both tall like their dad.

"Hey," I replied, giving them a small smile. I felt relief that my cousins, the two people I had grown up and shared everything with, were by my side for this evening.

Brian and Hannah are twins, and are six months older than me. From childhood into adulthood we remained close. Brian was visiting from New York - he is a doctor and moved out there after being offered the job of a lifetime to complete his medical training. Only, he now worked in the Accident and Emergency department in a hospital or "ER" as the Americans call it.

Brian's girlfriend Christine, an american elementary

school teacher, couldn't make it to London because there were still a couple of weeks of school left in the states. I had only met her once in the two years he had been away but she seemed like a no nonsense type of woman that possessed a beautiful smile and was easy to get on with.

Hannah was also a Doctor, a GP. She worked within London for a small but busy Practice, staying close to the family but in her own two bedroom flat with her boyfriend Keith, who was currently at a seminar in Wales. He was a dentist - they met when Hannah did a stint in Hertfordshire outside London at a hospital he was working for at the time. He left and moved to London to be with her in the most romantic of gestures.

Keith was cheerful, charming and funny. He would definitely brighten up the day with his jokes were he present.

Brian put his left arm around me and gave me a squeeze. We sat wordlessly for a few minutes soaking up the warmth of the evening. It was 7pm but light still. Hannah was the first to break the silence.

"So...aunt Audrey is looking like she may erupt like Vesuvius," she smiled mischievously, showing her perfect teeth.

"What's eating her this time?" I mused, a slow intrigued smile appearing on my face.

"I heard that her ex got in touch with her a couple of days ago," Brian whispers conspiratorially. Both Hannah and I laughed. It was out of character for Brian to contribute gossip to a conversation but he had recently become more in touch with his feminine side thanks to Christine.

"Where'd you hear that from?" I queried, genuinely interested in anything about Aunt Audrey that made her look more human. The truth was we all knew so little about her that we wondered if we were related to her at all. I did remember her being fun and loving when I was little and how she used to twirl me around in her arms. Then something happened around the time I was six and everything changed.

No one talked about it, so us kids at least didn't know what went wrong with her. We didn't have the guts to ask her either, our parents just kept quiet about it.

"I heard our mothers talking earlier in the kitchen. They saw me standing there and got off the subject quick." Brian shrugged and took a gulp of his beer.

"She should totally hook up with him. She has been a widow for more than a year now. Time to live life! Uncle Clive was a wonderful old man but I can't imagine him being a lot of fun at his age, she needs stimulation in a relationship," Hannah said, as usual spurting out exactly what she was thinking.

It often got her in trouble. The look of disgust on Brian's face and my own reaction to Hannah's honest opinion made us all laugh.

"I cant believe you just talked about aunt Audrey needing 'stimulation'! Ewwww, nasty!"

She was, of course, right. Clive was eighteen years older than Aunt Audrey. He died eighteen months ago of a heart attack having already had triple bypass surgery. He was a wealthy man, had left a sizeable slice of it to his widow, including their house in Kensington. The rest was split between his two older children from his first marriage and Tara. When he died, she had been distraught. She cared for him deeply but we all thought that saying she 'loved' him in the truest sense of the word would be stretching it a bit. I often wondered why she had married him. I didn't want to think of her as a gold digger, although she enjoyed her comfortable life. I mean, who wouldn't? But her hazel eyes held so much sadness behind the tough exterior she showed the world. There definitely was something painful in her past that no one wanted to divulge or bring to the surface again.

"So, you going to tell them about the New York plan?" Brian asked abruptly as he turned to face me, referring to my parents. His question immediately made me nervous again.

"Yes. Tonight," I said quietly, frowning at the thought

of actually doing it.

I hated having to argue with my family about what they thought was right and wrong for me. I could sense the reaction my overbearing family would have. Everyone had an opinion that they all felt they were entitled to make and advice that they thought I should take. They could drive me insane but I loved them dearly. The idea of hurting them made me feel sick.

"Bold move Lexi, you got a whole lot of crazy in the place at the moment," Brian smirked, raising his eyebrows in mock horror. Hannah made to slap his back but he avoided the contact by jumping up, laughing.

"I got Granna on my side Bri, she's got my back." I exaggerated a wink at him, giggling genuinely and relieving some of the pressure I felt.

As I watched my little cousins playing in the garden, I recalled the moment I had realised what I wanted to do with my immediate future.

A couple of sleepless nights ago in a fit of panic at approximately 03:45am...

Ring ring. Ring ring. Ring ring. Ring ring.

"Lexi? What the fuck are you calling me for at this time? Has someone died? Someone better have died..." Aisha's voice trailed off, but she was definitely sounding more concerned than pissed off. I heard mumbling in the background, the muffled voice of Aisha telling her husband Imran to shut the hell up and go back to sleep.

"Lexi?" I realised I hadn't said anything as yet. I was gripping my phone so hard my knuckles had turned white.

"No ones died." I heard my voice sound like the familiar panicky way it had started to sound like recently when I had been given the chance to be alone with my thoughts for too long. Panic attacks had started soon after the divorce proceedings had started.

I know that I had started to feel weak and
the life I had in me. It was so unlike me. T\
had woken me up in a panic and the only perso\
give me an honest opinion of my rambling thou\   \, ıny
bestie Aisha, or Ash as all her nearest called her. She had
never rejected or missed my calls. Ever. Even during her
cousin's wedding, she answered her phone to me whilst the
priest was reading the scared vows to the couple in the background. Now that was dedication to your friends.

"Whats happened hun? Did that spineless bastard say
something to you? I swear to God if he has I will show him
hell on Earth and wring his stupid neck-"

"No! No, he hasn't said anything Ash. I just had another funny turn." I don't know why I could never just call
them panic attacks. I felt like I'd become my mother by calling them my 'funny turns.'

"Oh honey...tell me what happened." So I let it all flow
out of me.

"I watched that program on Channel Four about
people that are super hoarders and there was this one
woman that just spent her whole life holding onto every
scrap of junk that was tied to memories she had and her
whole house was full of this crap and she couldn't even have
a relationship because she just closed herself off and when I
went to sleep I saw her house. Only it was my stuff in her
house and I was living there old and withered and full of regrets and what ifs and I woke up in a sweat Ash, I fucking
freaked out! Even now I'm shaking. I can't end up like that!
I'm so fucking scared I'm gonna end up like that. I would
rather throw myself off Tower Bridge into the Thames than
wake up one day realising I just wasted my life away."

The words came out in such a rush that I had to take a
deep breath at the end of my tirade. I could almost hear Ash
processing all I said, the wheels in her wonderful calm mind
turning at this late hour while her stupid neurotic friend
freaked out.

13

"Lexi, firstly I won't ever let that happen. I would bitch slap the sense into you pretty sharpish if you so much as even thought about becoming that way. I would send my mother in with her bin bags and rolling pin, mark my words."

I had a brief image of Ash's mother, who insisted I call her aunty Naj, with her Obsessive Compulsive cleanliness and neatness showing me who's boss and throwing me about the house in various wrestling actions and chokeholds.

"Secondly," Ash continued, "Your realising this is good news Lex. It shows us that there is a part of you that just wants to leave this crap behind and not keep it with you, to start fresh. So what you got to do is ask yourself what you regret not doing? What dreams you gave up for that asswipe? What would you regret if you didn't give it a chance?"

I didn't have to think hard about it. I knew the answer as soon as she had asked me the question.

"New York," I said without hesitance. That was my dream, that was what I gave up. I always wanted to go live out in New York, work there for a while. From the moment New York had captured my heart that first time I had visited it, I knew I left a piece of me somewhere along the tree lined streets and skyscrapers. I had told Tom about my dream and although he seemed enthusiastic about it at first, he seemed to let it slip away when he concentrated on completing his professional Architects qualification and working his way up in Reid and Clarkson, one of London's most prestigious Architectural firms, while I struggled to find a new dream having given up on Architecture as a career for myself. I just didn't know what I wanted to do with myself when I declared Architecture was just not for me, disappointing Tom with my 'defeatist attitude' as he put it.

"Sounds like you've known that for a while Lexi. Go for it, don't regret the time you've wasted, make up for it. There really isn't anything holding you here but your fear."

"But where do I start? There's so much to do, it's a big

decision to make. And my parents? Oh God Ash, my parents will freak out, thinking *I'm* freaking out! Oh no."
I felt the panic rise in my chest again and that familiar constriction of muscle and quick breaths.

"Oi! Nothing is gonna go wrong you nutter, calm yourself down! Deep breaths now, come on. Now let's count down from three...Channing Tatum....Two.....Channing Tatum in a suit...One...Channing Tatum in his birthday suit..."
I felt a giggle escape my mouth and my breathing relax gradually, the pain subsiding.

"Ash, what would I do without you?" I felt the tears in my eyes then, this woman got me so well. She was more than a friend, more like a sister and I felt undeserving of her.

"You're never going to find out. Now, open your front door in about ten minutes." I heard keys jingling and some shuffling about and more mumbling.

"What? You're coming over?" Looking at the alarm at my bedside table I realised it was now 04:11am.

"Yep. I'm not giving you any room to rethink this decision, not more regrets and what ifs for you. God knows you got too many as it is. We have got some planning to do. We haven't had a sleepover since we were in high school!"

"I love you Ash," I laughed, feeling happy for the first time in a while. What a relief to have someone watch your back and guide you to your happiness and to positivity. My runaway train had suddenly had a track switch from the boulder it was about to collide with, to the endless open track running smoothly towards so many possibilities.

Back the barbecue, reeling from the memory of my epiphany...

I started to wonder where my grandmother was. She had been the most sane and rational person in our family. Even if she drank and swore like a sailor. My maternal grandmother was American born, a real New Yorker. She had been the one who inspired Brian to venture out to the Big Apple and when I mentioned my plan to her a couple of days before, she was so encouraging.

I excused myself from my cousins when I realised I knew exactly where Granna was hiding.

I walked down the garden path to our little wooden shed. I opened the creaking wooden door to reveal Granna snoozing on an old deck chair with a bottle of Johnnie Walker whiskey and a glass tumbler resting on a crooked shelf by her side.

I stepped out of my Bubble because I felt safe here with her and considered taking a swig from her bottle for dutch courage but remembered the one time I had decided to get drunk with Granna. I was sick for two days from that stuff and vowed never to drink it again. Granna, however, could drink anyone under the table. Not that she was alcoholic. More like she liked to have a little tipple for down time.

I took a moment to soak in the sight of this woman I adored so much. I would miss her the most. In her youth she had been an attractive green eyed beauty with long wavy dark blonde hair. She was curvy in the right places with large breasts and I had been told that I have her figure, although I'm not entirely sure I could ever look as good as she did in her photos. Not that having large breasts was something to rejoice about. I mentally listed the disadvantages like having back and shoulder pain and the difficulty of finding clothes that fit perfectly without having them tailored.

Margaret Louise Stanton, a.k.a Mrs Richard Barker a.k.a Granna, had been the daughter of a wealthy property developer living in New York City in the late 1940's when she met my Grandpa Richie. He was travelling with friends, having finished his studies at Oxford when her stunning beauty caught his eye one day whilst he was out for a stroll in Central Park.

They started courting, as Grandpa called it, and he decided to stay longer in the city whilst his friends decided to travel onwards. When it became apparent that they had strong feelings for one another, Grandpa proposed to Granna and she accepted him but her father was livid and would not agree to them marrying because Granna would have to come back to England where Grandpa had a lucrative job offer waiting for him.

They were young and in love so she left her home and family for Grandpa and came to England. Her family eventually forgave them and she remained in contact with her parents siblings and even visited and had them visit us. I loved it when they would tell me their love story when I was little. It gave me hope back then in my young romantic mind.

I shifted to lean against the door frame when I accidentally dislodged a broom that had been propped at the side of the shed wall and watched it clatter onto the floor before being able to do anything to stop it. Granna jerked awake, her emerald green eyes wide with alarm, searching her surroundings. She visibly relaxed when she saw me standing in front of her and realised where she was.

She smiled lovingly at me and ran her hand through her snow white hair.

"Standing there against the light, you look like an Angel, Alli."

Alli was the nickname only my Granna used for me. As she said those words, I walked the few steps into the middle of the small shed, dropped to my knees in front of her chair and she enveloped me in her arms. I loved this woman so much, she was my rock.

"Granna, you always say the sweetest things," I muttered, as my head rested on her chest and she stroked my hair softly with her wrinkled but still beautiful long fingers. Her wedding band reflected the light of the fading summer sun, a constant reminder of my beloved Grandpa Richie who left us three years ago, after suffering a heart attack.

"I wouldn't say it if it weren't true darling." Her voice is so soft and soothing, her accent still thick after over fifty years of living in London and wise with years of experience. I lifted my head and smiled at her. She had always had more confidence and believed in me more than I ever had in myself.

"Drinking out here on your own?" I asked her as I stood up, raising an eyebrow.

"Do you really think I can get through the evening without a drop or two? Have you seen Audrey's mood today? And Jack's boys....sheesh! I love them dearly but they will be the death of me!" She chuckled and I couldn't help but laugh in agreement. Suddenly, she got up off her chair almost losing her balance and grabbed my arms as I offered them for support.

"You ok Granna?" I asked, concerned by her momentarily dazed look.

"I'm okay darling, maybe I've had a bit too much for today. Anyway, lets get this show on the road. You have got an announcement to make and I cant wait to see the look on your mothers face." She winked as her eyes glinted and she smirked mischievously.

Back on the patio everyone had assembled to grab fresh barbecued meat and the kids were thankfully occupied eating on the picnic blanket on the grass. My mum approached us as Granna took a seat on one of the chairs by the wall.

The stern look on her face warned us of the reprimand we were about to receive. I stepped right into my Bubble again.

"Mother! Where the hell have you been?! Is that alcohol I smell on your breath? And Lexi, how could you let her?" In my mind, I saw my mother stepping towards us with a medieval torture device ready to get the truth out of us.

Oh great. Mum was in uber stressed mode and that made me want to back out of telling her about NYC. I wanted to find anything, a bucket even, to hide myself in.

"Oh pipe down Elizabeth! It was just a drop of whiskey and I had already had it by the time Lexi came to find me. Stop being such a tight ass and live a little!"

I giggled at Granna's words. She was the only one that could make any situation better with her light hearted way of dealing with the family or even strangers. I knew exactly why Grandpa Richie fell head over heels in love with her and made her elope with him back to England.

"Oh mother!" My mum sighed, exasperated, but a hint of a smile touched her pink painted lips.

"Is everyone here?" Granna spoke to mum but looked at me. I felt myself shrink a bit when I realised Granna was taking the plunge as I was trying to back myself away.

"Yes, Audrey is just walking in now."

My mother never missed anything and immediately flicked us a suspicious look. In my Bubble I had somehow conjured up a heavy metal shield for defence. Shit was about to get weird.

"Good. Alli has something to tell everyone."

I felt a cold sweat work its way up my body and the hairs on the back of my neck stood as I shivered. Even Bubble was not going to be able to get me out of this - there was nowhere left to hide.

You're an adult, gosh darn it! Make a decision and stick to it Alexa. You owe it to yourself to do this. For you.

I hated that little voice in my head most times but she always made sense. I reminded myself that I was not asking for permission but simply informing them of my decision. Even if I felt like an errant child in the process.

My mother turned her suspicious look onto me and simply nodded. I glanced at Granna who had a strange look of peacefulness on her face. Her calm countenance gave me a little more courage. She obviously thought my move to New York would be good for me. And my Granna was seldom wrong.

Her clear and concise tone brought me back to the scene in front of me. She had already announced to the family that I had some exciting news to tell them.

Turning to me she whispered, "It's now or never kiddo."

Taking a deep breath, I stepped forward as my Bubble

popped, acutely aware of everyones eyes on me.

"Um...well...I just wanted to let everyone know that I'm really grateful for all the support I've gotten through the divorce and in helping me get back on track." I paused for a few seconds. I heard Brian mutter something about betting I'm going to chicken out and I turned around to see Hannah swat him on his arm and the turn to me giving me a flash of her perfect teeth in her confidence giving smile. I turned back to see the expectant eyes around me and continued.

"I've been thinking about it a lot and want to start afresh somewhere new...so...I...um...I've decided to move to New York." The words came out in a rush from my mouth and took a few seconds to register with everyone. There was pin drop silence for a few excruciating moments and I wondered if they would ever speak.

"Well, I think it's exactly what you need darling," Uncle Jack took my hand, breaking the silence, and gave it a squeeze whilst smiling broadly. I smiled back gratefully.

"Definitely, It's going to be amazing!" Tara squealed in delight giving my hand a tug.

"And we can come visit you once you're settled!" Megan looked equally enthusiastic and it was a little relief. But then I noticed that my parents were still silent. Aunt Grace was looking at mum cautiously. Mum looked frozen and dad was slowly making his way to her. Granna reached up to squeeze my hand from where she was sitting.

If there was one thing everyone knew about me, it was this - I hated the thought of hurting and disappointing my parents. It was the major reason that I had never been rebellious as a teenager. I could not live with the guilt of that possibility of hurting them or disappointing them. Finally my mother spoke.

"Lexi, I think maybe you are looking for an escape from what happened. Running away is not the solution. It is too soon after the divorce. I think you should reconsider." Her voice was deceptively soft. I felt my insides boil, my heart beat faster. That sickening feeling of doing something wrong filled me. I just couldn't handle making them worry. I got the shock of my life when I heard a calm and clear voice, just like Granna's, speak to my parents.

"Elizabeth, you need to let her go and do what she feels is right. Let her know what its like to live life away from this mess. She needs time to heal."

That voice and those words came from my Aunt Audrey. I wasn't surprised to see that I was not the only one shocked that she spoke, She hardly ever contributed to family discussions and usually was in a foul mood but today was like seeing a whole new side to her. Especially when looking up into her hazel eyes I saw sincerity and something else, a new emotion replacing the usual coldness. It took me a few seconds to place it but it eventually dawned on me. It was empathy and experience that came from the sadness in her eyes.

Dad squeezed mums shoulder and cleared his throat before he spoke to her, a smile forming on his face.

"I think Audrey has a point. Lexi should go. If she feels that its not for her, she knows she always has a home here."

I waited anxiously for mum to say something. She looked at me with sad eyes but smiled shakily and walked over to take my hands in hers.

"If it makes you happy then you should go. That's all I want for you."

Even though I knew she was reluctant to give me her blessing and I could hear the hesitance in her voice, I felt a tonne of weight being lifted off of my chest and relief that my family would be supporting me in my bold move to start afresh. I was in a state of shock that my parents had let it go so easily. There was definitely something different about them. I think It may have been aunt Audrey who won me this round.

Granna stood up and kissed my cheek.

"So, wheres the food? Are ya gonna let an old woman starve?"

CHAPTER TWO

New York, New York

I t took me another month to get my affairs in check and a visa sorted. I had gotten a good amount of money in my share from the sale of the house that I had shared with Tom. It would be more than enough to tide me over for a while in case I couldn't find a job soon after reaching New York.

Luckily I didn't have to change my name back to my maiden name - I had never taken Tom's surname, which always pissed him off. I liked being Ms De Luca and by the look of it, it was a bloody good idea I kept it. Less of the paperwork hassle.

Although Brian had offered me a place to stay in the large apartment he lived in with Christine, I politely declined, not wanting to be the third wheel in their home. I had contacted my friend Allison, better known by everyone from our high school as 'Bones' due to an incident involving a skeleton during a biology lesson. She had moved to New York three years ago and had a spare room going free in a town house in the upscale area of Manhattan. It was all working out perfectly, the rent was reasonable as there was another girl living there too and I knew that I was very lucky to get a room in Manhattan for what I was paying for rent. The house was not far from Brian and Christine which was comforting. Whats more, I got on really well with Allison since we first met at school. We were best friends and kept in touch as much as we could with the ocean between us. I looked forward to spending more time with her now that we were going to be living together.

I had given my notice in to my manager a few weeks back. Although she was sad to see me go, she seemed happy for me and shared my excitement. My work colleagues had planned a leaving party for me on my last day at work.

As a rule I didn't drink alcohol unless it was a special occasion and then too only a little. I had partied too hard in my university years with Tom and our old gang of friends and eventually one night I had drank so much that I almost ended up with alcohol poisoning. I sobered up pretty quick after that and vowed never to let myself be in that sort of situation ever again. Even when Tom left me for Rebecca (who shall be known as The Slut here on in), I didn't go do the obvious and drown my sorrows.

Okay, that wasn't exactly true. I had one night of drink infused madness post break up that I wished I could change.

Fourteen Months ago in a bar in Ealing...

I had been out with my friend Mandy for dinner in her bid to cheer me up. How did you explain to someone who was always changing boyfriends like she changed her knickers that breaking from a relationship, *a marriage*, after almost eight years together was not as simple as she thought?

Mandy seemed to think that I needed a rebound, forgetting the fact that I had only been separated from Tom for four months, and I thought she was crazy. Then she dragged me to a bar and kept egging me on until I accepted the pink coloured drink she kept thrusting my way. It was rife with Vodka. Possibly more Vodka than should be allowed in a drink. Before I knew it I had consumed three and I was the first to admit that I was a lightweight - I should never have given into Mandy. But I would also admit that it felt good just being a little carefree having dealt with so many emotions from the last few months.

Before I knew it, a hand slipped round my waist as I waited to be served at the bar. I turned around to see it was an old university friend, Max, who Tom used to be convinced had a thing for me. He was a nice guy, was in Tom's class two years ahead of me and he would always stop to talk to me. We hung out in the same group most of the time. Tom used to get really possessive when he was around and it would make me laugh. It was no secret Tom and Max disliked one another.

"Still looking gorgeous as ever De Luca," he said, his deep voice and cheery blue eyes making me smile for the first time in ages.

Okay, so maybe he used to flirt with me back then as well but it was all harmless fun. At least *I* thought so.

"Max! Oh my God! I haven't seen you since forever! How long has it been?"

"The last time I saw you was at your wedding." He looked at me with a pained expression when he realised what he had said. He obviously knew because as ever, word got around fast.

"Yeah..." I didn't know what to say, suddenly I didn't feel so high anymore.

"I'm sorry Alexa, that was a stupid thing for me to say."

"It's ok Max, it's a fact that we're getting divorced so no need to step around it." I smiled weakly, and saw him smile a little back and then he cleared his throat and kissed my cheek, whispering in my ear.

"Forget that arsehole. He doesn't know what he lost. Let me buy you a drink."

"Sure."

And one drink turned into two more that I shouldn't have had. We talked about everything and what we had both been up to since we last met, artfully stepping around the issue of Tom and my failed marriage. Mandy left quite early on in our conversation after I introduced Max to her, winking in a mischievous way. I had rolled my eyes at her insinuation but as the drinks kept coming and I turned into a happy drunk, I noticed how pretty Max's eyes were and I stopped feeling uncomfortable with the arm he had draped across the back of my stool and the way his thumb kept skimming my back through the thin satin of my top.

At one point of the evening, Max leaned over to whisper something in my ear and in my haze I turned my head quickly, only to brush my lips against his. On my part it was an accident but he didn't look too surprised himself. He leaned further into me to cover my lips in a heated kiss and I let him. I just let go. I didn't want to feel anymore. The fact that this gorgeous man was into me even after all this time and given my current state with the way Tom chose the slut over me, I felt flattered and wanted. And *damn* was he was a good kisser. He pulled away, both of us trying to catch our breath and steady heart beats.

"I didn't mean to be too forward and I don't want you to think that I am taking advantage of your current state but...I've wanted to do that since the moment I met you."

Even this drunk, I could see the sincerity in his eyes and it sobered me a little. Before I could stop myself, I blurted out what I should never have said.

"Let's go back to your place, Max." The look on his face was priceless, he clearly had never expected that.

"Um, Alexa, maybe I should take you home-"

"No. I want you to take me to yours. I want, for just one night, to forget everything and just give into something and someone else. You're gorgeous, I want you. One night only offer." Even as I said it, a part of me was standing over the situation watching in absolute horror. I had practically offered myself to this man on a plate.

"Alexa, maybe it's the drink talking. I don't want to be something you regret later." His honesty didn't hide the fact that I could still see how much he wanted me and the hunger in his eyes. Just a little push and he would lose all control. And I wanted him.

"I.Want.You. Take me to yours, please Max. Do this for me."

I saw the little resolve he had crumble as he slowly smiled and took my hand to kiss it. As he paid the bartender for our drinks tab and we got our coats, I saw someone I recognised in the corner of the bar but was too excited about what was about to happen on my dirty night out to pay attention. Seven months of no sex and a hefty amount of vodka did that to a person. For once, the sweet, loyal goody two shoes Alexa De Luca was going to let go and have what promised to be a night of hot steamy sex with a man that wasn't her cheating, lying husband.

And that night was just what it promised to be if not more. Max was an animal and I felt sexually awakened and wanted, something that I had lost way before when Tom had started distancing himself from me. Max worshipped my body all night until we fell asleep exhausted.

In the morning, however, things were different. I felt awkward and guilty. Even though I was separated from Tom, this felt like cheating. I was still feeling loyal to that bastard. And I felt guilty that I had used Max. He had been so good to me, apart from the mind blowing sex. He made me breakfast and massaged out the cricks in my body from all the various positions he had taken me in. I mean, for someone that loved sex, I had been sex starved and previously limited to one arsehole of a man.

When I was leaving I kissed his cheek awkwardly. I opened my mouth to speak but he stopped me.

"Before you say anything, let me speak. I know you regret last night, I can see it in your eyes, but I just want you to know that it really meant something more to me than just a one night stand. And I wouldn't have changed a thing. I only wish I had the guts to ask you out before Tom did all those years ago at university. He knew I liked you, bastard beat me to it."

The adoration that seeped from him made me start crying like a fool at his doorstep. He pulled me close into his muscular arms and I breathed in his male scent. I didn't know how much I missed being with a man until then.

"Shhh, it's going to be okay. You're a strong woman. You will come out of this on top. I know you will."

"I'm sorry Max, I feel like I used you," I blubbered, probably not looking very ladylike.

"Hey, enough! I would love to be used by you any time sexy. Last night was amazing..." He trailed off, looking into my eyes to make me believe what he said.

"Last night was amazing for me too," I replied, my cheeks flaming up a little and I suddenly felt shy.

"I'm glad." He smiled a cheeky grin that made me melt. If I hadn't been such a mess, maybe I would have fallen for him, given some time. The attraction was certainly there between us. I wiped the tears off my face and smiled.

"And just for the record," I said, pulling him by his shirt so that my mouth was close to his ear to whisper, "I won't ever regret last night. My body is deliciously sore, I'm pretty sure you will be on my mind for some time."

And then I kissed him long and hard because I was lustful and wanted to take something from the magic of the night before to remind me it was real as well as give him something to remember too.

Now people would ask why I would say I wished that night hadn't happened when I obviously enjoyed it. The reason is what happened exactly a week later.

I got a call from one of Tom's friends informing me that I had better go talk to him because he was going crazy. It wasn't unusual in the past when we had had arguments or if he was going through a difficult time for him to go off somewhere to vent and for me to be called by one of his mates to calm him down. Apparently I was the only one that had that unique ability.

I was about to tell him to take a running jump of a cliff with his friend in tow when he told me that Tom had found out about my night with Max and had gone to find him. They had a fight where things got violent. Grabbing my coat, I ran out of the house taking my mum's car keys without explaining anything to her. I had moved out of my own house as everything from our alarm clock to the cheese grater reminded me of Tom and I couldn't handle that.

I had been informed that Tom was sitting in the park near our former home which was now up for sale. I parked the car by the entrance, spotting his hunched over body from the distance. I could feel the connection we had, our electricity as potent as it was when we were in the height of our love.

I approached him as he sat on a swing, head in hands. It hurt me, every time I got close to him, smelt the cologne that I associated only with him. When those deep brown eyes looked up at me as I got closer, I almost reached out to comfort him when I saw the hurt on his face and the bruise on his jaw. Sitting down quietly next to him on a swing, I stared at my hands and waited for him to talk. The minutes stretched and I sensed him open his mouth to talk several times but it was like he couldn't get the words out. When he finally spoke, his voice was gravelly and thick with emotion like he had been struggling to control the pain.

"Do you really hate me that much?" I looked up at him and our eyes locked. I didn't even pretend that I didn't know what he was talking about.

"What Max and I did had nothing to do with you Tom." That was a total lie, I slept with Max after getting drunk on my sorrows over him, but I would never tell him that. I was surprised at how strong my voice sounded and silently congratulated myself. I was usually a dithering mess around him these days.

He looked taken aback and hurt by my words. *Good,* I

thought. *Now you have a fraction of an idea what it feels like, even if it was unintentional.* He cleared his throat before he spoke.

"So you did sleep with him then." I looked him straight in his eyes before I replied.

"It's none of your business what I do anymore Tom but I'm feeling generous today so I will answer you this one time. Yes, we slept together. I asked him to."

The anger bubbled to the surface as he stood up and punched the frame of the swings. Ouch, that must have hurt but I knew better than to approach him when he was that angry.

"Was he good?" he sneered, suddenly kneeling down in front of me and coming up just millimetres from my face, making me flinch. But I was beyond pissed, angry that he had thought he had the right to intrude on my life and be a hypocrite. I stood up fast pushing him away at the same time to feel in control.

"You want details huh? Fine! He was amazing, the best I've ever had! He has the sexiest body I've ever seen and he fucked me over and over again! We were at it all night and I LOVED IT!" I screamed, pushing his chest again. I could feel my the rage pouring out of me. As he shook with anger, I saw a single tear fall down his face. I was shocked, saddened and my heart broke a little more. You could never just stop loving someone. Our story was the living messed up truth.

"Alexa..." He grabbed me by my shoulders and then his hands cupped my face when I tried to look away, tears streaming down my own face.

"Baby please, look at me. I love you. You will always be the one for me. Can you find a way to forgive me? I will do anything you want, I swear it. Please."

I knew he meant what he said but it was too late for us. Considering he had walked out on me when I'd walked in on *them,* his realisation that he'd made a big mistake in choosing Rebecca over me had come too late. It was too late the moment he entertained the thought of screwing a woman that wasn't me.

"I can't."

"Please baby, I'm begging you. I can't stand the thought of anyone being with you other than me. I will go crazy," he said vehemently.

"You should have thought of that the moment you stuck your dick into that slut. At least you have a fraction of an idea what it feels like now. You didn't feel like this four months ago when you told me you were leaving me for *her*. And now you're here promising me *anything* when *she's* waiting for you, pregnant with *your* child. You're the biggest arsehole on Earth!"

I pulled myself away from him, the anger returning tenfold, only for him to grab my arm and pull me into his embrace and kiss my lips with an urgency I found myself matching in my anger, in my hurt, in all the what if's that filled the space between us. I finally got my wits together and pushed away but he dropped to his knees, holding me tight around my waist.

"Don't, please don't go. I know I don't deserve you, I'm a fucking screw up. I got stupid and weak and gave into temptation, ruining the only good thing in my life. But I don't know how to survive this. I won't be the same without you, you're the only good thing in my life." He buried his face into my stomach as I tried to control my tears and emotions. I had to ignore how i felt in close proximity to the man who was my home for so many years. I had to stop thinking about all that we lost. Instinctively I rubbed my belly.

"Was," I whispered. He looked up into my watery eyes, confused.

"I *was* the only good thing in your life," I continued. "I'm sorry Tom. We ended the moment you spent the night in another woman's arms. You have pulled out my heart and ripped it to pieces and I've got to do what is right for me. You're going to be a father Tom. Be responsible for that little life and do the right thing for you both. I didn't think I could live without you but I'm surviving. It won't be easy, it hurts like a bitch but I'm not about to ruin another life because of your mistake."

I pulled with a lot of effort out of his grip and knelt down, holding his face in my hands and kissed his lips for the last time. Leaving him kneeling on the ground, I stood up and left.

After that particular incident, I didn't let myself feel all the emotions welling up inside me as much as I had in the first few months. Maybe it wasn't good for me, in fact I knew it couldn't be healthy, but it worked for that time. I started to see things differently, I felt guilty about my actions post break up like slashing every single one of his BMW's tyres. And scratching the doors accidentally on purpose with my wedding band. Said wedding band was now lying at the bottom of the Thames under the Millennium bridge.

Okay, maybe I didn't feel so bad about that but I still cared for Tom. And now I was going to leave the memories behind to make new ones. Secretly, I wanted to be alone to grieve and get over him and us because for all their love and protectiveness my family and friends had started to suffocate me. Only Ash really understood.

***

The leaving party at work was held on the shop premises after closing. We often had birthday parties for our colleagues here and it was nice and intimate. With a couple of bottles of Prosecco and a few things to nibble on, we sat together, drank, ate and laughed. I was going to miss them, they were like my family.

After the separation, I had quit my job working as an Interior Designer at the Architects firm Tom worked at because things got really awkward since I couldn't help but give him dirty looks and want to rip his eyes out. That and the fact that the slut he cheated on me with was part of our office's admin staff.

In the end it worked out for the best. Leaving was inevitable, as I had started hating the profession I had chosen, so when I applied randomly at various businesses and a couple of Boutiques in Kensington, including Trinity, I was surprised to get an offer from them. Turned out they were desperately short staffed and needed someone in time for their sale and my part time arrangement worked out well for all of us. I could have stayed home but I needed to get busy and keep busy. Anything to get my mind off Tom, *that bitch* and his betrayal.

I got on well with the girls from the start and these ladies had been the ones to help me through the break up and the divorce.

"We got you something," Samantha, my manager, said suddenly pulling out a large black box tied with a red ribbon from under her chair.

"Aw you guys shouldn't have! Gimme!" I squealed in excitement, trying to hide how emotional I had been getting over the course of the evening.

I took the box and eight expectant eyes watched me pull the ribbon and pull off the lid. Inside was a brown teddy bear wearing a t-shirt that said "I < 3 London" which made me laugh.

"Whenever you miss home you have someone to hug," Natasha smiled, her blue eyes twinkling.

"You guys are determined to make me cry today aren't you?" I sighed, smiling sadly at them.

"Not yet! There's more. Then you have permission to get all emosh, okay?" Marissa said, trying to look serious behind the tears that threatened to escape her eyes.

"Okay, okay!" I laughed, picking up one of two tissue wrapped parcels. Opening it I found an A5 sized scrap book, on the front of which was written, "This is your life (at Trinity)."

Opening the scrap book, I found various pictures of us all and some of me alone taken on our company Christmas dinner, birthday parties and nights out. There were a few natural shots of me that I hadn't seen them take but were recent pictures from the past few weeks. There were some funny pictures of the girls posing and making funny faces and also pictures they had taken of each other holding up A4 sized pieces of cards that had funny quotes on them. Lucy was holding one that said, "Is easy after a couple of drinks" Her expression in the picture was inviting which made it more comical.

I kept laughing as we went through all the pictures recalling our good times together the past year. At one point we were in tears - not from crying but from laughing.

"Open the other one now," Lucy pointed to the remaining gift wrapped in tissue, wiping her eyes.

I pulled the paper apart and found a beautifully embossed notebook.

"For writing down every amazing experience you have in your new life in New York," Samantha said, answering my questioning look. At last I couldn't hold the tears back and I started sobbing like a baby. I felt like a right pansy.

"We know how much you like writing and stuff...we just thought you would like it...didn't mean to make you upset," Natasha said quietly, perplexed at my reaction and then looking to the girls for help.

"No, it's nothing like that...I..I..love...everything! I'm going to miss you girls soooo much!" We all had our little emotional cry party, allowed the drama for another few minutes then pulled ourselves together to act more 'ladylike,' as my mother would put it. Marissa picked up my wine glass and handed it to me, everyone followed suit with theirs.

"A toast, to New York! May you be happy and healthy and prosper in the Empire State!"

"May you eat lots of junk from street vendors and not gain weight!" Natasha chirped.

"May you find a dream job with colleagues as amazing as us!" Lucy contributed

"May you find the love of your life, a real American hot totty and forget all about the Shithead and super slut!" Samantha concluded.

"AND may the new man have a big-"

"CHEERS!" I shouted before Marissa could say anymore.

We clinked our glasses laughing in a loud, "Cheers!" This move would be more difficult than I had anticipated for sure.

***

Over the next week, I met with friends for drinks and goodbyes, packed a few clothes as a few of my bulkier items had already been shipped ahead to the address in Manhattan, and spent some quality time with my family, especially with mum and Granna. I did my utmost to make mum feel at ease with my departure and reassured her over and over again that I was happy with the decision and not running away from my train wreck life of late.

When the day finally arrived for me to leave, I made sure mum wouldn't come to the airport - I could not handle any theatrics there. Instead the drama unfolded at home with my mother clinging to my body as if I were dying and sobbing maniacally. Trying my best to comfort her I promised (for the hundredth time) to call her every other day and keep contact on WhatsApp and Facetime and blah blah blah. Thank you very much technology for allowing my mother to become my stalker. 'Preciate it.

Granna was gracious in her farewell although I knew she was sad to see me go but her excitement for me to experience her city won out over the other emotions. I promised to take a lot of pictures and videos to send her and she promised she would visit once her back was a bit better to handle the flight.

Dad and Megan dropped me to the airport and insisted on taking me all the way to security to say goodbye.

"Now, if you need anything just call, ok darling?" Dad said, looking worried and emotional but not enough to make a scene thankfully. He hated people making spectacles of themselves in public.

"I will dad don't worry, I promise. Don't worry too much, and try to make mum calm down. She stresses herself out."

"Telling your mother to calm down is like telling your aunt Audrey to stop scowling," he chuckled and we laughed as we hugged. I turned to my unusually quiet sister and gave her a squeeze.

"I thought you wanted me out of your hair?" I teased her. She looked up with he big brown eyes and gave me a small smile.

"Gonna miss you big sis." I squeezed her a bit harder.

"I wont be gone forever Megs. Come visit me as soon as your exams are over, ok?"

"Okay. And you will have to take me shopping!" She cheered up immediately at the idea of a shopping spree, expense paid by big sis of course.

I waved goodbye to them and took a deep breath, letting the adrenaline of leaving home behind and starting my new life sink into me. *This is the beginning of new and better things Alexa.* Today my sub-conscience was pumping me with confidence that I could do this.

***

Settling into my seat I found that I was sat next to a woman and her adorable little girl. I had loved children, wanted so desperately to have them with Tom. I was constantly reminded of that void in my life. The fact that the super slut had gotten pregnant so easily after a three month affair with my husband hurt a lot, especially when I had been trying for a year after we lost our first after fourteen weeks of pregnancy. That heart wrenching pain remained a constant reminder and the fact that Tom's sister Viola had called to let me know that his baby boy was born nine months ago, made the reality sink in that I couldn't give him that during our marriage.

Viola, who had been devastated when she learnt of his betrayal and our divorce, had stuck by my side and helped me through the divorce even when she was expected to take sides with her brother. She only gave me the necessary information about what he was doing and anything she felt I would hear better from her than from third parties. Tom's parents had been upset about the whole affair, disappointed with their son and the fact that couldn't keep it in his pants. I knew they respected me as much as I respected them, Tom had broken our family apart. Regardless, they wouldn't abandon their only son and I wouldn't ever expect them to and despite how supportive they had been towards me, I withdrew as much as I could from them to save awkwardness and pain for both of us.

The little girl sitting next to me started leaning more towards my side, giggling as she watched an inflight movie. Her mother noticed and smiled apologetically.

"Annie, you mustn't lean on the nice lady, sweetie," her mother said in an american accent. The little girl moved swiftly away, looking at me with wide eyes.

"Oh no, thats ok. It's not a bother, lean away Annie," I smiled at them both. Annie twirled her curly dark ringlet around her finger and stared at me with big beautiful blue eyes. She looked just like her mother.

"Whats your name?" she inquired in a sweet voice.

"My name is Alexa, but you can call me Lexi if you like." She scrunched up her little nose.

"I would like to call you Alexa. It's a pretty name!" She returned my smile and offered me some of her chocolate buttons.

"I'm Bonnie," her mother introduced herself shaking my hand. And just like that, we kept one another company for the rest of the seven and half hour journey. I learned that Annie had an older brother aged six who had travelled a couple of days earlier back to New York with their father and that she had just turned four herself.

Bonnie explained that they had been visiting her husbands family in London whilst she was still able to travel, revealing that she was at the end of her first trimester of pregnancy and feeling the sickness. We ended up talking and enjoying the journey and I was happy to help with taking care of little Annie as Bonnie frequented the lavatories when she felt naseous, one of the joys of pregnancy, I was told.

When Bonnie took a little nap, Annie told me all about the little rag doll she was carrying with her and gushed about her uncles and aunt who were waiting for her to get back to throw her a birthday party to make up for the one that they had missed while she was in London. She was so animated in her cute expressions and the innocence she radiated made me ache. If only we could all retain some of that within us as adults. I briefly wondered if I'd ever be able to have children and relive those precious life experiences children do for the first time again. I stopped my train of thought before I could radiate my melancholic thoughts to the little precious child beside me. *You wouldn't know what to do with a kid.* But I knew that was a lie.

I chatted away with Bonnie and found we got on easily. I surprised myself by feeling able to tell a complete stranger openly that I was recently divorced and starting my new life in New York. She was attentive and didn't pry which made it easier to share more information with her. She told me she was going to be attending a family wedding and was finding it difficult to find any clothes that were comfortable now that her baby bump had started to show and was funny. We talked about anything and everything whilst Annie slept and it was so nice to have a girly chat with someone so easy to talk to.

"I'm sorry for just prattling on," I smiled apologetically at Bonnie.

"Don't be silly! I enjoyed our time talking, It's been a while since I have had the chance to just have a girl to girl chat. I mean, I have a wonderful network of friends but we are all busy with our jobs, kids and husbands. No time for ourselves. It's great just talking to someone who is as easy to talk to as you." She smiled kindly and I new that she meant what she said.

"Ditto. On the easy to talk to part," I laughed.
When we landed at JFK, I helped Bonnie with Annie as we walked through the airport. We parted ways at arrivals having exchanged her number for Allison's home number. Bonnie waved at her husband in the distance and he began to walk over. I couldn't see Brian anywhere as yet.

"I will call you soon hun, I am sure Annie will remind me every day!" She laughed as Annie tugged at my jacket sleeve.

"You have to come visit soon Alexa, I want you to come to my party!" She said in her cute shy voice.

"Of course sweetheart, I would love to. Now you be good and help mummy and daddy out okay?"

"Okay!" She tugged me down for a hug, to my surprise, and gave me a kiss on my cheek. I felt a flutter of joy but the ache was there once again and the uncertainty of whether I would ever be able to have my own children was ever present and made me feel a little sick. I pushed the thought out of my mind. *You just got out of a longterm relationship, you're here to start afresh. You're young, you're just thinking of something that you lost. How do you know you were ready for it then anyway? Maybe life has other plans for you yet.*

My subconscious mind, the rational me, was giving me the

reasons. I just needed to let this go but it still hurt.

Bonnie's husband and son reached us and the way in which the family interacted warmed the hurt I was feeling. It made me smile that there were still happy families out there, it gave me hope for something better. *I must not dwell in the past.*

"Alexa, this is my English husband David and this little man is Tyler. David, Alexa has been helping me with Annie and her endless questions and has been so patient with us."

"It's nice to meet you Alexa. You must have a migraine by now," David smiled and held out his hand. He was blonde, blue eyed and tall and very handsome. He had a kind, warm smile and I liked him immediately. Tyler looked more like his dad but had mischief in his eyes that reminded me of my cousins. No doubt he would be fighting off the ladies soon enough.

"Not at all! It was a pleasure and the diversion was very welcome. Annie is a beautiful intelligent little girl, she has told me a great deal about her time in London." Bonnie and David looked lovingly at Annie as she hugged her daddy's leg and he lifted her up into his arms.

"Yes, she is a special girl, and chatty too. Just like her mother. Ow!" Bonnie playfully punched his shoulder and they smiled sweetly at one another.

We said good bye to one another with a promise of meeting soon and I watched them walk away with a smile on my face. I resumed looking for Brian when I felt a tap on my shoulder.

Turning around, I was enveloped in a bear hug and I didn't need to see the face to know Brian had found me. I struggled to breathe and laughed as I saw Christine's barely contained laughter as she rolled her eyes at her man.

"Bri, I think you cracked my ribs!" I laughed, and he slowly set me down and I saw the giant grin on his face.

"I am so glad you're finally here!" His blue eyes twinkled and kissed his cheek with affection.

"He's been up since five this morning," Christine explained smiling as she hugged me, firmly but a lot gentler than Brian had.

"He's had like fifteen cups of coffee too," she whispered in my ear as she let go and I giggled. I felt excited, less anxious and ready to see the great city that had been my unfulfilled dream for such a long time now. Brian grabbed my luggage trolley and we talked about the flight, I told them about Annie and Bonnie and then we discussed the plans Christine and Brian had made for dinner on our journey to my new home.

Driving out into New York City had me lost for words. I tuned out of the conversation, drinking in the sight of the Manhattan skyline as we crossed a bridge, taking the scenic route home. In that moment, I felt exactly the same way I had felt when I first came to New York years ago when I was at University. It was the only trip I had gone on without Tom, having met him on our degree course. He was in the third year of his Architecture degree and I was in the first year of the same degree subject. He had taken this trip already with his design studio in his first year and our relationship was still new. I remember arriving in New York and feeling so alive and amazed and I was beginning to feel that nostalgia again now. The tall buildings, wide roads and then the residential town houses all amalgamated into the great Manhattan area that I had promised myself I would return to.

It was late afternoon when Brian turned the car into the quieter residential Upper West Side area and drove down beautiful tree lined streets that housed the signature Brownstone buildings. I could see a few families out walking. A few dog owners were taking their dogs on walks, although a few of those dogs seemed to be taking their *owners* for walks. I smiled at how happy and laid back they looked.

The day was beautiful, late sun at the end of June, making

the surroundings look lush and invigorating. Brian slowed the car down to stop in front of a particularly beautiful Brownstone townhouse.

"This is where Allison lives?" I asked as Brian parked the car and moved to open his door. I couldn't keep the shock or the awe out of my voice.

"Yup." He chuckled at my expression and got out of the car to open my door for me. I stood on the sidewalk and gawked at the building.

This Brownstone was beautiful. For someone who appreciates architecture like I do, this was a dream. It looked to have a basement and three other floors. From my understanding, this was a Greek revival style townhouse and the attention to detail along with the way in which the building had been maintained proved that the owner took pride in his home. Allison had told me that the owner, our landlord, was a rich young man. Maybe a trust fund kid, I thought smiling. Who cared? This place was far beyond my expectations for the rent I knew I was paying for it. The little bit of lingering anxiety I had dissolved at the thought of this place being home for the foreseeable future.

"Look at you, living it up in New York," Brian nudged me with his elbow when he came to stand by my side. I gave him the biggest smile I could, and I knew my eyes were twinkling with excitement. Brian pulled me into a hug and kissed my forehead.

"You deserve it Lexi, you deserve so much happiness. I am glad I'm here to see you so happy." His smile and caring words prompted me to squeeze him tight.

"You're just the best Bri," I smile up at him, as he released me.

"I know." That cheeky grin reminded me so much of our grandfather.

Collecting my bags we climbed up the stairs to find the front door swing open before we reached the top.

"LEXI!" I heard her before I saw her. Allison "Bones"

Smart stood at the top of the stairs, wavy blonde hair, glassy blue eyes and perfect figure wearing black skinny jeans and a blue shirt the colour of her eyes. I could see she was containing herself from flying at me, seeing as I had a lot of luggage.

"Allison!" I managed to somehow drop my luggage with care and embrace my crazy hyper friend She squeezed me so hard I couldn't breathe after a few seconds.

"Allison...I can't breathe...Allison?....Alis....BONES!" The second I called her the high school nickname that made her famous, she pulled back and scowled at me, punching my arm playfully.

"I was happy to see you up until a few seconds ago Lexi. You just had to bring *that* up, didn't you?"

"You were squeezing the bejesus out of me, I had to defend myself!" I chuckled as I got my breath back and Allison smiled broadly, forgetting her gripe as she recognised Brian.

"Brian! Lexi told me you were in New York! How have you been?" Allison still looked at Brian the way she did when we were back in high school. She would try to come around to my house on the weekend when he would be there and would crush on him whenever he was not. I didn't enjoy hearing the details of what she wanted to do to him, considering he is like my brother.

Now, however, it was funny that she still looked a little flustered and her cheeks were a little pink. Considering she had a long term boyfriend, I guess some people still elicited the same reactions from one another no matter how much time had passed and circumstances had changed. And Brian was a good looking man. Back in the day, he was the bad boy, a grade above us, and all the girls wanted to be my friend to get to him.

"Allison, I'm good thank you. You look well," Brian said, sounding a little strange. I looked at him and then back at Allison. Something was a little off. He had a little smile on his face but it was his secretive smile. Oh dear...I had a bad feeling about this.

"And this is Christine, Brian's girlfriend," I interjected before this got more awkward for Christine. When I looked over at her, she seemed calm and was smiling. Hmm, maybe it was just me.

"Nice to meet you Christine," Allison shook her hand and smiled, remembering her manners as she ushered us inside the house.

"Wow." The word escaped my mouth before I realised I'd said it out aloud.

'You like?" Allison asked, knowingly.

"I...LOVE."

As soon as I walked into the hall, I was in awe of my surroundings. I'd never thought that I would want to live in a townhouse because of all the floors but my word, this was a mind changer.

The wide hall and spiralling staircase we had just walked past was painted white and I could see that the flooring throughout the hall, as it opened up into the open plan living and dining area, was a dark hardwood. The living room we were now standing in was just what I would want in a home. Just the right amount of classic with a wall of bookshelves reaching up to the high ceilings. Beautiful, plush dark purple velvet button tufted sofa's with matching single seat armchairs and expensive looking Persian rugs strategically placed.

And then there was the not too brash introduction of the modern interior aspect of the room. There were beautiful colours in paintings of abstracts on the wall to the left, and cushions of Moroccan blue, spice red, aubergine purple and saffron orange arranged on the furniture. The wall housing the impressive book collection had a break in the middle that housed a huge wall-mounted flatscreen and an even more impressive faux fire place recessed into the wall. More seating was arranged around the coffee table in front of the main feature sofa's, making the room seem more inviting. A beautiful Moroccan handmade glass chandelier hung from the high ceiling reflecting the beautiful colours reminiscent of the cushions on the furniture.

The size of the townhouse was becoming more and more apparent as my eyes fell past the large dining table and into the kitchen, as I walked further into the house, that was separated from the rest of the ground living space and situated at the back corner of the house. Large grand looking doors opened into the most beautiful granite, stainless steel and wood designer kitchen. I knew enough about the fittings as to estimate that this was a crazy expensive design. Definitely branded. Stools lined the breakfast bar and more kitchen appropriate lighting graced the room. There seemed to be every kind of appliance available there.

I idly wondered if any of it was ever used - Allison was not terribly fond of cooking as I remember and I had no idea what the other tenant was like. That was another thing I was nervous about.

I could see the deck and garden beyond the bi-folding doors. There was, what I liked to call, a free standing egg swing in one corner of the deck and some wicker garden furniture. A brand new looking barbecue range sat in another corner. I found myself thinking of dad and how much he would love to have something like that to conduct his barbecues on.

The lawn looked beautifully manicured and the summer flowers were in bloom - roses in pinks and yellows, chrysanthemums and peonies. It was such a beautiful symphony of colours and as I stepped out the smell was beautiful, I almost forgot that we were in the city.

"It is really impressive isn't it? Wait until you see the other floors!" Allison smiled, looking excited about showing the rest of the house off. There was a ground floor guest rest room that oozed luxury and a fully stocked pantry to finish off the tour of this floor.

Next we went down some stairs that were concealed by an ornately carved wood saloon style doors as an entry that led to the basement level. I was pleasantly surprised to find that the basement was far from dark and dank, as I had mistakenly expected, but light and airy. It had a similar ethos as the ground floor with white walls and hardwood floors but the main room had a feature wall on one whole side of the wall.

It was a big room and had been quite lovingly turned into a den of sorts - a games room. A bigger flatscreen than the one in the ground floor living room was mounted to the wall, a pool table was set up in one corner, a couple of games machines were beside that, some comfortable looking leather sofa's and chairs and a bar stood on one side which looked to be fully stocked. The room was actually big enough to double as a small scale club. Bi-folding doors opened up into the garden, under the deck with stairs leading up to it.

I was quickly shown the utility room through a door at the back of the vast room and then ushered upstairs to explore the first and second floors. All the while Brian and Christine followed, just as impressed as me although Brian was a bit more audible of his appreciation, especially in regards to the basement man cave.

I didn't think they could but things just got better the higher up we went. The first floor, where Allison and our house mate slept, had two bedrooms, another guest bedroom and a small study. I use the word 'small' loosely as the study was the size of my old living room.

Allison's bedroom was vast, walk in closet and en suite attached with her theme of lilac and white evident throughout. Her large windows opened out into a balcony facing the garden. Allison informed me that the two other bedrooms on the floor had identical plans only without the balcony. I was amazed at just how much space was available compared to what used to be mine and Tom's small London end of terrace house.

The second floor was much the same as the first, only there were two bedrooms and in place of a study there was a large empty study room slash office with very sparse furnishings besides the desk and a couple of chairs.

Allison had informed me before our ascent up the first and second floors that I would be picking from either the guest room on first floor or the two bedrooms on the second - I was that lucky that I had a choice. It wasn't as hard a decision for me to make as I'd initially thought it would be. I found my new room on the second floor, directly above Allison's, and fell in love. It was a mirror of the room below but was yet to be turned into my own comfy domain. Along with the balcony that was identical to the one Allison had in her room, this room had two beautiful bay windows that already had my head teeming with ideas for the room.

"Are you sure you want to be alone on the second floor?" Brian asked, going into big brother mode which was both endearing and amusing at the same time.

"Yes, one hundred percent. Don't look at me like that Bri, what could possibly happen to me sleeping alone on the second floor?" He thought about it for a few seconds and then reluctantly sighed his resignation on the argument.

"Great, so that's settled then! I'm so glad you're here Lexi!" Allison was beaming which was infectious as I found myself doing the same.

We decided to leave going to a restaurant in favour of a take away since I was jet lagged and we enjoyed one another's company as we caught up.

Around seven in the evening, as Brian and Christine started getting their things together to leave, the front door opened and in came a beautiful long wavy haired red head with piercing big green eyes. She was wearing a pastel patterned gypsy skirt and white cotton gypsy top. Her wrists were adorned with jangling bracelets, some with charms, others with beads and her large dream catcher earrings skimmed the beautiful porcelain skin of her nape. She was the definition of Bohemian. She smiled and it made her nose wrinkle as she winked at Allison and then came over to where I was standing and offered me her hand.

"You must be Lexi. I'm Sadie." Her voice was so soft and gentle that you would be inclined to believe she was a princess from a fairytale.

When I had released her hand, I smiled at her and knew this was our house mate that Allison had been talking about earlier during dinner.

I knew that she was a photographer, that she came from an influential family in Columbus, Ohio and that she was the sweetest person on Earth (Allison's words). I liked her already.

After Brian and Christine left, I spent another hour with the girls and felt happy and safe and *normal.* I had been feeling drowsy from the jet lag since I had arrived and the girls took pity on me and ushered me up to my room while they insisted on cleaning up themselves. I was grateful that Brian had transferred my belongings to my new room already and all I had to do was change into my pyjamas, brush my teeth and slip into the lovely fresh sheets of an impossibly comfortable bed. Tonight I felt like I was the luckiest woman in the world.

CHAPTER THREE

The Reason

The next day was a Saturday, which meant both the girls were home so we had a hearty breakfast. My jet lag wasn't as bad as I had anticipated and having slept a solid fourteen hours, I felt amazingly well rested and relaxed.

Once Breakfast was over, Allison pulled out a couple of sheets that looked like a contractual agreement - the rental agreement I presumed. She placed them in front of me and I looked them over. One of the documents appeared to be a Non Disclosure Agreement.

"Whats this for?" My eyebrows were raised in question because I seriously was at a loss.

"It's an NDA hun. We all have to sign one. It's part of the deal for living in this house. And probably why our landlord lets us live here with minimal rent," Allison explained.

"Ooookay..." I still didn't get what the reason was. I hadn't read the agreement properly yet.

"Let me explain," Allison said, sitting down next to me on the couch.

"Please," I murmured.

"Our Landlord, Mr Hamilton, only has three requirements from his tenants in this house. Number one is that he only wants females living in this house. Number two is that we try to maintain the house as well as possible. And number three, the most important one for him, is that we keep his identity and that he owns and lives in this house a secret. It is his privacy he wants to protect."

I absorbed what she said, although it didn't make sense to me that he would only want women in the house. Seemed unfair to men, not that I was complaining. Then I realised what she said last.

"He lives here?" I felt a little apprehensive, this guy seemed to be quite a presence and I didn't even know much about him.

"Not all the time. Very rarely actually. Every now and then he likes to escape from his life and camp out upstairs. You remember the locked door on the second floor next to your bedroom? That door opens up to stairs that lead up to a two storey extension of this house which serves as his personal apartment."

Wow. I remember seeing the locked door but not thinking much of it, assuming it was a storage space. I had no idea when we arrived yesterday that there was an extension to this house, I couldn't see it up close but now my designers mind was intrigued to see it, but of course that would be snooping. Plus it was locked.

"Where does he live otherwise?"

"In a penthouse not far from here." Hmm, odd.

"Why would he want to come stay here in the same city to get away? Has he got an overbearing wife or something?" Allison and Sadie both burst out laughing.

"Something like that!" I didn't bother asking anymore and signed the documents, keeping a copy for myself. Whatever it took to live in this beautiful palatial home for next to nothing rent.

***

The next week was spent settling into my new home. Allison and Sadie made perfect housemates and although Allison and I had history and an old friendship, Sadie fit right in with our friendship, her shy personality and easy going nature making it impossible to find fault. We had become friends in a very short amount of time and as I settled more, I felt confident enough to venture out on the weekdays when Sadie was working for a city fashion magazine doing photo shoots and Allison was in the financial district working for a big corporation as an analyst. I'd only been to local shops and Central Park but I enjoyed it so much, grateful to be living in the city I had always dreamed of living in.

I had yet to meet Allison's long term boyfriend, Brent. I'd initially taken the piss out of her the moment she told me his name, joking that he had a stereotypical rich boy name. He was also a close friend of Mr Hamilton, our landlord, which is how Allison got a room in the townhouse.

I knew that Allison had met Brent three years ago during a conference about some boring financial something or another and that he was an investment banker working a few blocks away from her. At the time she was a relatively new, young intern turned permanent employee.

They didn't hit it off straight away. Allison was openly rude to him and like I had done, she stereotyped him from the off set and avoided his attempts to ask her out even though she found him attractive. She always fell for the bad boys when we were at school. Then a few weeks later, she was asked to make a presentation for the bank Brent worked for. Unbeknownst to her, Brent was the man in charge and heading the meeting and she was presenting to him. In fact, he was a bigger fish than she initially thought; a very humble, serious man and a hard worker instead of the trust fund kid she thought he would be - even if his parents were wealthy.

She had to get through the presentation trying to avoid

eye contact with him because she was embarrassed thinking of the way she had treated him the first time they had met.

After the presentation, he asked to speak with her alone. She thought that he would ask her out again but instead he was professional and asked only work related questions and then let her go. She was gutted that she had lost her chance with this man because of her prejudice. The next day, however, she received a beautiful bouquet of flowers with a note:

"I know I shouldn't. You clearly don't want to
waste any time with me. But I couldn't help myself.
You looked so beautiful yesterday and
these reminded me of you."

The flowers were a blush pink. The dress she had worn for the meeting was the same shade. The fact that this man was being honest was a first for Allison, most of the guys she had been with were scoundrels.

The next thing she knew, Allison started searching through her handbag for the business card he had given her the day before. She dialled his personal number and to everyone's surprise asked him out after apologising for her behaviour. One date led to another and then many more where he acted like a gentleman and they got to know one another, finding that they did indeed have a lot in common. And then one thing led to another, fast forward three years and they were madly in love with one another. Brent had tried to get Allison to move in with him but she wouldn't - she loved having her own space too much. Besides, she told me, if she moved out of the house, it would be for her husband. I could tell she was secretly wishing he would hurry up and pop the question already. Okay, maybe not so secretly, she spent a whole day moaning about it to me.

Halfway through my first week, Allison called me from her office.

"Hey Bones, whats up?" I said cheerily, smiling at my

use of her nickname.

"Grr! I'm going to ignore that one! And only because I'm really excited! Brent wants to take me away this weekend - it's the Independence Day weekend and we were supposed to be attending a wedding that has now been cancelled. He hasn't booked the tickets yet because I wanted to check if you would be okay on your own. You know that Sadie is out of town visiting her family over the weekend too, right? Oh shit, maybe this is a bad idea. I don't want to leave you all alone on your first week here! I'm a shit friend!"

She always talked at the speed of a runaway train when she was flustered.

"Allison, please stop. Firstly, a cancelled wedding? That's just so sad! I mean, it's great for you but I digress...Secondly, I will be fine! I'm an adult and to be honest I'm looking forward to having the place to myself." And I meant it. I really wanted the time to myself to settle and explore and be a lazy arse for the first time in ages.

"But you shouldn't be alone in a new city and you've been through so much -"

"Stop! I'm not a charity case, I said I will be fine! And you are an amazing friend. I wanted the time alone. Trust me, I'm over the shithead so go enjoy time with your man and get a tan. Where you going by the way?" I lied about getting over Tom but she seemed to accept it for now.

"The Bahama's for four days," she sighed.

"You lucky bitch! If you don't go, I will and then you will be sorry. And don't you dare start that 'I'm a bad friend' shit again, okay?"

"You're the bestest friend there ever was Lexi. Still, it's not confirmed. We have to get leave approved, well I do, and then find last minute tickets at the busiest time of year."

"You will find them, don't sweat it. I'm so excited for you!"

***

To both of our benefits, Allison's leave did get approved and including the day off for July 4th, she would get a few days away with her man. She was due to leave the next day so as soon as she got home I helped her pack, giving her a thumbs up on all the skimpy bikini's she owned and throwing in extra lingerie when she wasn't looking. I had a good feeling about her up coming trip and some extra 'props' wouldn't hurt.

Sadie left for Ohio, the cab taking her to the airport that same night and since Allison's flight was early morning, we said goodbye to one another before we went to bed. Some alone time was exactly what I needed.

I went into my room, drinking in the beautifully decorated white vintage interior. I had since added a little colour with my patchwork throw Granna gave me years ago in all shades of gray and blue, my favourite colours, and some other personal effects such as my landscape paintings I had painted years ago that reminded me of happier times as a college student. I had decided that I didn't want too much colour to distract from the serenity of my white room so the only items that were placed in view were my jewellery box and a few bottles of perfumes on the beautiful dresser, my make up and other contents hidden in the drawers. There was a chaise longue that I had moved from in front of the bay window to a space in front of the floor to ceiling balcony windows/doors. This made more sense to me as I planned to make a window seat for the bay windows and use the area as a reading nook.

The walk in wardrobe was every girls dream. Enough space for all the clothes and accessories you could ever own. I found this space perfect for my large number of bags. I had no trouble admitting that I had a bag fetish and that this was an addiction. I couldn't seem to stop and owned some beautiful pieces, branded and non branded, that I treasured more than most things I owned. I had insisted on shipping them all with me as you never knew when you might need any one of them in New York. My mother had rolled her eyes and given up the argument.

Now, laying back in the sumptuous four post bed that felt like a five star hotel had procured it for me, I pulled out the embossed notebook my ex work colleagues had given me from my bedside drawer. I had been writing in it since the second day of my arrival. I used to write a lot before I got married and got wrapped up in being Tom's wife. Poems, thoughts and novels I never completed. I promised myself that I would start it all again.

I opened the notebook up to a fresh page and wrote.

Wednesday 3rd July

Today I actually didn't spare a thought about Tom...until now. How wonderful it is to spend a day just being selfish with my time and thoughts. I already know that I am well on my way to feeling indifferent to Tom. Just not quite there yet. I know that I am in the right place to heal what is left of the gaping hole in my heart. Mostly repaired, just waiting until its only a superficial scar that is my lesson learnt from experience and my good and bad memories patched in. Now I can start remembering the person I used to be. I hate that I forgot myself...I am a no longer the loaded gun, leaden with bullets and ready to fire...I am a leaf, falling from a tree. Weightless and uncaring, letting the wind carry me wherever it will. It's time for me to be me, I am finally free...

The revelation took me by surprise. I had never thought of things this way before and that in itself had become part of the learning process. *Realisation.* My Eureka moment.

I lay back in the comfortable bed, surrounded by fluffy pillows that were alien but needed and the welcome smell and texture of my patchwork quilt - a little home comfort. My eyelids felt heavy with sleep, a welcome sensation since with the crazy excitement of this first week, I had felt it hard to sleep for all the plans I had been making. Tomorrow I would put away the rest of my belongings, have a nice long bath and relax in this big beautiful house left on my own to deal with all my recent emotions and discoveries. Finally.

***

The next morning, I woke up with a big smile on my face. I couldn't remember the last time I did that. And that smile wasn't put there by someone else. It was all me. I didn't need anyone to make me happy, just me.

Sure, it still felt weird that the person that had felt like he was literally my other half had vanished from my life apart from the odd text message and phone call to discuss the legal stuff. That still hurt me, but not as much as it initially had. I guess the saying that 'time heals' was true. Every day the pain got a tiny bit less but that was still progress in my eyes. I had gotten past hating Tom a few months ago and the peace I felt at finally letting that anger go did me a world of good. I realised that the anger inside me only hurt me and not him. It was exhilarating that I could live my whole life thinking I knew myself well yet I kept surprising myself with just how strong I could be and how well I accepted change when I would previously loathe the thought of it.

I got up from my bed, sinking my toes into the soft rug on the hardwood floor and walked over to the balcony. Opening the french doors, I stepped out into the warm New York sun and thanked God for being able to enjoy it all. This was my routine since my first morning there. The view of the garden was refreshing in the morning and I found myself wishing I had a cup of tea to relax on one of the wicker chairs that was placed on the balcony.

Walking back into the room, I checked the time before heading into the bathroom. It had just gone past ten and I wanted to have breakfast and sort through my cd's, dvd's and books to put downstairs in the living room shelves where the girls had kept their things with their names on labels so that they didn't get mixed up. I had never shared a home with anyone, apart from Tom when we got married. Before that, I had decided to stay at home during university since I studied in London. It was exciting to have the opportunity to do it now with such accommodating ladies. My God, had I started to turn into one of those completely annoyingly optimistic people that find no fault with anything? This was definitely a 'LOL' moment.

Finishing from the bathroom, all minty fresh but still dressed in my pyjama shorts, vest and the bunny slippers my mum had bought me before I left London, I made my way down the winding stairs to the living room.

I had brought my boxes down the night before with help from Allison so all I needed to do was sort and place. I made myself a cup of tea in the designer kitchen (that had been well stocked with Tetley tea bags - the only thing Allison had asked me to bring for her) and got to work.

I turned on the sound system and figured it out quickly, plugging my Ipod into the dock. Setting it to shuffle I pressed play, turning up the volume on an old favourite dance song by Haddaway called "What is Love?" that took me back to school disco times when shell suits were all the hype and side ponytails were in fashion.

I was busy humming to myself and dancing a little as I reached up placing my CD's alphabetically onto the shelves (Allison had a system she wouldn't let anyone mess with) when I realised I hadn't eaten anything. My stomach rumbled in agreement.

Just as I was about to put my CD's down and turn to head to the kitchen to make breakfast, I was gripped from behind by two strong strong arms and pinned against a hard body. I screamed, dropping everything in my hands, but my assailant put his hand over my mouth to silence me

"How did you get in here? Who sent you?!" the gruff

and definitely male voice asked in anger as I struggled in his grip.

My heart must have been pounding like a jack hammer. My survival instincts kicked in and I bit his hand hard. He let go of me and growled in pain as I scrambled to safety, putting a sofa between us and grabbing the first thing that I could find as a weapon. My breathing had been fast from fear and adrenaline but my heart nearly stopped at the sight before me.

I think I went into shock the moment I clapped eyes on the half naked stranger in my new living room and what must have been over six feet of pure sex. Half naked sex. This man was a creature made up of fantasies.

My gaze travelled up his body slowly. Bare feet, long legs that I just knew had to muscular under the loose sweatpants. Now I knew what all those authors that wrote my favourite love stories meant by the sexy men in their books wearing jeans or sweatpants that just hung off his hips in 'that way.' His torso was a heavenly mix of tanned abs with a defined six pack, strong pectoral muscles, muscular biceps and oh my God. Tattoos. I had always had a thing for bad boy tattoos. This guy had a large tribal tattoo down the right side of his body and right arm, stopping before his wrist. He had a light dusting of hair on his body that just made him seem more masculine if that was even possible.

He was just the right amount of muscular without looking like a body builder but definitely enough to be boxing. And then I saw his face. I nearly pinched myself because it was impossible for that amount of absolutely perfect to exist.

Strong jaw with a light scruff of a beard coming through, manly cheekbones and a nose that was almost perfect but for looking like he may have broken it at least once at some point. It just made him more sexy and dangerous. He definitely must have played some contact sport.

His eyes were the most beautiful blue, the colour of a stormy sky - a blue grey - and dark thick lashes. His almost black hair was a beautiful thick mess that I just longed to run my fingers through.

He was my fantasy made real. I couldn't stop gaping at him, probably looking like a total moron. Then I realised that this man was a stranger and I was also inappropriately dressed. Plus he could be a maniac. He had just pinned me against him like I was some criminal. I was suddenly angry more than scared. I stopped ogling and found my tongue.

I was also vaguely aware that the track on my ipod had changed to "Single Ladies." I would have laughed were I not feeling mad.

"Who the fuck are *you*?" My voice came out angry and strong, which made me proud of myself for not wussing out. He, however, looked bewildered.

"Uh, I live here. Don't pretend like you don't know who I am! Who the fuck are *you*? You a reporter?" He was angry too which only made *me* angrier.

"I live here too! Jesus!" I was exasperated, still breathing hard from shock and the anger still hadn't subsided.
I then realised that he was stood silent, one hand nursing his left where I had bitten him. Realisation showed on his breathtaking face slowly but surely.

"You're Alexa De Luca." It was a statement, not a question.

"Yes I am. Again, who the fuck are you?" For the first time in the short few minutes we had interacted, he smiled a slow sexy dimpled smile.

"I'm Kade Hamilton."

CHAPTER FOUR

All American Male

"**E**xcuse me?" I thought I may have heard him wrong. But then again, that was the only plausible explanation as to how he got in and why he had reason to be there.

"I'm Kade Hamilton. You know, the landlord." Now he looked amused, his sexy smile turned into a grin and his eyes laughed with him as his dimples deepened.

"What are you doing here? I mean, I was under the impression I would be alone these next few days." I know I sounded rude but he was pissing me the hell off with his smugness. That and the fact that I really felt attracted to him, already fantasising about licking those dimples, made me want to slap myself.

"I got in just as Brent and Allison were leaving for the airport. It was not planned. I'm sorry I scared you, I was under the impression that you had broken in and were..." He stopped himself from saying whatever he was about to say, instead breaking into what could only be described as a lovable rogue smile before continuing. "Never mind what I thought. I forgot that I have a new tenant." He sure as hell didn't look sorry. I felt like punching that smile off his handsome face.

"Um, do I look like a burglar to you? Despite the fact that I am wearing pyjamas and bunny slippers, I was also *putting back* CD's, not taking them. And I'm not a reporter. What would a reporter want to do here?" I know I should have reigned in my temper a bit but this man had had me thinking I was going to get murdered not five minutes ago.

"Whoa there cowgirl, I'm sorry. I've been stressed lately, I just assumed the worst." He blew out a frustrated breath. "This is the worst first introduction ever. let's start over, okay?" He put on a practiced serious expression as he stalked over to me and I let myself break a little from my anger to drink in his flexing muscles when he came to a stop just a couple of feet away from me. He extended his hand and smiled.

"Hi, I'm Kade Hamilton. I like to grab innocent British girls and threaten them in my living room. I am also a black belt in Karate, like long walks on the beach and have a penchant for little stripy sleep shorts."

I looked down at my attire and went bright red. Laughing a little at his attempt to break the ice, I gave up and took his extended hand. The attraction was undeniable and the feel of my hand in his made me shiver. My natural tendency to shy away from male attention, especially a stranger, escaped me. I was surprised at myself. For so many years Tom was the only man I opened myself up to easily. I mean, I had male friends but they were *just friends.* And the thing with Max, in my defence I was rather intoxicated and therefore feeling brave.

"My name is Alexa De Luca, my friends call me Lexi. I like reading and not being attacked by my landlord in his living room. I never took martial arts but I'm vicious, I can kick ass. And I must warn you, I bite," I smiled before looking at his hand adding, "Oops, too late."

We stood smiling at one another for a few seconds before I pulled my hand out of his big strong one.

"You have a good strong hand shake," I said, trying to

break the silence. It was the lamest thing to say but I was famously known for not always being able to switch on my brain to mouth filter. My mother always said that it was because I was an honest person, saying what I thought. I just thought it was a huge dose of stoopid.

"Thank you. You have a strong bite," he laughed, examining his hand. Lo and behold, I had drawn blood. I suddenly felt really guilty.

"Oh God, I'm so sorry! I never would have done that had I known who you were."
He shook his head and grinned.

"Not your fault Alexa. I did give you cause to think I would do you harm. I'm truly very sorry. I had slept on the couch in the den downstairs this morning, heard your music and my sleep ridden brain didn't register that it would be you."

"It's ok, I guess there's no harm done. Well, apart from your hand." I paused a moment before good manners reminded me who I was. "Hey, let me take a look at that. You may need to clean it out and cover it. I'll do that for you, since it is my fault after all." He smiled and nodded his consent and we headed to the kitchen.

Kade propped himself up on a stool as I opened and closed every cabinet. I stopped when I realised he was chuckling softly, turning to give him a narrow eyed glare.

"What are you laughing about?" I did not like being laughed at for no reason.

"Um, the first aid box is in the restroom around the corner in the cabinet." I look up at him in exasperation.

"You could have told me when I've clearly been struggling here!" I couldn't believe this guy. Landlord or not, I was certainly not going to take his shit.

"I'm sorry! You just looked really cute running around like that..." I realised he probably also got a good look at my short cladded arse. I felt my cheeks pink as I huffed and made my way to the restroom to retrieve the first aid kit. *We've just met and he is being very inappropriate and I think there's a possibility he is trying to flirt with me!* My mind felt jumbled.

I heard him chuckle some more but he had wisely stopped before my return, looking a little sheepish. Sitting in front of him at the breakfast bar, I started tipping some antiseptic onto cotton and cleaned around the bite mark. He didn't flinch but I could feel his eyes burning holes into me. I was also aware of the heat of his hand in mine and that electricity that I felt between us returned ten fold.

Trying my best to ignore the tingling I felt in my body, I managed to cover the wound with a bandage and tied it securely around his hand. Once finished, I smiled at my handiwork and then looked up to the most breathtaking of faces I'd ever seen.

His brow was furrowed in thought and his eyes were more blue all of a sudden than grey as he looked straight into mine. It felt like an eternity had passed before his face broke out int o a slow sexy dimpled grin.

"Thank you." It was said sincerely yet it felt like it meant more. I felt a little shy as he stared at me, deep in his own thoughts and of all the emotions available, I felt shy.

"You're welcome," I finally replied trying but failing miserably to look away from his beautiful face. My stomach chose that exact moment to growl loudly. I closed my eyes in embarrassment and giggled nervously.

"You got some growler there. Had breakfast yet?" I could see he was struggling to contain his laughter.

"Uh yeah, I was about to make breakfast before I was rudely pinned down like a criminal in my own home," I rolled my eyes, turning to pull open the expansive fridge and taking out bread, an egg and some milk for my tea.

"Well, since you're making breakfast, I'll have two eggs sunny side up and four toasts thanks." I turned on my heel to see the sexy amused smile and a mischievous glint in his eye.

"Yeah right, like I'm going to make your breakfast for

you. I'm not your maid!" I started to get the feeling that he was intentionally winding me up and enjoying it too.

"Hey, you have incapacitated me! I can't use my right hand thanks to your vampire tendencies!"

"You have another hand mate, use it!"

"I need two hands to crack an egg," he pouted. This grown man actually pouted at me, giving me a glimpse of how gorgeous he must have been as a little boy.

"You're going to milk this for all it's worth, aren't you?" I looked him in his eyes and raised an eyebrow, a small smile creeping out on my face.

"Yes. Now make my breakfast woman!"

"If you say any more of that sexist shit, I will show you what real vampirism is," I shot him a warning glare before turning to get a frying pan from the cupboard.

"Promise?" I heard and felt the heat in the low tone of his voice. I didn't dare turn around for fear that my pink cheeks would give away his effect on me.

I felt his eyes on me the entire time I made breakfast, cracking eggs into the pan, buttering the toast that popped out of the toaster and making tea for both of us without actually asking his preference. The whole time, I gave myself a pep talk. *You will not flirt anymore with your landlord! You will not allow him the opportunity to get under your skin! Try not to insult him and stop being rude! Stop ogling at him!*

I knew that I was too messed up to *not* over analyse everything but once bitten, twice the cautious, bitchy woman. I couldn't ignore the fact that I had just met someone who was physically the most attractive man I'd ever seen. I could not deny that I felt a strong attraction but I would not read into his innuendoes and flirting. I couldn't believe I'd just met my landlord and that instead of being the old business man I thought he would be, he looked to be just a few years older than me.

I placed his plate in front of him and smiled a big fake smile before curtsying.

"Your breakfast, *sir*. Would that be all?" I know I should have stopped myself but surely this was better than flirting. He would just find me irritating and stop with the teasing.

Kade bit into his toast with perfect teeth, closing his eyes and moaning. The sound travelled up my spine and made me shiver.

"Never has toast tasted so good," he winked at me, a knowing smile on his face. He knew exactly what he was doing. My plan had backfired. I shot him an annoyed look and hopped onto the stool across from him at the breakfast bar.

Starting on my egg and toast I noticed with pleasure that he was eating his food with enthusiasm. A man who loves his food is a good sight. *He must work out a lot.*

He suddenly looked up and caught me staring, his lazy smile producing a sharp intake of breath from me. *Stop it now Lexi. He may be hot but he's also arrogantly aware of your reactions. Stupid sexy beautiful man. Stop!*

"You're a lot younger than I assumed you'd be," I said, saving myself from the embarrassment of being caught staring.

"Did you expect a middle aged balding business man?" He looked to be in good humour which put me at ease.

"Well, yes. I don't understand why a man living in an upscale penthouse would want to live here too. Are you running away from your wife or girlfriend?" I meant it as a joke but he suddenly seemed serious and a little sad too.

"No. No wife, no girlfriend." I could feel the tension radiating from the man who just a few seconds ago was so playful. I scrambled to recover the mood.

"So what's with all the secrecy and the NDA? Are you a mob boss or something, Don Hamilton?"

His mood lifted in an instant as he laughed heartily. He took my breath away.

"No, I'm not but but someone's been watching The

Godfather a lot. I'm just a very private person. I love this house, I like to come here as a retreat from work and sometimes family." I could tell it was much more than that but I didn't push him for the information. I was being nosy as it is.

"This is a beautiful house. I don't know why you don't just live here. I would find it hard to stay away." And I meant it, this house had felt like home the minute I stepped foot in it. I couldn't have wished for more.

"Ah, I have to keep up appearances with...work. I don't want anyone to know about this place. It's my sanctuary, you know?" I understood and nodded my agreement.

"So you like the house?" He asked seriously, as if my opinion mattered. It was evident that he was proud of his home.

"Like the house? I love it." I felt a little embarrassed of my overenthusiastic response but he just smiled sweetly at me. A different smile, not cheeky or flirty. His smile, his face was so expressive of his emotions. I felt that I could tell exactly what he was thinking at any given moment. I had never been able to do that with someone before.

"I'm glad. Should have seen it when I bought it. This here is a labour of love."

"I can't imagine this place being a dump. You have done a great job. Or the contractors have. I'm excited about the two storey apartment extension you got going on up there. Now that must be something else."

"You haven't seen it?" I shook my head no. "Ah, of course. It's been locked up. Allison and Sadie have keys but for some reason refuse to go up unless invited. I really don't understand why, I trust them." He looked confused at their respect for his privacy which made me believe he was someone who was used to having their privacy trampled on. His need for an NDA confirmed my assumption.

"Well, I guess they respect your privacy. Us women, we may be nosy but we know our limits not to disturb the man cave."

He looked dubious as if he knew better but laughed. I admired how comfortable and unashamed he looked sitting in just his sweats and bare chest.

"Do you want to come up and have a look at my man cave then?" he smiled his cheeky smile. I was quiet or a few seconds, debating the appropriate response. My curiosity got the better of.

"I though you'd never ask."

***

Kade led the way upstairs, filling me in on some the construction details with enthusiasm. Once we got to the door he pulled out a key from his pocket, while I ogled his naked back muscles and opened the door to his apartment.

The stairs leading up revealed white washed wall and once I stepped out onto the first floor of the two storey extension, I gasped in wonder. There was light radiating from every wall, mostly because each wall was entirely glass. What looked like automatic shutters were mounted above each glass panel.

The room was a very spacious open plan living room, a smaller scale but spacious kitchen area, what looked like a study area and a balcony looking out towards our garden. There were glass stairs leading up to a mezzanine floor and I could see a big bedroom and a few doors probably leading to the bathroom and maybe an extra room. The few support pillars of the structure were white, the furniture modern and minimalistic. The couch was an 'L' shaped white leather and the rug was black on hardwood flooring like the rest of the house. Art work couldn't be hung because of the glass so instead there were a few sculptures balanced on platforms and tables. What amazed me wasn't the high tech flat screen television or the Bang and Olufsen music system along with the other gadgets, but the sight of multiple bookcases I could see peeking from the mezzanine level in what must be

Kade's bedroom.

"Wanna come up to my bedroom?" He whispered wickedly in my ear. He must have seen my interest in the bookcases and I shivered as his voice trailed a delicious unspoken promise up my spine. I promised myself that I wouldn't let him see me blush so I ignored his chuckle of delight to my present reaction and stomped up the beautifully engineered floating glass stairs and gasped in awe of the collection in front of me. I was pretty sure he had every book in the library in here. A lot of history books on Egyptology and Greek Mythology and then there were the classics of Bronte and Austen, Dickens and Hardy. There were a few psychology books, an abundance of poetry books both contemporary and classic, books on religion and Philosophy and then a surprising number of cook books. Picking one of the "Baking made easy" books I raised a questioning eyebrow at him.

"Hey, I was alone in a foreign land without my mother and at university having to fend for myself. Don't judge me!" He looked defensive yet in good humour. I smiled and put the book back, biting my lip to stop myself laughing at his adorable expression.

"Kade, this is amazing. I feel like the whole library is stored in your bedroom. It's like I died and went to heaven." He leaned against a pillar and smiled, looking pleased.

"You are welcome to come up here any time you want, you know. It's not off limits to you or the other ladies. It makes happy to find someone as passionate about books as I am."

"I love books. I often lose myself reading. It is my escape."

I smiled back at him and for a few seconds something passed between us. An unspoken understanding of such. It was like we shared some of the brokeness of our pasts, even though I knew nothing of this guy apart from his name and that he owned this property and another more expensive one somewhere in the city

A book caught my attention from the corner of my eye and I immediately felt pulled towards it. Ignoring my manners, I picked out the old book that looked throughly read through with it's yellowing pages and creased binding and I touched the cover tenderly as if it were fragile.

"The Tale of Peter Rabbit By Beatrix Potter," I read aloud and smiled as tears came to my eyes with sweet memories of my Grandpa. Kade studied me for a second and then led me by the elbow to sit on the two seater sofa in the seating area of his bedroom under a skylight. The contact made me break my reverie to look at his concerned face. He didn't say anything, waiting for me to speak first.

"I'm sorry, I just saw this and remembered my Grandpa. He used to read this to me when I was little. My parents separated when I was very young, I'd just turned six. My mum took me and our stuff and moved us into my grandparents home. We stayed there for four years. He read this story and some others in the collection of Beatrix Potter books to me every night without fail. Then three years ago when he was recovering from a heart attack in the hospital, he asked me to bring my Peter Rabbit book for him. I remember thinking that it was so weird he would ask for it but I dug out my boxes of old books from the attic at my parents house and found it to bring to him. He told me to sit down by his side on his hospital bed and read me the story again. It was just so unexpected but I indulged him, and enjoyed the comforting feel of his arm around me as he read the story. The next morning we got a call from the hospital. He passed away in his sleep. When we went to hospital to see him and collect his belongings, I found that he had written a dedication in the front page. It said '*To my beautiful Lexi, you will always be the little angel with a big imagination and bigger dreams. Promise me you will live your life for yourself? Love always, Your Grandpa Richie.*' He knew he was going. And he chose to spend his last few minutes reminding me of all the things I had forgotten."

Kade sat there, listening intently. He smiled at me when I finished talking and I saw compassion in his eyes.

"I think your Grandpa Richie loved you very much." I looked up into those beautiful eyes, wiping away a stray tear that had fallen down my face at his words. I just kept surprising myself with the way I reacted to this man. I had just opened up about something so personal to a complete stranger. He just felt connected to me in some way. A kindred spirit.

"I'm not making a great first impression, am I? First I tackle you in the living room and now I'm making you cry." He reached up and wiped another tear off my cheek with his thumb. I stiffened at the intimacy of his contact with my skin.

"No it's not your fault. He's just the only man that never hurt me and let me down."

Grandpa was my hero, I had always wished my biological dad was like him and I always wanted to marry someone like him. Incidentally, Grandpa never liked Tom. He always said I was too good for him.

"So," I said, wiping my face and smiling up at him, thinking that I must have looked like a right mess, "What's you story behind this book?"
Kade gave me an enigmatic melting smile that made me warm inside my heart.

"My mom used to read this to me and my brothers and sisters. We would sometimes act out the characters. I was always naughty so naturally I was Peter rabbit." I grinned.

"You? Naughty? I would never have thought it!" I gasped in mock horror.

"Hey, I'm not so bad once you get to know me." He ran is hand leisurely through his thick dark hair and smiled that cheeky sexy smile. I looked away to stop it effecting me but that did nothing to stop me feeling a little hot under the collar.

"So you are not an only child?"

"Nope, one of five. I have an older brother and sister and then a younger brother and sister. I am the middle child."

I smiled at him, Imagining him as a younger brother and an older brother. I imagined that he would be respectful to the sister and a menace to the older brother, an overprotective brother to his younger sister and a hero to the youngest brother.

"What about you? Any siblings?"

"Yeah, a half sister from my mums marriage to my step dad and I have an older brother and sister from my fathers first marriage. Don't know how many more he may have, haven't spoken or seen him in years and I don't know his kids."

After my parents separated, and my father and his first wife reconciled, I only saw him on and off for about a year but after that he just disappeared and I would get an occasional phone call or card in the post. It was difficult for me to grasp because he was my hero as a little girl and I was very close to my dad.

He was originally from the States, a New Yorker actually, so I assumed he must have moved back there. I had never sought him out either. I felt that if I were important enough to him he would have made the effort but then things changed last year when he called out of the blue and spoke to my mother about how he wanted to be in my life again. My mum had left it up to me and I decided I didn't want the hassle because I was already going through so much. He would keep ringing every now and then to see if I would change my mind but I always told mum no. I felt that all those years when I *needed* him, he wasn't there and now that he wanted to be a part of my life, I no longer *wanted* for him to be. Mum had slipped his phone number and address into my bag before I came to New York, saying that maybe it would be good just to make amends and let go of the past and if I didn't desire reconciliation, I could always go for closure. It was still an issue I was unwilling to sort out just yet. *One life changing decision at a time.*

We spoke for a while longer, discovering that we had a lot of common interests, surprisingly. We shared opposing views on capital punishment. I found out that he'd studied at Oxford University and so had lived in the UK for four years. He had read Law there, thus surprising me further.

"Why do you look so shocked?" He smirked at my reaction.

"Um..I just...uh, didn't see you as a law graduate."

"You just thought I'm some drug dealing biker didn't you? It's the tattoos isn't it?" He smiled a knowing smile whilst somehow looking smug at the same time.

"No! Okay, maybe a little..." I blushed a little at being caught.

"Didn't anyone teach you it's wrong to judge a book by it's cover? Tut tut Alexa. Stereotyping me already." He bit his lip trying to stop his laughter at my discomfort. *Bastard.*

"Didn't anyone tell you it's wrong to assume that a woman in her pyjamas is an intruder and manhandling her is a gross invasion and violation of her personal space?" I smiled at my fast response. He smiled back and looked thoughtful.

"Touché Miss De Luca. You are a worthy opponent."

***

Before we knew it, it was two thirty and I remembered I was still sitting next to a topless hunk in my short pyjama shorts way too comfortably as would be socially acceptable with ones landlord, not to mention someone I had just met. I excused myself to go get changed and I could see the amusement on his face as I stumbled away. It seemed that I provided Kade Hamilton with constant entertainment.

Dressing in skinny black jeans and a baggy off the shoulder Rolling Stones t-shirt, I made my way back downstairs to the living room to resume un packing. Kade popped his head from around the corner. He was now dressed in blue jeans and a plain v neck t-shirt that just made his muscles look more delicious. I could see he had showered as well and the fresh scent was evident even from across the great room, his wet hair looking longish and unruly. Just so delicious. I willed myself not to drool and composed myself.

"Fancy a sandwich? I'm just making myself one. Thought I'd return the favour for breakfast." It was so unexpected and sweet of him to ask, I stood quietly for a few seconds.

"Sandwich, De Luca, yay or nay?" His one eyebrow raised, he seemed to have sobered from his earlier amused cheeky persona.

"Ah, yes please that would be great, thanks." I smiled shyly at him and looked back at the box I was unpacking.

"Anything particular you fancy?"

"Surprise me."

Twenty minutes later I was met with a salt beef and mustard sandwich with salad and crisps on a plate and also a glass of what looked like fresh lemonade.

"Wow, this looks great," I said appreciatively as we sat down on the rug in front of the coffee table. Kade turned on the tv to check the cricket scores.

"Oh dear God, please don't tell me you're into cricket..." I groaned. I hated cricket, Tom would make me watch with him and my step dad was crazy about it as well, not surprising since he coached the local boys team.

"What? It's a gentleman's game, surely this English lady would appreciate that?" My breath hitched in my throat. Tom always said that it was a gentleman's game whenever I complained which used to make me giggle and call him a posh boy.

I felt a pang of hurt in my chest, or was it a feeling of loss? Whatever it was, it made me feel those emotions I had been keeping at bay quite well so far. Kade picked up on the tension and slowly turned the television off. He looked concerned as he tapped my shoulder to get me to look at him instead of my fidgeting fingers.

"Hey, what's wrong? And don't say 'nothing' because I just saw the colour drain from your face."

Was I about to tell this man I had just met my sob story? He looked so sincere, so concerned that I started to let my guard down a bit. *Should I?*

"It's just that you reminded me of something my ex husband said. Well, almost ex husband, still waiting for the final papers." Now it was his turn to look surprised.

"You are...I mean, were, married? You look so young."

"I am young!" I gave him my 'I'm offended' face to lighten the mood, to which he smiled.

"You know what I mean."

"Well, any day now I will be receiving the final document proclaiming that I am a free woman. At long last." I should have sounded happier about that, given my drive to starting fresh.

"Judging by the look on your face, I'm guessing it was not something done amicably."

I sighed, not sure that I wanted to speak about Tom to have yet another person feel sympathy for me. Then again, the way Kade was looking at me right now - he looked interested and not pitying, so regardless of this man being an almost stranger, I started to think that maybe I could give him that little part of me and see if he ran a mile.

"You don't have to tell me anything about it if you don't want to Alexa, I didn't mean to pry." He looked so concerned and understanding, I felt that maybe talking to this man would be cathartic.

I took a deep breath and began my story...

Eighteen months ago...

"Shit. Shit shit shit!" I looked into my bag as my hand rummaged around feeling for the little box. Great. Mum had asked me over for a specific reason and that reason was sitting on my dressing table in my bedroom inside my house a twenty minute drive away. The earrings I had borrowed needed to be returned in time for her best friend, Aunt Edie's, fourth wedding. Yes, fourth. Aunt Edie still had it, whatever 'it' was. On second thought, I didn't want to know.

"Alexa Vita De Luca! Stop with the swearing! Dear God, this girl has no regard for manners!" She must have been pissed because she used my full name. It used to annoy me but now that I had grown up, moved away from her nest and missed seeing her so often, her scolding me made me smile with affection.

"Sorry mum." She couldn't stop herself smiling back, her annoyance forgotten.

"What's got your knickers in a twist?"

"I forgot the earrings at home mum, I'm so sorry. It will just take me a little time, I will go get them now."

"How did I know you would forget? One of these days you'll forget your own head! Don't worry about it, I will just wear one of my other ones. I'll go make us something to eat and we can catch up on everything we've missed." I would have loved that but I knew how much mum liked to match her clothes and accessories to look immaculate. I also had an ulterior motive to go back home. It was Saturday, my husband was home.

Recently he had been so busy with late nights at work, it had been like this for a few months actually, and I felt like we needed to connect again. We hadn't really had any proper action in the bedroom department for some weeks now. That was weird for us because we had always been active in the bedroom. But things had changed these few months, no matter how hard I tried to forget and move on, I couldn't.

We had miscarried our baby just three months ago. It wasn't planned, but that didn't mean it was unwanted. The surprise when we found out turned into immediate elation and we couldn't keep it to ourselves. We told our close friends and family who were all as excited as us. We kept being told that we would be amazing parents. I felt this completeness that nothing could compare to. And it was that little life growing inside me.

Before I knew it, days grew into weeks and I was suddenly 18 weeks pregnant and showing slightly. It was surreal but so natural at the same time.

One morning I woke up and didn't feel quite right. My stomach hurt as if I had eaten something bad and I pinned it all down to the large consumption of watermelon I had had the night before - one of my recent cravings. I told Tom that I would be skipping work that day because I felt sick. He kissed me and headed out saying he would be staying back at work to finish a project until late but to call if I needed him.

I spent that morning and afternoon resting and reading a bit and then cooking, the tummy pain having dulled and then disappeared. I settled back to watch an old RomCom, knowing I should take advantage of Tom not being home until late. That was until around 9:30pm when I started to feel the cramping get worse. This didn't feel like the earlier stomach pain I had. I felt damp in my knickers and looked down to see my pyjamas soaked in fresh blood. I panicked, my heart beating fast. I urged myself not to fall apart. I mean, people bled during pregnancy all the time right? Heck, I even heard some women would have their periods while pregnant.

I calmed myself down as much as I could and called an ambulance, trying Toms number next. It went straight to voicemail which was weird. He always kept his phone on. I tried over and over again to no avail. I realised I would need to call mum or Ash or someone. I decided on calling both. They both were concerned but tried to hide it by soothing me which only scared me more. Ash arrived at my house in record speed just as the ambulance did. Mum would meet me at the hospital so Ash rode with me in the ambulance, stroking my hand and trying not to look at the blood still dripping out of me. She was so strong for me, encouraging me and saying we would be fine.

At the hospital, mum took one look at me and went pale. I think in that moment I lost the last bit of hope I had left but I felt the denial take over me.

"Call Tom, mum. I need Tom. Please call Tom!" The tears I had held onto had started to spill in my frenzy as the doctors and nurses closed the curtains of the cubicle to examine me. The scan they took of my womb confirmed our fears. My baby had no heartbeat. I sat in shock, staring at the doctor as Ash held my hand on one side, mum on the other. I looked at them with disbelief. There had to be a mistake. No. This was not happening to me. To us. My baby. My tiny little life, gone before it had a chance. The pain I felt of the cramping didn't compare to the pain in my heart.

"Where's Tom?" I said through the tears that wouldn't stop.

"I tried baby, it's going to the voicemail." My mother was trying to be strong for me but I could see the tears she was holding onto. Pain was etched on both of their faces yet they tried to mask it for me. Ash got up to fish my phone from my bag.

"I'll try the office number."

The doctor came back to me, his look of sympathy put the seal on my predicament. I wanted to feel numb. The doctor told me that they would have to deliver the baby. As in, I would actually have to be in labour and deliver my dead child. A part of me died that day, along with my child. And I just kept thinking, 'Where are you Tom?'

The next couple of hours were the worst I'd ever lived. I was induced and they had to deliver the baby as my womb contracted and I cried and my mother held me close to her. They rushed it away, I couldn't bear to look. They sedated me and I think I must have slept forever. When I woke up, Tom was sitting next to me in the hospital chair, face in his hands. I could see from the clock on the wall that it was some time past 1am. Tom noticed me awake, his eyes looked red from crying. He moved on to sit next to me on the bed, taking my hand and rubbing it. He was still dressed in his work clothes, the tie and jacket had been removed.

"I lost our baby." My voice was hoarse, tears spilled of their own accord.

"No Lexi, you didn't lose our baby. Don't say that." His voice sounded hoarse too.

"I called and called, Tom. Where were you? Where were you when I was losing our baby?" My body started to tremble and the sobs started to take over. Tom held me to him and rocked me.

"I'm so sorry baby, I'm so sorry you had to go through all this on your own. Please forgive me. I'm so sorry." He seemed to be so broken up, barely containing himself for me.

"There was so much blood," I whispered, my hand touching my belly where a little life used to be. We held one another for the rest of the morning, silent tears slipping and broken hearts grieving.

After the miscarriage, we just tried to carry on as before. Poor Tom was working so hard for us. I knew he wanted to make the promotion to senior designer. He was one of the youngest in the firm to make it as far as he had. I was such a proud wife.

Our sex life had been strained. At first, I was relieved by Tom's hands off approach. I was grieving worse than him. But when I had finally felt able to connect myself with him again, he would be too tired or he was busy working late. The couple of times we did sleep together, he was so gentle. I knew he thought I was too delicate but I'd had enough of gentle. It was about time I woke his sleepy arse up and gave him a good seeing to. I smiled wickedly, congratulating myself on the excellent idea of wearing my new sexy lacy black underwear and bra set this morning.

"What are you looking so pleased with yourself about?" Mum looked at me suspiciously, pulling me out of my salacious thoughts. I stood up, hoping she hadn't noticed the blush creeping up my cheeks.

"Um nothing mum. Listen, you start lunch and I will go get the earrings. I really will only be a short while and I want you to look perfect tomorrow. Those earrings will be perfect with your blue dress. Just get started, I'll be back before you know it." I didn't give her much of a chance to protest and grabbed my keys and phone, leaving my bag on the table whilst practically stopping myself from skipping with delight to my car. The anticipation of long awaited sweaty sex was making my body tingle all over.

I started the car and switched my ipod on. I couldn't drive without my music. I couldn't do a lot without my music. Goo Goo Dolls *Iris* played on random. I smiled - it was our song. The first time we kissed this song was playing, a ploy of the DJ's to get all the couples on the dance floor. It was also our first dance on our wedding day. The smile turned to a stupid grin that followed me all the way home.

I had a plan. It made me giddy with excitement. Having a sex drought did that to a girl. I opened my front door as quietly as I could and closed it with even more care. Setting my keys down on the able in the hallway, I carefully removed my ballet pumps and pulled my simple t-shirt off. I popped the buttons on my jeans open and shimmied my ample behind out of them. I stopped to check myself in the hall mirror of my ultra modern house. My boobs looked great, lucky that my husband was a boob man. Then again, most men stared at my way above average bazongas. Tom used to get annoyed about me wearing anything that amplified that fact. It proved to be a difficult feat when they were not that easy to hide.

He is gonna have a coronary when he sees me. The wicked smile returned and I made my way up the stairs to our bedroom.

As I neared the bedroom door, I heard giggles and then suddenly a muffled moan. My wicked smile widened.

What's this? Is Tommy boy surfing the naughty channels? Hmm, maybe I can help him out... The door was opened just a tiny crack so I leaned against the door frame, trying for a sexy 'come hither' pose. With my foot I kicked the door lightly to open it wide.

"Baby, you don't need that when you have all of thi-" I stopped short. All the breath in my lungs left me, I felt like I was gasping for air. There, right before my eyes, my husband was pumping hard into a woman who was on her hands and knees and now moaning loudly as he smacked her arse. Loud enough to make the whole neighbourhood know what was going on in house number 426. The worst part of it all, as if that wasn't bad enough, was that they didn't even see or hear me come in. I watched in horror, unable to look away as he abruptly pulled out and laid her out on her back to continue fucking her. Because that was exactly what they were doing. Like animals. And now I knew exactly who she was. He bit her breasts, told her all the dirty things he wanted to do to her and then he kissed her slutty mouth as he increased his speed and they came disgustingly loud.

My chest constricted, whatever was left of my heart shattered into tiny fragments as silent hot tears blurred my vision. Through the incredible pain I felt, an eerie sort of darkness started to engulf me as i tried to hold onto the here and now. I was aware that I was losing consciousness but it happened in slow motion. I remember hitting the floor with a loud thump and seeing Tom break away from the slut. Seeing him look like a deer caught in headlights and the colour drain from his face. I remember his expression changing to concern then panic as he pushed her away from him like she was nothing but a piece of meat, cursing continuously and running in all his nakedness to my gasping body as I struggled to breathe and hold onto consciousness. I wanted to push away from his familiar arms and warmth, I wanted to get the hell away from there but my brain would not let my body move. Eventually, I let the darkness win, hoping against hope that I never woke up again. Because living with this pain would be unbearable. I'd rather never live to see another day.

When I came to, I felt a bit light headed. My chest hurt like a bitch and I lifted my head to look at my surroundings. I knew I was in my bed, I could see a blanket was pulled up over my body and despite the warmth of the wool I was shivering. And then I remembered why I was in my room, the whole episode replaying the ugly events in my head in slow motion. Had I imagined everything? Was it all just a bad dream?

I shook my head to clear the images. *Please God let it be a bad dream. Not my Tom. Please not my Tom.*

I raised my head to see Tom sat in the cushioned chair in the corner of our room, eyes red and despondent, wearing only his jeans, his brown hair disheveled and his talented architect hands fiddling with the arms of the chair. Damn. A tear slid out of the corner of my eye and a cry escaped my mouth.

He looked up and the first emotion I saw was relief as he rushed to my side.

"Oh thank God! You were out for almost an hour Lexi, I called the doctor over, he examined you and said you must have had a panic attack that led to you being unconscious. How are you feeling? Should I take you to the hospital? Lexi talk to me."

He looked desperate and if I could unsee and unhear everything that had happened today, I would have put him at ease. When I said nothing, tears still flowing out of my eyes, he panicked and started pleading with me.

"Lexi I'm sorry you had to see that. I'd give anything for you not to have seen that." He just seemed to be digging himself into a bigger hole. Was that supposed to make me feel better? He had been unfaithful and I was supposed to just think that him sharing his body with someone else was okay?

I wanted to slap him but I contained myself. The lack of his apology for the actual act of his unfaithfulness hadn't escaped me even in my fragile state. The heartache wouldn't stop but my hurt was turning to anger fast. I was scary when angry, even I knew that. I scared myself with how calm I could sound when delivering hateful words.

"Is she still here?" My voice never wavered.

"No." He looked worried. He should be.

"The office slut. Really, Tom? You couldn't find anyone else to cheat on me with?" I sat up when he didn't reply, looking down in shame. I suddenly realised that they had been fucking in the very bed I was now lying in.. Our marital bed. I jumped from it as if it were n fire.

"In our bed, in our fucking home!" I screamed with all the pain and anger I felt. Everything slowly started to make sense. The late nights in the office, the reluctance to have sex with me. My world was falling apart and I couldn't stop myself from crashing. I pulled the sheets off the bed, tearing at them in a rage. When I felt Tom put his arms around me to stop my rampage I realised I was still in my underwear and the skin on skin contact made my skin crawl. I clawed at his arms and screamed, managing to pull away from him.

"Don't fucking touch me ever again!" Tom was startled by the vehemence in my words. I had never spoken to him this way before, even when we argued. I started to get a throbbing headache, well on its way to being a migraine. The room spun a little again and I braced my hand on the dresser.

"How long?" My voice was steadier than I'd thought I could manage. When he looked down at his feet instead of responding, I couldn't hold back.

"How fucking long have you been fucking that whore Rebecca?! Tell me the truth!" If the neighbours weren't awake, they would be now.

He hesitated and looked up into my eyes. When he spoke his voice was not of the confident man I knew.

"About four months or so." Damn. That would coincide well with his more frequent late nights in the office. But I had the miscarriage three months ago. I felt the blood drain from my face, down my neck and slowly from the rest of my body.

"I need you to leave," I whispered, not trusting myself to talk and wondering how I was able to manage just those five words. He shifted slightly and it was then that I saw two suitcases by the door. I felt like I was going to faint again.

"Uh, I need to talk to you about that. I was going to tell you today but this all happened." He cleared his throat and couldn't quite look me in the eye when he continued.

"Rebecca and I are together now. I am leaving and I want to file for divorce." I stumbled back and luckily landed on the foot of the bed. My breathing started to get strained again from the anxiety building up. And another realisation forced its way into my head.

"That night when I was in hospital and our baby was dying and I was crying out in pain, you were with *her*, weren't you?" He didn't need to answer, he wore his shame on his face.

I thought things couldn't get any worse but boy was I wrong.

I heard the front door open and footsteps come up the stairs until we both looked at the bleach blonde office slut standing in the doorway looking smug and wearing a black bodycon dress almost showing her arse cheeks and black heels that I could only imagine prostitutes wearing. *So much for being gone.*

"Haven't you got your shit together and left her already, Tommy?" She slid her brown snake eyes at me and at that moment I just wanted to scratch them our with my nails. I knew we didn't really like one another at work but I would have thought Tom had more taste. Looks like he just wanted what was easy. *Bastard.*

"*Tommy* was just explaining why he was leaving his wife for the office slut," I replied for him, not hiding my hatred but trying to conceal my pain for my pride's sake. Rebecca's smile changed into one I could imagine a mental patient wearing, contorting her face into one of pure evil.

"He's leaving you because you couldn't give him what he wanted," she sneered.

"Becky, that's enough," Tom interjected nervously. *Becky? Tommy?* Bile started to rise in my stomach as I looked between the two of them. Rebecca looked at Tom with annoyance.

"You haven't told her, have you? Don't you dare tell me you changed your mind!" Now she looked angry and my curiosity piqued.

"Told me what?" I didn't want to wait for Toms lame arse to answer so I looked directly to Rebecca. Her face became the vision of evil once more. I thought things couldn't get any worse a few minutes before. I was about to proven wrong. Again.

"I'm eight weeks pregnant with his baby, Lexi," she spat the words in my face. I actually think I stopped breathing. And then I threw up right there on Miss Slutty Sluts nasty hooker heels. What happened next was a blur. I remember Rebecca screaming in disgust and saying something about how Tom had better buy her new shoes because I'd contaminated them. I heard Tom usher her with care to *our* bathroom to clean her up. I remember being In hysterics on the floor and wondering what the hell I did to deserve this from the man I'd loved more than myself. The man whose baby I had carried, the child that I had to give birth to as a corpse without him while he was having dirty sex with *Becky.* I realised at that moment that I meant nothing to him. I was just the wife he paraded to clients and colleagues and friends because I fit the bill. I gave him the best years of my life and he just threw them back at me.

That woman with whom he had spent little more than four months was carrying his child, something I had failed to give him. I felt like I was less of a woman as I clutched my stomach and cried my heart out on my bedroom floor. I saw Tom come in and stand above me looking down with an expression that made me feel as if he was torn between doing what was habitual and tending to me or going to his new lovers aid, the woman who was crying about her shoes and carrying his child. In the end he did what I knew he would do. Like a snake he slithered further into the room and picked up his T-shirt from the floor to put on, pulled on a pair of shoes, picked up his suitcases and left the home we had built so lovingly without another word.

I remember crying for what seemed like hours and then both my house phone and my mobile phone started ringing off the hook. Eventually, looking at the twenty odd missed calls from my mother, I answered the call from Ash as my phone rang in my hand.

"Lexi? Babe why haven't you been answering your phone? Your mums harassing me because she thinks you've been abducted by some cult trying to use you as a sex slave." There was a pause but I couldn't trust myself to speak just yet. "Lexi? Are you there? Are you ok?" I tried to take a breath but the hysterics took over once more.

"No. I'm not okay," I managed to cry out as I broke down in tears. And then it seemed like just a few minutes rather than the half hour it took for Ash to practically break down my front door, barging into my room and dodging vomit and ripped up bed linen to gather me in her arms and rock me against her as she soothed me into oblivion.

"H-h-he left me, f-f-for the office slut. She's pregnant."

Those were the only words I could manage, the only information that needed to be relayed, before I lost consciousness again.

CHAPTER FIVE

I'll drink to that

I could see I had shocked Kade with my soap opera story. True, I wouldn't have believed it myself were it someone else's story but I knew different. I couldn't make it up if I tried. I omitted the part about my miscarriage and Rebecca being pregnant with Tom's child, not quite ready to share that painful part of my story. Though I felt a bit stupid baring my soul to my new landlord, it felt good to tell my story to someone who didn't know me before or during Tom's presence in my life. At least I wouldn't have to be compared to pre-Tom Lexi and told how everyone knew Tom was bad news or some other words of wisdom selected carefully from Alexa De Lucas' Book of Fuck Ups.

Kade shifted from his position on the floor and I watched him get up and walk wordlessly to the kitchen. I watched his hard muscled back, sad that he'd put on a T-shirt and confused that he hadn't uttered a word. When he came back, he had a bottle of red wine and two glasses in hand. Settling back down on the rug, he placed the glasses in front of us and poured wine into both.

"I think you need one of these," he explained, "it's never too early for some wine with shockingly true story telling." His eyes looked like a deep grey-blue now and so positively stormy that I felt mesmerised. My throat felt a little dry from all the talking so I clinked my glass with his with a nod and took a sip, letting it warm its way down my throat and into my belly.

"I don't usually drink anymore," I explained smiling a little.

"Lightweight are you?" His cheeky dimpled grin warmed me.

"Yeah something like that. The last time I had more than a glass of wine I ended up in bed with my ex's arch enemy." I grimaced. Shit. No brain to mouth filter today, and I now had a glass full of wine to get through. Great.

"Now, that sounds like a good story..." The tease was back and I felt myself go a deeper shade of pink. I didn't dare reply for fear I'd say something more stupid than what I'd just let slip. Sipping on the wine quietly, I looked at him over the brim of the glass trying to determine what he was thinking. Since that morning, I'd been able to read every emotion correctly because his face and eyes were so expressive but just then I couldn't make head nor tail of it. Whilst I'd been bleeding my heart out in telling him my story, he had listened intently and nodded at the right moments. Now he just seemed blank. As if understanding my confusion to his lack of comment, he slowly put his own glass down and waited for me to do the same before he spoke.

"You've really had a tough couple of years huh?" I could tell he was trying to make light of it, perhaps not to upset me.

"Yeah I guess you can say that."

"I could sit here and tell you what all your friends and family members may have told you about what an ass he was etcetera but I think that gets old too quick. You've heard it all before, you get tired of being told how strong you are and how you're too good for him, regardless of them being right." I nodded, surprised at how accurate he'd been so far. It got me wondering if he had suffered the same fate.

"So," he continued, "I don't want to reiterate that. You don't need that. What I will say is that you have been given a chance here to start again, to do things on your terms and live for yourself. The best revenge you can get is to live your life and be happy."

His words permeated into my skin and fused into my bloodstream. He would never know just how much I needed to hear those words at that exact moment in time.

Without a thought I knelt up from my seated position and kissed his lightly stubbled cheek. The look of shock on his face was priceless as his lazy flirty grin slowly appeared again.

"Thank you. I needed to hear that."

"I'm that good huh? I should give you more words of Hamilton wisdom to earn me some more of those kisses." Cheeky bastard. I gave him a playful punch in his sexy bicep and giggled like a crushing schoolgirl.

"I am curious though, did he ever apologise? Guys like that usually come to their senses at some time or another."

"Well, the first time he realised the error of his ways was when he found out I'd been with Max, his 'arch enemy'. He said he wanted me back, despite the fact his girlfriend was pregnant with his child. It was a difficult time but even taking into account how much I loved him back then, I wouldn't ever take him back or give him an excuse to give up the chance of being a decent father to his child. After that time he only brought *us* up when we were talking to the estate agents about selling the house. He tried reminding me of all the wonderful memories we'd had there, the sly bastard, but all I could see was him with her on our bed and I felt like my heart was being ripped to shreds all over again. I refused to speak to him again after that unless through our solicitor."

I felt the twinge of anxiety in my chest again when I remembered his shaky voice begging for a chance. Kade soon snapped me out of my reverie by clinking the bottle as he filled my wine glass up to the top.

"Let's make a toast. Here's to getting the sweetest re-venge there is. Here's to the rest of your life," he smiled, lift-ing his glass towards mine.

"To the rest of my life," I smiled, clinking my glass to his.

***

Two and a half full glasses of wine later, I was getting braver than I'd ever thought possible and started probing my landlord on his private life now that he knew mine. We were both pleasantly intoxicated, Kade probably a lot sober than myself. Nevertheless, he had started to show me the extent of his flirtatious behaviour when he started to tickle me for making fun of his favourite football team, Manchester United. Being a die hard Chelsea fan myself, it seemed only natural I would. He tackled me to the floor on the rug and I laughed so hard I couldn't breathe.

"Take it back!" He breathed, trying his hardest to look angry but his laughing eyes broke the facade he was trying to put up.

"Stop it Kade, I can't breathe!" I giggled, trying to pull down my shirt that was now exposing my stomach.

"Take it back and I'll stop Alexa," he grinned, knowing he had as good as won this round.

"Okay, okay! Man United are not short sighted. And they don't wear stickers on their knickers," I huffed, trying to catch my breath.

"And?" He waited for my answer, earning a growl from me as I tried to free my wrists he had held in one big hand.

"And they don't wear rubies on their boobies," I whis-pered, giggling a little at the childish rhyme I used to chant at my die hard Man U supporter cousin, Brian, when we were kids.

Kade desisted with the tickling but I was suddenly aware

of his face inches away from mine, so close I could feel his breath on my face. His dark eyelashes fanning his cheek bones when he closed his eyes and took a deep breath. My eyes lingered on his full soft lips as I wondered what they would feel like against mine.

He released my wrists above my head and moved to hover his body over mine, holding himself up by his forearms on either side of my head. His eyes flickered open suddenly and don't know if I had imagined the lust in his eyes because I was projecting my own or if it was real. All I knew was that I was looking into the most beautiful eyes I'd ever seen, the depths of which I could get lost in. More blue than grey now, they pulled me in and as I felt the heat of his body just inches above me, his eyes were like magnets to mine and I couldn't look away. The trance we were in broke when I heard my phone shriek with a whistle, indicating that I had a message.

Kade quickly moved away as if my body were on fire. I guess I sobered up as fast as him when I realised the implication of where we were headed. *Note to self, do not stare deep into your landlords eyes when wrestling on the floor.* Geez, what was I thinking?

I could see that he regretted getting that close too by the way that he looked to be angry. I got up to find my phone on the book shelf. It was almost six in the evening and I'd received a text message from Allison.

Hey bbz! Got here safe, just got the chance
2message now...we been, ahem, busy wit other things hehe ;)
Its gorgeous here. Forgot 2 tell u, Kade Hamilton
will b around - unexpected turn up.
Aint he dreamy? dont tell Brent i said that!
See u soon chick. Enjoy the eye candy xo

The stupid cow didn't think I needed to know until now? If only she knew how much I was about to enjoy the eye candy a second before I got her message. I didn't need for things to get complicated when I had just started out again as an independent woman but I also didn't like the feeling that I'd been rejected. I shot a quick text back to Allison before heading to the kitchen where Kade was.

Thanks for the heads up you moron!
He scared the bejesus out of me, I nearly bit his hand off!
Anyway, long story, but yes he is just too sexy to be real.
Enjoy your trip, I'll make you pay later xx

I got an immediate reply from her, no doubt intrigued and needing more info. I just left the phone on a side table as I reached the kitchen. Kade was washing up dishes and muttering to himself. It sounded as if he was calling himself an idiot and cursed repeatedly. I watched by the door, admiring a domesticated man who obviously knew his way around a kitchen and all the time I thought to myself that even if I stood a teeny tiny chance with the Adonis, he was way out of my league. There was no comparison, so I decided in that moment to try my best to just be friendly, even if he flirted. Walking over to him I tapped his shoulder for him to turn his head slightly over his shoulder.

"Hey, you need any help?"

"Uh, no, I'm good thanks." His lack of warmth in his response just proved that he didn't find me attractive. He couldn't look me in the eye and I felt hurt by that. Things had been going so well, we were enjoying talking teasing and now he felt so repulsed by me that he couldn't look my way. *Best leave it be.*

"Um, okay if you're sure then I'll just go carry on with my unpacking in the living room." He nodded and I left as quick as I could, feeling dejected and confused yet resolved to getting on with my days plans.

Reaching for the stack of books I had yet to start on, I switched my iPod back in. Glad for the musical distraction, I felt Thirty Seconds to Mars' *The Kill* suit my mood as Tom lingered in my peripheral memories, mixed with confusing images of my new landlord.

***

By eight o'clock I had managed to sort the things I had in the living room and the walk in wardrobe I had upstairs. Now everything was the way I wanted it to be. How long it would remain that way, I didn't know but for now it was perfect.

I hadn't heard from Kade since he popped his head around the living room corner after washing up to say he was going to be up in his apartment, trying to get some sleep. He did look tired but also a little sad. I didn't pry any further and carried on with my work.

I made myself a simple and very English dinner of sausage, mashed potatoes, vegetables and gravy. It wasn't the same as it was back home but it helped ease some of the home-sickness I felt. I had made some for Kade too, it was only fair seeing as I'd 'incapacitated' him earlier. I couldn't be sure if he was up yet but I carried up two plates up the stairs. I hesi-tated at the door to his apartment, listening to see if it was possible to hear any movement upstairs. The faint sound of a guitar being played could be heard. I knocked as best as I could with the plates in hand but I doubt he heard me because the sound of the guitar continued. Reaching awk-wardly for the door handle, I found it unlocked and started walking upstairs as the sound got louder.

Reaching the top of his first floor landing, I found him slouched across his couch, guitar in hand wearing only his boxer shorts and engrossed in the music he was making. I had to stop and appreciate the sight of him. Legs as athlet-ically muscled and naturally tanned as the rest of his body, I watched the muscles in his arms flex as he played. That beautiful face, brows drawn in concentration, eyes stormy and biting his lower lip. I must have stood there, absorbing his perfection and the breathtakingly haunting tune he was playing on his guitar, for a while until eventually he stopped playing and looked up. I felt like I had intruded on a private moment but he just looked at me, like *really* looked at me as if he could see inside my soul. I started to feel a little conscious and stumbled to say something.

"Sorry for disturbing you. I knocked but I don't think you heard me. I made dinner, thought you might want some..." He smiled then, putting down the guitar and getting up to walk towards me.

"That's the best vision I've ever seen, a beautiful woman bringing me dinner. I'm a lucky man. No need to be sorry Alexa." I felt a shiver of pleasure run up my spine at his calling me beautiful.

"Flattery will get you nowhere Kade Hamilton. I am merely doing my duty since I rendered you useless in one hand, although I think you're playing that up a bit. No one with a serious hand injury can play a guitar as well as you did just there." I smiled deviously, happy with myself for turning the spotlight back onto him. I never took compliments well, my confidence was always low when it came to my appearance yet this sexy man was making *me* feel sexy and bold.

He reached me, taking both plates from my hands and walking over to his dining table, motioning me over to sit with him. He seemed so unashamed and comfortable with his body given he was half naked again. I admired his easy nature. Of course, who would be ashamed of a physique like his? Swallowing my desire, I joined him to sit at the table opposite him where he'd placed my plate.

"You found out my evil plan," he winked at me as he looked appreciatively at the sausages and mash.

"You play really well. I always wanted to learn but never found the time." He stood up and made his way to his fridge to pull out a beer and when I shook my head when he wordlessly asked if I wanted one, he pulled out a can of coke for me.

"I was taught by my older brother Jared, he was a bit of a rock star back in the day. I just wanted to be like him. Of course, he's now a boring old Banker and works so much that his wife and kids have to make appointments to see him." He smirked, obviously displeased with the way his brothers life had panned out.

"I guess life catches up with all of us."
He mused over what I said for a minute, picking his fork and knife up to start eating.

"I suppose you're right there. This is delicious by the way. Thank you for taking care of me, Miss Lestat." I smiled at him as he devoured the food on his plate and started on my own. You'd have thought he was eating at the Ritz instead of some pre made sausages and mash I'd lazily thrown together.

The silence was companionable as we ate. When we had finished, he insisted that I leave the plates in his sink for him to do as he walked me over to his living room couch. I loved this extension of the house. Obviously, you needed to have a good amount of money to be able to do these things properly and he had certainly paid well for his comfort.

I was conscious that it wasn't wise to get too comfortable there in his home but I couldn't help it. He insisted, after all, and I saw no harm in just sitting and talking for a while.

He turned on the tv to watch the fireworks for the July 4th celebrations. He'd gone up and put on a t-shirt and the sweatpants from earlier and I kinda missed the scenery.

"I'm sorry to sound nosy but why aren't you spending the holiday with family? I thought that's what everyone does?" I had been wondering what the deal was as a non American.

"Let's just say I needed some time away from them for now. It's better for me to stay here at the moment before work gets busy anyway." He seemed to be uncomfortable talking about it so I focused on changing the subject.

"Where do you work?" I asked straight up.

"Well, I work for the family business. I also used to give lectures once a week at Columbia University. I like to keep myself busy. Recently, I gave up lecturing to concentrate on work."

"Wow, you're not joking about keeping busy. I wouldn't have the energy to do all that."

"I'm sure you could do it if you wanted to. What do you do for work?" Hmm, good question.

"Actually, I'm not sure what I want to do. I have a degree architecture but I don't want to go further with architecture. I did the interior design thing for a while but it just didn't work for me. Was working in a boutique before I left London, I was hoping I'd figure out what I wanted to do whilst there but the truth is, I haven't got a clue. That's stupid, right?" Kade shook his head with a smile.

"No, not at all. A lot of people don't know what they want to do career wise. Some people have been established in their careers for years and been successful when all of a sudden they realise they hate what they do and start afresh."

"I've heard of that happening. I think I will start applying everywhere and see what works out for me. It's just frustrating not knowing what I want to do. I'm so jealous of those people that are so sure of their life plan. Mine just got shot to hell."

"There wouldn't be any excitement in life if everything went to plan, now would there?" His intense look showed wisdom beyond his years.

"That's true." I started to feel like I should leave, his mood had changed somewhat and he looked to be in deep thought about something.
I stood up and stretched, faking a yawn hadn't been difficult because I actually felt a little tired.

"I'm gonna go to bed. I think you need a good nights sleep too. Thank you for your hospitality." He laughed and shook his head.

"I should be thanking you. You did make me two meals out of three today."

"What can I say? It's my English politeness winning out," I smiled cheekily.

"Indeed. Well then my lady, I bid you adieu. Hope you have sweet dreams Alexa." He whispered his last sentence in a way that made goosebumps stand on my skin. His voice was delicious. I turned and gave him a weak smile.

"Goodnight Kade. Sweet dreams good sir. And happy Independence Day." Without another look I hurried down the stairs to my room, and didn't stop until I closed the door.

Sitting on my bed, earphones on and listening to Jake Bugg's *Broken*, I took out my notebook, fast becoming a habit and source of comfort.

Thursday 4th July

Today I met Kade Hamilton. I stopped breathing for a while, I think my brain stopped working for a while too. I started to believe that there was some kind of chemistry between us. There couldn't be, right? He's the epitome of perfect. So drop dead gorgeous that I can't stop looking at him. Why is it that I find myself drawn to him. The words 'moth' and 'flame' come to mind. God I wish I wasn't so messed up. He is so far out of my league, I don't know whether to laugh or cry. Kade Hamilton being around is going to be challenging for me. I don't even know how long he will be here and I find myself both wanting him to go because of his effect on me and wanting him to stay because I enjoyed his company so much today. Holy freakin shit. I'm done for.

CHAPTER SIX

The Eavesdropper

I awoke the next morning and stretched, smiling when I remembered the day I had spent getting to know Kade Hamilton. I'd only found out a fraction about him - after all it had only been a day, but still, I was desperate to know more. I kept getting this nagging feeling in the back of my mind to just leave him alone and get on with my life but I felt drawn to him, intrigued beyond anything. My promise to keep myself away from him was as good as broken.

A hushed voice in my head said, *be careful, don't get hurt again.* That familiar aching pain in my chest choked my hopeful feelings away from me. I remembered Tom, that image of him and Rebecca in our bed still giving me nightmares. Sometimes I'd just see him, cold and laughing at me as he broke my heart to pieces. Other times it was the scene reenacted of them in my bedroom only this time I was tied to a chair, being made to watch from start to finish as he told her how much better she was than me and said all the loving things he used to say to me, but to her instead.

In the beginning, after he had left me, the nightmares were frequent, occurring nearly every night. My parents begged me to see a psychologist and go through therapy. It took a while but eventually the nightmares decreased over time.

Now, I only had them once every few months when the stress got on top of me. But the anxiety attacks remained a constant reminder of the depression and pain I fought daily.

I knew I'd only just met Kade but at the same time I knew I had never had an instant attraction to a man that strong, not even Tom. In university, it was Tom who had pursued me and I had kinda fancied him but it was a gradual attraction that resulted in a deep affection and eventually love. I remember that he used to make me laugh a lot. Something I hadn't done in a while. *Kade seemed to have no problem making me laugh.* I started to think about the way he tickled me last night and how we had almost kissed. It was too much too soon and too darn confusing. I could see this was fast becoming an infatuation.

Okay, you get all your errands out of the way first, stall as much as you can and then casually make your way down to see if he is up. Sounded like a good plan.

***

I decided to make all my phone calls, face times etc. they were five hours ahead in London so I wouldn't be waking anyone up. First up was mum and she always insisted on face time, which wasn't always comfortable for me especially when I didn't feel like I looked my best. She also had a habit of showing me around on her iPhone screen if she was out when I called so her friends or other members of family could see me.

I rang her phone and immediately saw it connect. A few seconds later her face appeared on the screen of my iPad and she was wearing what looked like a tie dye kaftan I know Ash's mum had bought her from her recent trip to Pakistan. She looked funny because the colours were a bit bright for her pale skin but relaxed as she picked her cup up to take a sip of tea. I smiled and waved at her before I spoke.

"Good morning mum."

"Morning? Oh yes, I keep forgetting you're a few hours behind us over there. Good morning darling. Did you get all that unpacking done that you've been saying you had to do? Don't leave it too late." She gave me her stern look and I had to hide my smile.

"I've already done it. How's dad? And Megan?"

"Oh good. Yes they are well. Your dad had been driving me up the wall! He wants to clear out the shed and have it knocked down. After all the time we spent clearing it! And your sister, she's hardly been home because of some summer parties and what not. And now you're so far away. I don't get to see either of my children!" I knew she was just letting out her frustrations, looking a little teary but I smiled at the familiarity of it all.

"Mum, tell dad not to tear down the shed. There's too many memories there. Megan's a teenager so that's expected, and I'm still here available to talk to you where you can see my tired face all the way over there in London. Chin up! How is Granna? And Aunt Audrey and Aunt Grace? What's the latest gossip?" And with that foolproof distraction technique, I learnt that aunt Edie, her best friend, was going on her second cruise for the year with husband number four (still going strong), that aunt Audrey had taken an unexpected trip to Spain on 'business' and that our elderly neighbour Mr Humes had been taken to hospital via ambulance under suspicious circumstances. She told me this in a whisper because of the scandalous nature of the gossip. Apparently he had his girlfriend around and it was widely speculated that there had been some misadventure with a certain, ahem, enhancement product. I couldn't stop myself laughing as her eyes widened with every detail. I loved these chats with my mum.

I promised to call her again in a couple of days, not that she would stop harassing me on WhatsApp. I had to admit that I loved receiving her messages too, unless she was criticising me, in which case I avoided them.

Next I picked up the house phone and called Granna. She was having her hair dyed at the hair dressers when she picked up.

"How's my beautiful granddaughter?" Her cheery voice made me smile. She always told me I was beautiful. Maybe more because she knew about my low self confidence, always trying to hide myself in baggy clothes and looking plain so that others wouldn't see me.

"I'm missing you like crazy. New York is amazing, I wish you were here to enjoy it with me. Your old hometown after all." I could hear her chuckle and then a hair dryer in the background.

"Alli honey I will make my way to you soon I promise but you need to settle and make your friends before your old grandmother cramps your style."

"That is not even a little bit possible Granna. You are way too cool," I laughed, meaning what I said. Everyone loved her company, she was a firecracker.

"Aw stop it you, way to feed an old ladies ego. Anyway kiddo, you need to get out and absorb what this city has to offer you. I know you been sitting at home. New York is a fucking jungle of buildings and things to see so you better get your butt out of that house and onto the streets if you're planning on living and working there for a while. The people are different, the food is different." Granna was right of course, she always was. I'd been a little anxious about getting around the city and a tiny bit lazy too. Enjoying the comforts of the all inclusive town house, I felt like I didn't need to get out at all.

"I will Granna. Just waiting for the girls to get back from their trips and then I'll feel more comfortable going out."

"They aren't home? You're on your own?"

"Yeah kinda...the landlord is staying for a few days..." I could almost hear Granna's mind coggles working. She always caught me out when I was withholding, always called me out on my bullshit.

"Oh yeah? What's he like?"

"Um, we'll, he's nice..." I'm a shit liar.

"Just 'nice'?"

"He's, uh, really nice."

"Uh huh. Meaning, he's really hot. Alli, are you blushing?" I glanced at myself in the dresser mirror. Shit, I really was blushing bright red.

"Yes he's hot Granna, but he's my landlord! Now stop teasing me!" I heard Granna chuckle and then a muffled voice in the background.

"Ok my Alli girl, I'll stop. Just make sure you have as much fun as possible. I got to go now and get this colour washed out my hair. I got pins and needles in my ass, my backs stiff as hell. Fuck knows how I'm going to drive home!"

"Granna! Language!" I giggled. My grandmother had quite the potty mouth. She put sailors to shame.

"Don't you start on me darlin', I get enough of that from your mother and aunts. Now go feast on your hot landlord and give me the details later. Love you sweetheart."

"Love you too Granna." I heard the phone click and sighed. I missed her more after every phone conversation.

I had one last phone call that I wanted to make for the day. I dialled the number on the cordless and stood to stare out of the balcony.

"Lexi?"

"Hey Ash," I smiled into the phone. I hadn't been able to get in touch with her since I arrived. Apart from the WhatsApp messages, we kept missing one another's calls and it was frustrating because we always spoke every few days when I was back in London.

"Finally!" She squealed making me jump, "oh shit, I knocked over my coffee." I heard her rummage around her desk probably cleaning up the mess. She was at work but had her own office as the head of accounting at a medium sized firm. I felt a little guilty bothering her at work but I needed to speak to my best friend. It felt odd not being in regular contact. I wondered for a minute if the distance would make us grow apart, but then thought it a silly notion. We had been through so much together, our friendship was the kind that lasts.

"You there?" I asked after a few seconds passed.

"Yeah I'm here, I'm here. Bloody hell Lexi, it feels like ages!"

"I know babe. We just keep missing one another. Can you talk? I know you're at work..."

"Of course I can talk! They can take a running jump if they mind. Anyway, I got Pete by the short and curlies. He was in a tricky situation last week where he messed up some pretty important insurance forms and he owes me big time."

Ash's boss was a bit of a sleaze and could be a complete dickhead at times but she seemed to handle him well. He was truly lost without her.

"Good."

"Yes, it's good because I don't want us to be interrupted while you tell me all about Kade Hamilton." Ok, I was guilty of gushing very briefly about Mr Sexy eyes Hamilton to Ash the day before, when Kade was making lunch, in a message. I hadn't told her much but it was enough for her to know this guy had to be something special to make me behave like a teenager. I was also aware that I could be sued for talking to her about him, as stated in the terms of the non disclosure I'd signed upon arrival here. Luckily, I knew my bestie well enough to know she would never relay any information I gave her to anyone else. Nevertheless, I felt a slither of guilt for being so quick to blab. I squashed it down, still puzzled about the reason for the NDA.

"Yes, Kade Hamilton. Where do I begin?" I giggled. I then spent the next twenty minutes recounting every detail of the day before. When I finished talking, she was extra riled up and excited.

"You know what this means, right? You're finally thinking of other men! You can go out and date a bit, move on with your life. Get tarted up and go fishing! And even though you're being all 'oh no, Kade is my landlord, I can't have hot steamy sex with him,' I think you should give him a go. He's obviously flirting. I bet it's your ginormous tits. He's a boob man for sure. Although you have a nice arse too."

Somehow, even though we'd been friends for absolutely ages, Ash still could make me blush. The woman was so blunt, not ashamed of saying anything, and I wouldn't have her any other way.

"Shut up you! You make me sound like a super slut. Now I feel like I need to cover up, I'm gonna feel super self conscious. You're such a freak!"

"Yeah yeah super slut. Don't you remember that was my nickname for you at school? Better live up to it now!" That really was her nickname for me in school and it was funny because I was the complete opposite. I had a couple of non serious high school relationships but I still was painfully shy. Until I went to university. Tom found me a short time after and wore me down with his persistence.

"Okay you *ho.* I'm gonna be scandalous because you asked for it," I laughed, using my nickname for her which was also the complete opposite of her personality.

At that moment the front door bell started ringing. I went to the window in the front spare bedroom to look out to see who it could be. It was a pizza delivery guy. Guessing that Kade must be up and had ordered food, I ignored the bell, thinking he was downstairs to answer and continued with my conversation. However, when the bell continued to ring an unusually long time after, I had to go down.

"Stay on the phone hun, I'm going down to answer that." I skipped down the stairs as fast as I could with the phone to my ear without breaking my neck. When I reached the door, the delivery guy was turning around to leave.

"Hey! Sorry, I didn't know there was pizza coming. My

housemate must've ordered. How much do we owe you?" The teenage delivery boy looked frustrated but I seemed to have won him over with my apology slash explanation. He handed me the two big boxes and a bag of what looked like sides and drinks and then the receipt, choosing not to answer verbally. I realised that I'd stupidly not brought my wallet down with me and had turned to traipse back up the two flights when I saw the exact amount for the order on the side table of the hall and then a few bills that looked like a generous tip. I handed him the money and his eyes widened at the tip. He managed to beam at me now.

"Thanks!"

"Uh, you're welcome..." I kept the phone tucked to my ear with my shoulder as I hauled the items Kade had ordered to the dining table. Was he planning to feed an army?

"Hey, you there super slut?" Ash's singsong voice came through the phone as I set the boxes and bags on the table.

"Yeah ho bag, I'm right here. Man, this guy likes to eat."

"Oooo, I love a man that loves to eat. And you said he's fit. He must work out like crazy."

"It figures, that's why you married Imran, isn't it? The way he eats Nandos chicken, the way corn sticks to his teeth when he eats a cob and the peri peri sauce dribbles on his chin..." I giggled as she growled at me. The man took his chicken seriously but once he got going, the manners went out the window. It had got so bad at one point that Ash had sworn off going there with him unless he ordered a takeaway.

"Don't get me started on Imran! I'm seriously thinking that he will get banned soon if he scares any more kiddies eating like Nandos is running out of chicken! One of his mates got him a Nandos *gift card!* Now he's bugging me about going out for a date night. To freakin Nandos. To humiliate me. You can laugh all you want Lexi but you know how I suffer! That mate of his wont be invited to our New Years party this year, the bastard."

I laughed so hard tears ran down my face. I had wondered over to the living room bay windows and sat sideways at the window seat looking out to the tranquil neighbourhood.

"Okay, I'm sorry, but you got to admit that it's cute when he doesn't realise how stupid he gets over it."

Imran was a hot guy but more than that he treated Ash like she was precious to him. Which she was. But that wasn't always the case. Ash and Imran had their relationship tested to the limits. They had been together since forever, which for them was eight years, apart from a year where they had split up. The split had come three years into their relationship when she was twenty one and he was twenty four. They had just gotten engaged six months before in front of family and friends as was tradition. Imran had just started a new job and was being sent abroad to train a lot in Berlin and then to Washington where his company had offices.

He started to act weird and I remember Ash telling me that he'd been so cold and withdrawn with her. Not being one to fester in her insecurities like I had, she confronted him. He then admitted that he felt they had met too young and that he had major doubts about their relationship being what he needed. He didn't think he wanted to marry her anymore. She had invested all her love and time into their relationship, saving herself for him, at that point and what he said had shattered her heart. He left the country to train and work for three months after that and she cried so much. I remember I would come to her house and we'd just sit in the garden and tell one another what an arsehole he was and how he would regret it. And then she would cry that he'd broken her heart so bad that it hurt all the time and that broke my heart seeing my best friend, who was like a sister, in so much pain. It's probably what made her so amazingly understanding when I'd been hurting all this time.

We put a plan into action for the time that he was away. There was a wedding of one of their mutual family friend's taking place at around the time he came back from the states in three months time. Our plan was to transform Ash from beautiful to beautifully stunning for the wedding so that she would get so much attention he couldn't ignore it and would be made jealous. It was a childish plan, I admit, but we had no other option. Ash wanted him back, even after his cruel rejection. She couldn't see past their love.

So three months passed excruciatingly slowly. In that time, Imran had changed his relationship status to 'single' and had been posting pictures on Facebook that indicated he was seeing someone. Or a couple of 'someone's' by the looks of it. I guess he was taking his new found freedom seriously but that just ripped my best friends heart even more. After all, she had saved herself for him for after marriage. We were quite certain that he was sleeping with 'Callie' and then a month later with 'Laura' from the looks of their pictures together. That and good old Facebook stalking...

After that, Ash had gradually lost the fight in her to get him back. She felt that at least he was being true to himself, he hadn't cheated on her and that he had been honest to her too. But she suffered. She lost a lot of weight. She had always been voluptuous but the weight loss made her stunning features stand out and she started to get a lot more attention than usual. I remember how she got her new clothes fitted for the wedding because she still wanted to make him see what he was missing out on of course.

I had scored an invite to the wedding since Ash's sister was unable to attend. I still remember the look on Imran's face as she walked into the wedding reception hall in her beautiful cream coloured outfit looking like an princess. His jaw dropped, like literally. And the best part was that she hadn't even noticed him standing there - she was genuinely having fun and mingling. But I noticed everything and I'll be damned, our plan worked. Even though she insisted she didn't want him back, I could tell that the moment he walked up to her and their eyes met, that she could never really let go.

He told her she looked beautiful to which she said 'thank you,' smiled politely as if he were just an acquaintance and walked off. Because, you see, my best friend was never one to be won over that easy. You had to earn her respect and trust, even I had to when we first became friends.

The rest of the evening Imran could. Not. Keep. His. Eyes. Off. Of. Her. And she just ignored him. He hung on her every word as she talked to others. His brother elbowed him in his gut to stop him gawking at her.

A few weeks later, I got a phone call from him. I think I'd been expecting it.

"I screwed up Lexi," he mumbled miserably. "She won't answer my calls, she won't look at me if we're ever in the same place at the same time."

I drew in a deep breath before I decided to help him. After all, I always believed they were made for each other.

"If you want her back, you're going to have to fight for her. You know you have to earn her trust back and you can't rush her. If she's worth it to you and if you love her enough, you should do it."

"She's definitely worth it. Lexi, Washington was a nightmare. I met other...people...but all I could think about was her. I know I left her and I wanted to experience life without her but I was miserable. I tried to leave her alone, I really did, because its my own stupid fault but I want her back."

And so the chase began. It was really entertaining for me because I got calls from both Ash and Imran. Of course, I'd always tell Ash what he would say, which he knew and would always give me information he wanted her to have. Such a cat and mouse game. It took a couple of months for Ash to agree to talk to him and close to five months before they were back to dating to 'see where the wind takes us' as they said.

At around seven months into Imran's painstaking action

plan, he decided he would propose. Again. He was so nervous, bless him. He had help from me and Michelle, our close friend from school, to help set it all up for him. The perfect proposal. This is how it went.

The proposal - take two...

"You with her?" Imran asked, calling for the tenth time.

"Yes! Stop calling me! Relax! She's gonna get suspicious if I tell her It's Tom bugging me again. Just stay in position okay? I'll take her to the restaurant and you wait for the signal."

"I'm nervous, Lexi."

I felt myself melt. The poor man had been going mad trying to make tonight perfect for Ash. This was his grand gesture, his "go big or go home" moment. He was right to be nervous. Ash was unpredictable, you couldn't predict with 100% accuracy what her reaction to certain situations would be. As her oldest and closest friend, even I was sometimes at a loss.

"I'm sure everything will go smoothly. She will say yes," I hope, I wanted to add but didn't for fear of upsetting or stressing him out further. There was a pause before he spoke so quietly, I almost couldn't hear his words.

"What if she says no?"

I didn't get a chance to reply as Ash waltzed back into the bar from the ladies toilets.

"Look, she's coming back, I gotta go!" I quickly dumped my phone back in my bag and gulped down the last of my drink.

"Damn the queue in the ladies was loooooong! I had to do a Scottish jig just to keep it all in!" Ash grumbled as soon as she sat down at the bar. She had already consumed two virgin pina colada's and a few virgin mojito's too, so it was no wonder she was bursting.

Tonight was a big night and although I was nervous about helping execute Imran's meticulously planned evening, I was enjoying spending time with my best friend after weeks of being busy with work and life. We had met at a central London bar to have drinks *before we could set out for dinner. We'd been here an hour and now it was time to get moving for the second part of the plan.*

"I'm glad you haven't peed yourself, my love," I laughed, putting my phone into my bag and standing. We had a dinner to get to - possibly a life changing one. I smiled, feeling emotional all of a sudden. My best friend was possibly getting engaged again tonight.

We made our way to the tube station, stopping to throw some change for a busker singing Frank Sinatra's "The way you look tonight," not missing the flirty wink he sent us in thanks.

Once we reached the building housing the iconic rooftop restaurant, I felt the excitement bubble for my friend. Out on the rooftop on the warm summer night, the surrounding fairly lights and candles set on the tables and outskirts made the place seem like a scene out of a woodland fairytale. Vines and pink and white flowers weaved through the over head trellis and arches and adorned the table setting.

"Wow," Ash said, looking awestruck. I silently congratulated Imran for setting the perfect scene for her. I had to stop myself from jumping up and down in excitement.

"Yeah," I replied with a big grin.

"Are you sure this place is open though? We seem to be the only people here."

"Yeah...look! The maitre'd is coming over."

The smiling man greeted us with a knowing twinkle in his eye and seated us at a table right in the middle. I sat fidgeting for a few minutes whilst Ash perused the menu and chatted away, oblivious to the night that awaited her. I looked over her beautiful teal blue maxi dress, her dark hair styled in luscious waves over her shoulders and her make up perfect.

Soon I made an excuse to go to the restroom before squeezing her hand, for which she gave me an amused smile.

As I turned the corner inside the building towards the toilets, Imran stepped out looking dapper in his light grey suit and blue shirt over his broad and muscular frame.

"It's showtime," I told him in a low voice, smiling in en-

couragement. He looked like he might hurl. It was truly the first time I had ever seen him look anything but confident and cocky.

"What if she's not ready? Maybe I should have waited a little longer-"

"Imran, she said yes to you once before and she will say it again. Let her make the choice, okay?" I gave him a hug and a kiss on the cheek.

He nodded, blew out a breath and straightened himself as he took a determined step forward. I pulled out the camera he had set to the side, creeping out onto a part of the rooftop that had a screen I could hide behind as I got ready to capture everything.

I watched Ash look confused but happy to see Imran walk over to her. I saw the moment that she realised what was happening as he got down on one knee in front of her, producing a new ring that he had designed made from the old one with added new elements just for her. I saw her tears and happiness as she said yes and put the poor guy out of his misery. I witnessed their happiness, came out for long enough to congratulate her as we both cried and then left with promises of a real dinner together while the happy couple lost themselves in the beautiful warm London night...

I smiled, thinking about the happy ever after both Ash and Imran deserved and eventually got. Full of a sudden love for my bestie, I proclaimed it.

"I love you Ash, I really miss you *ho bag*," I pouted into the phone.

"I love you and miss you too *super slut*. Are you pouting?" I laughed.

"Yeah. You know me so well. Like people need another excuse to accuse us of being more than just friends."

"Well, I got a feeling that a certain blue eyed sexpot might find that hot and want to jump your bones if you mention it to him. You seriously could do with a good seeing to Lexi. Just imagine his strong sexy arms around you. Did you say he has tattoos? Damn that's sexy, I think I'm gonna dump Imran's arse and come over there to ogle with you."

I blushed because I knew that if I had the opportunity and I felt confident enough I would have loved to jump *his* bones. I'd not had sex for *fourteen long months.* I was seriously frustrated and had been made aware of it since meeting Kade yesterday. Just a day and he had captivated me. *Please don't let me get obsessed. I'm too old for crushing on guys!*

"Yes, yes he has tattoos. Really sexy tribal tattoos down one side of his body and muscles. Abs you could do your washing against. He's just too hot. It should be illegal. Yesterday I caught myself daydreaming about licking ice cream off them. Seriously, I'm officially the saddest woman on planet Earth with too much sexual frustration. I need to get this out my system Ash, help me!" I let out a frustrated growl.

"Babe," she cleared her throat, "just go have some fun. It doesn't have to be him, maybe you'll want to date? I mean, once you settle, I'm sure Allison will want to invite people over and drag you to parties. Remember what a party girl she was? She is going to make you get out. And I fully back her up with that because your 'mourning period' over shit stick is OVER okay? No more thinking of him. Go eat up your landlord or something. Maybe you should try eating various foods off his abs. Start with that truckload of pizza he's ordered. Lick tomato sauce and mozzarella off him." I giggled because of the mental image I got of me actually doing that.

"You know I won't be able to look at him without thinking of eating food off his stomach now right? Thanks for making things more awkward!" I laughed.

It was at that moment I heard a snicker behind me and realised...*I'm not alone anymore...*I turned my head towards the dining table to see Kade freakin sex-on-legs Hamilton leaning against the table, a slice of pizza in one hand and the other arm crossed over the very sexy torso we were just discussing. Behind the bite he was taking with that lush mouth of his, I could see that knowing, cocky and downright amused smile.

"Shit." That was all I could manage.

"What's wrong?"

"Um..."

"What? Did you accidentally pee your pants? Spill woman!"

"Uh, I got to go Ash..."

She was silent for a moment until realisation kicked in.

"He's there isn't he? Oh my God, did he hear what we were talking about? Oh shit," she started to laugh so loud, I'm sure her whole office must have heard.

"*Ash!*" I tried not to look at him, I could not be sure how much he'd heard but it must have been enough judging by the look on his face.

"Omigod omigod! He's so onto you now. Busted!"

"You've been upgraded from *ho bag* to *skanky bitch*," I grumbled as quietly as I could, feeling my face burn and his eyes penetrating the back of my head.

"All in a days work! Now go lick that man, he's probably excited by whatever he heard. He's a man after all."

"Bye Ash."

"Go get some muscular American man ass-"

"Good bye Ash!" I disconnected the call and slammed the phone on the window seat, closing my eyes in desperation to gather myself.

He couldn't have heard everything right? *The talk of his sexy tribal tattoos? Of eating food off his body? Shit, I can't even pretend I wasn't talking about him.* I was just glad I hadn't mentioned how long I'd been deprived of sex. How fucking embarrassing. No, wait. I'd said I was sexually frustrated. I'd said it out loud and it's possible he had heard it. *Now would be a good time to swallow me up ground.*

I turned slowly to face Kade, my head turned down and refusing to meet his eyes.

"Good morning. Or good afternoon now," he said in that deep voice and I could hear the amusement in it, laughter even.

"Good afternoon," I replied quietly. I was being totally obvious with my embarrassment, still not looking a him but I couldn't face him right now. I walked briskly towards the kitchen when his voice stopped me.

"I ordered us pizza, seeing as you fed me yesterday. No need to go the kitchen for anything, I got drinks and dessert here too." I could tell that he was going to make me look at him so that he could enjoy my humiliation. That sexy sadistic bastard.

"Uh, okay, thanks." I flicked my eyes up to his face and moved them away again immediately. He was trying his hardest not to laugh. Not only that, he just looked so breathtaking, freshly showered and his dark hair glistening as his blue eyes laughed with him. I immediately cursed myself for not thinking of an excuse and saying no to him.

I turned around, head still down and walked to the dining table where he waited for me to sit down before he sat down across from me. Face to freakin face. I wanted to both kiss him and slap him at the same time. Seriously. Sexually. Frustrated. Not that you needed to be to want to jump on Kade Hamilton.

"So...who were you talking to?" I had to eventually look up at him, glad that the large bottle of coke was slightly blocking the view.

"My friend Ash in London." I was not going to elaborate, just so he got the satisfaction. But of course, he couldn't leave it alone.

"Uh huh. So, Alexa, help yourself to some pizza. Do you need a plate?" He looked down at his stomach and then grinned mischievously right at me, locking his eyes on me before adding, "Unless you wanna eat off-"

"No!" I shouted, turning tomato red. How mortifying.

"Why not? Maybe then you could check out the 'sexy tribal tattoos' up close..." He lifted his t-shirt a little and I didn't know whether to orgasm or die of shame. I couldn't even deny that I was talking about it. Firstly, it was obvious and secondly, I was the worlds shittiest liar because I always blurted out the truth.

He chuckled when I continued turning red and refused to meet his eyes.

"Aw come on Alexa, no need to be embarrassed by the truth." That was it, now I was super pissed off.

"You shouldn't have been eavesdropping! You have such a big head!" I shouted, throwing the roll of paper towels at him which he dodged effortlessly.

"Hey! I cant help that I'm beautiful! And I was not dropping any eaves, lady." That remark earned him a paper cup to the head I mentally high fived myself for accuracy in aim.

"Stop with the throwing of things at me!" He was laughing as if he enjoyed my annoyance.

"Seriously, I wish I hadn't been overheard because I've managed to stroke your ego unintentionally and you're acting like a arse!" I huffed, annoyed beyond everything.

He quietened down with the laughter and I heard him say something under his breath that sounded like 'that's not the only thing I wish you had stroked.' I pretended not to hear although my blush had truly worked its way up to my cheeks, if it were even possible to get any redder.

After he had taken a breath from laughing, his eyes continued to laugh at me as he passed me a plate with way too many slices on it.

"I'm sorry, ok? You're just so easy to wind up. And you look so cute when you blush, which you've been doing since we met. Must be the Hamilton effect..." He grinned as I stared daggers at him but took the plate he was offering.

"So what, this is your peace offering?" I pointed at the plateful.

"Yeah...that and dessert. I promise I won't mention it again...today."

"Hmpf." He was displaying what he must have thought was an angelic face with a cute pout that melted me inside.

"Okay, fine. But dessert better have chocolate in it."
We ate in silence until I heard him chuckle again and looked up into laughing blue eyes.

"You think I'm sexy," He grinned.

"Argh!" I dropped my napkin on the table and stood to leave but as I passed him, he grabbed my wrist pulled me onto his lap. I gasped at the sudden move and then at the proximity of our bodies. I could feel our chests pushed against one another and his breath on my face. He looked serious all of a sudden, like he hadn't expected that to happen even though he instigated it.

We were silent for a good few seconds, confused yet unable to look away from one another. I could feel the attraction getting stronger between us like invisible ties and tiny magnets connecting us to one another. Enough to attract but just enough to pull away. It felt so impossible to feel like this having just met this man. I was well and truly in LUST with him. I had mentally slapped myself so many times since meeting him that I'd bruised my mental self.

I bit my lip, the rational part of my brain indicating that the warmth and the way his strong hard body felt was just not worth risking everything I had just rebuilt. He was just okay to like from afar. *Don't get too close, don't get burnt. Protect yourself.*

Snapping out of the trance, I stood quickly out of his lap and looked for an excuse to get away. His blue eyes seemed to break from the spell he had been under and a look of apology cast itself on his face as his mouth readied to say sorry but I decided to spare us the awkwardness.

"Um, I got to go send a few emails. Uh, I'll see you later." I turned without waiting for a response and hurried up the two flights of stairs.

CHAPTER SEVEN

Read all about it

I must have been locked in my bedroom for at least a couple of hours. At first I tried sending a few emails like I'd excused myself as doing but I only emailed Hannah and then I stared at my laptop screen for a good fifteen minutes. Solitaire and candy crush occupied some of my time and then I saw my notebook perched in my line of sight and smiled to myself.

As I reached for it on my shelf, my eyes settled on the little desktop calendar I had set by my books. My smile vanished off of my face instantly, replaced with that horrible heartache that had occupied so much of my time recently. Just when I thought I was on my way to getting over it, the memories just pulled me the hell back. It was 5th July, mine and Tom's wedding anniversary. It had not occurred to me until now.

I opened to a fresh page and pulled the top off of my pen. My eyes teared up as I wrote.

Friday 5th July
I can't breathe. Why does his memory still possess me?
I promised myself I wouldn't do this to myself. But I'm
sitting in this amazing city of possibilities, crying into
my pillow with this horrible pain in my chest. I remem-

ber EVERYTHING. I wish I could forget.
I remember the way he was so impatient to see me from the three days we had been forced not to see one another before the wedding, that he tried climbing the pipes up to my bedroom window. I laugh even now when I remember how he got busted by dad.

I remember how he and his mates tried to crash our hen party on their stag do. Luckily, the bouncers kicked them out before they got the chance to kidnap me.

I remember the way he looked adoringly at me as I was walked down the aisle in my white dress and red rose bouquet.

I remembered how our families laughed and took pictures, how my friends desperately grabbed the air for the bouquet.

I remember our wedding night, the promises he made and how he made me feel like the most beautiful woman in the world.

My heart aches for what we had. Our love is not yet dead in my heart, it's still dying a slow painful death.

I buried my face into my pillow and let my tears fall from my eyes as I sobbed quietly. I didn't hear the door knocking. I didn't hear it open. But I felt him sit down on my bed. *Um, hello? Is there no boundary this guy won't cross?* Now I felt like an idiot crying in front of him.

"Hey, I knocked for a while but you didn't answer. I heard something inside. I didn't mean to intrude but...uh...are you okay?" I raised my tear streaked face to look into Kade's worried blue eyes. Okay, maybe I instantly forgave him for just barging in. The fact that he actually cared about someone he didn't even know, showed that he had a good heart.

"It's nothing, I'm just being silly," I sniffed, trying to smile and conjuring up an image of what I must have looked like. A mess. That was my conclusion. He looked at me for a few seconds, not pressing for answers, before pulling me by my elbow and off the bed.

"Come on, shoot some pool with me." I didn't get a chance to decline his request as he gently pulled me away from my gloom.

***

"So, you wanna talk about it?" He asked, pocketing a red ball.

"No. Yes. I don't know." I grimaced at myself. Kade laughed. It was a kind laugh, an emphatic laugh.

"You don't have to unless it will make you feel better. I feel like I'm always being nosy with you. You can just tell me to mind my own business if you want."

"No, it's not that. You will think I'm being silly." Kade gave me an intense pointed look that made me want to continue. "Today was mine and Tom's wedding anniversary. Bit silly getting upset by something that doesn't exist anymore to even be celebrated. Tom always said I was the emotional sentimental type." I grimaced again, thinking of the way he must have viewed me when we ended our love story.

"Sometimes a relationship means more to one partner than to the other."

"You sound like you're speaking from experience." He was silent a few minutes, using his concentration to pocket yet another ball

"I've had my fair share of troubles. Trust seems to be something hard to come by. I don't think I have ever been in love to truly understand how you feel. Mostly, I've sought out companionship but I know what it's like to care about someone and have them betray your trust. Right now, I'm enjoying being single." He smiled as he missed a green ball and I took my position to attempt it.

He didn't seem uncomfortable revealing way more than I had expected for him to respond with. I admired his honesty and decided not to let my curiosity ruin the moment by asking any more personal questions.

"I need to enjoy being single. I just keep letting the past possess me from time to time. I have been...had been... with Tom for so long, I feel like I gave him the best of me and I have nothing left for myself. I need to enjoy this time, that's why I came here. Still haven't got out much."

I laughed at myself. Here I was in New York City, 'living the dream' and I hadn't been out in the city itself. Maybe, when the girls came back, I would take them up on their offer of showing me around. I liked exploring alone usually, I enjoyed my own company at the best of times but this big city felt intimidating on my own at the moment. I caught Kade looking at me with his beautiful sexy dimpled smile.

"I wish I could do that. Look at this city with fresh eyes." I smiled back at him, understanding what he meant.

"I feel that about London sometimes, but I really think how you are feeling at the times you go out makes a difference to your perception. There were times when I'd been sitting miserable outside the Tate Modern, looking out at the thames and I felt nothing, yet when I was happier I would stand on the bridge and think I was on top of the world and I hadn't seen the skyline look so beautiful before. Maybe you will get a chance to do that. As soon as you finish your 'staycation' here."

"My 'staycation'?" He laughed.

"Yes, your staycation. It's better than saying 'when you stop running away from reality by hiding out in a house you legally own for whatever secret reason you have.'" I knew I was being cheeky but he had crossed so many boundaries, why shouldn't I cross a few myself?

"Ouch," he laughed good naturedly.

We spent a little more time playing pool, which I lost miserably. After the game, he took my pool cue to hang on the rack and told me there was a pool on the roof of his apartment.

"Excuse me, what did you say?" Seriously? Could this

place get any better?

"Yeah, I had someone come in early morning to just clean it up since I've been gone a while, thats why I didn't show you yesterday. I also have a gym there. feel like taking a swim?"

I loved being in the water but I was very conscious of my body. I didn't think I was fat but I was curvaceous and my boobs made me feel extra conscious of the extra cushioned bits I possessed. Was I really ready to let my landlord see my partially clothed body? Then again, my sleep shorts yesterday must have left little to the imagination...

"You just want to see me in my swimsuit, you perv," I joked, trying to cover my indecision.

"Shit, you found out about my diabolical plan!" He laughed an evil laugh that was along the lines of 'muahaha' until he saw me fidget.

"Hey, are you really worried about me seeing you in a bathing suit?" *Blunt much?*

I fell silent and before I could muster up the courage to answer, he lifted my chin with his finger, the touch making my sensitive skin buzz from the intimacy. The seriousness in his eyes made it hard to look away.

"You are a beautiful woman Alexa. I don't think you even know it. You have nothing to feel insecure about. Please don't ever feel that way around me." I smiled a little, I felt a blush creep up but this time I didn't hide it. He held my gaze for what felt like an eternity before giving me a gentle push towards the stairs to get changed.

***

I went to find my one piece swimsuit in my room; I had packed it as an after thought. I changed into it and covered myself in my Rocky Balboa dressing gown. Yes, I was a proud owner of the film character's dressing gown. It even had 'Italian Stallion' printed on the back with a horse in yellow satin and 'Rocky' on the front left hand side on the black velour gown. I took this mens replica gown with me everywhere I travelled, forever the tomboy. In a silly way, it made me feel safe as if Sly Stallone himself had wrapped his mahoosive tree trunk arms around me as protection.

Making my way up the stairs of Kade's breathtaking apartment hugging my gown, I found a note taped to the wall beside the stairs to his bedroom when I couldn't see him immediately. Written in astonishingly elegant and neat joined handwriting was:

> *Make your way up the stairs and to the door at the*
> *end of the hall opposite the bedroom. Climb up the*
> *stairs Alice, into wonderland...*

I was intrigued. I wondered if he was exaggerating about the wonderland part as I found a door leading to another staircase up and out onto a rooftop terrace. I should have known by now that Kade Hamilton did not exaggerate.

In front of me was a big pool together with jacuzzi, what looked like a spectacular arrangement of lights for when the sun set and a beautiful view of the city in the near distance. To my left was another building, essentially making Kade's apartment a three storey home atop a townhouse. I immediately thought of how on earth he could have obtained planning permission for all of this.

This glass walled building housed a state of the art gym with a crazy assortment of machines that I both recognised and thought, 'what the fuck?' after seeing. In one corner was a punching bag and there were three television screens in front of the treadmills and cross trainers. Did one man need two treadmills?

I turned my gaze back to the pool where I spotted Kade leaning back with his back to the edge of the pool, gloriously wet, his body glistening in the afternoon sun and his wet hair calling my fingertips to touch. *Behave!*

He was watching me closely, deep in thought as he slowly pulled himself out of the pool. *Oh bollocks.* He just had to have perfect muscled toned and tanned legs like a freakin' model didn't he? And that too with his left calf tattooed. This tattoo looked like one piece and was Japanese. I recognised the dragon design that one of my friends had on her back. The colours vibrant reds, greens, blues, yellows and the black shading was unreal. I stood admiring his art, the dragon curling around his calf, detailed with the precision of a practiced hand and the bloom of a flower emerging from the pattern.

I continued shamelessly staring at his sexy ink and his sexy muscles until I felt his gaze on me again. I'd embarrassed myself a lot so far in front of this man, I didn't think there was much for me to lose in terms of pride and dignity.

"You got a thing for tattoos." It wasn't a question. More like a statement.

"Yeah, I've always found them interesting but yours are just amazing. Got anymore?" I'd become shameless, not employing the brain to mouth filter once again. It seemed like I was implying he had *hidden* tattoos. In places I couldn't already see, seeing as he was half naked in his swim shorts. Epic. Fail.

"Let's see. I've got the tribal down my right side, as you know from your food fantasy," he paused to give me a wicked grin before he continued, "then theres this Japanese on my calf. I have the scripture on my back and I have a piece on my lower abdominals, right above my, uh, you get the picture."

I blushed, right on cue. Damn him. I must have been in a permanent state of 'red' since I met him. And now I couldn't stop myself looking directly at his swim shorts, intrigued as to what lay under them. And then of course the dirty thoughts started and I looked up into laughing, knowing eyes.

"Um, so what's this piece you have on your back?"

Trying to change the subject was never going to be easy but luckily he smirked and turned his back for me to inspect.

I walked up closer to his sculpted muscled back, admiring how taut all his muscles were. Standing close enough to smell the chlorine and alluring cologne on his skin, I looked on with awe at his art. The tribal tattoo with its thick swirling patterns covered the right side of his back too, his arms more intricate and detailed. On his left shoulder blade I saw the elegant script he had mentioned, but it wasn't the way it looked that drew my hand automatically towards his flawless naturally tanned skin. It was what it said. My fingers traced the writing, feeling him tense and then relax under my touch. It read:

...and in time, this too shall pass...

The words spoke to me in a way that no one could. There was hope in the words but mostly it told me something very important about the man on whom these words had been permanently imprinted. He had been through something tough, possibly was still going through it, and he had needed these words of encouragement and hope.

"Beautiful..." I whispered, feeling emotional all of a sudden. *What is wrong with me?* I had been so good at hiding my emotions lately, keeping them buried because I needed to move on but this man had a way of pulling them out of me, even if unintentionally. And it felt good for once to be at ease with myself being this way.

I pulled my hand away and Kade turned around, a slight frown on his face. I started to worry I had crossed the line by touching him but he grabbed my hands his suddenly and pulled me into a hug. Shock at his sudden move, the closeness of his body to mine made me freeze for a second or two until I felt myself relax into his hold. Maybe it was the words I had read on his back, maybe the feeling that I wasn't alone in my pain and the recovery of my life. I don't know if it was one or all of these factors that made me start sobbing into Kade Hamilton's naked chest as he stroked my hair and back, muttering words to soothe me. I let everything out, my pain and self loathing and insecurities, my feelings of betrayal. And he just held me, this stranger that I'd only just met. In that moment I felt so safe, protected. I missed this feeling, the security in a mans arms and even if it was cliche I didn't care - the feel of this mans strong arms around me made me feel cared for and I felt pure bliss in my broken heart for just those few precious seconds. I pulled away from him but he kept a tight hold on me, allowing me just enough space to look up into his beautiful deeper blue eyes. It seemed like his eyes changed shade with his mood, and it fascinated me.

"W-why did you do that? Why are you so kind to me? You don't even know me." Why should I stop speaking my mind now and kill a habit of a lifetime?

Kade took a deep breathe and brought his hand up to my face, wiping a tear away with his thumb. I closed my eyes to his touch. Somehow, it just felt like *more.*

"Because you looked like you needed it. Because you have such sadness in your eyes that it makes my heart ache, makes me want to take it away. And because I feel like I've known you longer than just these two days." He looked so wise in that moment, reminding me that this man was possibly just as broken as I was.

His words sent a thrill through me of acceptance, grateful for his empathy but also selfishly pleased that he wanted to spend time with me to care for me. I gave him a weak smile and wiped the rest of the tears away.

"Thank you." I didn't need to explain to him what I was thanking him for. Damn, the list was endless from letting me stay in his home, for giving me so much of his time and attention and for that physical human contact. Of course, it helped that the physical contact was with a sexy hot man.

After what seemed like an eternity of gazing into his eyes,

the softness I saw turned smouldering and an intense jolt of attraction seemed to pass between us. I felt my nipples perk up beneath my robe. Could I really be feeling something so intense having just cried into his bare chest?

Suddenly, I was hyper aware of our proximity as I broke from his gaze and stared straight into his muscled torso. As if we both understood this was way too soon for whatever our thoughts were drifting towards, we jumped apart from the embrace that had started to feed a fire between us. The rush of cool air was all I needed to bring me back to my senses, whereas Kade quickly jumped into the pool. It made me giggle a little. It was like we were two horny teenagers. Jumping into the water started to look like a good idea to me too.

I watched him emerge, water trickling off his head and neck as he grinned devilishly at me. I returned his smile, deciding to just fuck it and give into the temptation of the water. I peeled off my robe, discarding it on a sun lounger and jumped into the pool, not giving Kade the chance to look at my swimsuit.

The water felt amazing as soon as I made contact with it. The New York summer warmth made this more than heaven. I emerged from beneath the water and raked my hair away from my face and moaned with pleasure. In an instant Kade was beside me.

"How do you make something as simple as that look so erotic?" To cover the embarrassment I splashed him full in the face. His shock was replaced with a hooting laughter as he tried to splash me back while I swam quickly away. Catching up to me, he grabbed me by my waist, raised me up and threw me into the water.

The childish enjoyment we were getting from getting one up on the other fuelled an adrenaline filled hour until we had pruned up so much we decided to get back inside and hydrate. Kade helped me into my robe, subtly trying to check me out, and looking impressed by it.

"So you're a Rocky fan huh? You are ticking all the

boxes Alexa. Great cook, has watched the Godfather and Rocky without being forced to and not to mention beautiful. You are every mans dream woman. Is there more?"

I know he was only flirting but it felt nice that I might be someones 'ideal' and it hadn't escaped me that he had just called me beautiful. Butterflies, the old almost dead ones that once resided in my stomach, found a little life in their wings and fluttered with the rejuvenation of his words.

"Uh huh. I also like motorbikes and tattoos and sexy man abs." Maybe it was the endorphins from all the fun we had been having together that had made me lust drunk.

"Motorbikes huh? I do happen to own a couple. I would love to take you for a ride sometime." One naughty grin and I'd melted. I wanted to say that I'd love to ride him but stopped myself before I looked even more like a moron.

"I'd like that very much."

***

After taking a much needed warm shower, I decided to go make a nice warm cup of tea. The air had chilled a little so a nice cup of tea or hot chocolate would be welcome. I pulled open the fridge door and saw zero milk. I should have gone shopping today at the local mini market but had been distracted by Mr sex-on-legs all day. It was after four so I could still run out to the nearest store and get some. There was no sign of Kade so I assumed he may have stayed up in his apartment for a nap or something. Pulling my light jacket from the coat closet by the door and pulling the hood over my half dried hair, I slipped out onto the street towards the local shops a few blocks away.

I was enjoying the walk back, having picked up huge bottle of milk, some ingredients for dinner and some ice cream I knew we could eat together while watching a movie. It was so weird yet so natural that I had just assumed that Kade would spend the evening with me again. I smiled as I saw a family walk by, the mother laughing as the dad ran after the toddler who had decided it was a good idea to chase a cat. The green of trees in the summer lifted my soul. It was just like how in London, even with the busy city life bustling around us, there were still parks and little patches of nature everywhere and I was happy I found it here too.

I was walking past a news stand when something caught my eye. A magazine, bright and glossy, shouting out at me. I stopped dead in my tracks. The picture on the front of the magazine was of a man with bright blue grey eyes, strong jaw and dark hair with a very distinctive amused smile. Not one magazine but damn well near all of them had similar pictures.

The main story heading of the one I picked up read:

> *"JILTED! Giselle Carr left at the alter by infam-*
> *ous playboy fiancé Kade Hamilton!*
> *Full story page six!"*

The breath left my lungs. The news stand guy looked pissed off.

"Hey lady, you gonna' buy that?"

"Uh, yeah, sorry." I handed him some money for the gossip magazine as I distractedly made my way home. I couldn't help but feel hurt and a familiar feeling of having my trust betrayed. I felt sick to the pit of my stomach.

All the butterflies had settled back into their previous state of distress as my image of Kade Hamilton 'the hero' turned to Kade Hamilton 'the villain' in a matter of a few pages.

CHAPTER EIGHT

I can explain

As soon as I slammed the front door shut I headed straight for the kitchen, furiously putting the few items I had purchased away whilst keeping the gossip magazine in my hand. Having read it twice on my way home, my blood was boiling. Things had started to fall into place and had started to make sense. I heard the distinct sound of bare feet on the stairs coming up from the basement. He appeared in the kitchen wearing a tight black t-shirt and blue jeans, his eyes matching the denim. But I couldn't let his beauty distract me.

"Hey, there you are. I was going to send out a search party...whoa, what's that look for?" He stopped mid sentence, no doubt silenced by the daggers my eyes were throwing his way.

I threw the magazine at his chest and he caught it easily, although somewhat surprised by my outburst.

"Care too explain?"

He took one look at the cover and closed his eyes as if he was in pain but at the same time exasperated. At that moment, I didn't give a shit. I felt like I could trust Kade to be honest with me, I trusted him enough to tell him something very personal and all this time he was keeping this huge secret about his identity. Moreover, he was hiding out in the house because he had broken this poor woman's heart! What an arsehole!

"Look Alexa, I can explain-"

"Save it Kade. All you men are the same. Have you any idea what this poor woman Giselle is going through? Have you read what is being said? Let me read it to you!" I dramatically pulled the magazine from his hands and finding the double page spread dedicated to the breakup, I started reading it out aloud:

"New York's sweethearts and power couple 'Kisselle' have split up! An Insider has revealed that Media Mogul Kade Hamilton and socialite Giselle Carr, who had been engaged almost a year, had intended to marry in a secret private ceremony with family and friends during the July 4th holiday. It is said that Kade never showed up for the ceremony, leaving Giselle distraught at the alter! Pictures show a distressed and broken hearted Giselle leaving her parents home with her bags on the evening of her intended wedding. A close friend has reported she is depressed and needs to 'get away from the reminders of Kade in the city.' We suspect she has flown to her holiday home in the south of France. Meanwhile, Kade Hamilton has gone AWOL and no statement has been issued by the Hamilton family as yet. It seems, ladies, our favourite most eligible bachelor is back on the market, cad or not!"

Below the short article were comments from the 'shocked and concerned New Yorkers' and a whole two pages dedicated to the pictures of the couple.

One look at Giselle and you couldn't deny that she was beautiful. Blonde straight wispy hair, emerald green eyes. High cheekbones, slim model like figure and tall. In each picture, her long legs were shown off in a skirt, shorts, dress or skinny jeans in a way that women would kill to look. And they looked so damn hot together. Kade in his casual jeans and button down smart shirts that were sometimes accompanied in some pictures with a sweater. There were a couple of pictures of them on the beach holding hands. Kade in his bare chested glory and Giselle with her beach perfect body wearing a tiny bikini. I would have to admit, that stung a little. Just to know that he had definitely tasted perfection and I would never come close to that. Not that anything could happen between us, but still.

Why was it that I felt so betrayed when this man meant nothing to me? I'd known him all of two days for heavens sake. Something was seriously wrong with my head or my hormones yet I still shot daggers at him. I felt a camaraderie with poor gorgeous model like Giselle without knowing her. I guess in this short time, I'd put Kade on some sort of pedestal, and his kindness towards me had blinded me.

"Alexa, do you always believe everything you read in the gossip columns?" His voice was calm but had an undertone of anger that I didn't expect to hear from him. A shiver ran down my spine as I took in his change of demeanour but quickly recovered from my shock when I remembered why I was angry.

"No I don't but answer me this. Did you or did you not cancel your wedding to Giselle just a short time before it was about to take place?" If it were possible, his eyes darkened further. His shoulders looked so tense that I thought he might never relax even if he wanted to. I felt like I was poking a bear with a stick.

"Why are you so concerned for Giselle?" he asked, avoiding the truth. When he said her name, it looked as if it pained him to let it slip from his mouth. I didn't let that stop me though. I was just getting warmed up.

"Because I know what it's like to be the one hurting from betrayal! Because men like you find it so easy to use and then throw away a woman like she meant nothing! Because she's probably thinking its all her fault! Was she too fat for you? Too needy? Too boring that you had to look elsewhere and screw the office slut and get her pregnant?!" I didn't real-ise I was projecting myself while shouting at Kade until the words left my mouth and I could't pull them back from the air around us.

"You don't know what happened between us Alexa. I'm not Tom." There was a trace of his tone softening when he said those words but his expression was still thunderous.

"What does it matter? You're all the same! You all take *everything* and leave us with *nothing!*" Angry tears surfaced and I wiped them angrily. Kade looked torn between anger and wanting to comfort me but he chose the former.

"Don't you dare paint all men with the same brush! I AM NOT THAT MAN!" His voice was loud when angry, as thunderous in expression as his face was. It ignited my fury more.

"Oh really? Then what kind of man are you?! You were flirting with me having just broken up with your fiancee! You are EXACTLY THAT KIND OF MAN!"

"So that's what you think of me? Because I'm a man, there isn't the slightest chance that she may have HURT ME?!"
He stood frozen as soon as he said it, as if he had not meant to let the words out. As if it were a secret and as if saying it out aloud meant it was real.

In the midst of our heated exchange, we hadn't heard Sadie come in quietly, watching our shouting match in shock, her big green eyes were even bigger as she looked at both of us. We looked her way when she cleared her throat to speak in her soft voice.

"Um, everything okay with you guys?" As if he had lit-erally melted, Kade's tension vanished and his eyes softened as did his voice while he approached Sadie as if he would a child.

"Yeah, nothings up. Just a misunderstanding. How come you're home early?" His voice sounded concerned. Why would he be so concerned for Sadie's well being? She'd only been in Ohio to see her family.

"Uh, things were just a little too intense up there. Mom and dad were trying to get me to move back home and my brothers...well, they kept asking a million questions that I couldn't keep up with. Over protective doesn't even cut it. But then again, they were happy that I turned up. I only left because I felt a little suffocated. Too many memories." She paused and then looked up at Kade and gave him a sad smile before she asked, 'How are you keeping up?"

Kade gave her a matching sad smile and I felt like I was an intruder witnessing an intimate moment, yet I couldn't leave.

"I'm okay Sadie, I'm holding up. I've had a while to digest this, I just sucked at doing the right thing."

The whole situation didn't seem to make sense to me. What memories was Sadie running from? What was the reality of the whole Kade-Giselle situation? I started to feel a little silly. If someone as sweet as Sadie believed in Kade, could it be that he really was the innocent party in all this. I must have been in a bitch mood because I just didn't buy it, or didn't want to. A pessimistic part of me just wanted to find fault with the so far perfect Mr Hamilton.

Sadie walked into Kade's arms like it was the most natural thing to do and it stung me a little. *Great, now I'm jealous of the sweetest thing that has ever walked this earth, over a non-relationship that I have with my landlord.* I needed to shake myself out of this funk before I did more damage. Sadie seemed to be upset and I couldn't see anything more than a deep friendship in the way they were acting with one another but it didn't stop me wanting to be the one in his arms. I'd turned into one twisted, silly school girl.

Stepping around them, as Kade hugged and rocked Sadie soothing her as she buried her face in his chest sobbing so lightly you had to strain to hear it, I stroked her back lightly before I left.

"I'm glad you're back home Sadie," I whispered

quietly. At that moment I caught Kade's gaze and all I could see was pain and empathy. I really did feel like a bitch in that moment. Was I incapable of thinking of no one but myself anymore? Had I lost the power to look at all things objectively? Shame on me.

I took the stairs feeling like the loser that I'd become and decided that a night of Jane Austen was needed to lift my spirits.

Once in my bedroom, I took out my BBC Pride and Prejudice dvd, the only one of two dvd's that had pride of place in my room instead of on the shelves in the living room, and stuck it into the wall mounted tv with DVD player. The other cherished DVD was a BBC adaptation of Persuasion. Yes, I am a Janeite, I'm living up to my Brit girl cliche. Don't hate.

It was late afternoon and still light outside so I drew the curtains and blinds, put on my cotton pyjama bottoms and one of Brian's old T-shirts I had nicked a year ago and cut the arms and neck of to make into a vest top and snuggled into bed with the remote.

***

Right about the time where Mr Darcy was proposing to Elizabeth Bennet for the first time, I small timid knock sounded at my door. I didn't need to ask to know who it could be.

"Come in."

Sadie popped her head of beautiful wavy auburn hair around my door.

"I'm not interrupting you, am I? I can come back later." I pressed pause just as Darcy opened his mouth to speak and smiled at Sadie, waving her over.

"Not at all. Just me and Mr Darcy in here. Whats up?" Sadie sat down next to me on my bed and looked at me with a kind smile.

"I just wanted you to know something about Kade. I

heard...you guys shouting at one another..."

"I'm so sorry you had to see that Sadie. That was just me getting stupid and judgemental. I've had a bit of difficult day." I felt embarrassed. Seriously, maybe I just needed to get some of my frustration out before I ended up eviscerating another person. Maybe buy myself a battery operated boy-friend or something.

"It's ok Alexa, you haven't known Kade for as long as I have. He told me what happened and how you found out who he is. Plus the mess with Giselle. He hates that he's be-come some sort of celebrity just by being the son of Alastair Hamilton 'the media mogul'. He hates the way people as-sume they know him from what they read. I know he should have told you who he is and all but I guess he liked that you didn't know who he was. He likes his privacy. Please don't think badly of him. He's the sweetest guy alive, he has saved me in so many ways, you cannot possibly imagine. I know I have three brothers already but really I have four." She smiled sadly and looked into my eyes with her expressive ones. "Give him a chance, I think he likes you."

I took a deep breath. When she put it that way, it made sense. The NDA's and him assuming I was a reporter breaking in when we met. And not answering the door for the pizza boy. Yeah, he thought I'd missed the fact he was in the base-ment den all the time the bell had been rung. I suppose he really had to take major precautions to keep his identity and whereabouts secret.

"Thank you for coming to talk to me. I guess you're right. I feel stupid about shouting at him about the gos-sip written in that magazine when I don't know the facts. I think it's the woman scorned in me sometimes rearing her ugly head."

I laughed about it, but deep down I knew it was something that would live with me. I couldn't help but think that Tom had ruined me for other men. Trusting people was some-thing I was finding difficult to do these days, even though

I thought I had started to get better since coming to New York. I guess it would take time.

"It's okay to form judgements Lexi, we're all human. Just make sure you take some time to analyse them when you form one that contradicts another."

She was right. Up until finding the magazine, my opinion of Kade was that he was this amazing Greek God.

I smiled and she returned it, her pretty face lighting up. It was hard to believe this woman had fallen apart just a couple of hours earlier. That skill of covering up your emotions came with years of practice. I pushed aside my thoughts that Sadie was hiding a painful past and patted the space beside me on my bed closer to the pillows.

"Why don't you come join me and Colin Firth here for some good old fashioned Austen era romance?"

"I'd love to! I think this is the best version of Pride and Prejudice they ever made!" God, did this woman have to be so perfect? I think I had just found my new best friend.

***

Around the time Elizabeth Bennet was rushing back to Hertfordshire to her family after Lydia's elopement with Mr Wickham, another more solid knock sounded at the door. Since Sadie was already in my room, it could only be a certain dark-haired, blue-eyed hunk.

My heart thundered in my chest. I felt foolish after shouting at him and I didn't know if I could look him in the eyes without feeling ashamed but good manners won out and I invited him in. I had no doubt in my mind that every female that ever looked at him would lose the ability to breathe at the initial shock of his perfection. I had to stop thinking like that, but who was I to deny that this man was a fine specimen. I was merely admiring God's creation after all.

"Hey," I said quietly. Sadie looked from me to Kade expectantly.

"Hey. I was getting bored, can I join you guys?" He sounded like a kid being left out of a game in the playground, it was so cute. I smiled at him and his easy smile returned too, brightening that beautiful face.

"If you're sure you want to watch a period drama..."

"Shit, is this Pride and Prejudice? My favourite!" he squealed with mock excitement. I looked at Sadie and we both burst out laughing. Kade looked amused as he made space for himself on the bed. Instead of coming to the side I had made space for him to sit, he bulldozed his way into the centre of my bed between Sadie and me.

"Kade!" I squealed as he snuggled between us.

"What? I get cold," he said, trying to look serious but I saw that naughty boy smile sneak onto the side of his mouth.

"Whatever," I smiled at him. We looked at one another with a mutual understanding. His eyes registered my apology and accepted, my eyes registered his regret at losing his temper and I accepted. He lifted my hand and kissed it. My stomach butterflies powered up and started their fluttering again.

Unable to stand the deep penetrating look in his eyes any longer, I looked to the tv screen for reprieve and settled in close to Kade to watch. How we were able to feel this connected this soon was a mystery. I never believed in anything like this being real, and I was a hopeless romantic at heart. I guess something of Kade's soul spoke out to mine. We had a *something* between us. It would take some time to figure that out and I was happy with that. For now, I enjoyed his closeness, the way he had put his arms around both Sadie and myself as if it were the most natural thing to do and how I rested my head on his chest. I never got that comfortable with strangers. But Kade didn't feel like a stranger, and I wondered if he ever had?

***

I woke up feeling strangely comfortable. Not that this bed was uncomfortable. Just that there was a strong arm holding me to a warm but hard muscled body and I didn't realise where I was for a while. I knew it wasn't Tom, he was not that muscled. I actually didn't care because it felt so good and the body smelt delicious as I wound in and out of consciousness.

As with all good dreams, I eventually had to wake up and when I did my heart was beating kinda funny. I stopped nuzzling into Kade Hamilton's chest shamelessly and looked up to find his eyes closed but a huge grin formed on his positively delectable mouth. Sometime during the night, we must have all fallen asleep.

It looked as if Sadie had crept out to her room but Kade had lost his shirt during the night and was just wearing his loose sweats. I was thankful I still had my bra on because my big breasts would have definitely been on display through my vest top had I not been wearing one. I squirmed when I realised that he must have woken up at some point to remove his shirt, knowing he was in my bed and had decided to stay.

"Good morning Alexa. Would you mind not wriggling so much, I'm trying to have a lie in." The cheeky bastard. I tried to pull myself from his grip but failed miserably as he held on tight without any effort.

"So many boundaries have been crossed between us, you do realise that don't you?"

He eventually opened his twinkling breathtaking blue grey eyes and smiled down at me. This smile was soft and sweet.

"I like the idea that there are no boundaries between us. That had to be the best sleep I've had in years. I never usually sleep overnight in bed with someone else, especially when theres no sex involved. It's a new thing for me. I may have to do this more often." He was serious yet teasing. That was both scary and hot. I felt *hot* at his mention of sex.

"Well, I slept well too but since this was unintentional - an accidental sleepover - it will not be happening again. I am not in the habit of strange men sleeping in my bed thank you very much."

"Strange men? Really? Do you really think I'm a stranger now?" He was laughing but there was a little evidence of him being offended.

"I suppose, once one has been manhandled by ones landlord and then wrestled in a swimming pool and tickled...it's not so much being a 'stranger' than just being 'strange'."

Kade's laughter rumbled through his chest through to me. God I loved how smooth his skin was, how hard those muscles were and how good he smelt. I tried, I really did, to hide the way I was inhaling him but of course it didn't go unnoticed. Especially when I closed my eyes when doing it.

"Let's stay in bed all day," I suggested after I had put my head back to his chest. I really was shameless. Somehow we both had been craving that physical contact with another human being. And as strange as this all was, it wasn't unwelcome.

"Hmmm," was the only response I got. I nuzzled back into him, our legs tangled together and drifted back off into a blissful sleep.

***

I felt someone kiss my cheek and whisper, "Thank you for letting me sleep with you last night Miss De Luca." And all too soon he was gone and my bed felt cold and empty. How the hell did he expect me to fall asleep again?

I waited a few minutes before I opened my eyes. His scent was everywhere. Like he had marked his territory. Something that had always been a turn on for me were men that smelled good. Tom always had these expensive colognes and body sprays that were heavenly and after we split, I would feel an ache in my heart whenever a man passed me on the street wearing a similar or same cologne. Those feelings of nostalgia would return and I'd want so much to be with him again.

Kade's scent was different. It was an amazing mix of cologne, soapy freshness and his own male, clean sweat. He was secreting major doses of pheromones and I was riding the high. And that sweet kiss? Yeah, I could still feel his lips on my cheek and wished they had been on my lips instead.

Lifting myself off my bed, I headed into the bathroom for a leisurely shower with the biggest grin plastered on my face.

***

The aroma of pancakes coming from the kitchen was making my mouth water as I made my way downstairs. Sadie was dishing up a pancake as I entered.

"Morning Alexa," she smiled her usual warm smile.

"Good morning Sadie. Is it still morning?" I glanced at the clock.

"It's eleven fifty seven, I'd say you are safe. Here, dig in." She placed a pancake in a plate in front of me at the breakfast bar.

"That smells delicious, thanks." I took a bite and moaned in ecstasy. "These are amazing! You are officially my favourite person in New York." Sadie giggled.

"Actually, Kade made those, I just flipped that batch because he's taking a call downstairs."

"Are you serious? Damn, that man is amazing." I closed my eyes on another mouthful, moaning my appreciation.

"I knew I could make you moan." I opened my eyes to a pair of mischievous blue ones. I threw a napkin at him, as if that would do any damage.

"If you weren't so damn good at making the pancakes, I would smack that grin right off your face."

"Yeah yeah, you wouldn't do that to me. You like my lickable abs too much." I knew what he was doing. One tomato red blush coming right up.

"I'm never going to live that one down right?"

"Nope. Eat up, I'm making a dozen more of these bad boys."

I watched him saunter over to the stove and busy himself, insisting that Sadie sit down too, as he made and served us pancakes. His arse looked so good in his stonewash denim jeans that were nice and worn in, with cuts and rips in the right places. Coupled with his plain white T-shirt, he looked just like a model. Barefoot and sexy. God I loved his body, I was like a hungry woman at a buffet when I devoured him with my eyes.

Stop objectifying him! Oh, Granna would just love him. She would think up a hundred ways to describe the way he looked in those jeans that would make the devil blush. I giggled and he turned around, throwing me an arrogant knowing look.

"Sleep well did you?" That shut me right up.

"Yes, I did as a matter of fact. Once the annoying bed bug left me in peace."

I could see a slight smile on Sadie's face as she pretended to be oblivious and ate her breakfast quietly. Kade grunted.

"Like you didn't enjoy being wrapped around my body." I couldn't argue and decided that instead of being flippant, a change in subject was needed.

"What's your plan for today Sadie?" That scored me another 'cat that ate the canary' smile over his shoulder.

"Oh, I have this project to complete for monday so I'm going to go into the office for a bit. I'll be back around six, wanna go out for a drink or two then? I know this great bar near work Midtown."

"Sounds great," I smiled, loving the idea of getting out

having been holed up in the house too long. I looked at Kade asked his back, "Will you be braving the storm and leaving your fortress Mr Hamilton?" He turned to flip his pancake to give us the full Hamilton effect and smirked.

"That depends."

"On what pray tell? The weather?"

"Well, figuratively speaking, yes. Depends on who is todays news. I've been in the news over two days now, I'm hoping one of the Richardson twins will do something crazy and knock me off the top spot for gossip in the next two days, so I doubt I will come out tonight."

"How can you be so sure," I asked, genuinely interested.

"I'm the son of a Media Mogul, don't you know? I know everything." He smirked again and turned back to wow us with his culinary talents as we ate.

***

Sadie had left for her office by one thirty and I sat on a comfortable sofa in the living room with my Kindle reading the latest romance from my favourite author involving a man who was part of a motorcycle gang with loads of tattoos and an unassuming woman meeting and falling in love. As much as I loved holding a real book in my hands, I loved the anonymity the e-reader provided to save the embarrassment that I always had my head in an adult romance these days to give me some hope of romance at all.

At that particular moment I was getting right to the naughty part, when out of nowhere my kindle was pulled from my hands by that sneaky bed bug.

"Kade, give it back! What are you, like five?!" I knew I'd die of embarrassment if he read it. He held it up and out of the reach of my flailing hands as he looked. It was worse than I expected. He read it...aloud.

"Ace pulled me closer and ran his big manly hands

through my hair. *'I'm going to take you right here Maddie. I'm gonna fuck you against the wall, on the table, on the floor and every other place I can find.'* I looked deep into his blue eyes and melted when I felt his hands cup my breasts. I let my hands envelop his shaft and closed my eyes. I couldn't breathe when his lips hovered over my breasts and he suck-OOOWWWW!"

"I hope that hurt the way you made it look like it did," I smiled through my red face, happy I got a punch into his rock hard stomach. My smile fell when he doubled over.

"Shit, Kade are you ok?" I dropped my Kindle on the sofa and went to him as he dropped to the floor. Just as I put my hand to his back he spoke.

"No I'm not okay. Maybe if you let your hands envelop my - HEY!" I flicked his ear. The bloody drama queen. I picked up my Kindle and huffed downstairs to the den, ignoring his hooting laughter.

It wasn't long before he was there, standing at the bottom of the steps as expected. I sighed loudly before I looked up at the sparkling baby blues.

"Are you stalking me?"

"Nah, I'm just bored. Cabin fever."

"So...you're stalking me."

"Basically, yeah I am. Thought I would come bother a pretty lady."

"Hmm, covering up your disturbing obsession with a compliment. Nice."

I didn't take compliments well, I had many insecurities when it came to people looking at me, and I mean *really* looking at me. Up until now I had been enjoying the attention I was getting from him but now I'd had a bit of time to dwell and the point of harmless flirting had passed us a while ago, I started to wonder why he was being so attentive to me. I used to be so confident. Could it be that Tom really had ruined me for other men?

"You don't take compliments well do you? You just

brush it aside like it makes you uncomfortable that some-one considers you as pretty. It's like you don't want to be seen, you want to hide in the shadows." He only had to go and hit the bloody nail in the head didn't he?

"Have you been looking inside my head? What are you, a shrink or something?" He came and sat next to on the couch as we watched it drizzle lightly outside.

"No, but I have had enough therapy over the years to open up shop myself." At my surprised expression he leaned over and whispered in my ear, "Don't worry, I'm not certifi-ably crazy. The stalking tendencies have just started since I met you." I flicked him lightly and he chuckled and moved back and relaxed into the comfortable sofa.

We were quiet for a few seconds, not really knowing what to say. There was also the air that needed clearing since we had our shouting match the night before. Nothing about the way we were progressing in knowing one another was con-ventional.

"So," he cleared his throat, "I guess I owe an you an ex-planation in regards to my cancelled wedding." He frowned as he looked at the coffee table in front of us.

"Look Kade, it's really none of my business and I shouldn't have shouted at you. I guess because of everything thats gone on with me recently, I have been very biased in my views. I'm sorry for being a complete bitch." His head snapped to me and he looked annoyed.

"Please don't ever call yourself a bitch ever again. I would never think that." His face softened and he looked sad all of a sudden. "You told me something very personal when we had just met, I know how much you were trusting me with that part of you that you shared with me. I think it's only fair that I do the same. The only reason I didn't want to tell you before is that I was kinda enjoying that you didn't know who I was. As in the 'celebrity' they've forced on me."

"In the context of everything else, I do understand now why you didn't say anything." It had to suck not being able to go anywhere without the possibility of people recognising you and watching your every move.

"It's hell having everyone know about what's happening in your life. Usually I don't get a lot of bother. It helps that the family business is news and show business. My dad owns a lot of the most prominent news agencies and magazines in this country and a few internationally. The gossips know to keep us out of the limelight as much as they can but it doesn't stop some of the opportunistic men and mostly women out there trying to paw at me, seeing if they can get something out of me. I suppose my colourful past doesn't help my public image much." He looked at my confused face and sighed. "I'm surprised you don't know about that, I thought you would have googled me by now."

In all honesty, I had thought about it but didn't get around to doing it. I was deadly curious.

"I won't lie, I want to but a certain someone hogged my bed last night so I didn't get the chance." He smiled his usual naughty smile.

"I don't recall you complaining at the time. You didn't exactly kick me out." I didn't really have a comeback so I just smiled at him, suddenly shy.

"Anyway, I digress," he sighed again as if it was difficult for him to part with the information he was about to share with me, "Let me relay some facts to you about my past to help you understand things better. When I was fourteen, my best friend Scott died. We were like brothers, we shared everything and it impacted my life in a bad way. I was a pubescent teen so of course I looked to ways of escapism."

He looked so distraught even after all this time, I had to resist comforting him so he could continue his story. My heart ached for him.

"It started with my behaviour at home and school. I was a popular kid, got on well with everyone usually but as I struggled to deal with Scott's untimely death, I lashed out at all the people that loved and cared for me. I tried all sorts of shit, I drank excessively and took so many drugs that I wouldn't even be able to tell you which one I had taken if you asked me, I'd just pop them as if they were candy.

At that age, I looked a little older than I was and I got a lot of attention but as soon as I got my 'bad boy' rep, the girls just flocked to me. And I slept with all of them. It seemed to rid me of the pain temporarily, relieve me of the guilt that I was alive and Scott was dead. You understand that right?" He looked desperately at me for understanding.

"Yes, I do." I did understand. After all, I'd slept with Max for the same reason, to escape the pain, even if it was my one irresponsible slip up. I still didn't understand what all this had to do with Giselle.

"I barely managed to get my shit together to graduate high school and then something happened that made me put my life into perspective. I was driving home from a friends graduation party with my sixteen year old baby sister, I'd had quite a bit to drink but had let my anger at Kirsty, my sister, cloud my judgement. She had turned up at the party wearing a next to nothing dress and was letting one of the sleaziest guys on my football team touch her in ways that made me see red. I know I was being a hypocrite. I mean, I'd been doing the same to a girl wearing worse clothes than hers but that was *my sister.* So I beat the shit out of the kid touching her and threw her into my car and drove the short distance to our house. I was shouting at her and she was screaming at me about how she was not a child when it was too late to see that I had veered onto the other side of the road. I crashed into an oncoming car, my car flipped over and spun a few times. When I opened my eyes, my little sister was bleeding from everywhere, it seemed. She wouldn't respond to me. Alexa, my whole world shifted. I was desperate to get to her, I didn't realise that I'd pulled my body over the broken glass and metal that had lodged into my skin to get to her. When the emergency services came, they had to cut us out of the car, it was literally crushed. The other driver was thankfully okay. But Kirsty wasn't."

His face looked so grave as he recounted his past, obvious pain etched on his face.

"Did Kirsty...did she...?" My eyes wide, I couldn't make myself say the word.

"No, no she didn't thank God. I would have died if I'd caused my sisters death. Contrary to our parents' belief, we actually do love one another a lot," he smiled sadly before he continued.

"No, Kirsty suffered a critical head trauma. It was pretty much touch and go, she had been in a medically induced coma for weeks before she was out of danger. I wouldn't leave her side, I refused. I would pray like I'd never prayed before asking God that, if he existed, would he please save her. I cried at her bedside, telling her I was sorry. She was lying there unresponsive and I had gotten out of that horrific crash with just the superficial wounds and a few bruised ribs. You can't imagine the relief when she came to. Those weeks in the hospital gave me ample time to really think over everything I was doing in my life. As soon as Kirsty was allowed home, I asked my father to ship me off to the army." He paused and I gasped.

"You were in the army?" That just amped up his sex appeal another notch, if that was possible, no matter how inappropriate it was for me to feel like that way when he'd just told me about a life altering experience. It explained how ripped his body was. He must be very disciplined with working out.

I loved a man in uniform. I reminded myself that now was not the time to think about that and in the process reminding myself how I had protested against the 'war on terror' to pour a mental bucket of ice cold water on my imagining him in uniform and gave him my whole attention when he continued.

"Yeah. I was in deep with the authorities as it were. My father has a lot of sway Alexa, don't get me wrong, he knows plenty of important people but justice still had to be served. He saw the opportunity in my request to make a suggestion for the punishment for my offences.

Two weeks later I was in training. My drill sergeant was a brutal but good man. I learnt so much in those tough months that I hadn't learnt in all my life. Much needed discipline and focus. It allowed me to forgive myself and relieve some of the guilt of my past. After intensive training, I was chosen to go into special forces. I was deployed to Afghanistan amidst the most tense years of the war. I was only twenty years old by then but I'd made quite n impression amongst my peers and I'd got quite a lot of 'action' on the field but you can't imagine the horror and the despair out there.

One particular incident involving a shoot out and a bomb almost cost me my life, earned myself a bullet wound too." I looked over his torso, wondering where it was hidden under his t-shirt. His skin looked flawless from what I remembered.

"Wow Kade, that must have been terrifying." He nodded and absentmindedly rubbed his chest over his right pectoral, giving me an indication where the wound was. Most probably covered by tattoos. I studied his face and all of a sudden he looked older, more weathered. His life experiences had aged him a little but that was hardly surprising. I don't know if I could deal with all the stress.

"It *was* terrifying. But I carried on with my assignments, I had a brotherhood out there that made me feel like I belonged. But as fate would have it, my mother found out about my third near death experience and had what can only be described as a nervous break down." *Third near death experience?* He had only recounted two incidents but I didn't press it as I listened.

"I didn't know about how she was deteriorating until about a year after the initial attack I had survived. Thankfully there was no way she could have heard about the covert ops we were involved in, I'm sure that would have sent her more over the edge. Soon I received word from my dad begging for me to come home. The timing was right I guess because I hadn't been healing from a wound I had to my leg from shrapnel and the medics were considering sending me home for better medical attention. It's good they did, there was a nasty mother of an infection there and I could have lost my leg had, they not sent me home.

My mom was hysterical when she saw me, she begged me to take an honourable discharge that was being offered due to my previous and current wounds at the time. I couldn't say no to my mom, she had gone through so much and I won't lie, I needed to get away from the horrors of the war. So I was discharged and started to applying to college to do a degree. Thats when I got accepted to Oxford and left to pursue my degree there. Those were some of the best years of my life."

He smiled at the memories and I couldn't help but smile with him. I was happy that it was my home country that had given him those happy times.

"So....how does Giselle fit into all this?"

"I'm getting to that, little miss impatient. I thought you should know the context of the situation first." He mocked annoyance and I lightly punched his stomach, gesturing regally for him to continue.

"Fine! You may proceed." He chuckled and pinched my nose.

"Yes ma'am! So," he settled himself closer to me on the couch, "after I came back from England upon the completion of my degree, I got involved with dads companies, learning the business and applying what I'd learnt. It was strange to be involved in what I always considered 'dad's work' but I enjoyed working with him. I still do. We made up for all the time we lost when I was being 'wild' as dad puts it. During this time I started to reconnect with old friends from school and the neighbourhood. That's how I got in touch with Brent again. I was at a party with him when I met Giselle. You see, Giselle is Scott's little sister." I took in his information overload and he sat back into the sofa and ran his hand over his face and through his hair.

"So you reconnected with her too?" Stupid question really but I wanted to fill the sudden tense silence.

"Yeah, I suppose you could put it that way. Giselle, well, she's gorgeous. You've seen her pictures right?" I nodded, feeling a sting of jealousy that he considered her gorgeous when I really shouldn't have - I mean, she was his fiancée until recently.

"Well, she mesmerised me. And the most important connection we found was our grief over Scotts death. We started to meet up more often as friends and quickly that developed into more. What I'm going to say next is going to make me sound like a jerk, more than you probably already think of me as," he looked into my eyes and took a deep breath. "I cared for her, adored her even, but I knew I didn't love her. Not in the way she wanted me to. It wasn't that crazy passionate love I heard people talk about. I like to think I loved her to some degree, but it wasn't enough. I knew she felt it, probably knew that I proposed out of being expected to and feeling pressurised to do so but she always said she would rather have something than nothing from me. So we continued in our comfortable relationship, as awkward as it must sound. I was faithful to her throughout and I thought she was too. Until about three months ago when I received a video message on my phone from Kirsty. She had been at some secluded restaurant a little out of the city with some friends when she saw Giselle. She was kissing someone. It was the kind of kiss that implied a certain level of intimacy. That 'someone' happened to be a mutual friend of ours."

Man I felt like such an idiot. I'd shouted at him for jilting Giselle when she had been the one breaking his heart!

"Kade, I'm so sorry. Did you confront her? I mean, obviously you said something but does she know you know?"

"Yeah, I confronted her. But thats where I've been an ass..." He looked ashamed. And the penny dropped.

"You confronted her right before the wedding." It wasn't a question. I could tell that was how it went down.

"Yes. It was a dick move. I knew for three months about her sneaking around behind my back, expecting her to say something before the wedding but she was happy to play along and carry on as planned. She was so relaxed and carefree, I convinced myself that everything would be okay and decided to just go along with it, even though I'd backed off from her emotionally and physically over that time. But when it came to the day, I just realised that I didn't want this for me, A loveless relationship in which there was already betrayal, I couldn't deal, and to know that she was intimate with another man? Not an easy thing to live with. So I confronted her and she cried and admitted everything. She had been having an affair for five months by then. She said she wanted me to love her like she loved me but she felt unloved and that Chris gave her that. It hurt that she betrayed me but you know what happened next Alexa? I actually felt relief when I walked away from her. I don't know if that makes me some sort of sadistic 'cad' as the papers want to label me but I actually felt able to breathe. I realised then that it was the right decision."

"Why are you letting them vilify you in the papers? It was obviously Giselle that cheated. You should give your story to them." I felt hurt for him, even if he was saying he was relieved.

"No, I wouldn't do that to her. The press hasn't hassled me like this for some time now, seeing as I usually just immerse myself in work and avoid the drama. Giselle, on the other hand, gets harassed non stop. She is that beautiful woman every man wants to take home and every woman loves to hate. I wouldn't do that to her. I can live with being the heartless creature that left her if that makes it a little better for her in the media. She's had to deal with a big loss after what happened to her brother and rumours of an eating disorder and endless other jibes of criticism. I still care for her."

"I should have realised that you're a man who is likely to defend a woman's honour, Mr Hamilton," I smiled at him.

"Well, you need to stop judging me Mis De Luca. If you allow yourself to loosen up a bit, you will see that being in my company has it's benefits."

"Are you implying that I'm uptight?!"

"Well, maybe more stand-offish..." He knew best to keep quiet when I levelled him with my death glare.

"I doubt I would have let a man I've just met sleep in my bed if I were. Anyway, now that I know how much of a gentleman you are, and seeing as you didn't take advantage of me last night, I'm inclined to think better of you."

The truth was I was feeling all warm and fuzzy inside that this man, who was any woman's ideal physically and mentally, was sitting here with me and that I had held his attention for even a few minutes of my life, which made me feel like I was privileged. But I didn't want to let him know that. A man like him with his size of an ego? I suppose that little flaw made this bad boy a little imperfect.

I smiled, knowing I was trying to deny myself Kade Hamilton. I was well aware that I was not as perfect as this man. And I was broken inside. I may have been attracted to Kade but the break up of my marriage was still fresh for me, I had major trust issues and I was only now starting to believe that I wasn't an ugly troll, which was something Rebecca called me when she listed reasons for Tom leaving me for her when we had a confrontation at work shortly after the event. Let's just say that it didn't end well for Rebecca as no one there actually liked her and her hair smelt like tuna mayonnaise for about a week...

"I can see the wheels in your head turning De Luca, tell me what you're thinking?" He looked worried as if I was again forming judgement of him.

"I was thinking of how perfect you are." *Shit. Why couldn't I lie?* Kade scoffed.

"Hardly. If only you knew. No one is perfect Alexa but I just want you to know that from all that I have found out about you, I think you are the closest thing to perfect I've ever known." I was silent for a few seconds as my brain battled to allow him to pay me such a big compliment when my natural instinct was to bat it away. He spoke before I could reply.

"Don't say anything Alexa, just accept it, thank me if you have to, but don't deflect a compliment. That is my opinion of you and you arguing it won't change anything." I felt self conscious and I naturally told myself that this was not real, that he was just being kind.

"Kade, I seriously don't think I'm in any way perfect," I looked deep into those soulful eyes, "I'm about as broken as the rest of them. But I'm trying to pick up the pieces and fix myself so that I don't have to be a mess. I'm happy with my imperfections, I have insecurities but I am learning to deal with them. You are right, I have trouble taking compliments but I will try to change that. For now I will take yours and I thank you for it. You really are a wonderfully generous man when it comes to the compliment department." He groaned.

"And yet you still manage to argue it when you've just thanked me. Well you will have to try harder in that case because I am going to bombard you with so many compliments every time I see you that you will run out of reasons they aren't true."

"Really? Won't you run out of compliments quick?" I laughed. He looked at me with seriousness in his eyes.

"I got a million I can think of right now. The first being I think you have beautiful eyes. I like the way there are flecks of green in the brown. I hope I get to see more of that." I was speechless and blushing but unable to look away from him when his phone rang and he moved slowly away, his eyes still on me, almost predatory, before he turned to go out of the patio doors onto the deck to take his call.

Staying away from Kade was going to prove difficult. He'd got me addicted to him like a drug in just this short amount of time and I hated to think of what withdrawal from him would feel like. My heart was in grave danger, the warning bells rang loud in my head as I buried my face in a cushion and let out frustrated growl.

CHAPTER NINE

Lost and found

I sat on the big arm chair with my earphones covering my ears as I listened to music, feeling lazy. It was Sunday after all. The night before, I'd met up with Sadie as promised near Times Square for drinks and we'd enjoyed ourselves just talking and getting to know one another at a rooftop bar. I didn't think I would ever stop feeling amazed by the allures of the city that had recently stolen my heart for the second time. I remembered why I had this dream of being here again. The lights, the bustle of people from all walks of the world and the sense of belonging was not unlike my beloved London. It was almost the same...but still different. I was in a different part of the world, lost and new to it all. I wanted the city to consume me, just as much as I wanted it to bring me a sense freedom.

It felt good to have a girlfriend in this big city. Allison had only been gone about four days but I missed her presence, although Sadie more than made up for it. She may have been soft spoken but she was actually really funny with her stories and the way her eyes lit up when she talked about her job and the people she cared about.

It turned out that Sadie was the youngest of four siblings and the only sister. I told her that I would give anything to have older brothers - that was until she told me that her three older brothers were extremely over protective of her. She then recalled stories of how they would make her life difficult when she was little, including locking her in her room on a night she was supposed to go out on a date with the school quarterback. She had managed to climb down a tree outside her bedroom window when her brothers had seen her fall to the floor through the downstairs window and tried to tackle her to the ground. Their parents had let it be, laughing so hard as she struggled to get free when finally her dad intervened and they reached a compromise. Sadie could go out for the date and the boys would stay a safe distance away to make sure the biggest player in school wouldn't make moves on their sister. I could only imagine what had gone down when Sadie, in revenge for her brothers' craziness, had made sure she was all but sitting on her dates lap kissing him at every opportunity. The poor guy was unaware of her brothers watching and let's just say that her brothers had to stay a night in jail and she was grounded for a month...

I had just got comfortable, snuggled into the arm chair, eyes closed and listening to my music when I felt him close by. I had started to recognise his scent and his heat. It was the kind of thing that happened when you were in constant contact with someone and I hated that I liked him being around, waiting for him to spend time with me. It only meant I would find it harder to detach myself when he decided to leave.

I felt one side of the earphones lift as he spoke in my ear.

"Whatcha listening to?" I opened my eyes to see his face so close, I was startled. He was wearing a button down white linen shirt and black jeans that just looked too sexy on him. Simple clothes made him look like a model, I couldn't imagine what he looked like in a suit. *Now that would get your knickers in a twist.*

I handed him my iPod to inspect and there was a look of horror on his face as he read the title of the current song. I laughed and paused the music, taking off my earphones.

"What? You don't like Selena Gomez? It's a catchy song."

"Do you listen to anything besides teeny bopper music?"

I laughed. I didn't know what I found funnier - the scowl on his handsome face or the fact he had just said 'teeny bopper.'

"No, I have a mix of songs from all genres and my sister happened to download a few new ones for me before I left London. I just don't mind them. This song is catchy. You should listen," I offered him my head phones but he lifted his finger to indicate I should wait a minute. He walked to the drawer of one of the wall units and pulled out a couple of things. Walking back to me, he held up his earphones head-phones and then showed me the earphone splitter in the palm of his hand. I felt a shudder of pleasure and couldn't hide my smile.

He wanted to listen to my music together. It may have seemed like a completely simple and innocent thing to others but for me this felt intimate. I loved music, I could map many moments of my life that I had soundtracks to. Music made me feel relaxed, it helped release emotions that were pent up inside me when I couldn't let others in to see them. When I was twelve, my mum had bought me a disc-man. I was so happy, I was inseparable from it. That week I must have rinsed so many double A batteries just constantly listening to my favourite CD's.

Looking up at Kade right now, a smile on his face as he went to sit down on the two seater and patted the cushion next to him, I felt happy. It was totally possible that I'd find a kindred spirit, something I thought I'd never find apart from with Tom. And it had been the first time that day that I had smiled.

After I woke up in the morning, I had been surfing Facebook

on my phone idly before pulling myself out of bed when I came across one of mine and Tom's mutual friends who had commented on a picture Tom had uploaded of his son. I usually avoided all things 'Tom' and had deleted him from my Facebook so that I didn't have to see his happy pictures after separating. I'd been declining his requests to reconnect as well. Even though we weren't 'Friends' on Facebook when I had left London, I had accepted his request after reaching New York having told myself that we were adults and it was only social media. But seeing the picture on my news feed made my heart burn with sadness. It was a picture of his little boy, Matt, in his mothers arms and the caption quite simply read, "Bliss." My heart hurt. He felt blissful with his family, something I couldn't give him. I'd been in a dull mood all day and I kept telling myself I was an idiot and that we were not together anymore so it was only fair that he found his own happiness but that didn't help because it felt unfair. Why should he find happiness so soon, before he even left me, when he's broken every bit of my heart, every one of my dreams and shattered any hope I had left? Had he really ruined me for anyone else? I felt like I'd been discarded, like I had no value when once I was invaluable. The insecurities of being the one left behind returned ten fold and made me question if I could really find happiness again.

Snapping out of my thoughts I sat next to Kade, my thigh accidentally brushing his and causing me to jump a little from the shock of it. I tried to disguise my over reaction by subtly shifting away and giving Kade my ipod to plug the earphone splitter and then our headphones.

"This is going to be interesting," he said, playing the track from the start. He listened intently for a while and made a few faces of disgust here and there. When the track finished, he scrolled through my songs, humming and hahing at some of my choices. He selected a few tracks along the way including 'Ordinary world' by Duran Duran and 'Clint Eastwood' by Gorrilaz. Then he handed me the ipod to select a few tracks to listen to together and I went for a few mellow girl power tunes to annoy him like Alicia Keys 'Girl on fire' and good old Spice Girls.

He laughed when I played 'Wannabe' and then the track changed on shuffle to a song that tugged at my recent melancholic mood again. It described how I felt about Tom. It was a song called 'Lost and Found' by Lianne La Havas.

The lyrics almost suffocated me with emotion and I didn't realise I'd been quietly sobbing until I sensed Kade's eyes on my face. I turned to see him leaning against the arm rest having turned his body to face me. His face was etched with concern. It just made me feel more broken. The lyrics swirled in the air between us as a soulful voice sang my feelings.

...you broke me, and taught me
to truly hate myself
unfold me, and teach me
to be like somebody else...

Kade pulled off his earphones and set them on the coffee table. He took mine off from around my ears and pulled the iPod out of my surprisingly hard grasp on it, putting them down next to his earphones. He took my hands and pulled me into his arms. I automatically placed my head on his chest and drew my legs up onto the couch to get more comfortable. His arms enveloped me protectively and I sobbed into his shirt, glad I hadn't been wearing any make up.

"If you want to, we'll talk whenever you are ready," he said softly when my sobs finally subsided. I was shaking still from the overwhelming emotions. I nodded and buried myself further into his body, enjoying the warmth and a perverted part of my mind remembered just how ripped his body was under the shirt, I could feel his abs where my hand rested on his stomach.

Was it really so weird that I felt this comfortable with

a man I knew little about? But then again, who wrote the rules and a timeline on how long you should know someone before you *actually* knew them? It was fast becoming an experience I'd accepted was safe to let myself have and that I should trust my instincts instead of questioning everything for a change. He was making me forget my worries with just a shoulder to cry on and kind words of wisdom. I had started to think friendship was on the cards. I told him exactly that.

"I think we're becoming friends." He laughed at me as I peered up at his face.

"Are you asking me to be your friend?" His bad boy smile had reappeared, making me sit up straight to look him straight in the face as I wiped my tears with the sleeve of my cardigan.

"Um, I'm saying that I think we already are." I narrowed my eyes at him when he laughed again.

"Well, you didn't ask me. And I expect you to bring me a gift as an incentive." He looked serious all of a sudden but the humour in his eyes made me sigh exasperation because he was winding me up like no one I know.

"What, like a friendship band or a frog? What are we, like, five?" He grinned as I tried to scowl at him to hide my smile.

"I wouldn't mind a frog..." I smacked his rock hard stomach and jumped off the couch before he could get to me, smiling as he chuckled.

"Such a doofus," I mumbled as I headed to the kitchen for a drink. I heard him get up and follow me which made my smile widen. I was insanely attracted (understandably) to an insanely hot millionaire. Funny how I never thought of him as a millionaire before even with the knowledge of his family business and properties, including this one. He just didn't act like the stereotype I had in mind for this kind of man. He was modest about his wealth and it was endearing

He walked up to one of the kitchen cabinets and pulled out Oreos and then leaned over where I was standing by the refrigerator to pull out the milk. I watched him with fascination as he poured milk for himself and started pulling out one Oreo after the other, dunking it in the milk. He demolished the entire packet in a matter of minutes as I sipped on my Diet Pepsi.

I didn't realise I was staring until he looked up and smiled.

"You want some? I have a whole load of these things in that cupboard, you are welcome to help yourself." He smiled that dimpled boyish smile I'd only seen a couple of times that was cute and not flirty. I liked it a lot and returned it with my own shy smile.

"No thank you, I just enjoy watching you eat. As weird and creepy as that sounds..." *Oh shit, I'm blushing like a fool and sound like a* creeper.

He laughed and downed the rest of his milk in one go before washing the glass in the sink and sat next to me at the breakfast bar. We sat in silence for a few minutes and I knew he was waiting for me to talk about my wimpy outburst a few minutes back in the living room. I wanted to stop blurting out my personal life to my landlord but somehow I'd passed the stage of being appropriate when I fell asleep with him beside me a couple of nights ago.

He waited patiently for me to speak, so I decided to get chatty.

"I'm sorry Kade. You probably think I'm a stupid hormonal woman crying over a stupid man." It was the first thing that came out of my mouth as I looked up at him. I didn't want him to have this impression of me being a weak woman with severe emotional mood swings. Even if I felt like I was.

"Firstly, you have just been through, and are still recovering from, a difficult break up. A marriage break up. I think you are allowed to be emotional. Secondly, never apologise for showing your true emotions. Trust me when I say that there are very few women I know of that allow themselves to show how they feel as freely as you do. For me, it's a very attractive quality in a woman. I hate women that act a certain way because they think society asks for it," he paused, giving me that delicious 'panty dropping' smile of his, making me blush before continuing, "and thirdly, I would be happy if you shared your troubles with me. We are friends after all - with or without the delivery of the frog." His smile remained but his eyes showed a warmth of compassion and I thanked divine providence for allowing me to meet this wonderful, seemingly perfect, man.

I returned his smile, took a deep breath and proceeded to tell him about the picture on Facebook, the relevance of the song and my current feelings. I felt like a total idiot considering how long it had been since Tom had left my life. I mean seriously, why was it taking longer for me to heal? Was it all my abandonment issues because I had unresolved 'daddy issues?' I cringed at the thought. Despite having those feelings of animosity towards my biological father, I was fortunate enough to have a wonderful step father that I called 'Dad' who wasn't perfect but did his best to raise me, another mans child, without ever making me seem like a burden. I was lucky, so that excuse wasn't one I was willing to use, regardless of how much of the truth lived in it.

"Stop doing that Alexa." I looked up at the stern face, wondering what he was annoyed with me doing.

"Stop doing what?" I finally asked, fiddling with the label of a dish cloth in my reach.

"Stop over analysing your life, stop trying to make sense of it and just let yourself feel what you feel in the moment you feel it. In time, you will make your peace with it before you even know it because burying these things causes long term damage. And thats the kind of fucked up shit that doesn't go away." I looked into his eyes to see a darkness that flashed across his face as he stared off into the distance past me, brow creased from some memory that seemed to cause an untold amount of suffering. Again, I was astonished that I was able to read so much of him so easily.

"You sound like you speak from experience," I said softly. My voice brought him back to the here and now and he looked at me with a soft smile, the tension seeming to have dissipated almost as quickly as it had struck him.

"I'm just your average wise ass," he joked and stood up from his stool. "Listen, I got some work stuff to do since I've missed a few days of work so I'm gonna head up to my office. Later, let's make a plan to counter your loser ex and his very public display of showing how happy he is. Which, by the way, is an indication that he really isn't." I gave him a curious and confused look.

"You actually work? And what exactly is this action plan Mr Hamilton?" He smirked down at me before answering in his sexy voice.

"Yes Miss De Luca, I actually do work. I have a demanding job and I like to think I'm good at it," he tapped my nose with a long finger that I had to stop myself from biting. "And to answer your second question, we are going to do what you ladies do best. We're going to get you dressed up sexier than usual, into a club with yours truly, take a hell of a lot of pictures and post the shit out of them on your social media networks. Let him see what he missed out on." He moved in closer to me, bringing his lips closer to my ear as he whispered, "and then when you are done with playing adolescent games, you are going to let yourself go. Let yourself live and make that way you look in those photos a reality, live the way you want to. Be that sexy carefree woman that I see you becoming. And you already got the sexy bit down to a tee."

With that he left a lingering kiss on my cheek before giving me an unobstructed view of his broad muscled back and sexy arse as he left me standing there, blushing and feeling the machinery of desire, that I had thought was rusted, start working and fuelling a fire at the pit of my stomach that made my heart (and some other muscles down south) clench with need.

***

It was getting dark outside and I was closing the living room shutters and flipping on the lights when I got a phone call from Brian. Kade had been holed up all afternoon in his apartment and Sadie was out helping a friend move into her new place so I'd been enjoying the solitude with a good old romance book.

"Hey nutcracker," his tired voice came over the noise of the phone line.

"Hey Sloth." Yes I called him sloth, like the character from the Goonies, because thats how he would sound when he talked whilst eating when we were kids. I guess some habits follow you into adulthood. To this day we stare at him in horror as he continues to talk with his mouth full. He had named me 'nutcracker' because...well, its a long story.

"How you been?"

"I've been good. Wondering where my so called big brother has been. I started to think you had been abducted. Or that maybe Christine's dad had put a hit out on you or something," I joked. Christine's dad was a devout Catholic and had taken the news of the two of them living together, out of wedlock, badly. Hannah and I had laughed so hard when we found out about the little threats Brian would receive veiled in casual conversation whenever he would go with Christine to her parents house for dinner.

"I'm sorry Lex, I got so busy at the hospital, these days I don't know whether I'm coming or going. I got your messages, I just kept getting called for emergencies before I could reply. I'm so sorry." He sounded like he felt so bad about it and I felt guilty for joking around with him. I knew how demanding his job was and how important the time he gave his patients was.

"Hey, Bri, it's no big deal. I'm just happy to hear your voice. I know you're out there busy saving lives, you hero.

Way more important than sitting on your arse eating ice cream - which by the way tastes a lot sweeter than the stuff we get back home - and watching pointless television."

"Rub it in why don't you! I still feel bad, I'm supposed to be looking out for you-"

"Oi, I'm not a little kid! And I know where you are if I need you. Stop sounding like my mum. Or yours for that matter. Just come have dinner with me when you get a day off."

We spoke for a short while longer and then we hung up with a promise of having diner together on the following Friday night.

***

I was about to plop back down on the couch with my kindle when the front door burst open and an excited Allison bounded into the living area followed by the man I knew was Brent from his pictures, carrying the two suitcases Allison had taken for the four day trip. Because a girl can't have enough beach wear, of course.

"LEXI!" She shrieked, scaring the living hell out of me. She was jumping up and down and seeing my confused look she shoved her left hand closer to my face for me to look at a colossal freakin' diamond ring on her finger. And thus began the screaming and jumping around that we both partook in, leaving poor Brent possibly considering the ramifications of his recent actions.

We were still hugging one another and squealing in glee when Kade joined the chaos. I saw him give Brent a curious look and Brent shrug in reply.

"I take it that she said yes?" He asked Brent. The reply was a smile and a nod to which Kade gave his best friend a man-hug, hand shake thing.

"Omigod! Omigod!" I squealed loudly again
"I know, right?!"

"You have to tell me EVERYTHING!"

Allison walked over to Brent's waiting arms and formally introduced us.

"Brent, this is my crazy friend Lexi," she beamed up at him with eyes so full of love, it could make any single persons heart ache. Like it did mine, remembering what it was like to feel like that for someone. I pushed the feeling away, determined not to let my melancholy ruin my friends happiness.

I surprised everyone including myself by giving Brent a bear hug, my heart full of adoration for the man that had broken the mould for Allison. Brent hesitated only a moment before he reciprocated laughing and giving me a huge grin. I decided I liked Brent from the moment I saw him. Tall, built and blond haired, he was the perfect half to complete Allison in the perfect looking couple department but apart from that, his brown eyes showed a kindness that looked genuine and you felt comfortable in his presence.

"I didn't get a hug like that when we first met," complained Kade, an amused smile on his face. I shot a narrow eyed glare at him before responding.

"That's because you mauled me like a man bear for allegedly trespassing on your property." Brent and Allison exchanged amused yet confused looks before we all sat down on the chairs and couch in the living area.

"My bad," he replied, sexy smile back on his face as he held his hands up in his defence. The guys started talking about the trip and the weather there whilst Allison pulled me close to her to whisper harshly in my ear, "What the hell have I missed?!" I gave her a wicked smile and shook my head.

"First, you spill about the proposal, then we'll talk Kade Hamilton."

It wasn't difficult to get her to open up, since I knew first hand that newly engaged couples (mostly the women), loved talking about the proposal. It turns out that Brent had hired out the entire beachfront side of the resort and proposed while they walked hand in hand down a sandy beach, with candles lit in a path on either side of them.

"Lexi, the way he told me that he could never imagine a life without me...I cried like a baby," she said reverently, tears in her eyes as we picked up the bottle of wine and the wine glasses in the kitchen to head back to the boys. I paused, setting the bottle down.

"Allison, you deserve nothing less. God, I'm so happy for you! He's a keeper! You forgot to tell me he's Brad Pitt in 'The Legend of the Fall' sexy!" We hugged tightly and laughed.

"He is, isn't he," she said dreamily, eyes fluttering and all.

Back in the living room, Sadie entered the house as we sat down with our drinks. Again, a similar shrieking jump around dance thing was repeated once she saw the huge rock on Allison's finger. We sat together in companionable chatter. I got to know a lot more about Brent and found we actually had a lot in common, especially with our views on current affairs of the world. We laughed and I got to know my new friends better. We stayed up late until Brent decided to go crash upstairs as he had an early meeting the next morning. Kade left shortly after.

"Good night ladies, I have to go get some beauty sleep now." The girls giggled giddily as I snorted in the most unladylike manner and looked away from the beauty that could not possibly get any better.

Miffed at my response, or quite possibly pleased with the challenge, Kade stalked over to me as the girls looked on with mouths open. He bent down and whispered audibly in my ear making me shiver.

"Good night Alexa. If you feel the need for company tonight, you're more than welcome to come sleep with me. Again." With that I got another soft kiss on the cheek and pulling back, he winked at me as he waved goodnight to the girls again and left the room. My mouth was hanging open too as I turned to see the accusing awestruck face of Allison and the knowing look on Sadie's face.

"What the fuck just happened Lexi?" Allison asked. "And what does he mean by sleeping with him, *again?*" Oh shit. *Shit shit shit!*

"Um, not *sleeping* with him the way you are thinking..." I realised that more of an explanation was needed for both of the girls to stop looking at me in shock and the slightest bit of awe. Okay, maybe quite a bit of awe.

Grabbing another bottle of wine, we sat huddled on the persian carpet amongst large throw cushions as I recalled the last few days with Kade Hamilton, sex God extraordinaire. I left out the near kiss. Not that it had been on my mind. Not at all.

"So, it's just a bit of friendly flirting and nothing else?" Sadie asked, unconvinced by my insistence.

"Yep, just being friendly and messing about."

Even as I said it, a voice in my subconscious was saying *yeah right* as I twisted a ring on my finger. There was no way any living breathing woman would deny thinking as far as 'what if?' and 'should I?' with Kade. I wanted to be single a while longer and I doubted Kade meant anything more than harmless fun with me. And yet I still smiled thinking about him and that made me melt a little more inside. *Pathetic.*

"Lexi, Kade doesn't do friendly flirting. I mean, he jokes about with us all the time but he's never come all the way across the room to kiss us goodnight," Allison prodded, a knowing smile on her face.

"Yeah, he's different around you," Sadie smiled, her expression matching Allison's. I looked at them both in bewilderment.

"Guys, this is nothing more than a mutual appreciation of one another. I find him attractive, he finds me funny. We are becoming friends and besides, we just met! So stop insinuating things when we barely know one another!" Allison chuckled, shaking her head.

"You already slept with him. Now, you may not have done the *deed* but you still shared a bed with a guy you '*barely know*' so that says something in itself. Damn girl. If I were you, I would be basking in the compliments he gives you. Which, by the way, did not escape our notice. He kept complimenting you on, like, everything!"

That was true. Kade had held up his promise to compliment me into submission. It started off innocent enough until he was complimenting the way I held my wine glass and the buttons on my blouse. Talk about ridiculousness! Of course everyone had noticed. Who compliments a button on your blouse when its just an ordinary plain white plastic button? I laughed at the memory of just an hour ago and explained the reason behind his attentiveness.

"I love playful Kade. You are bringing him back," Sadie laughed. I must have looked confused because she explained further.

"Ever since he got engaged to Gisselle, he has been this walking talking robot. He knew he was just doing it to make their parents and her happy. He never really loved her, anyone could tell. He cared for her, yes, but never truly loved her. And it took a lot of guts to stop the wedding. I'm glad he did it and saw sense. God, he was so unhappy. It's good he has found a kindred spirit in you Lexi."

It made sense that he felt relief after what he had told me about Gisselle cheating on him with his friend. I had to remind myself that he had not divulged the details of this affair to everyone else and to keep quiet about it.

After a half an hour more of poking and prodding for more information, we each retired to our rooms. I heard Allison squeal as soon as she closed her bedroom door, no doubt being mauled by her fiance.

I smiled to myself as I waved good night to Sadie and climbed up the next floor to my bedroom. Oh how I missed being mauled.

CHAPTER TEN

It's a small world

I awoke the next morning to a loud knocking on my bedroom door. Glancing at the clock I saw that it was only 6:30am.

"What the fuck?" I murmured to myself as the knocking commenced again.

Rolling myself out of bed, adjusting my long t-shirt over my bare legs, I walked to the door and pulled it open to see Allison's beaming face.

"What the fuck?" I repeated now to her. She was dressed in her gym clothes and looking radiant. No doubt from her sexathon with Brent Pitt. And she had work. The girl must have got by on Red Bull or espresso drips all day.

"Lexi, you have to get your work out gear on and hurry up to Kade's gym! He stopped me and Sadie before we left for the gym before work and insisted we use his place instead."

"That's incredibly kind of him, but what does this have to do with me?" I was starting to get annoyed. Not only had I been rudely woken up after just four hours of sleep, I'd now passed that stage where I could make myself go back to sleep.

"Because he *sent for you!* Lexi, you would have to be an

idiot to pass up the chance to train with Kade freakin' Hamilton! He's just so sexy to watch. I'm in a loving relationship and Sadie thinks of him like a brother and yet *we* ogle him when he's there in the zone. He is fucking HOT!" She whisper shouted the last bit.

Well. Now I was intrigued. I hurried to the bathroom, peed, brushed and changed like lightening then ran up the apartment stairs and then up two more flights of stairs to the rooftop gym.

***

"Right, I'm done! I got to hit the shower and get to work," Allison declared, pushing the stop button on her treadmill. The past hour, we'd been doing cardio work outs and stretches as advised by drill sergeant Hamilton. Although I had a feeling he was being extremely lenient when I watched him work out. The three of us were gawking at him through the mirror, and then pretending like we were unaffected by the way his shirtless self was lifting weights at the bench. Allison only had to be spot on right about him being a sight to behold in full work out mode. I would have kicked myself if I'd missed out on this.

For the past hour whilst we were also getting a Kade workout on our eyes, rippled muscles and all, Allison had been whispering crude things to make me blush and giggle.

"I bet you want to be that water bottle pressed against his lips! Lucky bastard bottle! God, okay, I need to stop imagining that for myself...Brent Brent BRENT!" She shook her head to clear the image and reminding herself of her fiancé. Sadie and I just laughed our tired arses off.

Sadie pulled the plug on her stretches and decided to leave with Allison. They waved good bye as I watched Allison sneak a look back at Kade and then wink at me before she left. Sneaky insinuating bitch. I was pretty sure they didn't need to leave so early.

From my position on the cross trainer, I could see Kade set his weights down and pick up a bandage to start wrapping up his hands. *No way. How can this be even the slightest bit possible?* Kade Hamilton, boxing? He was a boxer? There was no way this guy could be all that hot.

My questions were answered as he stood in front of the punching bag and started working it out, hard and fast. Each punch and jab showing the delicious contraction and release of his muscles *everywhere.* I didn't realise that I had stopped my workout to stare until he turned his sweat soaked body towards me, no doubt feeling my penetrating stare through the mirror. His sweat soaked hair was choppy about his face, as if he was a model posing for a fitness magazine. *Perfection.*

"Liking what you see here, De Luca?" His smirk told me he *knew* that I liked what I saw. I hoped my exercise flushed cheeks would hide my blush. I stopped and stepped off the machine and walked over to the smirking hunk.

"You a professional?" I asked, hoping my voice sounded contained and not girly high pitched. My first observation of him having a boxers body, upon meeting him, was obviously on point I'd impressed myself.

"Uh, not in the sense you would think of what a professional is. I used to box at underground boxing gigs."
I suddenly felt hot. Serious, consuming desire was flooding me picturing Bad Boy Kade throwing punches in an underground arena, half naked and sweat dripping over his muscled body, just as it was now.

"You used to?" I had to swallow the lump in my throat and mentally slap myself for being such a lusting whore.

"Yeah, while I was at Oxford and then when I got back home I did it for a a couple of seasons in New York." He shrugged like it was no biggie. Now I wanted to slap *him* for turning me on so effortlessly.

I had a thing for boxers. I read so many romances about them and had a crush on a famous boxer. He was unknowingly ticking all my boxes. There was hardly anything left on my hot male fantasy checklist that he hadn't ticked. I had a little moment where I thought that this was really too good to be true. I'd have to make sure to knock him off the pedestal I'd put him on before I got infatuated with him. Although in all likeliness, I'd already boarded the train from 'My-God-You're-Hot' avenue to arrive at 'I-Wanna-Have-Your-Babies' Central station. I needed some sense slapped into me.

"Wow." That was the only word I could manage.

"You're intrigued, which means you have some interest in boxing," he smiled, eyes glinting with teasing thoughts no doubt.

"I, uh, have this thing for Jack Mangle. Since I was in my first year of secondary school. I have his posters in my room back in London still. I know, it's silly." I looked up to catch a glimpse of just how silly he thought I was but instead it looked as if it were his turn to be impressed.

"You like boxing and Jack Mangle. You're seriously ticking all the boxes here, lady." *Ditto.*

He was grinning at me and the most intense feeling of newly revived butterflies flew from my stomach up into my heart. He observed me for a few seconds before he bent forward to look me in the eyes, only a couple of inches separating us.

"Jack Mangle is a friend of mine." I felt like I was going to hyperventilate.

"NO WAY!"

"Yes way," he smirked with that pleased glint in his eyes.

"Oh my GOD! I LOVE HIM!" I was acting like a teenager but I didn't care. I had obsessed over this guy since I hit puberty - he was my fantasy man. Correction - *one* of my fantasy men now.

"Theres a match he's fighting for a charity event next month and I've been left dateless so, if you aren't otherwise engaged Miss De Luca, I would love for you to accompany-"

"YES! Of course!" I shouted jumping up and down like a kid before letting him finish. I jumped up to his tall frame, hands on his muscular shoulders and on my tip toes as I kissed his cheek to his surprise.

"If I'd known I'd get that much appreciation from asking you to help me out, I'd have asked earlier." His eyes penetrated me with that hot look he got that made me feel naked.

"Thank you," I replied shyly. I was turning to leave him be when he gently gripped my wrist and pulled me to where he was standing.

"You can't leave without showing me how much you know about boxing." Naughty was written all over his face again.

"I enjoy *watching* boxing. I don't actually box myself, Kade."

"Let me show you then." I scoffed at the thought of my limp wrists flailing to hit the punching bag but when I saw the serious determined look on his face, I knew I would get hell for trying to get out of it.

"Fine," I huffed, "But don't say I didn't warn you!"

***

The next half hour was filled with excruciatingly close body contact. You could cut the tension between us with a machete. It was definitely no secret how attractive I found him. If my previous behaviour had not alerted him as yet, then my breathing, my inability to stop looking at his muscles as they worked with his demonstrations of punches and the way I had to keep saying 'huh?' when he asked if I had heard anything of what he had said, had pretty much confirmed it.

After attempting to get me to punch with more energy for the millionth time, he finally took pity on me and called it quits.

"Maybe you should take some self defence classes or

something. You live in New York City now darlin' and you need to be street smart," he chuckled.

"Psh! I've lived in London my whole life and nothing has ever happened, touch wood." I tapped the bannister on the way down his stairs. As we left through his apartment door he spun me around by my elbow outside my bedroom looking serious all of a sudden.

"It doesn't hurt to learn a few basic moves."

"I'll be fine! Honestly, you're starting to sound like my mother!"

"I'm serious Alexa. No place is safe. Just promise me you will think about it?" His concern was so touching, I felt myself melt even though I was certain I smelt nasty from all the sweat dripping down my body. Talking of sweat and dripping, didn't he just look like a divine piece of ass standing there? *Sigh.*

"Alexa! Did you just hear a word I said?" He still had his serious face on and looked so cute but I could tell that now was not the right time to blurt that out, he was dead serious.

"Okay, Okay! I promise to think about it mum! Now can I go take a shower?" He broke out into a cheeky smile and whispered in my ear, "Can I join you?" Cue cheeks flushing. I swat him on his arse as he turned to go back to his apartment and guess what? His arse cheeks were that firm my hand stung instead of causing him any damage.

"Now now, Alexa, I know you're impatient to have me but I'm not *that* easy. You got to take me out on a date first!"

I couldn't respond since he'd already made his way back up and my jaw was on the ground.

"That cheeky arse!" I grumbled to myself, allowing a small smile to slip out of me. I really hoped he wouldn't be around me all day. I had work to do and I needed zero distraction.

As luck would have it, after a quick breakfast Kade excused himself to go deal with work related matters and even though I needed him away I felt a pang of disappointment that he had other things to do. I think any woman would feel the loss of his company. I could see why Giselle was desperate not to lose him, even after her indiscretion.

***

I sat down with my laptop at the dining table and started my task of the day - 'Find Your Lazy Arse a Job.' I felt redundant just sitting around all day, even though it had been nice to have that luxury for a while, especially with Kade here. But I had to be realistic. Soon he would have to leave to go about his normal routine, back to his penthouse no doubt, and as he had said he did have a regular job.

Truth is, I had always been used to doing *something*. My Granna always said that the body should be treated as a machine - if you didn't use it the way it should be used and often, it would rust and not work properly. Since I had no responsibilities and no real reason to just sit at home, I felt kinda useless and the lack of routine was weighing heavy on my mind. Plus, I needed to save what I had and start earning again.

I started searching sites for jobs with no specific idea of what I wanted to do. I was happy my CV was up to date and I applied to absolutely every job I felt I could possibly qualify for.

I was in the process of filling out an application form for an admin job when I heard Kade coming down the stairs, talking on his phone. Clean shaven, unlike in the morning, he was wearing a blue polo shirt that complimented his eyes that had turned a darker shade of blue. He wore tan colour pants and converses, somehow making him look younger and also a bit preppy.

Refusing to let him catch me looking at him again (as was becoming an embarrassing habit), I pulled all my concentration back on the job at hand. It seemed futile in any case. I felt his presence everywhere, even when he went to the kitchen for something. It was like he owned the room, and I don't mean it literally, although he technically did. He just *owned* the atmosphere *and* my thoughts when he was near. God I wished I could see sense whenever he was around.

I tried to make myself look busy and struggled not to listen to his conversation although that was an entirely impossible thing to do when he came to stand right beside me.

"Yeah, Linds, just tell them I'll be back on Friday and can you just call Mr Davison back and say that we will discuss the legalities in person. I don't like this whole email and phone call bullshit. I need to see him face to face, he needs to find his balls and face me. Uh huh. He said what?! No, no. I suppose not. Okay, thats fine. Now let me speak to my baby."

Baby? I looked up to see him staring off into the distance with a cheeky smile on his face. I also heard a loud reprimanding voice on the other end of the line and then silence. Then he spoke.

"How's my little munchkin? Is mommy taking care of you? She eating pickles and ice cream? Sickening isn't it, huh? Don't worry, when I get back I'm taking your mommy's ass out for proper food. None of that nasty crap, you need a real greasy burger and fries. And a large milkshake, your choice. Now you be good and kick the shit out of mommy if she gives you grief, just like we discussed. Love you baby."

That had to be the weirdest conversation I'd ever heard and I stared at him open mouthed as the voice of the woman finally came faintly from his phone. He looked down at me and winked.

"You take care of yourself Linds, make sure you take the rest you need. I will see you as soon as this shit clears up. Okay great. Sweet. Catch you later."

Kade plonked himself on the chair next to me as he dropped his phone down on the table.

"You having a baby?" I blurted out, anxious for some reason.

"Nope. Watcha doin'?" I watched him silently for a

few seconds and when it seemed like that was all the response I was going to get, I sighed and gave in.

"Job applications. Some places just ask you to send CV's. I feel like I've bombarded the entire city of New York with my resume. So tiring when you don't know what you want to do."

Kade scratched his chin, a frown of concentration on his face, making him look more alpha male than ever before.

"Why don't you try out at Hailton's? There's a temporary post opening up soon. Apply for it, probably won't start right away but I think I could have a word with the boss," he winked with smiling eyes. From what little he had told me about his family's company and the organisations and businesses that came under the Hamilton umbrella, I could tell they were a big deal.

"You think so? What kind of position?" It would be great to work for such a big reputable company and it would look amazing on my CV. I should have felt a little wary of accepting his kind offer but at the moment, the idea of having a stable job was a dream come true.

"There are a couple of roles opening up in Admin and there's a Personal Assistant's role too. Send me your resume and I will forward it accordingly."

"Thank you Kade, that would be awesome. I'm seriously grateful for the help. What is your email address?" He rattled off his address and I could feel my spirits lift somewhat.

I had just sent the email to him and he confirmed receiving it on his phone when we heard the front door open in a rush and thumping footsteps in the hall coming towards the living room. We both looked at one another, not expecting the girls to be back yet from work. I heard her voice before I saw her. Standing there and looking angrier than the calm and sweet woman I had met a short time ago, was Bonnie from my plane journey. I think the 'what *the fuck?*' look I had on my face spoke volumes.

"What the *hell* are you playing at Kade Hamilton!?"

I saw little Annie scurry in from the hallway. I'm assuming that she had not done as she was instructed to stay in the hall when her mother turned to give her a reprimanding look. I didn't blame her for coming in to watch the drama, I was just as curious.

"How the fuck did you know where I was Bonnie?" He sounded equally angry. I sat there like a spectator at Wimbledon watching the tennis match to-ing and fro-ing of the ball.

"Kade, watch your mouth! Annie is listening!" She cupped her hands over Annie's ears as if it would help now that the profanity had already left Kade's lips. He looked rattled, and stood and walked closer to Bonnie.

"Okay, let me rephrase - How the F-U-C-K did you know where I was?" He spelled out 'fuck' and I wondered how effective *that* particular idea was when it looked like Annie may be trying to figure out the phonetics of the word.

"Oh come off it Kade, I've known about this place for two years now. Ever since the last press fiasco. I had Jenson follow you. You should have known better than to hustle me." Kade looked furious but one look at Annie and he seemed to have been counting to ten under his breath with his eyes closed.

No one had acknowledged me being present for all of this as yet and I couldn't really walk away unnoticed. Plus I was crazy curious about what was going on.

"Who else knows about this place?" He spoke in a tone that seemed to be practiced for times of frustration. Bonnie looked irritated.

"Just me and Jenson. And Annie. Look, don't worry, no one else will know. Jenson swore he would not speak of it. But you should know better than to disappear for a few days when everyone is going stir crazy looking for your as- um, behind."

"Well thank you for your concern. As you can see, I am

alive and well so you can leave now." He turned away from Bonnie when she spoke in an authoritative tone.

"No, you are going to come home with me right now. You know what times like these are like on her." Kade let out an exasperated breath and ran his hand through his hair in frustration.

"Is she okay?" Now he had me wondering who *she* was.

"She'll be better once she sees you. Just come over for a bit. The storm seems to have calmed down a bit around you in the media. The Richardson twins have taken the press's attention once again to save your a-s-s," she smiled as she rubbed a hand over her pregnant belly.

"Oh yeah? What was it this time? Throwing hotel furniture out of the windows? Alcohol poisoning?" Kade was smiling too now, the earlier tension fading.

"Worse. They ended up in vegas and drunk. Neil got hitched to Naomi and Nat of course had to do what his brother did so he grabbed some ditzy and tied the knot with her. The reports say Nat is looking for an annulment. Apparently he didn't know she was a H-O-O-K-E-R."

They laughed and suddenly Bonnie's eyes landed on me and she squinted as if she couldn't believe her eyes.

"Alexa?" She walked towards me and now it was Kade's turn to look confused.

"Hey Bonnie." She hugged me and looked questioningly at me and then Kade.

"So, not to be rude or anything but how do you know Kade and what are you doing here?"

"Um, he's my Landlord." It wasn't much of an answer but it was enough information to clear the confusion on her face as she smiled.

"Right! Well, he's my brother." There was silence for a few seconds as I absorbed this information. It all made sense now. And I felt stupid not recognising the trademark blue eyes and dark hair and similarities in features. I finally found my voice and smiled.

"Oh! That's Annie's uncle Ade!" We laughed.

"How do you two ladies know one another?" Somehow we had forgotten Kade was there as we laughed at how small the world is. He pouted as if we had deliberately left him out of our private joke or something. Bonnie sighed and rolled her eyes.

"We met on the flight back from London. Alexa was sitting next to me and helping me out with Annie. Annie was quite taken with her." Bonnie smiled at me.

"She's not the only one," I heard him say under his breath with a wink in my direction. I had hoped that Bonnie hadn't caught onto what he'd said but one look at the confusion on her face made me blush.

Annie managed to garner our attention at that moment as she spoke quietly to get her uncles attention.

"Oh, I'm sorry Annie. Uncle Ade is silly. Come here, I haven't seen my favourite girl in the whole wide world for so long! I need hugs and kisses, stat!" Annie giggled in a liberating girly pearl of laughter that made my heart smile as Kade lifted her up high and then smothered her with kisses and hugged her tight.

I loved seeing him with her like this. It was always something I loved to see - the way men behaved with their children, or in this case, nieces and nephews. Maybe it was some basic instinct for women, to see a 'mate' prove that he was the best choice as a partner, that you did right in choosing him. An animal instinct and every bit as necessary for me.

A pain seeped into my heart, the memory of what I lost still lingered and joined itself to this happy moment, watching Annie laugh, to remind me that it was possible that I may never have this.

Bonnie must have noticed the sadness in my eyes when she touched my shoulder and looked worriedly into my eyes.

"You okay Alexa?" Her concern made it a little harder to smile but I managed one anyway. Even though I had blurted out my abridged version of my marriage breakdown on the plane to Bonnie, she didn't know about the baby I lost.

"I'm fine. So, you're the older sister of the elusive Mr Hamilton?" I was master of the subject change. Bonnie was kind enough not to push me further and grinned.

"Yes, that's me! Has he been behaving himself? Our mother has been going crazy with worry while he's living it up over here."

"I can't comment on his behaviour as it has been...interesting...but he is definitely been living it up. Have you seen his apartment?" Bonnie's eyes grew wide and a smile of curiosity lit her face.

"Seriously? I need to see this. This idiot hasn't got the manners to show his beloved sister around his secret lair." Kade lifted his head from blowing raspberries on Annie's little stomach and scowled at his sister.

"You were never supposed to know about my 'secret lair' Bon Bon. You're a sneaky woman!"

"Well you should know better than to doubt my excellent spying skills, ALIKADOR! I always find out about everything! Now come show me your house, moron."

"And how do you suppose you are going to get up all those stairs?" he grumbled and Annie immediately hugged his head to her and the sweetest smile I'd ever seen, that was meant just for her, blessed his lips. My heart melted more and I felt myself be pulled more into him.

"I'm pregnant, not an invalid! I'm not even *that* pregnant! And if I get tired baby brother, you can carry me."

Kade muttered something under his breath about a whale and Annie giggled as he begrudgingly made his way towards the kitchen and started the tour which I couldn't help but follow like the nosy twit I was. After seeing the first three levels, we entered the piece de resistance with Kade's apartment and he set Annie down on the sectional couch while he took Bonnie's hand and led her carefully up the stairs to show her around. I decided to remain downstairs with

Annie. Being in Kade's apartment was enough to exhilarate me but to be in his bedroom again with that amazing over-powering scent of his cologne and clean man sweat would have just been much. I was afraid that I had already been pulled under too far and needed to break to the surface to breathe.

"Hey Annie, do you remember me?" I sat next to the little angel who smiled and blessed me with the same dimples her uncle had.

"Yes, you have a pretty name, I never forget a pretty name, Alexa." This little girl had to be the sweetest little thing ever.

"Well, I'd never forget a pretty little girl that is as sweet as you," I laughed as she moved from her seat and parked her bottom on my lap. I pulled a ringlet of her dark hair to bounce and she giggled.

"So, Annie, did you have your birthday party already?" Her eyes lit up.

"It's going to happen in a month! Mommy says we had to have it later and that its not so far away but I know thats too long! Will you come to my party Alexa? I'm having it at my house in the yard and we will have a big bouncy castle and a clown and lots of balloons and we will play games and you can meet all my friends...." Annie kept talking excitedly and I laughed and gently played with her beautiful curls, listening attentively.

She asked me a million questions, mostly about our families cat back in London once she learned I had one. Annie was trying to plait my hair, talking animatedly about their dog Spot when Kade and Bonnie approached us having completed the grand tour.

"There's my girl," Kade said in his deep voice, sending shivers up my spine. I knew he was talking to Annie but for a second I imagined that he meant me and instead of scaring the shit out of me, the idea of being his girl made me *feel something.* What this could possibly be, I didn't care to explore just yet.

I smiled up at him and as he reached over to pick Annie up and hug her long and hard.

"Alexa is coming to my party!" She told her uncle excitedly. He smiled fondly at her and then at me.

"Oh, no Annie honey, I can't just come to your party-"

"Nonsense! You're coming Lexi, we agreed on the plane remember? The party plans have just been finalised so I didn't get the chance to email you. Kade knows the details, you can come with him."

Bonnie left me no chance to reply as she made her way down the stairs. I looked at Kade for an explanation but he just shrugged with his naughty smile playing at his lips.

I didn't really want to decline the invitation since Annie was adamant I be there. It would be rude not to accept. It had nothing to do with going with Kade. Nothing at all.

CHAPTER ELEVEN

Finality

Kade left shortly after with Bonnie and Annie, not to return until it was close to midnight. I was in my bed when I heard a knock on my door.

The girls had both returned home from work at different times looking shattered and were grateful for a home cooked meal prepared by me before retiring to bed.

I found myself feeling restless. An hour after Kade had left, I received a telephone call from my solicitors in London. My divorce had been finalised, the papers had come through and they would be posting them to me as fast as they could. A numbness had taken over me as I mechanically thanked them for all their help and support, accepting their congratulations at the demise of marriage - my biggest investment in life thus far. I'd placed my life's worth of trust and love in that marriage, all my savings. All of me. Everything that was even the smallest bit of value was trusted into that partnership and it had all been dissolved with the receipt of some papers.

After I had hung up, I walked around in a daze, not really doing anything in particular but thinking. It was as if a showreel of images was passing before my eyes of the years I had with Tom. Those haunting good memories of holidays and simple days spent together in love and full of hope. Those bastard memories that threatened to break me completely. Funny how I had a shit memory when it came to everything else in life but when it came to Tom, I remembered everything.

Eventually I left the empty living room I'd been standing in for the best part of an hour and found the smallest bit of comfort in my room. I hadn't told my family yet. I know they would worry for me and I didn't want them to worry about my worries. I'd only end up worrying about *them* worrying about *me* worrying, which would just leave me worse off than before.

I let myself have a long cry as I gave in to the overwhelming feelings that washed over me before I drowned and had another panic attack. I knew I'd have to tell my family soon but I would rather charge Ash with that duty. She was good with keeping my family calm, I would ask her to break the news to them.

Just when I thought that I had let all the tears out, my monsoons worth of water running dry, I received a text message from a familiar number.

> *Tom: I got a call too. I'm sorry I ruined us. I'll always love you baby.*
> *You were the only one for me. I will never forgive myself for letting you go. T x*

True to his style, Tom always managed to pull at my heart strings. And my tears. After that message, I couldn't hold back the tears and the volume of my crying because I didn't have to look in the mirror to know I was ugly crying.

Now, someone was knocking on my door. I couldn't make myself talk through my hiccupping and crying but the door opened anyway. A half asleep Allison and Sadie walked in, worried looks on their faces,

"What's wrong babe?" Allison climbed onto one side

of the bed and Sadie took the other.

"It's o-o-over. F-f-finalised!" I cried hysterically as Allison and Sadie looked at one another in alarm.

"What's over sweetie?" Sadie asked soothingly stroking my hair from my wet face as I half buried it in my pillow face down.

"The d-d-divorce came through! Then Tom messaged me!" I pointed a shaking finger at my phone that Allison picked up and checked. Having read the message and passing it to Sadie, she lay down next to me and enveloped me in her arms. Sadie set my phone down and did the same. They made me into a big Lexi sandwich, my sobs shaking them both. They didn't need to speak, they didn't need to do anything because them just being there was enough.

***

I felt the strain on my eyes when I woke up. I must have cried myself to sleep. The spaces next to me were empty and rightly so because it was past midday when I checked my bedside clock. I closed my eyes to relieve them from the sliver of sunlight coming through the exposed part of the curtains. It took me a few seconds to register that someone was there.

I almost jumped out of my skin then placed a hand on my chest to relax the thumping in my chest when I saw that the figure casually sprawled out on the chaise was Mr Sexy Hamilton reading the newspaper in his white t-shirt and stonewash denim jeans, looking fresh and as if he just came back from a photo shoot on the beach. All tanned and gorgeous. And it was at that exact moment I chose to remember what I probably looked like at that precise moment. My assumption was proven to be correct when I glanced at my reflection in the mirror across my bedroom on my dressing table. Red and puffy eyes, hair looking like a birds nest and red swollen lips.

He hadn't seen me yet so I contemplated faking sleep. Unfortunately that option was taken from me the moment I realised Kade had in fact put his newspaper down and sat up, now with his full attention on me. His muscles bunched up as he rested his forearms on his knees and a shiver ran up my spine as the desire to touch them invaded my senses.

"Good morning...I mean, good afternoon," I managed to croak out. Great. How unattractive. Not that I wanted to look attractive to him. Not at all.

Of course he just smiled with his perfect teeth and dimples on show, making me forget for a moment where the hell I was.

"Good afternoon Miss De Luca. Get your sexy butt out of bed and into that shower, we're breaking you out of this joint." I couldn't quite understand what was happening here, so I told him.

"I don't understand."

He sighed with mock exasperation and got up off the chaise taking the two strides it took for him to reach the side of my bed. He took one of my sweaty hands and pulled me up to sit with a gentleness I didn't expect of a man with his masculinity. He sat down by my side, facing me as his deep blues penetrated my soul.

"I know you've been crying over the loser. I saw the girls this morning too. They were worried - I'm worried about you. So I'm taking you out of here." I sniffled. I actually sniffled. And then I started sobbing like a fool, no doubt ugly crying in front of the Adonis. He looked confused, bless him, and a little bit scared. Then I felt his arms come around me and he comforted me.

"Don't let this define you babe."

"It's not that...th-th-this is the sweetest thing anyone has ever done for me!" I'm sure if I could step outside myself and look at this scene, I'd want to slap myself for being such a wimp.

I pulled away from him to see that I had transferred snot and tears onto his clean white shirt...and I cried some more.

"I've ruined your shirt!" Seriously. I was totally pathetic. And then I heard that deep laughter rise from his chest out of those delicious looking lips and his eyes seemed to laugh too at my silliness in what was supposed to be a serious situation. Naturally, this started me off too and the giggles that rose from me after the sadness and pain of what I had felt just moments before provided me with the right release. It felt like it was just what I needed. Cathartic and nonsensical. Two words I'd have never imagined putting together.

***

Kade had coaxed me into relaxing for much of the afternoon, distracting me with silly stories until it was time to get ready. This was when I was surprised to find that he would be leaving the house in disguise when he mentioned needing time to dress. It shouldn't have really shocked me, given that he had been all over the pages of gossip magazines and tabloids everywhere just a few days ago but I took the opportunity to tease him as much as I could about it.

"Are you going to wear a 'Village People' tribute disguise? May I suggest the cop with the handlebar moustache?" I giggled as he stood there rolling his eyes.

"You done?"

"Um no," I giggled some more. I think the pre clubbing drinks had gotten me a little silly. He gave a long sigh and took my hand in his as he looked sincere before he spoke.

"Alexa, unfortunately in the world that I live in, there is a lot of crazy out there. It wouldn't matter if I looked like a donkey with two heads - as long as you're a 'celebrity' and your name means something to the masses, everyone wants a piece of you. They won't leave you be, no matter how much you try to escape or hideaway. Honestly, I haven't used a disguise in a really long time but right now my face is still in some of the magazines out there."

He looked serious and I felt contrite. Biting my lip and my tongue for a few seconds, I squeezed his hand.

"I'm sorry I took the piss. But I understand, really I do. I'm looking forward to meeting your alter ego."

Kade smiled a beautiful boyish smile that felt rare, because it wasn't the usual naughty or casual polite. It was filled with the emotions he felt from having shared a little bit about the real 'him.'

"You don't need to apologise, it is quite funny. What say you and I play a little dress up? Have you got any costumes? maybe a little nurses outfit - ow!" I pulled my hand out of his and smacked his rock hard stomach, flinching in the process from the sting on my palm. There he was again. Sexy, arrogant and teasing Kade Hamilton with his cheeky grin, dimples and all, never really leaving the room in the first place - always near the surface.

"Any excuse to feel me up huh?" He grinned, earning him a growl from me and a fierce scowl, leaving him and making my way swiftly out of his way and across the room as the sound of his uncontrollable laugh followed me.

"Sexy bastard," I grumbled under my breath, the earlier guilt I had felt dissolving into annoyance that he got me blushing again.

This is becoming a bit too regular an occurrence to ignore.

***

"I look like a tart."

I'd been standing in front of my bedroom mirror for the past twenty minutes scrutinising my look. It was a Tuesday evening - a work evening - yet somehow Kade had managed to rally the girls and Brent for a night out. Despite the fact everyone must have been exhausted and had work the next day, I was well aware of the fact that they were doing this for me and being there for me, despite the fact that I was the new recruit in their friends' circle.

"You look stunning Lexi, stop bloody ruining the atmosphere with your negativity!" Allison scolded, standing next to me and putting an earring on whilst doing a jig to get into her high heels simultaneously. I swear this woman only needed to put on a bin bag to look amazing. Her baby blue shift dress may have looked plain when on a hanger but on her perfect model body, she looked like she just stepped off the runway.

I, on the other hand, looked like a hooker. Well, at least I thought I did. And this was my own doing. I had impulse bought the black body con dress before I left for New York. It was on a day I had been particularly stressed out having had an argument with Tom about something stupid, I think it was about DVD's that we had bought together and wanted back. Deep down, I knew that the DVD's weren't the reason for the argument. It was more so the fact that he had found out through his solicitors that I was moving to New York and was 'acting out' for use of a better term. Whether he liked it or not, it was none of his business but I could hear the hurt in his voice and despite how much damage he had done to me, I still didn't like that it upset him. Still, him being a complete arse urged me to pick up the tight black number and I even went into Harrods and bought Louboutins. I know. Every girl needs a pair of those bad boys in her closet and I splurged.

Standing here now, looking at my curvy figure and the ample chest I was gifted with, I looked different. A good different, just not a comfortable one. Allison had decided I should go with a smokey eye look and since make up was a hidden talent of mine, I complied. My lips were a harlot red, the blush just right, the smokey eyes making the green pop out of the hazel. My hair was in loose curls and I had borrowed some bangles from Allison, teaming them with my simple diamond studs and pendant. I wanted to feel as confident as I had made myself look on the outside.

Sadie walked into the room in her black skinny jeans and

cropped off the shoulder fitted black top with red bra straps showing underneath looking every bit like a red headed Sandy from Grease. I loved her style - so classy and yet fun and girly. She always looked good in clothes that no one would have thought would work in todays fashion conscious society. She made it work and I noticed the way other people would stop and look to admire her and she would shy away. Yet she would still be confident. Why couldn't I be like her?

"You look so hot," Sadie smiled genuinely, looking at me up and down. I returned her smile a little less confidently but decided there was no use trying to talk myself out of wearing this dress since it was I who had pulled it out of the closet in the first place.

"Nah, I look like I overdid it. You look stunning, I feel like you're ready to dance with John Travolta on a west end stage somewhere!" Sadie laughed, a slight blush appearing on her cheeks. At least the girl could take a compliment graciously unlike myself.

"I will seriously kick your arse if you put yourself down one more time!" Allison said sternly, shaking her finger at me.

With a sigh, I nodded and smiled at the two most amazing girls in whole of New York. Of course, I was biased, but they truly were beautiful inside and out. It made up for not having Ash here with me. Mostly, anyway.

***

"Are you coming down anytime soon or do we have to literally pick you ladies up and place you into your awaiting carriages?" The loud voice coming from the landing below was clearly Kade's.

Shuffling across my bedroom, I grabbed my clutch and we hurried down the two flights to the hallway where the men stood with tumblers of amber liquid in their hands laughing about something. Brent was wearing a white shirt with smart dark trousers and his hair neatly styled looking like Brad Pitt in Oceans Eleven. Kade's back was turned to me but as he heard us approach he spun around and froze on the spot. The feeling was mutual.

Although he had on a black trilby hat and had miraculously grown a beard courtesy of his bureau of disguises, he was still *him*. Sparkling blues and muscled body under the black button down shirt and ass hugging black Levi's. I think I may have actually sighed looking at him. He looked yummy.

He took off his hat to reveal what I always called a 'Clark Kent/Superman' hairstyle side parted. Just. Wow. Kade took a couple of steps toward me and looking deep into my soul, his eyes spoke volumes.

"You look beautiful Alexa." His eyes told no lies, my cheeks flushed but I bit down my refutal of his compliment. He noticed and smiled, picking my hand and bringing it to his lips to kiss before whispering, "Thank you."

Nothing more was said as we quietly stepped out into the night. A black limo waited outside for us to get in, no doubt Kade had these ready for him whenever he so desired. As we huddled into the back, I started to feel a bit more relaxed. It was about time I let my hair down.

***

"This is the best night ever!" I shouted over the music. Everything was thumping in my body from the vibrations of the music and the alcohol making its way through my system. I was tipsy and well on my way to being flat out drunk.

Once we arrived at the club in Brooklyn, it was apparent this place was made for dancing. There were no pretentious plush interiors, just functional seating and a massive dance floor with a bar to the right hand side of the vast space. People that came here were there just to dance and enjoy the atmosphere. A host of guest DJ's were lined up throughout the week and tonight this guy spinning the decks was right on my level with the music preferences. It was surprisingly packed out for a Tuesday night, I guess everyone was still in the holiday spirit. Plus this DJ was damn good.

After much insistence that I didn't want to drink, I finally gave into Allison, who knew exactly how 'relaxed' I became when inebriated. She had a mischievous look in her eyes as she prodded me.

"Come on! Just this one night let loose and enjoy. I miss fun Lexi!" Apparently I was easy when it came to peer pressure.

And now I was dancing with a stranger out in the middle of the packed dance floor. I didn't realise just how close he had gotten until I felt his hand on my ass. Definitely not a line I was willing to cross with anyone tonight. I wasn't quite that drunk yet in any case, not that I'd want to repeat past mistakes.

Just as I was about to say something to Mr Handsy, I saw that he was suddenly not there anymore. I looked around confused but didn't have time to think when I found myself being pulled into the strong and very capable arms of Mr Hamilton. I felt like I couldn't breathe. The whole evening, I watched as he sat at the bar with his drink, not approaching the dance floor as us girls danced, even when Brent joined in. He seemed to be keeping himself sober, surprisingly, even with the amount he had drunk. But I did feel his eyes observing me and every now and then he'd take out his phone. I felt disappointment when I saw him looking intently at his phone screen, stupid as that was. It just made me wonder who the lucky person diverting his attention was. So I pushed the thought aside, because that in itself was alarming, and carried on taking the drinks Allison plied me with and kept dancing. The giggles got louder, the moves got kinda raunchier and it did cross my mind that if I remembered this all the next morning, I would cringe.

Looking up now into Kade's eyes, I could see a flicker of emotion. Jealousy? Possessiveness? I couldn't make it out but it was animal, consuming, and it drew me closer to him in his arms as my arms slid around his neck and his hands snaked around my back to hold me close. The song playing was 'Closer' by Ne-yo, by no means a slow song but somehow it felt like we had our own pace, our own tune. The intensity of his stare, and the alcohol, forced me to break the silence between us.

"You didn't have to save me you know." His eyes narrowed a fraction. If anyone else had seen him, they wouldn't have noticed the change in his demeanour but I did. After the hours I spent with him in close proximity for however little time that may have been, I had become attuned to him.

"Are you telling me you enjoyed that guy having his paws all over your ass? Did you want him?" I knew now was not a good time to poke the bear with a stick so I appeased him by smiling and shaking my head.

"No. I just didn't want you to get noticed is all." That seemed to make the tension in his body shift a little and he flashed his dimpled smile at me under that real looking beard.

"I don't like my girls being harassed, so I took care of it. Don't worry, I was not noticed."

We danced in silence, swaying to the fast paced song and not really caring. I placed my head on his shoulder and he pulled me closer, letting me breathe in his scent. This was fast becoming my favourite place - in his arms. I wondered how lucky a girl would be to call this man 'hers' and then quickly squashed the thought out of my head and enjoyed the attention I was stealing in this moment from him.

***

A few more hours and tequila's (amongst other drinks) later, we were walking, well I was stumbling, back to the limo. Kade had practically held me up as I wavered.

"Hey," I giggled, falling drunkenly against him again.

"Well hello there," he grinned back, chuckling as he shook his head.

"You have pretty eyes. Like deep blue oceans, I could drown in them." Oh shit, did i just say that out aloud?

"You're drunk. Let's get you home and into bed."

"That's what he said." For the love of God. Kade laughed and grabbed my waist with both hands to steady me.

"Okay, definitely drunk. Time to go home." He bundled me into the limo and we drove off.

I didn't even realise we were home until I felt strong arms carrying me up some stairs. I opened my drunk eyes to intoxicate myself further with the kind smiling face of the gentleman carrying me to my bed. He lay me down so gently, as if I might break if he didn't and started pulling off my heels. I watched in my haze, half conscious yet my body aware of his closeness. He pulled the covers over me and leaned over to kiss my cheek but as he started to pull away, something made me pull him back. His face was so close to mine, I could feel his breath on my face. My eyes trailed from his blues to his soft lips and I found myself closing my eyes and pulling him closer to me. I felt him suddenly pull away and I knew he'd seen the hurt and confusion in my eyes when he did. Instead of leaving, he stroked my hair away from my face and touched his forehead to mine.

"Not like this," he whispered, kissing my forehead. He stroked my cheek and then left quietly. I didn't have much time to process how I felt before I passed out in a confused daze.

CHAPTER TWELVE

New City, new job, new man?

I awoke with a splitting headache and the need to pee really bad. Not to mention the bile coming up my throat. I ran into the bathroom and promptly threw up. From my very few past experiences of being drunk, I knew I'd feel much better after that. After relieving myself and brushing my teeth, I splashed water over my tired face and sore eyes, wincing at the pain in my head from the assault of the day light filtering in from the window. I stalked back to my bed to lie down, noticing that it was 12pm and I had yet again slept in. As I set my phone down on the dresser, I noticed a couple of pills, a glass of water and a note by my bedside. Picking up the note, I read:

> *"Take these and rest today. Now I know why you*
> *don't drink - the things you were saying to me*
> *last night...*
> Kade
> *P.S. Your hair looks great this morning :)"*

Ever conscious, I grabbed my phone to look into my front facing camera. It looked like birds had started to nest in my hair. Argh! Damn him and his mission to compliment me every day. Especially when he thought he was being funny.

Even as I tried to relax in my bed, something niggled at the back of my mind about last night. Something had happened or something had been said. I couldn't quite remember at that moment but I knew undoubtedly that it would come back to me later. I was one of those unfortunate drunks that remembered everything the next day or so. Thats my shitty super power folks - I remember every terrible moment that occurs when I've been drunk and disorderly.

I sat up and swallowed the pills as prescribed by Kade and took the welcome drag of cool water, giving my parched self the much needed relief before drifting off into oblivion.

***

I awoke again to the sound of my phone ringing after what seemed like five minutes but was in actuality, a whole two hours later.

Noting that the number was unknown, I frowned and cleared my throat as I answered it.

"Hello, may I speak to Miss De Luca?" a smooth male voice came from the other end of the phone.

"Speaking," I managed to reply, wincing at the raspy sound coming out of my mouth.

"Miss De Luca, I am calling regarding your application to work at Atlantis Art. Having reviewed your resume, we would like for you to attend an interview at our premises. I know it is a bit short notice but could you possibly come down today?"

I wracked my hangover clouded brain for which of the million applications this could be referring to. *Atlantis....atlantis....Ohhhh, the art gallery!*

"Absolutely, I am free today. What time would you like for me to be there?"

"Would you be able to make four o'clock?" I looked at the bedside clock and inwardly groaned. It was already a quarter past two. But I was desperate to get myself working and settling fast into a job so that I wouldn't feel like a loser sitting at home with too much time to think about stupid things.

"That would be perfect," I replied as cheerily as I could muster.

"Thats wonderful. I won't be there for the interview but you will be meeting with Jason Ford. Good luck Miss De Luca."

"Thank you Mister..."

"You can call me Michael."

"Thank you Michael," I said, a little taken aback at how informal this mostly formal sounding man was being. He had a nice warm sounding voice, I could only imagine him being an easy going guy. In a strange way his voice was comforting.

I pulled myself out of my thought. I had a lot to worry about like getting myself to an interview in little more than an hour and a half. After hanging up the phone, I shot into action, showered and feeling somewhat better after Kade's magic medicine, I was able to pull out what I thought was an appropriate outfit for an interview at an art gallery. The position was for Gallery assistant at what seemed to be an exclusive gallery in the Upper Eastside part of the city. I decided to play it safe and wear smart black trousers with a white loose blouse tucked in and a black mixed material blazer. I broke the monotone with a red scarf and I left my hair out in long natural waves. Pulling my smart black heels on, I rushed out of my bedroom, happy that I'd manage to get my make up done in time.

Downstairs I saw no sign of Kade and everyone else had to be still be at work. Thinking nothing of it, I stepped outside to try flag down a taxi as I walked down the street.

***

"Thanks, keep the change," I told the taxi driver,

jumping out of the cab as if it were on fire. The dude was driving like a bat out of hell! I felt lucky to be alive. *And I thought London cabbies were bad! Actually...its a tie...*

I gathered my bearings, patted down my clothes for wrinkles and finally looked up at the grand glass building that was Atlantis Art.

It seemed to be made entirely of glass from the facade. I could see that it was a modern, clean cut style that the designers of this gallery had gone for. It remained elegant, the white walls within the building visible from outside and wonderfully high ceilings.

Taking a deep breath, I pushed through the glass doors, admiring the antique ornate looking door handles as I stepped into the cool clean air inside the vast space of the gallery.

At the sound of my heels clicking on the expensive wooden floor, the blonde head of the person sitting at the reception desk shot up with an instant welcoming smile.

The girl couldn't be more than eighteen years old, innocent looking with her big blue eyes and cheery smile. I smiled back, approaching her slowly. I got the sense that this gallery was repeatedly cleaned over with a toothbrush. The dark wood floor looked like it could sparkle in the right light.

"Hello. I'm - "

"Miss De Luca?" The deep voice definitely couldn't have come from the cute blue eyed doe sitting in front of me. Spinning on my heel, I found myself standing face to face with a Calvin Klein underwear model. Or at least he probably doubled as that.

Standing behind me in a well tailored and fitted light grey suit was the breathtaking face of a dirty blonde, green eyed fine specimen of a man. Positively drool worthy. I took a deep breath and smiled, trying to stop myself from glancing at his shoes. I have this thing about grey and navy suits being worn with tan shoes. I know it is silly but theres just something about a man who is sensible enough to make the pairing that makes me unbelievably happy. Tom never did pair his suits and shoes correctly - it drove me up the wall and I think he enjoyed annoying me.

"Yes, I am Alexa De Luca," I smiled, taking his outstretched well manicured hand. He had a strong handshake, impressive. That and the model smile he just gave me. *Must not look at his feet...must not look...stop...aw shit, you looked two seconds too long you freak...but tan coloured shoes non the less, mini fist bump!*

"My name is Jason Ford, I will be interviewing you today. This young lady at reception here is Denise. I hope you didn't find it too difficult getting here?" His polite and professionally friendly manner put me at ease from the nerves I had been feeling before.

"No, not at all. I took a cab." Something in my face must have showed my distressed memory of the experience that made him laugh.

"I gather you may have found one of the more enthusiastic drivers out there." I laughed too, shaking my head.

"I think its an unwritten rule that in every city there must be at least one in every three cab drivers that can give you a formula one experience."

"Yes, I guess you were lucky to find one of New Yorks finest then." Something about the way he was looking at me, made me feel a little nervous again. His gaze missed nothing and the expression on handsome face seemed to sink into deep thought for a few seconds until he broke the silence.

"Let's talk in the office Miss De Luca." I followed his tall broad form across the large gallery space to an office at the other end.

Usually, I would be feeling more nervous than this. I was never much good in the company of good looking men, being too self conscious, but the past few days spending time with Kade had made me feel less self conscious and a little brave. I mean, if you can stand being alone in the company of Mr Perfect Pecs then you can pretty much do anything. It was that and maybe the fact that although Jason Ford was undeniably attractive, I was not thinking about the attraction because my mind was still lingering on Kade. Now *that* man was my kind of perfect. I shrugged off images of the blue eyed dark haired devil, preparing myself to impress Jason Ford and perhaps get this job.

***

Half and hour later I was completely relaxed and laughing at the jokes Jason was making. Turned out he's a really laid back guy under the posh suit and professional demeanour.

"Well, Miss De Luca, I don't usually do this but I think Michael and the team would be happy to welcome you to Atlantis Art as the newest employee. The offer for the role is yours."

Wow. I couldn't help the beam on my face. What started as a *meh* kind of day had suddenly turned around ten fold.

"I would love to accept, Thank you so much. And please, call me Alexa."

"As you wish, *Alexa*. So long as you call me Jason."

In the short time I had spent at the gallery, I had learnt that the gallery had been owned by Michael, the owners', family for three generations. Jason took me on a tour of the gallery and I got to see some of the most beautiful paintings I'd ever seen.

"We have a current exhibition based on fantasy landscapes. It's a step away from the usual classic art most people expect to see here but Michael loves to mix things up a bit here and the patrons always tend to appreciate the work," Jason explained.

I was a sucker for this kind of fantastical artwork. I stopped walking as I approached a piece depicting a landscape in which a red haired fairy like creature sitting with its back to the beholder was sitting on the edge of the Earth and looking out onto the blazing sun. Only, the blazing sun seemed to have its own landscape - there seemed to be pink clouds and hot red mountains and life on the blazing sphere from a close up birds eye view.

"This is incredible. If I didn't know better, I'd say this is the work of Enzo." I'd been a fan of Enzo's since I'd first seen his work a few years ago. He was a well known artist, known for his beautiful fantasy art work. His talent knew no bounds. I had to try my best to stop myself from touching the painting, I felt so drawn to it.

"Uh...yeah, it actually is an Enzo piece. I painted it." My jaw must have literally dropped to the floor. He did not just imply that he is Enzo, the world renowned artist whose face I've never really seen because, well, his art work was so great and distracting that I never had a reason to want to know about him as a person.

"Are you serious? You're Enzo?" Jason smiled sheepishly whilst rubbing the trim beard at his jaw.

"In the flesh."

"B-but you're Jason Ford." I promise you, I felt stupid later on for saying that.

"My name is Jason *Lorenzo* Ford. My mother is Italian. I'm assuming you are part Italian too?" At my nod, he continued, "I chose to keep my nickname as my artist name. Otherwise I'm just known as Supreme Court Judge Fords' son." Well...that was a revelation. Composing myself, I gave him a genuine smile of appreciation.

"Mr Ford, your art work is simply amazing. I'm sorry for my reaction, I guess I always assumed that Enzo would be...different...in person." *Dig another ditch for myself.*
He laughed out loud and I turned an appropriate shade of red, given my level of ignorance.

"Alexa, please call me Jason. And I know what you're thinking - most people expect for me to be in overalls or jeans stained with paint all the time. When I'm painting, yeah I usually am. I just came back from a business meeting this morning. I don't usually work here, I help Michael out from time to time but I'm meant to be a silent partner. He asked me to come for the interview today since I live nearby. I hope you're not disappointed."

For the first time since meeting him, I saw a sort of sparkle in his eyes and a hint of flirting. My cheeks felt a little hotter.

"No not at all Jason. Thank you for taking the time to see me." His smile widened making his already handsome face a work of art in itself. Still, a voice in the back of my mind criticised that smile for not producing dimples like those of a certain blue eyed devil.

"The pleasure was all mine Alexa. I hope to be seeing a lot more of you from now on. I will let Michael know about the progress we've made here and he can send you the details as to your start date and salary etcetera. He will probably arrange a day for you to come in and meet the rest of the staff before you start."

With another handshake and an exchange of pleasantries, I left the gallery to make my way back home with a skip in my step and a smile that refused to leave my face.

***

I'd been been home only for a few minutes when my phone started buzzing with Facebook notifications which was weird considering I hadn't posted anything recently. I had forgotten to switch on my mobile data so as soon as I got home to wifi connection, it was buzzing like mad. *76 notifications? 38 comments?!* Since when was I so popular? Wasn't even my birthday! In addition, there were five whats-app messages.

Confused, I fired up my laptop in my room to check on the bigger screen what the heck had people riled up. Worst case scenario would be someone hacking my account and leaving spam. What I didn't bargain for was my account actually being hacked and posted with pictures. Of last night...

I looked in horrified amazement at the pictures Kade,

Brent, Allison, Sadie and I had taken of last night, of us all. There were quite a few group shots and a few of Brent and Allison being an annoyingly cute couple, a few of me and the girls, a couple of the guys making faces behind our selfies. But the pictures that got the most 'likes' and comments were the ones of me and Kade. I don't remember these being taken but wow. In one picture, I couldn't recognise myself as the same person. I looked carefree and as if I had been laughing, looking back at Kade who was leaning down close to me from behind me, also laughing. I looked sexy, and happy and more confident than I could imagine myself ever being.

Another picture showed me in Kade's arms, his hands on my waist. My body was pressed close to his and my arms around his neck staring with half closed eyes straight into his as he looked seriously down into mine. The moment could be interpreted into something intimate if you didn't know the context of the situation. But then again, did we share a moment back then?

I started reading the comments, most of them stating, "looking hot girly!" and "so sexy!"

One comment caught my eye and didn't allow for me to look on. It was a comment from Tom on the intimate looking picture of myself with Kade:

"Glad someone is having a good time."

I knew he was fuming. I knew him well enough to know that he was definitely angry and upset and jealous. If you had asked me a week or two ago, I may have felt bad about it. I may have felt like it was a spiteful and hurtful thing to do, even after everything he did to me because I was not like him. That was Alexa in the past. Alexa of the present and hopefully the future would never again be made to feel guilty for living her life. I especially wouldn't let adulterer Tom make me feel bad for having legitimate fun with whomever I damn well pleased.

Checking the time of the upload, I could see that there was only one person in possession of my phone that could have uploaded to the new album entitled "celebration." *Talk about rubbing salt onto the wounds.* I silently scolded him and smiled at the thought that Kade had helped me get an upper hand on what had been a shitty day yesterday, helping me conquer the last shred of pain and the memories and get a fresh start.

Now, if only he were there to tell off for invasion of privacy and thank for being so amazing to me.

***

It was 8pm before I heard anyone come in through the front door. Leaving my book on my bed, I made my way down to the second floor in time to see Sadie smile tiredly at me as she made her way up the stairs to her bedroom.

"Hey Sadie, let me help you with those," I smiled, taking the two portfolios and her camera bag from her.

"Hey Lexi, thank you so much." She looked like she could do with a good rest. Opening her bedroom door, she dropped her bag onto her bed and flopped backwards on a sigh, eyes closed and patted the space next to her. Laughing, I placed her things on her desk gently and joined her in a similar manner.

If I could design a mood board describing Sadie's personality, her room would be it. There were family and friends' photos everywhere - in a collage on the wall beside her large fluffy bed, by her desk and in frames on her window sill. Her desk was like an organised mess of photo's and layouts and clippings. A variety of pictures and articles were pinned to the board on the wall in front of her desk and there were quite a few soft toys. The colour scheme was all white with purples and pinks thrown in and there were so many cushions on her comfy bed. The room smelt of roses.

"Rough day?" I asked, turning my head to the side to

observe her face in profile, eyes still closed. It was then that I noticed a slither of a scar on the base of her neck that started just under her left ear and ended at the middle of the throat. It looked jagged but seemed to have healed well enough that it was only noticeable to you if you got close enough. I couldn't begin to imagine what could have caused something so sinister looking.

As if she could feel the burning intensity of my stare, Sadie turned her face and then her body towards me, ultimately hiding the scar. She curled up a bit defensively, her arms hugging herself. Her eyes begged me not to question her and I understood immediately not to push her, not to ask. So I changed the subject to something that had been niggling me since morning.

"Where's Kade?" Sadie breathed out in relief and gave me a thankful smile.

"He went back home this morning." *Um, excuse me, what now?*

"He went home?"

The confusion and the beginning of what felt like my stomach dropping must have shown on my face as Sadie sat up, which made me sit up and face her.

"Lexi, he had to go back and resume his 'other' life. I hate it too when he comes here and we enjoy being normal and can be friends away from his 'other world,' where he normally lives, without the constraints he has to protect his relationships in public. The reality of the situation is that he is a celebrity. He's famous and handsome and rich and that means no one will ever really let him have a truly private life. Please don't feel bad about it." I suddenly felt defensiveness pulling through all the other emotions.

"I'm not feeling bad about it, he can do what he likes but I just thought he would say good bye before he leaves." Sadie gave me a knowing look as she took my hand in hers and I felt like an idiot for being so transparent.

"I can tell you feel hurt he didn't say bye in person.

Don't take it personally Lexi, that's just how he is because he hates the good byes too. But I know he probably left you a note somewhere, he always does find a way to redeem himself. That's how I know he went home - he put a note inside the Cheerio's box because he knows thats always my breakfast on work days. Thinks he's being funny." She giggled and I couldn't help but smile at their friendship and this soft spoken resilient, yet shy, woman sitting next to me. She had definitely gone through something horrific. That scar on her neck looked sinister, her reaction confirmed my fears. Yet here she sat as if everything was fine again and she could deal with whatever came her way, giving me the reassurance that a man I hardly knew well enough to miss didn't just disregard me when he left.

We spent some time talking about our respective days. I told her about getting a job at Atlantis art at which she got really happy and we celebrated by eating M&M's she had stashed in her side cabinet. I mean, the girl really loved her M&M's - there were literally packets and packets of the stuff.

"What are your co-workers like?" She asked whilst popping a blue peanut M&M in her mouth.

"I haven't met them yet. The guy who interviewed me doesn't exactly work there either...he's actually a very well known artist." At this, Sadie's eyes grew wide with excitement.

"Who is he?"

"Enzo!"

Sadie's face went blank. I gave her an incredulous look.

"You have no idea who I'm talking about, do you?"

"Uh, sorry no," she apologised, shaking her head.

"Well, he's only the best fantasy artist ever! Wait until you meet him and see his work. It's amazing."

I continued fan-girling for another ten minutes as Sadie patiently listened. Finally I realised that I should probably let her rest and eat and retired to my room for the night.

***

My laptop indicated an email from Atlantis Art as I logged in. It was from Michael. All the details were there for me to start on the coming Monday, as was discussed with Jason a.k.a Enzo. The salary was better than I had expected, the hours were perfect where I worked four days a week and every other Saturday. There was an opening night for a new and upcoming artist in three weeks time where I would be required to work with the rest of the staff until late into the evening. Lunch was one hour, etc etc. I couldn't help but smile. My first instinct was to call Ash. I touched the screen to FaceTime before remembering that it was 2.30am in London and started to end the call when it connected to a very wide awake Ash grinning back at me.

"Oh my God Ash, I'm so sorry I didn't think about the time! Such an idiot!" Ash laughed and shook her head.

"You're not disturbing me my love, I've been waiting all day for you to call me so I can look at that sly mug of yours and ask you to SPILL THE DETAILS ON KADE SEXY HAMILTON!" Ash's excitement helped fuel the memories of last night and I gave her all the details as she asked more and more questions. After I'd finished telling her about Kade and then about my new job, I felt better. Every person needs an Ash they can talk to about anything and everything. She is the one person on the planet who knows absolutely everything about me and vice versa. She looked at me with a knowing smile.

"You like him don't you?" I looked at her as if she was stupid.

"Of course I like him, everyone does." Now she looked pissed.

"You know what I mean Lexi. You *like him*, like him." I started fidgeting with my hands. I hated when she put me on the spot because she had some psychic ability to look into my soul. That is what you get when you know one another so well, I guess.

"I like him," I admitted, "but I don't know him well enough. Plus he's a rich famous person and way out of my league. And he just got out of a relationship, I just got divorced. It would never really go anywhere if we even thought that way. And I don't think he sees me in that way, it's just harmless flirting." Ash's face softened and she smiled that enigmatic all knowing smile.

"Lex, I saw those photos online of you two. Alcohol or not, and in his case you said he hardly drank, you can't mistake the look in both of your eyes. He knows theres something there. He is seriously attracted to you. You are not out of his league, and you both have time so let it be and see what happens. Theres no rush. In the meantime, however, if you just happen to have crazy monkey sex whilst figuring out your 'feelings' later then thats just what nature intended." We burst out laughing. Subtlety was never a strong characteristic for Ash.

"I think I've made enough bad decisions for a lifetime in these past few years Ash. I'll be happy for things to be simple for now."
"True. But a girl can dream! I'm an old married woman now, I want to live vicariously through you Lexi, don't let me down. Did you look for the note Kade might have left you by the way?" Honestly, I hadn't had the chance. I got up and searched my room whilst Ash remained connected on facetime.

"I have no idea where he would have put one," I complained, wondering if there even was a note for me. It was highly presumptuous of me but still a big part of me wanted that attention from him and for the first time I allowed myself to admit it.

Having searched for a couple of minutes and finding nothing obvious, I tried hard to swallow the disappointment, said goodnight to Ash, changed into my pyjamas and flopped onto my bed. Leaning down to the mains socket to charge my phone, I found a post it note stuck to my slippers by the side of the bed. A note from Kade.

> *"Hey pretty girl, you have the most annoyingly cute*
> *bunny slippers. But that's not why I left this note.*
> *I'm going back into the wild, so to speak. I may not*
> *be back for some time but you can stay in touch -*
> *I programmed my number into your phone. And*
> *I apologise for the pictures. I'm sure you want to*
> *kick my ass. Save it for the next time we meet.*
> *Sweet dreams.*
> *Kade."*

I grabbed my phone and searched for his number but couldn't find anything under 'Kade.' I did, however, find a new entry. Under the name "Lickable Abs." I couldn't help the laughter bubbling out of me as I turned off my lamp and lay my head onto a pillow of thoughts of just how lickable those abs were.

CHAPTER THIRTEEN

Eat, Sleep, Work, Repeat

The next two weeks went like a blur. I started work at the gallery on the following Monday as planned and was introduced to the rest of the employees.

Skylar, who was a part time model, was a tall slender and beautiful mixed race woman with piercing blue eyes. Incidentally, I knew I felt like I had seen her before when she told me she was the face of a brand of clothes marketed to teenagers, with her advertisements displayed all around the city. She looked like she was a teen but revealed her real age to be twenty eight. I found that we got on quite well due to her maturity and knowledge on how the gallery was run. She helped me find my way around the first few days, especially with tips on how to remember information about the very important Artists whose work we displayed and sold.

Mary was the walking example of everything my mother was scared I would become when I grew up. Tattooed and pierced and totally working the Goth look, I was shocked to find out that she was in fact a chartered accountant who dealt with all things finance in relation to the gallery. Her tough exterior matched her personality but she was warm and welcoming even if she was not overly affectionate. It was actually a breath of fresh air having her around. Her parents were celebrated scientists who were currently travelling through the Far East. Every time she talked of them she seemed to smile wider than I'd ever seen her smile. It made me miss my family more.

Clyde was our resident art expert as well as fashion expert and a terrible flirt. You wouldn't think he was gay, the way he flirted with us ladies, but unfortunately it was true. This handsome clean cut dark haired and dark eyed devil in pristine designer suit was, to our dismay, off limits to all women, which I knew a lot of our female clients found irritating.

In my first week, Clyde forced me to go shopping for 'smart sexy work clothes' which he insisted were part and parcel of working at Atlantis. He made it easy for me though, since he had such good taste and I loved that we got looks from passers by who thought we were a couple every time he pulled me close to him. There was nothing camp about Clyde, he just exuded confidence and I felt like I could take a leaf out of his book. Which is why I didn't argue much with his selection of pencil skirts and silk blouses for me. The heels took some convincing but eventually I'd procured quite an impressive arsenal of work clothes.

And so, Alexa De Luca had turned from the tracksuit wearing tramp to the sexy smart heel wearing, well groomed assistant at the Atlantis Art Gallery.

I amazed myself with how quickly I had settled into my role and with how much I actually enjoyed being around the different art pieces that told so many stories. I felt welcomed by my new work family, something I had missed from my days at the boutique. The ease with which we conversed and joked and worked gave me a good structure and purpose to my day. It also kept my mind off the fact that I hadn't heard from Kade for the past two weeks. Neither had anyone else for that matter but still, it felt weird that he was away.

I had seen the odd magazine front page displaying his

arrogant abandoning beautiful face and articles about how he had returned to work and that he had given one interview exclusive to Flick magazine about his split with Giselle where he stated they had split amicably having realised they were not as compatible as they had once thought they were. It felt annoying to read that ridiculous cliche response when I knew the truth. But alas, he had to play it his own way to protect the ones he loved.

***

It was a Friday night, the second full week I had completed at work, when I came home only to be ushered out again by Allison, closely followed by Sadie as they pulled the door closed behind them and filed us all into a waiting cab.

"Um, guys? Mind telling me why I am not allowed to go inside and why we're in a cab going God knows where? This is kinda like kidnapping." I saw the cab driver raise his eyebrows in the rear view mirror to which Allison rushed to explain.

"We're having dinner at *Kaleb's* place. He asked us to come over to thank us for our hospitality." She didn't have to give me the exaggerated eye signals for me to remember 'Kaleb' as being Kade's alter ego disguise name.

Having wondered how he was and being incredibly curious as to where he lived, I still felt super annoyed that someone I had shared so many intimate details about my life with had just up and left. It made me want to stay home so I made my feelings clear, never mind the cab tearing down street after street.

"I'd like to stay home please, I've had a terribly long day and need the beauty sleep." Allison gave me her sternest of looks while Sadie tried to hide a small smile.

"Listen Lexi, he asked specifically that we make sure you come. We're all tired from work but it will be nice to hang out since we hardly get to these days."

"True," I laughed, "but mostly because you are always away being loved up by Brent and Sadie has to work on her recent project. Not my fault lady."

"You're not allowed to back out so you have no excuse to say we don't spend time with you. Sadie's project was handed in today and Brent will be meeting us there. Gives us all a chance to catch up." There was never any arguing with Allison. Somehow that woman always got her way and I was just too tired to argue anymore.

We pulled up outside an elegant skyscraper in the sought after Upper East side. You could almost smell the money around there. Incidentally, I had passed this building every day on my way to and from work without even knowing that this is where Kade lived. So close yet so far. I realised that I may have started to sound a little like an obsessed teenager with a crush and pushed the thought out of my head.

The doormen greeted us with smiles and called the lift for us. The penthouse was on the 42nd floor and security in this building seemed to be paramount and high spec. Sadie entered a special code that would take us straight to the penthouse. I could only imagine who the other occupants here were. We stood silently, checking out our faces in the posh marble and mirrored elevator as we ascended up the building seamlessly.

Upon reaching the floor, the doors opened to a cream marbled foyer and a single dark wood door in front of us. Allison stepped out first and straight up to the door that she knocked on, ignoring the bell, three times. I cowered at the back, not quite sure how ready I was to see Kade again. A few moments later the front door opened and I could hear rather than see Kade. The deep and playful voice sent shivers down my spine.

"Good evening ladies, please come in. I will just be a moment." I could hear Kade walking away into the room and shuffled in behind the girls, Sadie giving me an inquisitive glance after observing my timid behaviour.

I like to think I was prepared for the grandeur of Kade's mostly permanent residence but I think it exceeded my expectations. It wasn't too dissimilar to his apartment with us but it was at least triple the size and expense for sure. The floors were all a grey veined white marble, the walls white and the furniture looked too expensive to sit on. I knew this because in my time working with the Architecture firm, I had spent some time with the interiors department looking at the catalogues of designer furniture and gasping at the monstrous prices.

This place was huge. The living room was the first room you walked into after walking through a wide hall, and of course the pretentious rich boy had a Piano in the far left hand side of the room. The sofas were white leather but the room was accented with grey and splashes of blue. A grey throw here, a few blue and grey cushions there. There was a fire place, the modern kind that you would imagine being in a place like this but it looked good with the sofas facing it. Kade had had the foresight to have it turned on for a homely effect even though we were at the beginning of a sweltering August. The rug in front of it looked like it was the softest fluffiest thing in the planet. I could testify that it was as soon as I sat down and quietly slipped off a heel to feel the comforting softness on my tired foot.

I could see a bi-folding door leading to the kitchen, and noticed another couple of doors further away.

The spiral stairs leading up to the second floor were grand, made of marble and wrought iron balustrades leading up to what looked like four or five more rooms.

The high ceilings held intricate light fittings and from what I could tell, with my recent experiences at the art gallery, there were expensive paintings and sculptures on every surface acceptable. This place looked like the ultimate millionaires lair.

Not long after taking a seat we heard the door being knocked and Kade shouting from the kitchen for someone to open it. Seeing as I was at the end, I volunteered to go and open it. As expected, Brent stood on the other side of the door looking tired but happy to be here.

"Hey Brent," I smiled and savoured the warmth of his brotherly hug.

"Hey Lexi, I am so glad this day is over." We walked into the living room where Allison proceeded to give Brent mouth to mouth resuscitation as it would seem. They had not seen one another the whole week so I suspected we wouldn't see Allison this weekend after dinner tonight. They usually ended up staying at his place when they had 'catching up' to do. I really wished I could hate them and their PDA but the truth was I felt happy seeing them. It gave me the reassurance that not every relationship had to be a train wreck. Besides, I couldn't begrudge the people I loved the simplest of joys.

I was about to rejoin the group from the entrance of the living room when I realised Kade was standing at the other end by the kitchen, staring at me with intensity I couldn't quite decipher. And then he started walking towards me with lazy, measured and assured steps. He smiled that sexy teasing dimpled smile that I had begun to love as he got closer, stopping a foot in front of me. I couldn't help appraising him the way he was appraising me. Wearing his navy suit trousers and a crisp white dress shirt that had a few buttons undone at the top revealing a teaser of the delicious chest underneath. His hair was still its neat mess of waves and even though he looked like he'd had a tiring week of working, his eyes sparkled like pools of the deep blue ocean. He was breathtaking to behold in his smart casual appearance. I started to wonder what he would look like a full three piece suit.

"Alexa." His voice sounded a little husky as he smiled down at me, pulling me from my thoughts of him to the reality of him standing in front of me, so close and so very real. I forced myself to hold onto some dignity as I responded.

"Kade." I couldn't think of a word to say apart from that. How could I when Kade was staring at me like that? I felt self conscious as his eyes seemed to suck every thought from my mind. At some point I acknowledged Brent fake coughing from the living area, drawing my attention to the others but Kade was still looking at me. I could feel his stare on my face as I looked from Allison's smirking face, Sadie's happy face and Brent's confused one.

I felt Kade take my hand and gently pull to draw my attention back to him. He made a slow scan of my body, toes to face, making me feel like I could melt under his gaze.

"I love the sexy secretary look you got going on there Alexa." There was no use in hiding the blush.

"I even have the glasses to complete my look." I think I heard a gasp from one of the girls but I couldn't look because I had shocked myself with the blatant flirting back.

Kade lifted his eyebrow as he smiled wickedly at me.

"Welcome to my humble abode." Humble my arse. This place exuded power and money. Nevertheless, I smiled graciously and thanked him for inviting me as well as the others.

He led me to the seating area, placing my hand in the crook of his arm like a gentleman.

Kade went away to get us all drinks as we sat and chattered away about our week. Brent made a joke about Kade being a domestic goddess as he carried in a tray of drinks and pulled out coasters, to which he mocked offence but winked at me when I laughed at him and then sat down next to me. Once again we had shifted into our comfortable pattern in the group, lighthearted and warm in one another's company.

Dinner was served shortly after and tasted divine. I tried not to show how impressed I was with Kade's culinary skills with his full chicken roast and the trimmings. When Sadie made a comment on how he had outdone himself once again, he smiled and shrugged his shoulders saying that a roast is the easiest thing to put together and he'd got it all made in an hour like it was no big deal. I admired that about him, his effort for his friends and the energy he had to do this on a work day. I wanted him to know how appreciated it was, so I told him and the answering smile was breathtaking.

**

"Let's play truth or dare!" Shouted Allison a little too loudly by Brent's ear that he jumped a little. Nearly everyone had drank a few glasses of wine or bottles of beer but I had steered clear of alcohol and Kade seemed to have a high tolerance for the whisky he had in his tumbler. Allison, however, seemed to have gone from sober to tipsy really quick, Brent looked buzzed and Sadie just kept smiling. That was until Allison mentioned truth or dare.

"Oh no, let's not," she replied turning a little pale.

"Why not?" Allison frowned at her.

"Because last time you dared me to go kiss a random stranger in the street! He turned out to be my dentist! I had to change practices because of that - he was damn good too!" Allison giggled as did the guys at the memory.

"He was a damn good kisser?" Allison said with fake shock.

"He was a damn good dentist, you cow! You know exactly how to wind me up!" Sadie seemed to have loosened up, I had never heard her talk like that to anyone but I knew she was joking. Her lips kept twitching to break into a smile.

"It's not my fault that you never choose a truth and always a dare," Allison laughed. Sadie suddenly looked a little sober and glanced at Kade quickly before answering.

"Dares are a lot more fun anyway." No one else seemed to have noticed the little slip of Sadie's bravado but I looked at the way she seemed to have closed up a little and Kade's concern.

Allison soon commandeered everyones attention, loudly

proclaiming she would go first, without anyone actually agreeing to a game.

I caught Kade smiling at me, winking when our eyes met. I stuck my tongue out at him in an admittedly childish way, to which he raised his eyebrows.

"Okay honey, seems like we won't be able to leave until you have your way. Truth or dare?" Brent asked, smiling up lovingly at Allison and she pecked him on the lips. *They are so sweet it makes my teeth hurt!*

"TRUTH!" She bellowed, causing us all to cover our ears. I could see a question form in Sadie's mind as soon as she smiled and the tension lifted from her face as she asked Allison, "What really happened that day last week when you called me on my day off sounding anxious and asking me to bring you a change of clothes...including panties...and leave them outside your office door?"

I saw the moment Allison regretted suggesting the game.

"Oh shit." Brent couldn't seem to contain his laughter, earning him a swat on his thigh from his fiancee.

"Aren't you going to answer us Allison?" Kade joined in, looking from Allison to Brent with a grin that seemed to have sussed out what could have happened.

"Can I switch to dare?" Allison asked Sadie with pleading eyes. She suddenly looked a little sober too.

"Rules are rules sweetie," Sadie smiled brightly, enjoying beating Allison at her own game.

"You may as well tell them babe," Brent said through his continuing bursts of laughter.

"Ugh! Fine!" Her eyes fixed on Brent's as she gave him a scowl and looked like she had the beginning of a blush creeping up her neck before she continued. "Brent came over that day to discuss an account. It was a business meeting-"

"A naked business meeting," Brent interrupted, shocking me with his blunt admission. The others looked less surprised, obviously having seen Brent this relaxed after a drink or two. Judging by the massive grin on his face and the scathing look Allison was giving him, he was enjoying winding her up too much.

"Yes, a *'naked'* business meeting," she grumbled whilst leaning into Brent's ear and whispering so loud that we could all hear, "trust me, that will never be happening again!"

Brent raised his eyebrows suggestively, the shit eating grin still on his face as if he had heard her say that before to no avail.

"*Anyway,* during the discussion of...business...Brent managed to tear my dress. And, um, under garments. I had a hugely important meeting with the directors in an hours time, I was desperate. This *man,*" she poked at Brent who had tried unsuccessfully to pull her into his lap, "just got up and left me to my peril!"

"I had to get ready for the big meeting too!" he protested in defence whilst trying not to laugh.

"So that's why you called and wouldn't let me inside your office," Sadie laughed.

"Yeah because my dress was ripped from here," she indicated from the neck line, "to here," to the bottom of the dress. Kade raised his eyebrows at that.

"Brent, you animal...I have so much respect for you bro," Kade smiled as they fist bumped. What a pair of teenage boys. Allison glared at them, I swear I could feel the heat of it.

"That's not the worst part," Allison continued.

"What happened," I asked, trying not to laugh at the visual I was getting.

"As soon as I got changed and entered the room for the meeting, *that man* says quite loudly, disregarding the fact that most of these men and women know that he's my fiance, 'Good afternoon Miss Smart, you look lovely. Is that a different dress from this morning?' I wanted to die right there."

Poor Allison looked so red and she tried not to smile as we laughed at her. Eventually the giggles got ahold of her too when she finally allowed Brent to pull her into his lap and kiss her tenderly.

I watched them in awe as she placed her hand on his chest and lay her head on his shoulder as he whispered to her and soothed her. It was then that I caught Kade watching me from the corner of my eye. I didn't want to but I couldn't help but turn my head towards him slowly as our eyes met. There was an emotion there that I wanted so much to believe was real. Affection. His face was close, *too close,* and I could feel his breath on me. Those blues focused on me in a way I could only stand for so long before my body reacted.

After what seemed like forever, Allison finally broke the tension between us and I managed to look away.

"Okay, here's a bottle so take a spin. I gave you a nice juicy truth there so it's got to be one of you guys next."

After a few moments of deliberation Sadie grabbed Kade's glass, downed the liquor in one and took the bottle from Allison's outstretched arm. I looked at Kade, the worry evident in his eyes but he said nothing as Sadie set it down upon the coffee table and spun the bottle.
And of course it landed on me.

"Truth or dare?" Kade smiled at me, his eyes laughing at my discomfort.

"Um...truth?" I don't know why I said that.

"Oooooo I got one, I got one!" Allison squealed. I knew she was going to embarrass me to the absolute limit.

"Oh shit," I murmured as Kade got more comfortable shifting closer to me.

"Is it true that you only took part in the school talent contest so you could dress like a tart and get Simon Ward's attention?" The bitch was looking triumphant as I silently vowed to strangle her in her sleep.

"Wait, wait, we need some background on this Simon Ward guy," Kade piped up. *That's two on the shit list.*

"Simon Ward was the hottest guy at school. He was the school football teams captain, that's "soccer" to you, and super intelligent so he had everything going for him. We all fancied him," I replied.

"Well, we all did but Lexi liked him most. And there was a rumour that he liked her too. So she 'allegedly' hatched this plan with some of the girls in our class, tried to get me on board but I managed to get out of it. And then on the night of the talent show, Lexi became...Britney Spears!" Allison actually shrieked that last part.

I was fully aware of the laughter coming from all around me as I face planted into my hands, the loudest noise coming from Kade beside me.

"And did it work?" Sadie gasped to catch her breath as her laughter died down. Lifting my head from my hands I finally looked up at everyone with my bright red face filled with embarrassment and from the memory, trying not to laugh myself.

"Well...I did manage to get his attention when the buttons of my school shirt popped open during my rendition of 'Baby one more time' to reveal my bra to half the school and the staff," I cringed.

"Mr Rogers nearly had a heart attack from seeing your barely covered boobs!" Allison guffawed and then we all erupted in laughter.

"You get your guy in the end?" Brent asked.

"Yeah, I got my guy in the end. We dated for six months before he moved to another school. He was my first proper boyfriend. We kept in touch for a while. Last I heard, after he had graduated from Kings and was fully qualified as a doctor, he travelled to Sudan to help the less fortunate. I knew there was a reason he stole my heart."

"Lucky bastard," Kade mumbled beside me so only I could hear. I turned to look at him, his eyes burning with an intensity that I didn't want to let myself explore. The moment passed quick enough when Allison insisted we spin the bottle again. The game continued with more hillarious truths and dares until the bottle settled on Kade, who had dodged all the truth or dare until then.

"Come on Kade, choose!" Allison said in her gladiator voice. Unfortunately she had continued drinking but had gone into the 'funny accents' stage of her drunkenness.

"Dare."

"You sound quite confident there Mr Hamilton," I teased, "You think you can handle what comes your way?" He turned towards me with a mischievous smile and a glint in his eyes.

"Anything y'all throw at me."

"Well, since I spun the bottle last, I get to decide!" Allison interrupted, before anyone could say anything.

"What would the lady have me do?" Kade asked in his mock Shakespearean accent as he turned his blues onto Allison.

"Hmmmm, let me think..."

"Oh boy, this could take a while," Sadie murmured. Suddenly Allison was looking at me. And smiling that wicked smile she had when she was about to make someone pay. Somehow I knew whatever nefarious plan Allison had in mind, I wasn't going to like it.

"You have to kiss Lexi. As in, proper make out. No pecks."

"WHAT?!"

"Really?"

"Oh God."

Yeah, the first mortified reaction was mine followed by Kade's confused one and then Sadie who was in a fit of giggles.

"Seriously Allison?!" I was turning beetroot red at the thought of Kade's lips on mine. I mean, it was pretty obvious that Allison, who could have come up with a thousand better dares than this even if she was twice as drunk as she was there, was trying to play match maker. Not that I didn't want to kiss him. My lips were tingling at the thought but embarrassment of him being forced to do so was eating at me.

"Aw come ooon Lexi, stop being such a prude! Don't act like you don't want to!"
Seriously I could hit the bitch right this very second, ruin her beautiful corporate face and not feel bad about it. Not even a smidgen.

"No, I will not take part in this." I stood up, noticing Sadie had sat next to Brent and the two of them were laughing like children do when someone farts loudly. I hadn't dared look at whichever mortified expression Kade must have had on his face. That was until he grabbed my hand and pulled me to face him. And all I could see were his eyes, the burning heat in them and his delicious looking lips smiling in that mischievous way. He also looked a little annoyed.

"Are you saying you don't want to kiss me, De Luca?" His slight frown confused me a little because a moment ago he seemed taken aback at Allison's demand for the dare.

"Uh..yes...I mean no..." *Fucking stupid melting female! Stop losing your marbles over a man!*

"It's either a yes or a no, It can't be both," he whispered moving closer to me, sliding his hand around my waist and pulling me abruptly close to him so that my body was flush against his. He'd never been this physically commanding before, so in control of my body. I could feel the warmth of his body and his breath against my face that sent a shiver down my spine. I felt annoyed with my reaction, with the fact that I allowed him to just pull me into him with such little effort because my body betrayed me and magnetically pulled into him. But still, I didn't dare move from his arms. Because in the few seconds that we stood silent looking into one another eyes, thousands of babies were born, millions of people fell in love and a billion hearts were broken yet time stood still for me and I felt that I was the one person on the entire planet that held this incredible mans full attention.

"Do you want me Alexa?"
Dear God. That was a stupid question if I'd ever heard one.

I must have emitted some semblance of agreement from my Judas body because Kade's arm around my waist tightened to squeeze my breathless self even closer to his hard and warm muscles as his free hand brushed my hair back to cup the back of my head and draw my face up and close to his. My arms instinctively went around his neck. And then I lost myself in his kiss.

First his soft lips skimmed mine in a teasing invitation and I followed his lead as if it was the most natural thing to do. He gently bit my lower lip and pulled it between his teeth before letting go, the whole time looking into my eyes with heavy lids. The raw need in his eyes awakening a boldness in me that I had never expected. I licked his lips and watched as his mouth curled into a smile before I closed my eyes and let him lead me in the breathtaking kisses this man was annihilating me with. His tongue swept across mine and I allowed myself this one pleasure that I'd never have normally let myself have. I knew the exact moment we had both let go of whatever it was holding us back when our kisses grew hungry and consuming. He bit at my lips as I sucked his, I could hardly remember where I was. It was as if we had forgotten where we were and *who* we were. I felt Kade's hand slide down from the back of my head, down my neck and then my back causing shivers to run through my body. I had let out an embarrassing moan of pleasure when I heard someone clearing their throat in the background.

The show had ended before we'd gotten to the really good part. I pulled my lips and body away from Kade's as if he were on fire. We both stood breathing hard looking at one another, me in shock and him with that brooding intensity I sometimes saw when he was deep in thought. His hands had fisted at his sides as if he was trying to gain some sort of control over himself and the situation. I didn't dare look at the others, noticing the painful silence in the room. It was a good few seconds before Allison spoke.

"Wow, you guys that was hot, like watching po-"

Brent cut her off with a quick kiss to her lips and an embarrassed yet apologetic smile on his face as he coaxed his fiancee to her feet and started for the door.

"Hey man it's quite late, we had better get going home now. I'll catch up with you during the week. Sadie, we can drop you off on the way." I vaguely remember Sadie agreeing hastily.

"Yeah sure," Kade replied quietly, not taking his eyes off of me. The intensity in his eyes was shredding me yet I still couldn't look away. In my peripheral I could make out the others saying goodbye to me and mumbling goodbye back to them yet the power of this mans gaze kept me rooted to the spot. I mean, surely I should've left with them, right? After all, I lived with Sadie. I should have left. I should have left but I couldn't because he was keeping me there with that invisible chain around my body, *my heart.*

The silence once they left was immediate. I felt like it would consume me but I couldn't think of a single thing to say as my eyes remained locked on him. Finally, after what seemed to be forever, Kade spoke.

"You have witchcraft in your lips." Those words stole my breath away. My brain leapt for something clever to say to make the moment light. This was too much for me. Way too much too soon, no matter how much I wanted it.

"Did you just quote Shakespeare to me?" I tried to effect a light tone of voice but it was hard to be convincing when the object of my desire was openly staring at my lips again with what couldn't be mistaken for anything other than hunger. And then his eyes snapped to mine again and that smirking mischief ever present in his features made me sigh with relief.

"Always seems to work with the ladies."

"Player," I laughed, taking a small step back. I needed space from him, his presence was just too big even in this huge space of his home. He engulfed it and I felt like an ant.

"Alexa, look at me." It was impossible not to obey

225

when he sounded so imploring. The air felt thick with tension and lust lingering from our kiss. I started to fidget when his intense eyes locked onto mine.

"Alexa, are things going to get awkward between us now?" I wish he wasn't so blunt. I was quite happy to pretend nothing had happened.

"I don't know." It was the truth. Kade slowly reached out to show me his intention of taking my hand and sitting me down.

"I'm not sorry that we kissed. I may be sorry that it happened in a way that has caused you to feel embarrassed in front of our friends. I know you're out of your comfort zone but I won't apologise for it. I think you know as well as I do that this was going to happen between us sooner or later." His words made my body tingle. I felt the blush but I looked at the turbulent emotions in his eyes and I wanted to believe this was the real deal. That he meant those words and the ones that were left lingering unsaid in the space in between. I searched for the words to speak and when I found my tongue, I surprised myself with my answer.

"I'm not sorry either." In another life, I probably would have denied any feelings and shot him down but something had made me bolder and I realised that I didn't want to spend my new life blocking the things that could well give me happiness for however long it lasted. But things were moving faster than I would have liked.

Kade, looking a little surprised at my declaration, moved closer still and then tilted my chin up so I met his gaze.

"I'm glad we got that cleared up. I thought you would deny it and fight me about it."

"I'm always honest Kade."

"That's quite a fortunate thing for me," he smiled, rubbing his thumb gently over my chin before dropping his hand. My eyes remained trained on his. He seemed to think something over then shake his head at the thought.

"Since the others have ditched us, you wanna hang

out some more?" I couldn't ignore the butterflies. They seemed to be my companions in his presence.

But bubbling under the surface of my own feelings of excitement, having gotten his attention, was panic. Panic that the situation was something I was not yet ready for and it was not in my control how we may, from this point on, hurtle into something we were unprepared for when we were both a little broken.

"I can't." The words left my mouth as the uncertainty set in. Kade frowned.

"Why not?"

"It's just..." I suddenly felt nervous. He chuckled as I remained silent a second too long.

"Alexa, I promise I will be a complete gentleman. I won't even sit near you." He made a show of sitting on the single seat opposite me. I laughed, which it turn made him smile and continue.

"Look, let's not let it get weird between us because of that kiss. I would hate for you to get all embarrassed and quiet on me now. You said no regrets, so did I. As much as I would like to explore that chemistry between us, we've both just got out of long term relationships and I don't want to mess you about Alexa. You're not the type of woman any man should just have a fleeting romance with. If I were with you, I'd make you mine in every sense of the word and I damn well wouldn't let you go. I don't want you to feel uncomfortable around me."

Despite everything he said being truthful and appeasing to my disappearing panic, I felt a pang of hurt and disappointment that I wasn't sure was justified. It sounded like he wasn't looking for anything serious once he started looking again and that coupled with the memory of a drunk me being rejected by him stung a little. I covered my reaction with a smile that I hoped was convincing.

"I'm glad you're so honest, and yeah now I don't feel so weird about it."

"Good, then you can have something to drink with me. How else are we going to get to know one another better?"

"Uh...I could always google you I guess," I tried to joke, wanting to ease the tension between my heart and mind. It seemed that might have been the wrong thing to say. His eyes grew steely, there was a slight scowl on his face. The only consolation was that he was looking past me with the fierce look on his face and not directing it at me. Almost as soon as the look had crossed his face, the iciness in his eyes melted as it returned to me, perceiving me warily.

"I'm surprised you haven't already. Maybe you should." The manner in which he said it showed disinterest but I could tell he felt tense about what I might find out about him on the world wide web. Feeling a little confused at his change in demeanour, I got comfortable in my seat, tucking my feet under me and trying to relax.

"Maybe I will." He looked away again for a second but returned with his soft smile.

"Tea?" There was that knowing smirk again and he was back in the room with me again instead of far away.

"Only if it's Tetley's mate," I joked.

"Funny you say that..." he held up a finger for me to wait and disappeared into his kitchen only to come back with a packet of fresh Tetley's tea bags.

"You are seriously like my favourite New Yorker," I laughed.

***

Hanging out with Kade Hamilton in the evening, as it turned out, complied of a lot of laughter and the evening news.

After an hour of banter about nothing in particular, he had turned on the TV and put on the local news channel. Then he proceeded to discuss current affairs and ask my opinions which was refreshing as I hadn't really bothered with the news since moving to NYC.

He would be passionate on some subjects and concentrate on the news reports when he turned over to the national and international news.

I smiled even wider at him as he caught me looking. A little off-balance, it took but a few seconds for the cheeky man to return a smile.

"I'm a little boring and old aren't I? You're going to not want to hang out with me any more." He pouted. He *actually* pouted, which was so ridiculous for a grown man to do and at the same time confusingly hot.

"I was actually thinking that you have so many sides to your personality and I've just seen a little bit more. When you spent those few days over with us, I thought I had you all figured out but you have so many interests. It's nice to see that, it's not boring. But I do have to go home now. It's been a long day and I've overstayed my welcome here."

"You're always welcome here Alexa so please don't feel that. And I've learnt a lot about you through your opinions so it's been a pleasure. I'll arrange for my driver to drop you home."

Before I could protest, he picked up his landline and tapped a few numbers.

"Luke. I'd like for you to take Miss De Luca home please. Yes. Thank you." He looked up at me as I stood up. "Luke will meet us downstairs and will take you home."

I wanted to ask him, so I did.

"When will I see you again?" I wanted to pinch myself for sounding so needy but I had enjoyed the few hours we had spent together, after so long, to let it go. What looked like hope, sparked in his eyes that in turn sparked in my chest.

"Soon," he said with conviction. "You have my number and I have yours. I'll be in touch with you."

His phone beeped to alert him of a message.

"Your ride is here, let me escort you."

Placing his hand on the small of my back, he led me out of

his home, ever the gentleman if it weren't for his index finger stroking me softly and absentmindedly as we stepped into the elevator, that had left heat in the places he had touched me.

In the underground parking just outside the lift lobby was a black BMW 7 series. The driver was waiting for me and as we approached Kade introduced him to me as he ushered Luke aside to open the door himself. Such a gentleman.

"I'll see you soon then," I said feeling a little shy.

"You can count on it," he smiled, reaching out to move a few tendrils of hair from my face.

I stepped up on my toes and kissed his cheek. He seemed pleasantly surprised at the simple yet familiar gesture. I had surprised myself too.

"Thank you for tonight." I settled into the back seat.

"You're most welcome Alexa. Good night."

"Good night." He shut the door and waved as Luke drove me home.

I didn't know what was going to happen with our friendship but I felt an excitement that had long been suppressed finally spill out of me with my every breath. Or maybe that had been happening for a while. Probably since I had met him.

CHAPTER FOURTEEN

Fucking Google

I was staring at the message on my phone when it lit up, alerting me to a FaceTime call coming from Ash. I pressed accept and her perfectly fresh looking face came into view on my screen.

"Well?" she practically screeched.

"Uh, hello to you too Ash," I muttered. She sighed and rolled her eyes. From the looks of it, she was in her living room having a cup of tea.

"Yeah yeah hello, how are you blah blah! Let's cut to the good stuff! Have you done it yet?"

I sighed in exasperation as I ran my hands down my face. Last night as Luke drove me home, I had received a message from Kade. It simply read:

Google me. K x

Before, the idea of googling him made me feel like it was silly and nosy. His insistence now that I do it made me nervous. Naturally, I confided in Ash about the events that led up to this request, having been unable to sleep with all my nervous energy. And surprisingly my 'sunday is my day of rest and you shall not awaken me before noon' best friend was up bright and early which was a cause for concern.

I looked at her excited and annoyingly bright demeanour and sighed.

"I've typed his name and not hit enter yet. I don't know what I'm going to find once I do."

"Duh! Thats the freakin point, love! Just do it already!" I swear, if I didn't love her, I'd strangle her and her new found love of early mornings.

"You bloody well know what I mean, woman! I'm just scared he's some crazy nymphomaniac or that he has a long sordid criminal history or something that I've been bliss-fully unaware of." I shuddered at the thought. Ash rolled her eyes and put her mug down on her coffee table before ad-dressing me up close in her camera.

"Lexi, do you really think that this guy, who has made such a big impression on you that you cant seem to act like a normal person around him, can really be any or all of those things?" I thought for a second before inhaling and letting out the deep breath.

"No," I grumbled, knowing she was right.

"I think he's very thoughtful. He's encouraging you to read about his past, his life, through the eyes of the bastards of the media. He's edging you to look at him through prob-ably the most critical eyes out there and probably asking you to read words that he has despised all his life. He's open-ing up to you babe. It's a big sign of trust. He doesn't know how you'll react yet he's giving you this. I think I'm in love with him myself." She looked away dreamily, causing me to giggle.

"Such a tart. Go and ogle your own man!"

"Oooo, possessive already! And you've already put him in the friend zone lady, tut tut! Keep him. I prefer my smelly, snoring, hairy ape anyway." I couldn't stop my laugh-ter at the look on her face.

It was at that very moment that Imran decided to make a topless entrance behind her, scratching the scruff at his jaw and looking a little confused. Taking in his well defined body mixed with his adorably dazed look, I pointed at him and laughed harder.

"Ugh! Immy, go put on a shirt or something, you're scaring Lexi." He finally noticed that Ash was talking to me and grinned as he walked over and sat next to his irritable wife, attempting to grab her mug of tea before she snatched it from him and growled. Yeah, she actually growled at him.

"Hey Lexi."

"Hey handsome. Your wife was just telling me how much she loves you," I laughed as she tried and failed to swat at his arms to stop him from pulling her into his lap. Now, snuggly settled in his lap, it was hard to miss her irritation melt away and the mutual looks of love and adoration on their faces as they stared at one another for a few brief moments. I felt the pang of longing that always came when I saw other couples interact. I longed for that feeling again. Suddenly, I felt like an intruder in their very private moment. As if they had realised I was still there, Ash turned back to face me with a small smile while Imran kept looking at her.

"Did you tell her," he asked his wife. She immediately looked back at him with a death glare.

"No," she bit out as she swat his arm hard.

"Ow bleedin' heck woman!"

"Tell me what?" I inquired, feeling a little trepidation at Ash's reaction. God, I hope nothing bad had happened. Ash sighed and turned to look at me with an almost guilty look on her face.

"Whats going on Ash?" I didn't mean for my tone to sound so harsh but I was starting to freak out now.

"I was going to tell you Lexi but I just didn't know how to. Please don't be mad," she pleaded, looking as worried as the time she had forgotten to bring in her final English Literature coursework for the deadline at school.

"What the hell are you talking about?" I was starting to get annoyed now. This was Ash, my best friend for absolute years. She had never hidden anything from me. Not a single thing. And now it seemed I was the last to know something important.

"Lexi don't be upset with me, I wanted to tell you first, even before Imran!" He gasped in shock at her traitorous thoughts and if my mind wasn't going crazy with all the possible scenarios in my head, I would have laughed at how comical he looked.

"ASH-"

"We're pregnant!" Imran blurted out. Ash covered her face with her hands and I couldn't quite contain my shock. Not shock at the news. Just shock that my best friend chose not to share the most life changing news she could ever receive with me.

"Ash? Why didn't you tell me?" I asked, still letting it all sink in. She moved her fingers slightly to peek at me. My breathing was coming out difficultly. I couldn't deny that I was upset but I needed to know why she held onto this news from me. Imran gently pulled her hands from her face and kissed her forehead in encouragement.

Taking a deep breath, Ash finally faced me. Her eyes were red rimmed as if she were about to cry.

"I didn't know how to. When I found out, I wanted to call you straight up, I swear. But then I remembered what you had been through and I didn't want to remind you of that. To rub it in..." She trailed off and I understood perfectly what she meant. My best friend had been keeping her happiest news from me to spare my feelings. To stop me from thinking of what I could have had with Tom and what he already had with another woman.

I couldn't stop the tears that started falling from my eyes as I watched Ash mirror me. I heard Imran mutter "oh shit" and grab the tissue box from the coffee table for his wife.

"You stupid, daft, beautiful girl," I sob. "How could I ever feel sad about my best friend, my sister, making me an aunty? I'm not sad. I'm so over the moon happy for you that I can't contain the feeling. I want to shout it out to everyone I know and then to everyone I don't know! Don't you ever feel like you can't tell me about all the good, and bad, things in your life because of how you think it will affect me! I couldn't be happier for you both and for myself. If you ever do this to me again, I will find your shoe collection and pull off the heels to all your stilettos!" Imran laughed at Ash's horrified look at my threat but soon we were all laughing. As soon as we calmed down (and wiped the tears away) Ash told me she was eight weeks pregnant and that she had found out two weeks ago. Since then she had been having on and off morning sickness and had been overly tired during the day but full of life during the mornings, explaining her chirpy Sunday morning demeanour.

"I can't wait to see baby Malik!" I gushed.

"Well, due date is second week of March. We want to try come see you before I get too big to travel," she smiled. For the first time since we started this conversation, I saw the vulnerability and nervousness take over her pretty face.

"Hey Ash, you know everything is going to be okay don't you?" I saw my normally composed friend breakdown in front of my eyes and the slightly panicked look on her husbands face as he held her close and rubbed her back.

"I think Ash is a little overwhelmed Lex," he said, giving me a small smile.

"I know what you're thinking Ash, I know you saw what happened to me but that doesn't mean it will happen to you. You're a strong person and this baby will be just as strong as its mama. If you let the negative energy in, it will harm you both. God, this totally sucks that I can't be with you right now!" I felt frustrated that I was unable to console my friend. Imran gave me a tired smile and hugged Ash closer.

"I know. You're right. I wish you were here, you ho," Ash gave me a watery smile and wiped her face.

"Me too, Ash, me too." After a little more cajoling, Imran left us to get showered and shaved and Ash got me to finally hit the 'enter' button on the search engine.

As expected, a million articles, pictures and pages popped up. This was going to be a long morning for me.

**

Two hours later, I was staring at the articles I had saved. It took a while to sift through the early years that had Kade Hamilton's name on every gossip website and magazine available. Ash had retired back to her bed for a nap half an hour ago after an information overload, leaving me alone to contemplate once more.

His early years were shown in an almost nostalgic way - the pictures were always of him as a young boy smiling and surrounded by his family and some friends. Various family holidays and public events that he would attend with his parents. There were pictures of his siblings, all similar in their looks. In my search, I came across a picture of Bonnie's wedding from a few years back and she looked gorgeous. Kade had been right, their father had tried his hardest to keep minimal media interference in their lives as there only seemed to be only a few private occasions that the paparazzi had gotten their hands on from that time. Kade was as hand-some then as he is now, his face rounder as a child but show-ing the promise of his evolution into a man.

That all changed after, what I assume to be, the time Scott passed away. Apparently the guy had a penchant in his teens to date many women and party hard up until his late teens. Honestly, he didn't discriminate with age, race or looks. There were just that many women in his life, the oldest rumoured at being forty and one of his fathers employees. There were the various news articles about his and his sis-ters car crash and the implications of that event on him. The pictures of him through this time were drastically different from the ones from his childhood. He looked like a hardened youth, angry at the world yet devastatingly handsome. His clothes...damn. Biker leather and white t-shirts, silver rings and a hoop through his lip and eyebrow. There were a few tattoos too but not as many as he had now. He was a delicious bad boy dream in his teens. I could see why women even back then were so attracted to him. An assortment of pictures were readily available of Kade stumbling out of clubs, hands inappropriately exploring the women he was with in public, under age drinking. God, he must have been every parents nightmare.

Then abruptly came his army years which were less publicised, probably because of lack of information and due to the fact that he had been part of covert operations for part of that time. There were a few photo's of him returning home in his oh so sexy army uniform that had my mouth watering. He looked so sober in those photo's, all of a sudden very mature and serious.

My favourite pictures had to be the ones of his time in Oxford and his trips to London. Those were the ones where he looked happiest, with friends or alone, he had immersed himself in his studies and enjoyment, taking advantage of his time there. The articles were more positive since then until the recent scandal with Giselle.

He seemed to have many paparazzi after him and Giselle, the worlds dream celebrity couple. They all wanted a piece of them and I can imagine that kind of attention putting a lot of pressure on their relationship. Despite everything that had happened between them, I could see the level of respect they had for one another and the friendship they shared. I had no doubt that Giselle was in love with him. It was hard not to fall for someone like him.

I decided to go down and get a coffee, since I hadn't slept the whole night and felt groggy for it. Sadie had left early to go meet some friends and had left a note saying she would be back late evening. Allison was still spending her weekend with Brent so I assumed I wouldn't be seeing her until

Monday evening. I sat down at the kitchen counter with my coffee and a croissant and checked my Facebook. I had still been getting comments and likes on my clubbing pictures with *Kaleb*. I smiled when I looked at those carefree moments where he allowed himself to let loose, lost in his alter ego. I knew the moment was meant to liberate me but I couldn't help but feel like it was liberating him more. Or maybe this was a moment of liberation for *us.* The beginning. Either way, it was a revelation at that moment...that only sought to confuse me further.

I was reading a friends comment when my whatsapp messenger alerted me of a message from Ash with a link to an article.

> *Ash: You know how you said there were very few pictures and articles about Scott Carr?*

> *Me: Yeah...but then again I didn't search very hard for it to be honest. If I just search for him maybe I'll come up with something*

> *Ash: Well there's no need because I'm way ahead of you. You're going to want to read this article...it took a lot of digging to find it in some local articles from a small Colorado town.*

> *Me: Okaaay Sherlock, I'll check it out now.*

I tapped on the link on my phone whilst settling into my stool at the kitchen island. Nothing could have prepared me for the article.

August 30th, 2003

Body of respected Senator's son found on hiking trail.

The body of Scott Carr, son of Californian Senator Stephen Carr, was found yesterday - exactly two weeks after he had been reported missing - on a hiking trail near the Rocky Mountains.

Carr, aged only fourteen, had been on a hiking trip with some

classmates when he failed to return to his lodgings from a planned hike on August 15th. His friends and chaperone reported his disappearance within a few hours having found his discarded jacket on the trail with what appeared to be blood.

Authorities were unable to give us a detailed account as to what the cause of death was but sources say that Carr had been a victim of a gruesome attack. Witnesses report that the body of the fourteen year old, found at 6.40 am local time, seemed to have been viciously attacked by some kind of sharp instrument. Police denied foul play, indicating that it was rather an unfortunate case of an animal mauling the fourteen year old to death.

Among his friends on the hiking trip were Reese Stark (13), son of oil tycoon Ryan Stark and Kade Hamilton (14), son of Billionaire Media mogul Alastair Hamilton.

An earlier report from locals stated that the missing persons report filed with the police included the disappearance of Kade Hamilton who was said to be missing at the same time. These reports were neither confirmed nor denied by the police.

The junior Hamilton was seen huddled in a car with his parents this morning a few hours after the discovery of the body of his best friend.

Senator Carr was called in to formally identify the body of his only son early this morning and is said to be in shock.

There is a lot of speculation as to what really occurred after Carr's disappearance, leading to his untimely death. There is talk of a kidnapping of the wealthy Senators son gone wrong or just a case of a mugging gone wrong. In any case, a young life was taken carelessly and the authorities have not responded to the devastating discovery in the way that would be expected in a high profile case such as this and locals have been left confused and frightened by the unknown threat to their community.

The air seemed to have left my lungs. Scott may have been murdered. And if what the reporter was insinuating was true, Kade was with him when he disappeared and possibly when he died. Shivers ran up and down my spine. I felt little sick. *Is this what he wanted me to find?*

The fact that Scott, the son of an American Senator, was possibly murdered and it didn't really make the international news made this all seem like a cover up. What had really happened?

I hadn't realised that I had zoned out until my phone buzzed. It was a message from the devil himself.

> *You look cute when you're concentrating on something.*
> *Want to have lunch with me?*
> *K*

I jolted from my stool, looking around myself to check if he had somehow installed cameras in the house. Realising this was just one of his 'a compliment a day' things, I relaxed back into my seat. Then re-reading his message, I was surprised at what he had asked. I had just assumed that he would be difficult to reach now that he was back to his normal routine. His straight to the point message seemed a little strange, almost like he was thinking too hard about asking. I could picture him typing it out a few different ways before sending this version.

The words from the newspaper article were floating in my head, scaring me with the questions I wanted to ask him about it. I typed out a message as quick as I could.

> *Sure. Where and when? x*

I then proceeded to worry whether I should have added the 'x' at the end of the message. It was stupid, I know, but the written word was often interpreted in a thousand different ways by different people of varying dispositions. A reply sounded almost as soon as the message was delivered.

> *"I'll have a car pick you up at 12.30pm. Wear*
> *smart casual. See you soon.*
> *K x*

I smiled at the 'x' I got in return then frowned at his order to wear 'smart casual.' It was all a little ominous and the lingering uneasiness from my recent google discoveries, courtesy of Ash and her expert google sneak search skills, was making me feel nervous about meeting him. It wasn't that I was afraid, it was more that I didn't know how to ask him questions about his past without it being awkward due to the sensitive nature of the subject.

Glancing at the time on the clock in the kitchen, I realised I had little more than an hour to get dressed and rushed upstairs to make myself ready for the tense ride ahead.

***

"Good afternoon Miss De Luca," Luke greeted me as I walked down the front steps to the black heavily tinted Mercedes parked right outside. It became apparent that Kade owned more than a couple of cars, as was standard with the wealthy around these parts.

"Good afternoon Luke, thank you," I replied as he opened the door to the back seats for me. I sat down and then turned in surprise when I caught sight of Kade sitting a seat away next to me.

"Hello Alexa," he said in a low rumble. The skin on my arms prickled at the timbre of his voice.

"Hey...I didn't think you would be here," I replied still wondering if this was an illusion.

"Where else would I be?" Now he sounded amused and I was treated to a dimpled smile.

"I thought you would be at the restaurant."

"Well, I wouldn't be much of a gentleman if I didn't come and pick you up, would I?"

I finally allowed myself to take a good look at him, drinking in his dark designer jeans, white shirt and navy blazer. He looked tired, as if he had been up all night thinking. Or drinking. Possibly both. The tension in his body seemed to fade with his laughter when he caught me staring at him and that made me smile because *I'd done that.*

He sat back again and looked me up and down, making a show of it as I had done with him. An appreciative look took over his features. I was wearing a navy and white polka dot summer dress that came up to my knees. It was my favourite summer dress because the flared skirt made me feel really feminine. I teamed that with a navy three quarter length sleeve blazer and strappy tan leather gladiator sandals that tied up my legs. Red lips and subtle smokey eye make up with a light blush and my hair out it natural waves completed my look. Inadvertently, we were wearing clothes that matched. I looked good and for once didn't have anything to criticise about myself. But I still couldn't take his complement when he paid it.

"You look beautiful Alexa."

"Yeah, with bags under my eyes," I laughed. He moved fast, crowding me in my seat, making my breath hitch at his sudden movements and closeness as we whizzed past streets going God knows where.

"I'm going to repeat my compliment and you are going to accept it Alexa," he said in a stern voice. He looked me hard in my eyes, causing me to swallow some of the nervous excitement building in my body from breathing him in so close.

He moved his lips to my ear, stroked my cheek and in a low voice repeated, "You look beautiful Alexa."

He didn't move from his position, his breath fanning my hair, sending chills down my spine. I realised he was waiting for my response.

"Thank you," I whispered back. He moved to look down at me, still leaning close, one arm behind my headrest and one hand supporting his weight, pressed to the seat between us. He smiled sweetly at me as he shifted back into his seat as if he hadn't just taken my breath away. I also felt a little annoyed and from the smile on his face, he knew it.

Before I could contemplate this any further, the car slowed down to stop.

"We have arrived sir," Luke answered from the drivers seat. The whole journey had whizzed past without us noticing.

Kade smiled and exited the car. I went to open the door on my side when I found that he'd opened it for me, offering a hand to help me step out. This man left me speechless with more than just his good looks. I don't remember the last time that I had been in the presence of a real gentleman.

Placing a hand on my lower back, he led me into a quiet looking restaurant. From what I could make of my limited knowledge and terrible navigational skills, we seemed to be close to the Museum of Arts and Design in the Upper West Side, a place I had visited one weekend with Sadie, and a twenty minute drive from Kade's Lenox Hill residence.

I didn't have time to absorb my surroundings because Kade briskly walked us into the restaurant and nodded to the Maitre d', who immediately led us to a closed off private section of the venue.

"What's the rush?" I laughed as he looked determined to reach our destination without eye contact with anyone else in the building,

Once we reached the table for two in a beautifully decorated intimate setting, he pulled out my chair before anyone else could and settled himself quickly, waving the waiter away with some instructions for wine. Finally he looked relaxed and relieved as he smiled at me apologetically.

"In case you have forgotten Miss De Luca, I garner a lot of attention when I am out and about." I *had* forgotten. It was so easy being with him alone in the confines of the house or in his penthouse that I hadn't really thought about his social status much and the attention he would stir on this first real 'outing' together. His behaviour now just made it more scary and real.

"You're so humble and modest Mr Hamilton," I joked, smiling back at him.

"That I am, lass." The thick Scottish accent he put on made me giggle but it also made me ignite from within. *Damn that was sexy.* And so began our easy conversation about his heritage as we ate our way through starters and the mains. He told me more about his grandfather and great grandfather settling here having travelled from Scotland. How they had encouraged them to learn about their ancestors and never forget their roots. It was fascinating listening to their traditions and how his grandfather was initially against Kade's father marrying his mother because she was not Scottish but of Italian descent. She had eventually won her father-in-law to be over with her perfectly baked Scottish shortbread and oatcakes. I had to laugh at that.

"The way to a man's heart is through his stomach, as they say." He grinned at me as he took a healthy bite out of his desert, a little of the chocolate sauce staining his bottom lip. He licked it off and I felt it right in my naughty bits. And apparently I had started to think like a teenager again.

As we enjoyed the rest of desert, the memory of the early morning google search started creeping back in, ushering the elephant into the room with it. I swallowed my last bite as if it were lead and not a delicious and expensive signature desert made by one of the finest chef's in the world. I cleared my throat and bit the bullet.

"Kade...I found something about you online that was confusing. About Scott." I saw Kade visibly shrink into his seat as his eyes darkened with memories and his tan skin looked pale. At first his silence had me chastising myself. I had figured that when he had asked me to search for him on google, he wanted me to find these things out about him. It seemed that this particular information wasn't something he wanted to be found, judging by his reaction.

I started to feel nervous as the sudden change in our pre-viously carefree rendezvous turned cold. Kade stood sud-denly, grabbing his wallet and dropping a ridiculous amount of money on the table. The wait staff immediately flus-tered about grabbing our blazers and helping us put them on. Kade grabbed my hand this time, not sparing a look at the staff he had just two hours ago been so courteous to. I made to speak, to ask if he was ok or apologise or both but he turned swiftly before exiting, his face bent close to mine and through clenched teeth said, "Not here."

The journey in the car was tense as Luke drove us to Lenox Hill and Kade rubbed a thumb across his wrist absent-mindedly as he stared out the window. Halfway through the journey I swear I heard him curse, "Fucking Google."

CHAPTER FIFTEEN

All Hell Breaks Loose

"Drink?"

"Uh, yes please. Just some coffee." We'd been back in Kade's penthouse for ten minutes now and so far those were the first words he had uttered to me. The first thing he had done was go to his bar and pour a large amount of whiskey for himself, which he had then proceeded to knock back. After the third glass, he seemed to relax a little although the tension was still present.

I wondered if he had forgotten that I was there and contemplated leaving when I heard him ask me about a drink. Watching him walk back to me with my coffee from the kitchen, I felt a little relief when a small smile appeared on his face. He sat down next to me on the couch, leaving space between us as he turned slightly and leaned back so he could see my face.

"Thank you," I mumbled and took a sip, hoping the hot liquid would soothe my dry throat and nerves. I'd never experienced Kade in this kind of mood. I felt out of my depth.

"I'm sorry for the way I behaved earlier." I wasn't expecting him to apologise but I appreciated it anyway.

"It's not really your fault, I shouldn't have brought Scott up. It obviously upsets you."

Sitting forward he set down his glass on the coffee table and leant his elbows on his knees as he rubbed his face with both hands. When he sat up again, his smile was sad but in his eyes was a determination.

"It does upset me but you couldn't have known why it still haunts me to this day. Where did you find that article you read?" I put down my coffee cup and dug into my bag for my phone and handed it to him once I found the link Ash had sent me. He looked at it for a few minutes, his face not giving away much of his emotion but I could feel the tension still.

When he eventually handed it back to me, he sat back on the sofa and sighed.

"My dad put an enormous amount of effort into burying those few stories and speculations. The perks of being the 'media mogul.' Looks like one got away. It's not enough that I can't escape the memories..." He trailed off, looking into the distance at a harrowing memory. I gave him a few moments before I gently placed my hand on his arm and brought his attention to me as I spoke.

"Kade, you don't have to tell me anything. I just didn't know what you wanted me to see when you asked me to Google you last night."

"I thought you should get to see the negative publicity I've had from my earlier years of recklessness so you got an idea of what you're dealing with being associated with me. I didn't think you'd find this," he gestured to my phone. I smiled as I realised his was apprehensive that I would judge him because of the wild ways of his youth.

"I don't think you are so different from a lot of young professionals with a past they feel they should be ashamed of. You were a kid and then a rich 'heir' at twenty and you had an excess of wealth and alcohol and women. I think a lot of guys would have done the same. I'm not making excuses for it because yes you made bad choices at times but you were also hurting. I get that, I see that. I'm not about to judge you." I felt his hand remove mine from his arm and take it in his, the smile on his face was beautiful.

"And that's why I find you irresistible Alexa." Trying to keep my emotions (and hormones) in check, I returned his compliment the best I could. The mixed signals he gave me would forever be my companions, or so it seemed.

"Ditto." He laughed, a full manly sexy laugh that broke some of the tension around us.

"You're cute Alexa. And perceptive. Which is why I know that you can tell there is more than meets the eye with me. And although that should make me weary, it doesn't. So I'm going to share with you a truth that only my parents, Scott's parents and Giselle, Sadie, my lawyers and the relevant authorities know. James and Bonnie found out at some point too. In my opinion, that's still a large number of people that know what really happened the night Scott disappeared and how he died."

I sucked in a breath, steeling myself for what I knew was going to be difficult for him to tell me and difficult for me to hear. He squeezed my hand once before he settled himself better and cleared his throat to begin.

"We were on our annual hike, the kids of rich influential families trying to be 'normal.' Our parents would insist on it every year so we could have a relatively normal holiday just before school started again. That particular year was the fist time we weren't accompanied by our parents or siblings. We wanted to have a strictly boys only holiday. My dad agreed that we could go as long as we took a chaperone. In the end Colin Stark, Reese's older brother who was eighteen, agreed to go with us provided he had his own cabin next to us." He paused and looked at me, smiling as a memory found it's way back to him.

"We were like brothers, the three of us. Reese was the youngest just by a few months but me and Scott had birthdays in the same month. Reese was a prankster, always pissing us off with the shit we would find in our beds and scaring the crap out of us by hiding in the most stupid of places. Scott was more mature but he could take a good joke. He constantly reprimanded Reese but he would always laugh with him. We had so many good years together as children, it used to seem like we were invincible. Scott's mom called us the 'Terrible Trio.'"

Kade stood up and walked over to a cabinet I hadn't paid much attention to before, at the side of the room. He pulled out what looked like a small leather photo album. He walked back over to me and placed the album in my lap as he sat down then flipped open the first page. I saw a picture of three young boys, maybe aged six or seven, in scouts uniforms looking muddy and standing at the end of a dock. One was unmistakably Kade with his beautiful blue eyes framed by long dark lashes, a mischievous smile on his face. The other two boys were blonde but one boy had green eyes and the other brown and was taller than the other two. Both the blonde boys had an arm around Kade's shoulders as he stood in the middle holding a string of fish they must have caught that day. I smiled at the picture, having never pictured Kade as a boy scout.

"That's Reese with the brown eyes. He was always tall for his age and proud of it. Scott was the shortest but just by a couple of inches. It never daunted him though, he always said that he knew when he grew up he'd be taller than us both. If only he knew how short his life would be." Kade's smile died on his lips and I found his hand again as I squeezed and allowed him some time to collect his thoughts as I flipped more pages of the album. So many memories had been placed into the album, smiling photo's of these young boys that looked like they didn't have a care in the world. Pictures taken in various iconic places on holiday and the at family barbecues with their parents and siblings. I saw the roundness of youth melt into more defined features and taller bodies up to the last photo's of them aged fourteen.

My hand lingered on the last photo in the album of the three of them standing by the sign for the Rocky Mountains National Park, gang signs and thumbs up beside an older teenager, presumably Colin Stark, who looked like he'd rather have stayed home.

Kade rubbed his thumb along the picture of his best friends and him reverently.

"This is one of the last pictures of the three of us together. Scott's mom made these albums and gave them to me and Reese on the day of his funeral. She said she wanted us to always remember him this way and not the way we found him." He seemed to lose some of the colour from his face at the memory.

"Do you want to take some time Kade?" I asked tentatively. I didn't want the man I was growing too attached with to relive the most painful memories of his life if he was hurting.

"No. I'm ok Alexa, I want to tell you everything. I feel like I want to."

He squeezed my hand this time and rubbed soothing circles with his thumb on the back of it as if I needed the calming gesture. Taking a deep breath, he started the story of the day everything changed.

***

"It was the last day of our trip, the sun was about to set and we decided we'd get our smores on the fire outside before it died out. You know, real manly stuff," Kade smiled. Sitting back he closed his eyes and continued.

"Colin was shacked up in his cabin with some girl he'd coaxed into his bed with his stash of beer and vodka he'd snuck into the trip. He was...getting busy...so we preferred to be outside where the noise level coming from his room was a little more bearable. Scott went into the cabin to get his jacket because he was getting a little cold when we heard

250

him scream and then shout and curse. Turns out Reese had put ants and lice in his bed and some other bugs in his sleeping bag. Man was he pissed when he came back out, shouting at Reese for being a dick.

That whole week that we'd been there, Reese had been ribbing him the most and I think he finally just snapped. Reese was shouting back at him and they got into the worst fight they had ever been in. I even had to break them apart at one point. And then Scott stormed off into the woods. I don't know why he didn't just stay. He'd never stormed off before, I mean, he was the most level headed of us all. If he had just stayed..." Kade's eyes clenched at the memory. I pulled his hand into my lap and rubbed the soothing circles he'd been soothing me with into his skin. He took another breath to continue.

"Scott was gone for five minutes, just five minutes, and I knew something bad had happened. I'd been ripping into Reese for being such an asshole and when I realised Scott hadn't come back I started to panic. We were both banging on Colin's door to get him to come help us look. When Colin stumbled out stinking of alcohol, it took us another five minutes to explain that Scott hadn't come back. To anyone else it might seem like a silly amount of time for someone to be missing to start worrying but out there in the forest surrounded by the unknown and with it suddenly pitch black outside, we just didn't want to take a risk. He could have fallen and hurt himself or gotten lost. But what happened was worse." He stood up and slowly walked over to the mantel over his fireplace, his back to me as he spoke.

"Colin finally pulled himself together and we decided to take our flashlights out and call for Scott. By now, it had been about fifteen to twenty minutes since he'd left us. Colin was still a little unstable so Reese went with him on one route through the trees and I went on my own down another. I walked as far out as I could but couldn't see anything or hear anything. I was about to give up and go back when I saw something glint on the ground. When I bent down to take a closer look, I saw it was Scott's Foo Fighters button that he always wore on his jacket. Worse still, there was torn blue fabric on it and what looked like blood. I was panicking so much about what this could mean that I didn't really register the faint sound or the shadow stepping out of the dark to hit me on the head. I blacked out instantly. When I came to, I was covered in scratches and blood and in some dark dungeon behind bars and Scott was there too, unconscious and hurt worse than me. We'd been dragged like hunters game through the twigs and dirt and splinters of the woods to this place and we had no way to know where we were."

I couldn't contain the gasp that left my mouth, involuntarily standing up and moving towards Kade. My natural reaction was to put my arms around his waist from behind him, feeling him shiver from the recollection. I had an indication that Scott had met foul play but never had I even thought for a second that Kade was involved in any way. Especially as a victim. God knew what he had witnessed and been subjected to.

He squeezed my arms around him, his back still facing me as he tried to steady his breathing. I didn't know what to say to him so I let him continue in his own time.

"I felt like I'd been screaming and pulling at those bars for hours before Scott regained consciousness and started screaming with me. It was a long time before he came for us. He was old, to us anyway. He must have been in his early fifties. He looked like a hobo from a distance but up close I noticed his shiny white teeth and even though his clothes looked hand stitched they were clean. His hair was long, beard was long and dark with bits of white. But it's his eyes that I still cant get out of my head. Dead, evil and calculating eyes. He just stared at us screaming and begging to be let go and started laughing like a maniac. His spit was flying out of his mouth, eyes crazier than before. He was enjoying our pain. I didn't realise how right I was until I saw just how depraved he was." I started to shiver myself and Kade pulled my arms away from him to lead me to sofa again to sit down. I couldn't speak and somehow knew not to. There was nothing I could do to comfort him just yet and it made me feel useless.

"He would leave and then return after a few hours and we'd pass out somehow and wake up again, in pain. I found out later that we were subdued by some kind of taser. At some point he dragged Scott outside the dungeon into this hall that was bathed in light. There were some medieval kind of devices there, a chair with shackles where he secured him and so many blades and knives. Thats when I saw the dried blood all over the ground. I threw up and passed out. When I woke up the next time, Scott was in the chair facing me from the outside, his stomach had been cut open, h-his intestines were out and he was just gurgling blood from his mouth. I just - I -" Kade covered his face with his hands as the big man I had come to see as a strong and confident man let himself break and shiver with the fear and deep sadness in front of him, his eyes watering with emotion.

"I'm here," was all I could say as I curled myself around him on the sofa. He eventually looked down at me, eyes so blue, haunted and glistening with emotion I wished I could soothe.

"The man had removed some of Scotts flesh. He was sitting at a small table eating it." I couldn't stop myself from gagging. The horror and dread I felt was just a fraction of what he must have felt.
Kade shook his head as if to clear the image and rubbed my back to settle me.

"After some time, the man left. I hadn't realised I'd thrown up all over myself. The stench of death and decay was overwhelming but all I could see was my best friend in pain, dying slowly. His breath was so shallow and his voice raspy but he kept trying to say something to me. Eventually I could only make out the words "go' and "run." I didn't know why he would do that for me, I couldn't leave him. And even if I could, how would I be able to leave undetected? I sat there and cried, he was dying and all he cared about was getting me out of there. He was dying, Alexa. I couldn't do anything."

I felt the tears as he buried his face on my shoulder while I gripped him as hard as I could, unable to stop my own tears. We stayed in each others arms for a while, soothing one another from the horrors of the past. When we had calmed enough to breathe normally, I asked the question that was plaguing me now.

"What happened after Kade?" He took a shaky breath.

"Somehow in and out of consciousness Scott knew the man was a little further away from the part of the dungeon we were in. He kept trying to indicate slowly with his eyes, mouthing for me to go. The man had left the cell door open, I dragged myself up from the floor and crawled as quietly as I could. I hadn't realised until then that I had a sharp pain in my side. I pulled my shirt to see a large cut, it had definitely been made with a knife. There were also other knife wounds all over my body but not quite as deep. I was in a lot of pain but Scott started to convulse in his desperation to get me away.

I hesitated for a moment, he was looking into my eyes and I could see my best friend still there frightened but strong. Man, was he the strongest bravest person I've ever known. His body may have started to give up but he was still there. He just kept trying to say 'go' and I did. I tried to go quietly through a narrow dark hall and I couldn't see any sign of the man. It was cold down there, and I had the pain from the stabbing wounds on my body but I just kept thinking that if I get out I can get help for us both.

I reached the end of the dug out hall - we'd been in a cave in the forest this whole time. People must have been looking for us. I didn't know how long we had been out there but it was day time now and I could see the man out in the woods a little ways away. I watched for a second before I summoned all the strength I had and ran. I ran barefoot and bleeding and I could hear the man shouting in confusion but I had an adrenaline rush and fight for survival on my side. He couldn't keep up or find me. I ran for so long, I don't know where and how long but I didn't dare stop. Eventually I heard helicopters up ahead and reached a clearing where I started shouting and screaming for help. They found me eventually. We'd been missing three days, they told me. I'd lost a lot of blood and needed a transfusion and some surgery for the deeper stab wounds. I was hysterical, trying to get them to go back for Scott.

In the time I'd been held captive with Scott in that cell, he kept telling me that if he didn't make it to tell his mom, dad and sister that he loved them. It was almost as if he knew he wouldn't make it. The emergency care and the cops kept trying to get information from me but they couldn't figure out where this cave was. I was shipped to the hospital and knocked out with sedatives because I refused to stay down. They didn't find him until ten days later. He'd been stretched and had his bones broken on some medieval device called a rack and his body wasn't completely decomposed. The man had removed parts of his body. His heart was missing. My best friend suffered the most horrific and painful death and I couldn't do anything to stop it."

CHAPTER SIXTEEN

Phone jacker

My mind was reeling from everything Kade had just told me. The horror of a real personal experience coming from someone that seemed to have his life almost perfectly put together, made me pause for some time to gather myself before I spoke.

"You can't put blame on yourself for something you couldn't have possibly been able to stop. How could a four-teen year old overpower a grown man? Kade, Scott died an unimaginably painful death but he still wanted to save you from that. He had accepted that he was going to die."
Even as the words left my mouth, I knew it wouldn't be enough to really console him. The situation was bigger than I could have imagined, his burden and pain from the past just too big to soothe with just words.

Suddenly, everything made sense - his spiralling out of control, the lucky escape from the crash and his sisters stint at the hospital driving him to join the military. His leaving the military due to his injury and mothers delicate state and then moving to London to study just to start afresh. And most of all his connection to Giselle. He'd been carrying his past around with him for years, even though it wasn't com-mon knowledge, but it was his cross to bear.

I glanced at him sitting back on the couch, staring up at the ceiling. He looked like he'd aged ten years all of a sudden, the tension evident in the muscles of his body and the frown on his beautiful face. I moved closer to him, careful not to startle him, and put my arms around him. He surprised me by pulling me flush against him in a one arm snuggle.

I could smell his cologne and his natural scent and felt the kind of relief, comfort and security that I hadn't felt since... since...Tom. The realisation startled me. I didn't think I could feel that with someone else and so soon. In my mind, getting over Tom should have taken longer. My reaction to Kade made me feel like maybe I wanted him out of lust. It was one of the reasons I wanted to back away from him because although I really liked his personality and he made me happy and laugh every time we were together, my brain kept telling me to slow down and think rationally.

Kade cleared his throat to speak and I collected my thoughts. *Concentrate on Kade right now. Think of what you're feeling later.*

"I couldn't handle it Alexa. When they couldn't find Scott I was hysterical. My parents, Scotts parents and Reese's Parents flew out as soon as they found out we had gone missing. The state in which they found me made my parents break down. When they found out Scott wasn't with me and after I had given my statement, his parents just gave up on life. I refused to come back home after the surgery despite everyone trying to force me. I said I wouldn't go until Scott came back, even though I knew we wouldn't get him back alive. When we finally got his body, everyone left. My dad had paid off everyone he could think of to keep this out of the media. No one should have even gotten a scent of it. Mr Carr, Scott's dad, is one of my dad's best friends. He didn't want to cause him more pain and he didn't want me to live with the constant reminders of being a victim and the harassment in the public eye."

"He was protecting you all. He sounds like an amazing dad," I smiled sadly at him.

He gave me a small smile in return. "He is. I'm lucky."

"Did they ever...catch the guy?"

"My dad and Mr Carr managed to hire some of the best private investigators in the world on the case, alongside the police detectives. They collated a file of over fifty similar cases in the region that somehow had been overlooked as suicides or accidents with animals being the reason for the state of the bodies when they were found. There were still a lot of missing people in that list. All the information was presented to the lead investigator in the FBI and they had profilers come in. Within three months they got a lead.

Along with my description of the guy that had been sketched by an artist, we found out that I was not the only one of his victims to survive an attack. A woman who lived in the locality came forward when the investigators started looking for the man with the sketch. She didn't say anything at first, I mean who would? She lived nearby, she was in constant fear that he would come back for her. But something made her speak up later, when she walked into he police station. She asked to speak to a female officer. When alone she revealed she knew the guy personally. He was her old neighbour as a child and he'd been overly friendly with her when she was growing up, to the point that she felt uncomfortable. He started peeping through her window when she was a teenager but she had been too scared to tell anyone because he'd threatened her a few times when she had caught him. His obsession reached boiling point when he kidnapped her one night and subjected her to hours of sexual abuse and torture in the basement of his house, just a few houses away from her own. He said he would let her live and leave her alone if she never told anyone. It was bizarre because she thought he was definitely going to kill her. But he let her go and she fabricated some story, telling her parents that she had snuck out to see a friend and got grounded. Sure enough, the next day he just disappeared. No one heard from him or saw him around for years. She lifted her shirt to show the officer marks from blades made years before and carved into her stomach were the words, 'Property of M.Bates.' The guys name was Marlon Bates."

"You mean like Bates from the film Psycho?" I said with my mouth agape. Kade gave a dry laugh without humour.

"Yep, you can't make this shit up."

"That's so fucked up." He was silent for a few seconds, collecting his thoughts.

"Bates didn't really stay away though. He started to live out in the forest after selling all of his property and belongings. He'd built shelter for himself out there and had lived like some kind of survivalist."

"The cave," I stated the obvious.

"Yeah, the cave. But he made a mistake, he came back every year on the day of the woman's birthday. He would make her stand in front of him and show him his mark on her stomach and then he would rape her. It was like he owned her and she couldn't shake that. He would always be there. Thats why she could recognise him from the sketch of him as an older man. She couldn't live her life as a normal person, couldn't form a relationship with another man or have her own family. She was terrified of that day she would turn a year older and he would arrive and continue his control and abuse over her. She would think of running away but he would somehow always know and be ten steps ahead of her, sending her a note telling her that he knew what she was doing. He'd been watching her. So that day when she walked into the police station she demanded that they keep her there until he was caught or she would kill herself."

Kade stretched his legs out and I felt conscious that I may be tiring his arm and went to move but he pulled me close again. I settled into his arms again, feeling the warmth seep into my soul.

"Please tell me they caught him before he could run," I

asked, absentmindedly drawing circles on his chest with my fingers.

"They caught him. Bates thought he had been clever but he had underestimated the woman. She may have been terrified of him but she had many years to think and plan how to end his life or hers because she couldn't take it anymore. She had followed him back twice to see where he went. She drew a map and it turns out he was never that far from her. She was his obsession, after all. The longest tortured victim. And what was even better was the fact that he would give her his trophies from all of his murders on her birthday. She had kept them knowing they belonged to other people. She led us to him."

"My God. What a brave woman." I don't think I would have survived all that abuse over so many years.

"She is an exceptional woman. Whilst some may argue that she had allowed him to carry out all those murders by staying silent, I can only imagine what it must have cost her to keep it to herself all those years, fearful and tortured. She was the key witness when we went to trial and she was so amazing. The thing is, this man is evil even behind bars. He started sending letters to me, I became his new obsession and he would contact me for a visit nearly every month with a letter but obviously my parents intercepted those and by the time I was older he knew more about me thanks to the media so he would send me birthday cards and on Scott's death anniversary he would send me a 'gift' in the form of another body buried out in the woods of one of his many victims on the missing persons list. His condition for me receiving this 'gift,' as he calls it, is that I meet with him before my birthday." I felt his muscles tense as he revealed this information and I could tell he was clenching his jaw without even looking at him.

"The bastard! I hope he rots in jail." I couldn't help the dread I felt for him, having to meet with the man who murdered his friend in front of him and had tortured him for so long. I knew without him telling me that he had kept his end of the deal because there was no way Kade would let a family suffer when he could do something about it.

"He was found guilty and sentenced to death by lethal injection. He's been on death row all these years and the date has been moved a few times due to appeals etcetera because of his now old age but I'm waiting for news of the date being set any day now. As time passes, he's been found guilty for almost 67 murders, of which only 32 bodies have been found. Some were locals, some were tourists but a lot were troubled souls or homeless people he had picked up from somewhere in his car - people whose family members would expect to be gone for some time without contact. Each and every person on that list of missing persons is being found each year having been on the scoreboard of one of the worst serial killers the world has ever seen."

I balked at the number of his victims.

"You're amazing Kade, to go there and sit near that vile man just so you can get those bodies back to their loved ones. I don't know how you do it." Kade pulled back slightly and smiled sadly at me.

"It's the only way. And since the year began and he knows he's running out of time, he's been asking for me to come every month for two names and burial sites at a time. It's been the shittiest year of my life."

"Im sorry you have to go through all this alone. I want you to know I'm here for you Kade, as your friend. Thank you for sharing this with me, I know it couldn't have been easy to relive it all."

"You made it easier just by being here," he smiled easily and I felt a bit of the tension slip away. "I'm not used to being seen as the weak emotional type," he joked as I play punched his arm.

"I don't think there's anything wrong with being emotional but I definitely don't think you could be mistaken as weak," I replied, eyeing his muscled arms and torso with a giggle. *God I'm such an ogler!*

"Subtle, Alexa," he laughed for the first time since he'd sat me down in his apartment to tell me about Scott.

"Can't blame a woman, can you?" I smiled up at him, still comfortable in his arms. He laughed it off and peeled himself away from me to grab the television remote.

"Enough of the horror stories. How about we watch a movie? Your choice." I was relieved he was able to let go and relax a little after his revelation and with that started a marathon of comedy, pizza and a thousand laughs trying to get through the tenseness of the air around us after his revelation, as Kade allowed me to be his friend. The kind that lusted after him with a vengeance.

***

The following day I woke up feeling contemplative. I had been dropped off late at the house, a kiss on the cheek.

Pouring a mental bucket of ice over my lingering thoughts, I got up to get ready for work with the thoughts of Kade's ordeal with Marlon Bates heavy on my mind.

Throughout the day, I was quiet and deep in thought. The huge secret I'd been entrusted with weighed heavy on me and I kept thinking of what Scott and Kade went through. I felt horror and sadness and loss and anger all at once.

Tuesday was much the same only I was annoyed because I'd only received one text message from Kade on Monday saying he was out of town for some business and he hoped I'd have a good day. So by Tuesday afternoon I was stewing and annoyed with myself for behaving like a teenager. Again. I was happy to have his friendship, he had made it clear we weren't going to have anything else and I had no right to feel like a needy girlfriend.

An hour before the Gallery was to close that day, I heard a phone ring behind the reception desk.

"It's Britney Bitch...."

Denise, our young part-time receptionist and full-time student, looked stunned for a second before bursting out laughing as the first beats of Britney Spears "Gimme more" rang out from what looked like my phone in her hand. Turning bright red and checking that there were indeed no patrons in the gallery, I grabbed the phone from Denise in a hurry to silence it. Sure enough, "Lickable Abs" was calling.

"What the hell -"

"You look particularly seductive this afternoon, Alexa," the smooth voice came from the other end of the line. I tried to keep the smile out of my voice as I responded, my heart pounding faster.

"You couldn't possibly know how I look today Mr Hamilton since the last I saw you was two days ago. And you really need to stop invading my privacy."

"Madam, if you want me to stop invading your privacy then you had better set a code to lock your phone. And if you insist on leaving your phone unlocked, at least log out of Facebook. Also, I know exactly how delectable you look because I'm standing right outside your establishment."

I turned to face the windows to the street and sure enough, he was standing there in his suit, one hand behind his back and the phone to his ear in the other, grinning from ear to ear. God, he looked delectable in a three piece designer navy suit with vest, white shirt and blue tie. His messy hair slightly tamed. *Please let them be tan shoes with that suit... please tan shoes...RESULT!*

When he walked inside, I couldn't stop my own grin as he brought his hand around from behind him holding a large bouquet of calla lilies mixed with roses in the most beautiful shades of red, orange and yellow.

"For you." Could I look more like the cat that got the cream after the past two morose days I'd spent just thinking? But talk about giving a girl mixed signals.

"They are beautiful," I gushed, taking the bouquet from him.

"Just like you," he winked.

"Oh please, that was just cheesy!" I scoffed.

"Yeah but that doesn't mean it isn't true. And that further proves that you're still incapable of accepting compliments. Tut tut Alexa."

"You're such a goof ball," I laughed. He raised his eyebrows.

"An americanism...interesting. Are you already becoming 'Americanised?'"

"It's all the time I spend with these guys at work and Sadie. Don't worry, theres still a Brit in me yet. I cannot live without my english tea." He took my hand and kissed it, sending little shivers all over my body.

"Wouldn't want you any other way."

I was suddenly aware that I was still at work and although our last customers had left half an hour ago, Denise was trying hard not to look at us whilst reading her book. Jason was in the back in the office, Mary going over some accounts with our boss Michael, with whom I had yet to meet, at his residence and Clyde was due back any minute from his meeting with a buyer. Skylar had a day off.

"Um, Kade, is it okay for you to be seen here?" I hated that I was the one bringing this up but I didn't want to make the tabloids and gossip mags any more than he did. He laughed and pointed to two burly men standing guard outside of the gallery.

"The cavalry comes with me to the very public of places. Just until everything blows over in celebrityville in regards to my very public personal life. I estimate another week. There is bound to be another controversy caused by the Richardson Twins. So long as your colleagues don't say anything, I think we will be okay." He was still holding my hand and looking at me with his smouldering eyes.

"I don't think these guys will say anything if I ask them not to. Besides, we're friends." I swallowed the lie because even to my ears it wasn't convincing. *In my heart of hearts, I know I will always want something more.*

He smiled and let go of my hand as he turned away to admire the art work.

I hurried to put the flowers safely behind the reception desk and ask Denise for her discretion about Kade after explaining we were 'just friends' which she automatically agreed upon.

I caught up with Kade after giving him some space to explore. When I reached him, he seemed to be in a good mood, standing and admiring one of the renaissance pieces we had managed to procure ahead of the Gallery event exhibiting the beautiful art work produced by 'Enzo' or Jason, as I now knew him, that I had been asked to help organise and plan the coming Friday. Kade had been invited and I reminded him.

"Ah, yes, I received the invite. I'll be coming for a couple of hours. Is this the gig that Atlantis has got you organising?" I loved that he was showing a genuine interest in what I was doing.

"Yes, I'm handling the guest list, caterers, special client lists and viewings but Jason is helping me."

"Jason?" His frown was cute.

"Jason Ford." A look of recognition passed his face as his easy smile made an appearance again.

"Ah. I didn't know Jason was out here helping."

"It is his show after all. You know him?" I shouldn't have been surprised given the circles their families travelled in but still.

"Yeah, our dads know one another and we kinda all grew up *knowing of* one another. Plus our moms are friends, what with them both being of Italian heritage so it was bound to happen. There were always these parties and events. We'd get bored and sneak off and drink vodka in each others rooms or play pool. Or darts. A word of advice though, never play darts when drunk." I laughed as he winced at the memory.

I heard footsteps and as if on cue, Jason in his immaculate suit stepped into the room, smiling at me. His smile turned into a grin when he saw Kade.

"Well if it isn't Mr Gossip Central himself!" he bellowed. Well, he probably didn't shout it but in the usually quite gallery space, his voice echoed unforgivingly.

"Jason! I knew I could always count on you to enjoy my misery, bro." They did their man hug/pat on the back thing and I felt a little self conscious in front of two of the most handsome and sexy men I had ever seen. Though Jason exuded this fierce passion in his personality, it was Kade who drew me in every single time with his deep blue eyes promising more adventure than I felt I could ever bear.

"Hey, I was forced to buy a new tux for your wedding. My mom had been on my case since the invitation arrived. And then the reign of terror started with all the 'why can't you find someone to settle down with?' and 'Look how sensible Kade is! You need to be more like him!' So you freakin' owe me man." At Jason's revelation, Kade laughed a full belly laugh.

"I can imagine your mom giving you hell. She's planned your wedding since the day you were born." Jason laughed but gradually stopped as his brow furrowed.

"Seriously though Kade, how you been?"

I chose that moment to excuse myself to the staff room. I couldn't be there intruding on something so personal, even though I knew so much that others didn't know about Kade. Or maybe I just didn't want to know about Kade's feelings for Giselle. A feeling akin to jealousy and inadequacy crept over me but I shrugged it off. I was a woman, not a teenager. I needed a better way to deal with these emotions that crept up every time I saw the pictures of them together from the past and the articles I would read from time to time. She was in his past, I kept telling myself. He'd stopped having a relationship with her months before the official break up. We'd just started getting to know one another as friends. His personal affairs made public were part and parcel of being a Hamilton and everyone close to him had to accept that.

Making my way to the gallery lobby, I took my time arranging some of the printed information we were to hand out at the event, or *soiree* as Clyde kept reminding me. I could hear the men approaching and looked up when Jason called my name.

"Lexi, I'm gonna head out now for my meeting. Denise and Mary have already gone home, Clyde called to say his meeting had run over time so he will be going home from there. I'm gonna lock up so get yourself home to rest, you've been rushed off your feet with all the organising. I'll get David to check everything is secure." David, our security guard and a polite mammoth of a man, nodded and headed to the back of the building.

"Thanks Jason, I'll see you tomorrow." I gave him a hug and kiss on the cheek. before going to grab my light jacket and purse. I felt Kade's gaze burning into my back and then felt the full force of it as I faced him head on with my return. Jason was on his phone and waved goodbye.

"Are you ready to go? I'll drop you home. I needed to discuss something with you."

"Yeah, thanks Kade." We stepped out of the building and magically Kade's car came to a stop right before us, Luke at it's wheel. Settling in, I turned to Kade, noting how quiet he was as the car pulled away.

"What's wrong?" I asked. He shook his head as if to shake his thoughts and gave me a small smile.

"You're going to think I'm an idiot if I tell you." Now I laughed.

"I don't think thats possible. Try me."

"I felt a little jealous that you gave Jason a kiss and hug when leaving and I didn't get the same kind of reception when I walked through the door."

Well that was honest. I was a little taken aback but I wouldn't be a red blooded woman if I said that it didn't flatter me. It took me a few seconds to answer, I was still searching for the words.

"I guess I didn't know how you would feel if I did that to you..."

"It's not like we haven't kissed before Alexa." I blushed at the memory and I knew he got the reaction he wanted when he smiled knowingly as he continued.

"I guess I like to think that you're comfortable enough around me to treat me like you treat Jason."

"I...uh...guess I'll, um, keep that in mind next time."

We were quiet a few seconds, me looking at him from the corner of my eyes and seeing him grin, before I broke the silence.

"So, what did you want to discuss with me?"

"Oh, yeah. Annie's birthday party is this Saturday, you're my date remember? She was persistent that I remind you. And Jack Mangle's big fight is this Sunday. I really hope you didn't have any other plans because you're going to be seeing a lot of me this weekend." The excitement at the thought of spending the entire weekend with Kade was obvious from my face and it made him happy. Plus, it was Annie and then freakin' Jack Mangle on Sunday. Hardly a hardship.

"I am looking forward to it."

When the car pulled up in front of the house, I leaned over to hug Kade and kissed his cheek softly, conscious of the smile I got in return for being more familiar with him as he'd requested. Looking up into his eyes, I poured every ounce of sincerity into them with mine.

"I'm really excited for this weekend to start."

"Me too," he replied.

CHAPTER SEVENTEEN

Breaking Glasses, mending souls

T he last few days of the week before the big event at the gallery had me exhausted. The realisation that I had truly taken on a huge task and responsibility dawned on me with each day and I had to admit that I had actually started to enjoy all the event planning, despite being tired. When I wasn't busy at work, I'd get to text Kade.

He had continued sending his daily compliments via text. The latest was, 'You have beautiful ankles,' which had made me laugh so hard, considering they were a little swollen from the week of running around like a headless chicken.

It was now the day of the exhibition and I felt the biggest sense of achievement I had ever felt before in regards to my job. Everything had been executed perfectly and Jason was happy with the way every piece of his art work had been presented in the vast space and on the galleries white walls.

I had enough time to change in the back room into my navy blue long mermaid style lace dress with long sleeves. The lined fabric reached above my knees over which the lace fell in the mermaid style tail of the dress in a clever way that required no panelling. The sleeves were not lined, fitting the lace over my arms elegantly. The neck of the dress was a boat neck style and it fit like a glove.

It was a contraption that Clyde had picked out for me the week before upon finding out that I was going to go in a regular black dress. I laughed at the memory of his horrified expression when he saw the dress having followed me home to see me in it.

"I can't talk to you right now," he'd said, clearly upset. And then I'd been dragged the next day to Saks to try on every dress he could find for me, all of which were vastly out of my budget but then I remembered that I work hard and I might as well splurge just this once...and that was the thought that spiralled me out of control. I found myself with matching heels and another bag to add to my growing collection.

Standing there now, I admired myself in the mirror. *Not bad.* I smiled at my reflection. My hair was out in styled waves with a side parting. My lips were painted a matte rose pink, light blush, light smoky eyelids and eyeliner with the final brush of mascara. I felt as elegant as the dress looked and I couldn't help but wonder if my enthusiasm was amped up to this level because of my excitement and anticipation of Kade's arrival. Knowing that he would be coming here this night made me want to look good for him. It would be the first time he'd see me dressed this way, trying to fit into the society he was used to. The rebel in me argued that he would like me in anything I wore and I shouldn't have to conform but I squashed the thought. The event required it and besides, I liked looking pretty every once in a while.

I ran my hands down my dress and gave myself another once over before leaving the room to start the evening and wait eagerly for that mischievous smiling devil.

***

The guests had filed in soon after I had exited the back

room and in no time at all, nearly all of the people invited filled the huge Gallery space and mingled. Michael was due to arrive at some point in the evening so I was looking forward to finally meeting him.

The wait staff made sure everyone had a drink in their hand and the hors d'oeuvres were being served consistently. I was pleased to see that everyone passing me was as in awe of Jason's work as I was. There were a lot of serious art collectors in the room, willing to spend ridiculous amounts of money to procure their favourite pieces. Since Jason had entered the art world a few years ago as Enzo, his work had been an instant success with the elite of the art world. His most famous and his commissioned paintings and sculptures had, at their highest price, sold for millions and grew even more in value after. Yet this talented man that I had begun to form a wonderful friendship with was just so modest and humble. He would always come into the gallery in his suit but there would be a smudge of some kind of paint or something on his hands, sometimes even on his clothes. It was endearing to know he was just a regular guy in love with art, using his talent to gift us with the beauty he could create.

Said gentleman was currently a few metres away looking particularly polished and suave, being accosted by a bevy of beauties fawning over him asking questions about his work. Questions that were already answered in the literature I had tirelessly compiled and printed for the patrons.

He smiled easily at them and patiently answered their questions and laughed when he caught me rolling my eyes at them.

I checked my watch and turned to find myself facing a broad suited chest that was unusually close. Letting my eyes travel upwards, I found the smiling face of the highly anticipated Kade Hamilton. I took a step back to allow myself to breathe but I was happy to find that it seemed as if he needed it too. As he soaked in my appearance, I took my time to appreciate his. In his tailored black suit, crisp white shirt and black tie with black dress shoes and his slicked back hair he had confirmed to me that the theme tonight for the men was definitely suave. *Move over Henry Cavill!*

"Beautiful," he murmured, taking my hand in his and kissing it.

"Not too bad yourself," I replied, suddenly feeling very shy in front of him and noting a few heads turn to see the famous younger Hamilton.

I caught a movement to the right of Kade and realised we weren't alone. I tried to hide my reaction when he placed his hand on the lower back of a woman about his age, dressed in a fitted black off the shoulder gown, blonde hair tied back in a chignon, red lipstick on smiling lips. She was beautiful.

"So this must be the lovely Alexa," she said in her bright and cheery voice. I hated it.

"Yeah...Hailey, this is Alexa. Alexa this is my friend Hailey," he said looking a little embarrassed. Was Kade actually blushing? *He's been talking about me and she's his friend... retract those claws Lexi.*

"It's nice to meet you Hailey," I smiled genuinely, although a little surprised still. Why would he be telling his friends about me?

"And it's nice to finally meet you! God, that dress is beautiful! You look amazing!" Happy that this woman, unlike the many others giving us daggers, was not a bitch, I applauded Kade's choice in friends once again.

"Thank you," I blushed as I noticed Kade smiling intently at me. He looked proud as if I had passed some test. "You look stunning in your dress Hailey. I really don't have a clue where to start when it comes to choosing appropriate evening wear for events like these," I laughed.

"Well, you're in luck today because this lovely lady here is an up and coming fashion designer," Kade said proudly, hugging Hailey to his side as if she were his little sister. She one arm hugged him back and laughed.

"More like a 'struggling to meet the deadlines' designer! You should come into my studio one day, I can show you some of my designs. With a figure like yours, you would look gorgeous in them! Like this dress," she gestured at her attire, "it's one of my signature designs. You would look like a stunner in this girl, trust me." And from there the conversation continued about fashion and somehow ended up on the latest episode of our favourite drama on TV. Kade had hastily excused himself to talk to some older gentleman beckoning him from the other side of the room.

"God, I thought he would never leave," Hailey laughed.

"I think all our lusting over Count Leonard made him queasy," I giggled. Hailey suddenly grabbed my hands, a serious look on her face.

"Alexa, I just want to know something truthfully. Please don't mind when I ask you this but I need to know that you're not going to hurt him." I could see in her eyes that she wasn't joking and although I felt uncomfortable and a little offended because she was making a massive assumption as well as interfering, I knew the inquisition came from a good place and wasn't meant to be malicious in any way. Looking at her just as intently, I gently squeezed her hands and answered truthfully.

"Hailey, Kade and I are just friends. He's made it clear he's not ready for a relationship and I've only legally been divorced for a month. I've come out of a *marriage* and although its been over a year and half since I separated from my ex I just need some space to breathe. Kade has made it clear that we're friends and I'm ok with that." Hailey smiled and squeezed my hands back.

"I'm sorry Alexa, I know that made you uncomfortable and it's none of my business but I'm a blunt person, I have to say something when I feel it. He really likes you, I see it when he talks about you. He may say he wants to be friends but I think he wants more. He has this fire in his eyes that has never been there before now. He didn't get that when he talked about Giselle or anyone else he's been with. He's so very dear to me and so many people, we just want what's best for him."

"I understand and yes it's not anyones business but I understand where you're coming from and I promise you that whatever happens, it's not my intention to hurt him in any way. I hope that can reassure you enough."

Hailey just smiled and nodded and we resumed a walk around the gallery as I pointed out some of my favourite Enzo pieces.

Hailey's talk had jolted me. I wanted to believe he saw me as more than a friend because of this attraction between us but I knew if we ever crossed that line, like we did with the kiss dare, it would ruin the new friendship that was blossoming between us.

Every once in a while my eyes would seek out Kade. He was usually surrounded by important looking people, deep in discussion and every now and then his eyes would meet mine and he'd smile and wink causing the usual blush fest. He was currently being accosted by a beautiful brunette woman and her friend. It was a bit of a shark tank in there with all the man candy and I could see quite a few women closing in on my man. *My man? Since when had I become the possessive type? Since when was he my man?*
Something about this woman putting her red painted claws on Kade's chest and rubbing up and down, as if he was more than an acquaintance, just majorly pissed me off. I knew I didn't have the right to be but I couldn't help it. The brunette man hunter must have sensed my scathing looks her way as she turned around and looked me up and down from across the big room and scrunched up her nose as if she had smelt something unpleasant and continued man handling Kade. Kade noticed the exchange but before I saw his reaction, I walked off into one of the private viewing rooms housing Enzo's more valuable pieces of art to be viewed by

appointment only. It was dim in the room, only low intensity light shining down on the painting and backlighting under the benches illuminated the room. Hailey followed me in and sighed.

"You got it bad, girl," she chuckled.

"That obvious huh?"

"Yup."

"Ugh! I'm such an idiot! I shouldn't be feeling like this." I let out a breath and looked up at the most beautiful painting I believe Enzo had ever painted. It was the piece I saw when I came for my interview at the gallery, of the redheaded fairylike creature sitting on the edge of the earth looking towards the sun. I let the colours bring into me a sense of calm as Hailey stood next to me.

"Alexa listen, have you not seen the way he looks at you? The way he's been watching you all night like you're the most precious person in the world and if he loses sight of you, that you'll disappear? God, I could only dream of that happening for me!"

I smiled at Hailey, a doubtful but grateful look on my face.

"It will happen for you. How could it not? You've spent an hour and a half with me and in that time you've offered me free fashion advice and services, all but threatened me to not break Kade's heart and perved on all the hot men and let me match make for you. You would be a hard person not to love."

Hailey hugged me and we giggled a little because I was match making *hard* once I found out Hailey had been single for a year following a bad break up and seeing as there was a lot of potential in the room...why not?

I heard the door to the private room open and shut and we left our embrace to see Kade standing in the doorway looking at me with intense eyes but a knowing smile on his face.

"Yeah...I'm just going to go talk to shortlisted hottie number two," she whispered in my ear and patted Kade on his shoulder as she sauntered out with a confidence that I wished I could possess even an iota of.

Kade crossed the small room. He took in the painting I admired so much, smiling as if he got what it was about.
I hadn't realised I was still holding my empty champagne glass and in an attempt to stop myself reaching out to touch his face on impulse and squeezed my hand around it, causing it to break. I dropped the remaining shards when I felt the sharp pain in my hand.

"Shit!" he shouted, grabbing my hand to inspect. A small piece of glass had cut through my palm and caused it to bleed quite a lot. He pulled a handkerchief from his pocket and wrapped it around my hand to stop the bleeding, lifted me over the broken pieces of glass as if I weighed nothing, even though I stated I was perfectly capable of walking, and sat me on a bench telling me not to move as he left the room. I hardly had any time to process what was happening when he appeared again with one of the onsite catering staff and a first aid kit we kept in our staff room. Kade turned on the main lights.

Whilst the flustered girl cleaned the broken glass, Kade tended to me.

"Are you sure you're not a doctor," I joked as he unwrapped my hand, cleaned the stinging wound, applied some antiseptic and placed a dressing and then a bandage neatly over my hand, securing it. He kissed my injured palm, sending shivers down my spine.

"I've been in plenty of situations where I've needed to know how to treat a scrape or two." His smile melted me immediately.

"Thank you good sir for taking such good care of me," I smiled back. I felt like he wanted to kiss me but was conscious that the girl was still in the room picking the last bit of glass.

"You're welcome ma'am. You need to take better care of yourself." I looked past his shoulder to see the girl leave and shut the door behind her before I impulsively put my arms around his neck and kissed his cheek softly and lost myself in his arms. He felt like home. That both scared me and made me want to just give in to my confusing feelings, consequences be damned.

Getting past his initial shock at my sudden act of affection, he gave me what I needed returning my embrace and kissed my temple affectionately. I adored this man for letting me have this. There were alarm bells in my head but I hit the snooze button on them. I needed this.

Eventually I pulled out of his arms, gently placing my head on his shoulder, one arm behind him, his one arm around me as we stood side by side in front of the beautiful art piece.

"This is my favourite of all of Jason's work, even though all his work is amazing. This one just makes me feel something different. The colours, the metaphor for looking to the sun. It's like giving someone hope."

"It is a beautiful piece. Jason is exceptionally talented. He's garnered a lot of attention today as well from his fans," Kade laughed.

"I see he's not the only one with 'fans,'" I half joked. *Shit. I sound like a jealous girlfriend.*
He turned and held me by my shoulders, peering into my soul.

"I don't care for fans. I never have. My politeness is a hazard but my reputation from my past dealings in the public follows me wherever I go and its hard to explain to some of those women that I'm not as interested as I may have been when my life spiralled out of control."

He leaned in closer, an invisible force pulling me closer too. I looked up into his eyes, pain of the past reflected there and my breath hitched. How could a person be surrounded by so many people yet feel so lonely? *You should know,* said the voice inside my head.

He stroked my lips with his fingers until I couldn't take it anymore. I couldn't decide whether to give into the temptation or pull away. A movement by the door made the decision for me as I pulled away and gasped. If I wasn't so worried about what had almost happened, I would have been in a fit of giggles because of the shocked look on Mary, the Gallery's accountants' face. She looked almost comical with her unusually tame appearance. Instead of her usual goth get up, she was wearing a grey dress and the least amount of make up I've seen her wear although there was no hiding her beautiful tattoos and piercings. She looked beautiful either way. But right now I was scared of what her reaction might be to seeing us, even though her open mouthed bewilderment was a clue. We were still standing close to one another and the way Kade had been touching my lips must have given her enough of an idea to jump to a conclusion.

"Hey Mary," I almost squeaked.

"Hey girl, whatcha doing over here?" I wanted to slap my new friend.

"I was just showing Mr Hamilton my favourite piece by Jason."

"Hmmm, were you now..." Mary was quite close to getting on my shit list. I turned my red face to Kade's laughing one.

"Mr Hamilton, why don't you get yourself a fresh drink? I'll meet you at the bar." This seemed to amuse him more.

"Of course *Miss De Luca*, I shall see you in a short while. Nice to meet you Miss..."

"Mary Oliver."

"Miss Oliver."

"And you Mr Hamilton," she nodded her goodbye.

He thankfully left us and I breathed a sigh of relief. Which was short lived.

"What in the *what* were you just doing here, you hussy?!" Mary pulled at the collar of her dress, clearly uncomfortable with the closed neck hiding a pretty tattoo of her black and white cat, Petunia.

"He's a friend Mary, nothing was happening," I lied

uselessly.

"Lexi, I think I know what a "come hither I want to suck your face off and then spank your ass" face looks like, 'kay?" My face heated a little more.

"It isn't like that! I mean, I'm attracted to him but we're both not in the right state of mind. It's...complicated." I sighed and sat down on the bench, head in hands. Mary sat down next to me, rubbing my back.

"It's ok. I get it. I guess I was shocked to see you here with mister sex god of the decade. And before you say something, I did not make that up. He was voted Mr Sex God of the year by Strut Magazine." I laughed when she gave me a goofy grin.

"I am so confused, I think I'm pissing everyone off with my issues. I still think about Tom, and his betrayal still hurts when I shouldn't care but then I feel...something... when I'm with Kade. I wish it was simpler."

"If it makes you feel any better, I stalked my ex Kyle for three months after he dumped me. I couldn't get over why he left me for that fake tit barbie. I would look into his bedroom window, steal some of his stuff from the trash. Real crazy shit. He threatened me with a restraining order when he found me outside his window one day. One particularly low day I found myself in front of my bathroom mirror with a used razor I picked out of his trash, holding it to my wrists. I didn't think I wanted to live without him, he was my first love. And then something made me look up, really look into the mirror and look at myself. That voice in my head asked me, is this really what you've become? You're not pathetic, you're not worthless. You're a freakin' genius, you're worth more than a sad ending. You're twenty one years old you psycho, go live your life!"

Mary turned to fully face me, her eyes showing wisdom beyond her years. I felt sad for my kooky, crazy friend and the pain she had been through.

"The point of my telling you this is that we all go

through a 'lost time.' We all become lost girls or boys. I have had a very few moments but they taught me so much. Mostly that the pain I felt was temporary. And I had to believe that it would pass and I would be awesome again. If I didn't think that then I wouldn't have met my Frankie because honestly I would have just been a sucky sad person. I've told Frankie all about my messed up shit and he still loves me. Go figure. So chin up, honey buns, that man is a hunk of candy every woman in that room out there wants to lick and su-"

"Okay! I get the picture love, thanks!" I gave her hand a squeeze in gratitude.

She smiled a wicked smile and stood up, dusting the skirt of her dress down.

"My pleasure. Now, what happened to your hand?"

CHAPTER EIGHTEEN

The Hamilton's

I awoke to the alarm on my phone and a knock on my door. It was Saturday, the day of Annie's birthday party. Sadie flew into my room as soon as I uttered the words, looking bright and cheery as always. She was dressed in a pretty summer dress, holding a plate of toast and cup of tea for me, setting it down on the bedside table. I couldn't grumble at her when she had brought me food. Plus, she was coming with us to Annie's party, seeing as she was a friend of the family.

"Thanks Sadie, I need to get my arse out of this very comfortable bed."

"You're welcome. How was last night?" I got out of bed to pee and then proceeded to tell her of the events of the evening through the bathroom, leaving out mention of the incident with Kade. After I had peeled myself away from Mary's inquisition, I had found Kade with Jason at the make-shift bar at the far end of the Gallery and had enjoyed their stories and jokes. I felt myself smile remembering them as I pulled on my clothes behind a vintage screen I had picked up for a bargain price in Brooklyn.

"Where were you? I thought you were supposed to come take photographs for us? *And* you were asked to come as my personal guest." I had actually invited Allison and Brent too, who had showed up for the last couple of hours having had dinner with Brent's parents earlier.

"I got stuck at the office so I sent Emily instead. She is amazing, don't worry. And I'm sorry I didn't show up to your first big event. I was really gutted but Allison said you did great hun," she smiled as I stepped out from behind the screen in my colourful maxi dress.

"I was nervous it wouldn't go as planned and I'd mess it all up but I'm relieved that it all went well. Michael, the owner of the gallery, didn't show up because he was unwell so I didn't get to meet him. Again. That also left me and Mary with a lot of the responsibility, in his stead, of the sales of selected paintings. But it was good," I smiled back, picking up the simple jewellery I'd set aside to wear.

If I were honest with myself, I had been shit scared I would mess up the deals and transactions with the ridiculous amounts of money being exchanged for Jason's incredible art. Luckily Mary helped me with that, even though she kept making if difficult for me not to laugh out loud at her dirty jokes when the clients were out of earshot.

Grabbing my sandals and bag we headed outside to a waiting car, in typical Hamilton fashion, to be driven to Bonnie's place for the kiddies party of the year.

***

The whole hour and half ride to Westhampton was filled with our tales of childhood parties and mischief. I enjoyed the way Sadie's face would light up when she talked about her brothers and although she feigned annoyance at their behaviour towards their only sister, I could see the affection she held for them in her eyes. Her parents sounded like a fun power couple, deeply involved in politics and business but very proactive in their children's lives.

I smiled, remembering my own mother and step father. I

missed them. I missed my little sister. Most of all I missed Granna with her sarcasm and wit. The more I thought about it, the more I missed everyone. I made a mental note to contact my only family member in New York, Brian, as soon as I got some time.

Before we knew it, we were driving up a beautiful winding drive to Bonnie's spacious home. The front door was open as we approached and made our way through the wide hallway into a big living space and towards the backyard, passing a few parents and children on the way. Sadie seemed to know a few people, smiling, waving and moving me forward quickly before she could be accosted.

"A few of my parents' friends, their kids and their kids' kids," she explained in a whisper.

"And you want to bypass them because...?" I replied, trying to contain my laughter at her comical expression.

"I don't like the Spanish Inquisition that ensues engaging in eye contact. 'Oh Sadie! How is life? I heard you're working as a photographer? What an exciting *hobby*! Are you *married*? No? *Boyfriend*? No? Oh...' " Sadie's high pitched imitation tickled me into a giggle as soon as we got out into the spectacular garden and pool. I was still laughing when Kade walked out to us in his swimming shorts and flip flops all Hasselhoff style complete with dazzling smile and wet hair, carrying Annie on his shoulders. She looked like a little princess sitting perfectly perched, waving at us.

"You came, you came!" She shouted, wriggling to be let down as Kade gently placed her onto her little feet.

"Happy birthday Annie," I smiled at the little pink birthday girl, handing her the gift that I had wrapped in rainbow coloured paper.

"Happy birthday princess," Sadie said, kissing her cheeks.

"Thank you! I have so many presents! I'm going to go give them to momma." And with that, the birthday girl was gone and we hardly saw her for the rest of the party since a horde of kids were surrounding her the entire time with the poor entertainers trying hard to tamp the hyperactivity of some thirty or so little dears.

"Thanks for coming," Kade said sincerely.

"I wouldn't have missed it for the world. Even if my feet are sore from being in heels the whole night last night." I felt a sliver of pleasure, remembering the way he was the night before. A quick glance in his direction told me I wasn't alone with the memory. I quickly looked away, knowing that if I stared at him any longer, I'd be in trouble.

Sadie seemed to be a little preoccupied as she tried avoiding people who knew her parents or brothers. It was so odd being in an environment where everyone knew one another and had to keep up the appearances. I guess family gatherings at home may have been stressful for me but at least all the nosy questions came from concern and not just being a busy body.

The thought of my family brought me back to the present and made me realise just how nervous I was, knowing I was being surrounded by a lot of Kade's family and friends. It felt odd to be such a new acquaintance and having an invite to a private family event. It made me feel honoured to be included in their fold but I also felt a little bit like I was the freak *and* the entire freak show. Fresh meat, so to speak. Luckily, most of the people there were close family members and young parents with their offspring. Most of the time I felt like the insecurity was on my part but every now and then I would catch a puzzled or inquisitive look my way from one of the guests. I guess this was to be expected as a new face in their sphere. I tried to just shrug it off and in time I forgot the looks as Kade made us laugh and then took us to meet his family.

"You made it!" Bonnie smiled and hugged first Sadie and then me. She looked a lot bigger in the baby bump department than the last time I'd met with her, but she informed me that she was now in her second trimester.

"You must be excited," I smiled, taking in the fact that Bonnie looked amazing even when tired. This family had seriously good genes. A fact that was confirmed as we saw an older man and woman walking towards us and introducing themselves as Kade's parents. Kade's father had a head of salt and pepper hair and piercing green eyes. His strong features were so alike his sons that I could see what Kade would look like at that age. But Kade's eyes were his mothers alone. Beautiful blue and devastating. Although her dark hair had the natural silver streaks age brings, she looked like a model. Super genes indeed.

"It's a pleasure to meet you darling," she said with a hand squeeze after which Mr Hamilton seized my hand to plant a small kiss at the back of it causing me to laugh when Mrs Hamilton smiled and rolled her eyes muttering "like father, like son."

"And how do you know my lucky son?" he asked, his eyes smiling with mirth at making Kade squirm at the question. I could see he was worried that I would mention his secret lair to his father.

"We met through Allison at the gallery I work at," I replied, surprised I could lie so easily. Truth was, I felt the need to protect his secret too. I wanted it to be his safe haven, and for that safe haven to be near me. Bonnie knew but had promised not to out him. I still just wanted to keep something for *us.*

"Alexa and Allison know one another from school," Kade piped in, looking at me gratefully. From there, the conversation turned to Allison and the news of her and Brent's engagement and how happy they were together and then to my life in London. Soon Mr Hamilton was insisting I call him Alastair and Mrs Hamilton that I call her Andrea. I couldn't remember the last time I enjoyed a family occasion as much as this and was grateful to Bonnie and Kade for inviting me.

***

Later in the afternoon as the party wore down and most of the families and children had gone home, Bonnie and her husband David insisted we stay and have a few drinks outside on the deck around a fire pit that was lit, more for ambiance than warmth, while the children were put to bed and we waved good bye to the older Hamilton's. I finally got the chance to meet Kade's other siblings.

Jared, the eldest Hamilton, was a quiet but observant man. Handsome like his father, hair dark blonde like his fathers used to be with his mothers beautiful blue eyes. From what I knew, he was a banker and took time loosening up to others. However, Kade kept passing him drinks and soon he was laughing as much as we were. His wife, Shannon, was a warm petite lady, nothing like the tall supermodel I would have pictured him with. One look at them and you could tell there was a love story right there waiting to be told. They had two children, Parker and Sophie aged ten and eight respectively.

Kade's younger sister, Kirsty, sat there speculatively looking from me to Kade. Considering there was no open romantic relationship between us, I got the feeling she was trying to suss me out. From talk around us, I found out that she worked as an assistant editor for one of the magazines her father owned.

She had dark blonde hair like Jared but green eyes, also like her fathers. Pretty and elegant is how she came across - but also untouchable and unattainable.

The youngest Hamilton was also one of my favourite Hamilton's. Cameron Hamilton was a mini Kade. Tall like his brothers and father, lean muscles that his brothers teased he was building up, dark hair and sparkling blue eyes and dimples to match his brothers' - he was a young girls heartbreak waiting to happen aged only nineteen. He made it his mission to make me laugh well into the evening, unfazed when his siblings teased him about being mom and dads 'mistake.'

Sadie, Kade and I sat with his siblings and their partners, enjoying the summer night and easy conversation.

"They're just jealous that I got the best of the gene pool," Cameron winked at me, making me giggle when Kade threw an inflatable ball at him.

"You got what was left, doofus," Kirsty said dryly, trying not to smile.

"Whatever. Y'all love me really."

"Yeah, we do Stammeron," Bonnie said ruffling his hair after struggling over her bump to reach him.

"Stammeron?" I asked puzzled to which Sadie laughed and shook her head.

"When he was a kid, we could always catch him out on a lie because he'd start stammering to hide the truth. Mom and dad thought it was cute but obviously we just teased him about it forever," Kade answered.

"Do you guys have nicknames for all of you?"

"Yeah. Jared was 'Jarhead' because of his obsession with the Marines in his early teens," Kade laughed as Jared threw a cushion at him, "Bonnie was Bon Bon because it pisses her off and thats just too much fun to miss out on. Kirsty was Crumpet for a long time because she auditioned for a part in My Fair Lady at school and her cockney accent was just so terrible. And these miscreants called me Alikador because they thought it was funny to poke fun at my fear of reptiles." His siblings groaned as we laughed.

"These guys are always on at each other," Sadie said, lips twitching with mirth.

The easy flow of conversation had us sitting there late into the evening until we remembered that we had a journey back home to consider. Saying goodnight to the others, Sadie, Kade and I piled into the waiting car as Luke drove us back into the city and home. Kade dropped us home, with a promise to pick me up the next day for a night to remember.

***

"You're going to watch Jack Mangle?! Why didn't you tell me this before?" my cousin Hannah squealed on the other end of cyberspace as we face timed one another. Myself, Brian and Hannah had an obsession with Jack Mangle right from the beginning of his career and that hadn't really stopped. It helped that he was only a couple of years older than us so he had been a figure we could relate to these past eight years of his fighting career. Now I was telling Hannah that I would see him live in action and would meet him in person, thanks to Kade.

"Because you would obsess over it and nag me to get you pictures and autographs - even when you know I'd do that anyway!"

"Okay...you have a point De Luca. But don't forget to tell him I love him! And that I'll wait for him forever!" She said this whilst pulling a dramatic damsel in distress pose which was quite impressive considering she was holding her phone whilst doing it.

"Hannah, don't quit the day job." Hannah stuck her tongue out at me and we laughed.

"Let's see what you're wearing. I want you to look presentable when you meet my future husband."

I stood my iPad up by the dresser mirror and stood back to twirl and show Hannah my red skater dress paired with black tights and heels. I had pulled my hair up into a high ponytail and accessorised with a long necklace, hooped earrings and some bangles.

"Wow, hot stuff! Look at you! I wonder if this new hotter version of your former hot self has anything to with that guy you told me about?" Hannah was, of course, referring to Kade. Not that she knew exactly who he was. I was still bound by the NDA and Ash was the only person I had told. I felt guilty keeping it from her and my family, especially since Kade and I enjoyed a good friendship - even if the boundaries were sometimes unclear. I knew it was a matter of time before the media got a picture of us together and I was dreading it. Kade's father could only have so much control of the media, even if he owned so many of the outlets. I needed to talk to Kade about it as soon as I got the chance.

I managed to steer Hannah away from conversation about Kade and focussed back on her fantasy husband until I had to say good bye when the doorbell rang.

As soon as I sat in the back of the car, I felt disappointed. Kade was not there.

"Mr Hamilton will meet you at the venue, Miss De Luca," Luke spoke, looking at me from his rearview mirror as if he could read my mind as well as my expressions. I thanked him for letting me know and then sat back to take in the passing sights. It never ceased to amaze me that this was where I lived now. Opening the window slightly, I closed my eyes, breathing in the night air.

CHAPTER NINETEEN

Mangled

The Madison Square Garden venue was vast. Going there for the first time having seen it on television made it another site on my 'to do' list that was getting crossed off.

As Luke opened the door to the car and I stepped out, I was unprepared for the camera flashes and the red carpet experience. I managed to quickly hide my shock. I mean, I really should have remembered how I was arriving to the fight and exactly who my new friends were. I briefly enjoyed the look of confusion on the paparazzo's faces as well as the interviewers who were anxiously awaiting the arrival of the celebrities.

I wasn't really sure where I was meant to go until I heard a woman call my name. I turned to see a stunning blonde, who was very pregnant, come up to me with a huge smile on her face.

"Hi, I'm Lindsay," She surprised me by hugging me. When she saw me looking confused she rolled her eyes and continued, "Typical, he forgot to tell you. I'm 'Linds' - Kade's personal assistant." Understanding dawned upon me.

"So that time he was talking to 'his baby' on the phone, he was talking to your baby bump?"

"Yeah...he gets excited like a little kid high on candy when he sees a baby bump. He's lucky my husband thinks he's great otherwise there would be a smackdown. Seeing as my husband is a boxer too," she laughed, seeing my look of disbelief.

"Does he do that to all the ladies he meets?"

"Nah, that would be highly inappropriate. Just the ones he cares about. I know it sounds and looks crazy but it's his way of showing he cares for the little life I'm carrying here. I'm sure you may have seen him try with Bonnie's bump. She's a lot snappier when pregnant so I don't think she tolerates it." I thought back to the party last night and seeing Bonnie slap Kade's hand off of her baby bump and his wounded look. My heart softened to butter at his thoughtful weirdness.

"I have no idea what to say to that. It's nice to meet you Lindsay, you must have a lot of patience to work for him." Lindsay laughed prettily, her bright blue eyes sparkling. She actually was the personification of a glowing pregnant woman.

"I do but he's a sweetheart. I'll be going on my maternity leave soon so he will have to fend for himself for a little while. He asked me to come find you because he is arriving in a bit and didn't want you to get harassed or confused where to go. We can just wait here," she pointed to the foyer just inside the entrance of the building.

Lindsay and I talked for a short time before Kade arrived. I found out that her husband was a retired boxer, an injury making it impossible for him to fight any longer at the age of thirty two. He was now coaching some of the younger fighters and presenting on some sports channels. He would be there tonight supporting Jack Mangle. It was so exciting knowing I was so close to meeting my hero.

Soon there was a commotion up at the front of the red carpet as another black car pulled up. The door was opened and out stepped Kade Hamilton, solo, buttoning his blazer as he took off his sunglasses to tuck them into the front pocket. It felt like I was watching it all in slow motion, like in a dream. The way his hair moved in the slight late afternoon breeze, his hollywood white toothed smile, the twinkle in his eye that I like to think was just something to do with the camera flashes because otherwise there would really be something wrong with me.

Kade stopped for a couple of the cameras for both pictures and interviews. He was too far away to hear exactly what he was saying but he smiled and laughed along with the interviewer and posed politely for pictures with other celebrities the I recognised from TV. It was hard not to be impressed and awe struck by the number of famous people milling around. I was also impressed by the number of them that came and said hello to Lindsay, who in turn introduced me as her friend. I felt a little underdressed in my simple dress looking at some of the celebrities and their spouses in sparkling dresses and sky high heels.

We waited for Kade to find us as he made his way inside, hands tucked into his trouser pockets. It didn't take long for him to spot us and warm me up with his grin.

"Well, if it isn't Alexa and Linds," he said as he kissed Lindsay on her cheek and then pulled me into a hug that felt more than platonic. I could swear that he was breathing me in just as I was him and felt his lips brush the shell of my ear on their journey to press a kiss on my cheek. I could see Lindsay looking at us from the corner of my eye and let go from his embrace to shrug it off. As we followed Kade into the main arena, I met her eyes. She had a knowing smile on her face and it made me a little paranoid. I didn't want anyone to speculate about us when nothing had even happened. *Yet,* the greedy voice in my head said.

The anticipation and excitement was high as we moved further in, people already seated and waiting as others poured into the venue. Kade, Lindsay and I had seats at the front where we could see the action up close. We were lead to our seats where we found Lindsay's mountain of a husband seated and waiting. His name was Stuart Foster and under that frighteningly built body, he was a softy. He told jokes that had us almost crying with laughter and after a time Lindsay had to excuse herself to go to the ladies room, the joys of pregnancy she said. Stuart went with her to help push past the growing crowd of people. Kade turned his attention to me.

"Alone at last."

"Yeah." I felt conscious that someone somewhere would be watching our every move, especially seeing as Kade was sitting right next to me.

"So, how did you like my crazy family?" He said it with mirth in his eyes, making me think of the happy day we had spent together yesterday.

"They are all wonderful. I really didn't know what to expect when we got to Bonnie's but everyone is so down to earth and easy to talk to. I know you and Bonnie are great but I honestly thought it might be difficult starting a conversation with the others, which turned out to be quite the opposite. And your parents are amazing. I think it's my family that you would find crazy." I laughed at the thought of him meeting them.

"I'm glad they made such a good impression on you. I'd love to meet your family one day. No doubt they only know what the press say about me. It would be nice to change that opinion." I looked down at my black painted fingernails.

"Um, my family don't know about you." At seeing his wounded expression I hurried to add, "The Non disclosure agreement kinda makes it hard to say anything." Understanding filled his eyes and he laughed humourlessly.

"Yeah it does. I don't mind you telling the people you trust that you know me. I guess it's not always been easy to find trustworthy friends outside of my usual social circle.

I'm surprised you haven't told anyone."

"I told Ash but she's practically my sister. If I with-hold anything from her, I swear it comes to her in a dream or something. She hounds me like crazy until I tell her what-ever I haven't told her. It was impossible not to. Plus you can trust her with your life, she wont tell a soul. I don't even think she told her husband." Kade seemed happy with that answer.

"I'm glad you have a person like that in your life."

"Do you have a person like that in your life?" He was quiet for a few seconds.

"I used to think I had a person like that with Giselle but there are things I haven't even told her that I've told someone else. Can you guess who?"
I found my voice sounding small when I replied.

"Me?" He just nodded his head, a sincere expression on his face.

"I'm honoured," I said, my hand pressed to my heart and truly meaning it.

A look passed between us but before he could reply, Linds and Stuart came back and we settled into our seats to watch the warm up fights and then the main event.

***

"Mangle hiiiiiiiimmmmmm!!!!!!" I screamed at the top of my lungs, jumping out of my seat with just about every other Jack Mangle maniac there in the venue. Lind's was screaming with me, which only seemed to encourage me to out scream her. It was a bit of a bloodbath, and that was just our 'supportive cheers.' Kade seemed genuinely worried about the level of enthusiasm we were showing, whilst Stu-art just laughed and held onto his wife lovingly in support of their precious cargo.
The moment the hot and sweaty six and a half foot, dark haired and dark eyed muscular giant Jack Mangle laid out his

opponent for the last time, the screams and cheering were deafening. I couldn't contain my excitement. I was about to meet my teen crush in under an hour!

"Oh my God, he is so amazing!" I gushed as the referee held up Jack's hand, naming him the victor and then presented the charity title belt before they exited the arena for interviews and check ups.

"That man has crushed many a mans ego just by pummelling them. Physically and metaphorically," Kade laughed, pointing first at the bleeding opponent who was being led out and then at himself.

"Aww, do you feel threatened?"

"Duh. If he can get that much of a reaction from the ladies for doing that, it doesn't leave much hope for us regular guys."

"I'd hardly call you a 'regular' guy."

"Are you saying I'm extraordinary?" I smiled as I placed a hand on his chest and whispered in his ear.

"Absolutely." His answering look made me shiver and my shivering lit a fire in his eyes, as if he felt it right through his body. The moment was short lived as the venue started to clear and we were ushered to the after party in limousines towards a Manhattan night club.

**

The excitement from the fight spilled into the party at the club and everyone was buzzing. Drinks flowed easily and people chatted away excitedly while they awaited the arrival of the man everyone had come to meet. Forty five minutes later there was a roar of applause from the entrance of the club where Jack Mangle entered with his entourage. There was screaming from outside that followed him in as women shouted out offers to have his babies along with other unmentionable things.

Once he was in and the outside world was shut out, the

congratulations poured in. The fight had been amazing with both opponents evenly matched but along with that, the proceeds from the ticket sales and generous donations made by people throughout the fight, a record amount of money had been raised by them for a children's charity. Ironically, a violent sport was funding so many children's projects. Most of these projects were run by the Hamilton's and I found out that Kade and his brothers and sisters all had invested their time into quite a few of them. Kade's mother had been the spokesperson for the group of charities, herself a Human Rights Lawyer (something I had googled about her after I had met her and was immediately impressed by her extensive career).

I stood nervous and excited when the crowd that had initially surrounded Jack Mangle started to disperse, having had their piece of him and a picture proof they rubbed shoulders with him. My eyes widened when he approached and loomed over us, his beautiful face marred only by a small cut on his eyebrow and a bruise on his jaw. Even that made him look handsomer, if that was possible. I couldn't help my reaction, he was my teen idol after all. Jack smiled first at Kade and then glanced at me with a wink that actually made me want to swoon. I mean, who swooned anymore? I didn't even know such a thing actually really happened in real life, it was so confusing.

"That was some fight there Jack, for a second I thought you weren't gonna look too pretty when you got out," Kade joked as they man hugged. Funnily enough, standing next to Kade, Jack didn't look so intimidating.

"Yeah right, like Ruthers could ever get that lucky! I had to give the crowd something to watch, otherwise the fight would be over in minutes," he laughed back, his voice deep and mesmerising. I looked at him in awe until he caught my eye again and gave what can only be described as a panty dropping grin.

"Ah, sorry, Jack this is Alexa De Luca. Alexa is a big fan

of yours," Kade said, his voice laced with laughter at my goo goo eyed expression. Jack took my hand and kissed it. From the corner of my eye I saw Kade's eyes burning into Jack almost in a warning. *Maybe I'm reading too much into this.*

"Alexa."

"Jack." I stood quiet staring for a short time when I heard Kade clear his throat next to me.

"Um, it's lovely to meet you. The match was amazing," I managed, blushing at how inarticulate I had become just from being in his presence.

"The pleasure is all mine Alexa. And where has Kade been keeping you all this time?" Seeing Kade's face looking a little stormy, I decided I needed to get over my star struck self and have some fun.

"Locked in his basement," I whispered in fake seriousness. Jack raised his eyebrows and a smile spread as he decided to play with his friend too.

"Oh yeah? How selfish. Depriving the world of such beauty," he made a point of looking me up and down. Kade looked annoyed.

"He just wants me all to himself. To cater to his every whim. He only lets me out when I've been good."
Jack leaned closer conspiratorially.

"Does that mean you're usually a naughty girl?" I inched closer too.

"Absolutely."

"Do you two need a room or something?" Kade asked, looking positively stormy.

Jack and I looked at one another and burst out laughing with Jack smacking Kade on the back hard, which would have sent any normal person flying. Kade stared at us poker faced but eventually rolled his eyes and signalled to the bar tender for another drink.

After some more outrageous flirting, Jack eventually asked me to dance. Kade appeared nonchalant and let Jack pull me onto the dance floor. I felt a little disappointed that he now seemed indifferent when initially he was annoyed. Maybe he wasn't that into me anyway. The thought made me feel down but I didn't have much time to dwell on that when Jack pulled me into a close embrace to some techno dance music that was playing. He was a seriously funny guy once you got to know him and very easy to get on with, not to mention easy on the eyes. The shirt he wore looked like it had to be custom made to fit all his rippling bulging muscles and his dark hair was long and brushing his shoulders. He danced light-footed which was amazing for a guy so built. He would twirl me around and then bring me closer and dance to the beat and make me laugh at various comments on the people around us. I could feel eyes on me because I was with him but mostly the eyes of one particularly broody male, even though I couldn't see him. Eventually I started to wonder where he was in the crowd. I didn't have to wonder long.

Kade was laughing and being half mauled by a lithe leggy brunette on the dance floor, his hands on her waist and dancing like he had never danced before. It pissed me off.
I knew that Jack and I had basically decided to mess with Kade the moment we noticed his behaviour when I was fangirling. I hadn't expected Kade to just not give a shit. And now he was dancing with some gorgeous *whore.* Whatever. I was dancing with Jack Mangle. I didn't care. Not one bit. Not even when he looked over at me and gave me his regular smile and wink. *Bastard.*
So I hung onto Jack and flirted harder, danced faster, laughed louder. We posed for selfies all night and drank a few shots and laughed but all the while my eyes sought *him* out and all I really wanted was to dance with *him* and laugh with *him*. It made my heart hurt. *What am I doing? Why are we playing this game?*
A couple of hours in, I excused myself and sat down in a booth reserved for the man the party was for. He followed almost immediately, concern on his handsome rugged face.

"Hey Alexa, you ok? You feeling sick?" I smiled at how this tough guy that I had barely known two hours ago (apart from all his bio data I had on my wall on a poster of him at my parents' house) was secretly a cartoon watching nerd and such a sweetheart, showing concern to a lady he barely knew.

"I'm okay Jack, just exhausted. It's been a pretty full weekend." He nodded, looking into the distance. I noticed Kade looking at me and not listening to something the brunette *slut* was saying to him, worry on his face.

"You know, I've really enjoyed tonight. It's not every day you meet a girl who is ready to screw with your friends' head with you. You're pretty brutal, lady. I am in awe of your talents." He saluted me as I laughed.

"Thanks Jack, not too bad yourself. You're pretty convincing."

"Not hard to flirt with a beautiful lady," he grinned.

"Stop it! You're making me blush," I laughed.

"Kade has got it for you big time, Alexa. He looks like he wants to take me on in the ring," Jack motioned with his head at the direction where Kade was on the dance floor.

"I don't think so. We're just really good friends. He's said that he's not looking for a relationship."

"Yeah, we all say that until one day she's standing in front of you and you can't take your eyes off of her."

"You sound as if you're talking from experience," I nudged him playfully. His expression sobered.

"No, not my own experience but from seeing it happen for others. I'm still looking for that special someone. Only time will tell if theres someone out there for me."

"I'm sure there is. You're a sweetheart and no lady will ever be able to resist." I kissed his cheek and I'm not sure if it was the low lighting or something but I swear I made the formidable Jack Mangle blush. I made to move out of the booth and Jack stood up to let me through when I did.

"I'm gonna make a move. I have work tomorrow and

I'm exhausted. I'm so glad I got to meet you Jack, it's surreal."

"Like I said before, joke or no joke, the pleasure was all mine." He kissed my hand again and I made to leave when something he said stopped me in my tracks.

"I know he's crazy about you. He's never been jealous with any of the other women he's been with. Giselle could flirt all night with me if she wanted and he wouldn't think anything of it, he'd know I was fucking with him and laugh it off. With you, he's so high wired that he can't help himself, he looks like he's gonna bust a vein or something. Just, be easy on him if he's irrational tonight, okay?"

I turned and smiled sadly at him, not sure I wanted the huge responsibility of being the girl that made Kade a little crazy. It's not like he was bothered now anyway, he had a new brunette *strumpet* with him.

"I'll try. Take care Jack."

I had walked out towards the front of the club and had almost reached the exit when I heard him call my name. I turned to see him, hair tousled and buttons of his shirt open. His sleeves had been rolled up, showing off his corded and tatted forearms.

"You okay? Are you unwell?" His genuine concern drowned my annoyance that he'd been letting that *thing* rub herself all over him.

"Yeah...I'm just tired. Got work tomorrow so I'm going to get home and sleep. It's been a packed weekend."

"You must be exhausted. Just give me a second and I'll get our coats."

"No! It's okay, I'll get a cab home. You should stay. I'm sure you must still have a lot to discuss with your friend." Okay, so maybe not all of my annoyance had drowned, because I felt the bitterness in my voice on the word 'friend.'

"Ah." He gave me a sly knowing grin.

"Ah? Anyway, whatever. I have to go home now."

Kade grabbed my wrist gently but firmly before I could move away. He pulled me to a quiet alcove.

"You came to this event with *me*. You didn't dance with *me*, didn't spend time with *me* but you sure as hell will be taken safely home by *me*." There was a complaint in his voice as he said it and no matter how much he tried to hide it, it was there. Kade Hamilton was jealous and I could finally believe it. I couldn't help it. I smiled.

"Is that a complaint?"

"No. You can do what you like, you're not mine for me to have the right to tell you what to do but as the person responsible for you being here, I will be taking you home."

"If I were yours, I'd have had an issue with you letting women maul you while I'm there," I retorted. It was out before I could stop myself saying it. And now he knew that *I* was jealous.

"If you were mine, you wouldn't be flirting all night with Mangle. You'd be in my arms, feeling my body against yours and I'd be breathing your citrus sweet scent into my lungs and not that nasty perfume I can still smell on myself," he replied, suddenly so angry and close that I could feel it radiating off of him and into me.

I hadn't realised he had cornered me until I felt the wall meet my back and I was pressing against it as he moved closer.

"If you were mine, I'd never let you get close to those skanks." He lifted a hand to cradle my head and his other arm snaked around my waist.

"If you were mine, I wouldn't have to feel like ripping my friends arms off because he touched you all night when you know you're mine."

I couldn't tell what was real anymore. Did he mean I was his or was he still speaking hypothetically?

I could feel his muscles against my body and his breath on my face when I looked up into his eyes. The intensity in them was killing me. I didn't know if I was strong enough yet to handle that. I could feel the tide pulling me in, so I panicked.

"It's just as well that I'm not yours then."

Just like that, the magic seemed to dissipate from the air. His eyes cleared of the lust and focussed a bit more and he took a step back.

"Right. Just as well." The mental bucket of water seemed to wake him and he took a couple more steps back and walked away. I stood stock still not sure what just happened. A minute later he was back wearing his blazer and helping me into my coat then leading me out the back exit of the club to where Luke was waiting for us with the car.

The drive home was silent and Kade looked thoughtful as he stared outside the window at the passing streets. I kept my head down, not sure what to do or say to lighten our moods. Soon enough we were parking in front of the town house and I was stepping out with the help of Luke. Kade rolled down his window and smiled but the smile didn't reach his eyes, it was strained.

"Thank you for a lovely night and a wonderful weekend," I said. I leaned in to kiss his cheek but he moved and I brushed his lips instead. The shock of the softness of his lips made me touch my lips when I withdrew.

"Pleasure was all mine," he said, equally surprised. "Good night Alexa."

And with that, Luke drove him off to his luxury fortress in the sky when we both knew he would rather be here, at *home,* in this warm and comfortable house where his presence roamed like a ghost.

CHAPTER TWENTY

I am not your 'Baby Girl.'

The following morning was busy. The artwork that had garnered attention and buyers had to be sent away to be professionally stored and prepared for their new owners and many people were calling in to say how impressed they were with the event.

I hadn't even had time to think about the awkward moment from the night before when Mary ran into the staff room during lunch break and threw a magazine at me that I managed to catch. Skylar didn't bat an eye lid, obviously used to Mary's outbursts of drama, and continued to eat her salad.

"What the hell Mary?!"

"Look at the front page!"

"What?"

"Look at the *front damn page*! You're on it!"

I looked and first I didn't see it but sure enough, in the bottom right hand corner of the front page of 'Gossip Girl' was a small picture taken from the Jack Mangle fight the night before. In the picture was me with my hand on Kade's chest when we were sitting in the arena, right about the time when Kade had told me he trusted me. I should have known that even in a crowded venue like that, we would get papped.

The picture was small and you could only see our profiles but our expressions were easily read. The caption made it glaringly obvious:

> *'Kade Hamilton spotted getting close to mystery woman at the Jack Mangle charity fight! Page 7 for more!'*

"Fuck."

"Yep. Read page seven." I turned the pages to read the short excerpt accompanied by the offending picture in a larger scale as well as a picture of Kade looking dapper when he arrived for the fight. Skylar looked over my shoulder as I read out loud.

> *"The illustrious Kade Hamilton was spotted out at a public event for the second time after splitting with fiancee Giselle earlier this summer. Kade smiled broadly for the camera and was reported to have had a good time but the question on everybody's lips is this - who is this mysterious brunette? Kade was said to have been sat all night with the red dressed beauty and they were reported to have left together for the after party at Club Vibe. Could it be that our favourite Hamilton has found himself a new beauty so soon after his break up with Giselle? Is this girl the reason they split? Let us know your opinions!"*

"You're dating Kade Hamilton?!" Skylar asked, wide eyed.

"NO! He's my friend. Why do these guys twist everything? Ugh! Now there's speculation that *I'm* the reason for his break up with Giselle. I'm gonna get found and trolled by the die hard *Kisele* fans. Great!" I threw the magazine down.

"Honey, with a picture like that, it's hard not to assume. But look, it's not a full face picture and I'm sure the Hamilton's will bury the story," she consoled me.

"I say you own that shit!" Mary proclaimed.

"I just hope it's not going to cause issues for Kade."

The rest of my day was spent distracted and checking my

phone in between work to see if Kade had sent me a message but there was nothing. I wondered if I had created a bigger problem by teasing him and then denying him the night before. I was never the kind of person that liked to play games and for some reason I thought it would be fun to wind him up, but instead I was left feeling guilty for toying with his emotions only to pull away when he got closer. I desperately needed to sort myself out and fast.

***

Cards and calls were still coming in on Thursday morning when news came that our boss was going to be paying us a visit, finally, to thank the staff personally for all our efforts.

By the evening, the gallery was spotless and we were all waiting in the large staff area for Michael to arrive. It would be the first time I was going to meet him and my colleagues seemed to love him.

It was a quarter past six when Jason walked in and greeted everyone. I was hugging him hello when I heard Michael's voice behind me. I turned around...and froze.

"Alexa, this is our boss Michael. Michael, our newest most talented recruit, Alexa," Clyde said warmly. When I remained quiet a bit too long, Mary nudged me and gave me a questioning look.

"Alexa," Michael said, his expression cautious but mixed with something else I couldn't quite place.

"Dad?" The shocked gasps came from four of my colleagues. Jason seemed not to be shocked, which made me angry. I turned to him and gave him the dirtiest look I could muster. He had the decency to look sorry.

I hadn't seen my father in years. After he left my mother and returned to his wife, whom he was separated from, when I was six years old, he had tried once to reconnect when I was thirteen, which counted for nothing. At that one meeting, he had introduced me to his two older children on a trip to London, both of whom seemed to hate me. After that,

I'd receive a card for my birthday for a few years until they stopped too. Recently, my mother had received a few phone calls from him, the two of them very amicable on the phone, which irritated the shit out of me. He'd always want to speak to me and I would never be interested.

And now he was here, in the flesh. In my mind he was always that dark haired, green eyed handsome man who had turned my mothers brain to mush. Now he stood in front of me, the once dark hair turned salt and pepper but still full, age lines around his still vibrant green eyes. Still every bit the handsome Italian American my mum had fallen for but somewhat tired looking and older. He was looking at me like he had so much to say. Unfortunately, so had I. Over twenty years worth of words.

"So you own this gallery?" I managed to keep my voice calm.

He looked sheepish. Everyone else just looked on with rapt attention.

"Yes...it was my idea to keep this from you. Only Jason knew and he was sworn to secrecy. I'm sorry Alexa, I didn't see any other way to get you to talk to me. Your mother-"

"She knew as well, didn't she? What the hell dad?! I haven't seen you in years! You have had zero input in my life and now you're telling me that this was all an elaborate *scheme* to get me to talk to you?"

I was fuming and I knew I should tone it down because these people around us were my friends and I didn't want them to see the years of hurt, feelings of neglect and my anger towards their boss - my biological father.

"That's not what this is Lexi. You applying for the job and talking to me was pure coincidence. You've proved to be a valuable asset to us, I knew you would be." His praise softened my approval seeking heart for a moment, but then the ugly feelings of neglect sunk in again.

"I can't do this right now. This is the reason you never

showed up at the event? I can't compute. I need to get out of here." I walked past my father and grabbed my belongings. I didn't want to cry in front of everyone.

"Lexi, wait. Just let me speak with you in private," he pleaded, taking hold of my hand in both of his to stop me yanking it away. The tender fatherly gesture made me give in and I let him lead me into his office.

He sat in his chair and motioned for me to sit too. I felt too vulnerable to sit down in front of him in this setting - something about feeling like a reprimanded child had me hovering behind the chair instead. He ran his hand through his curly hair and sighed.

"I didn't want you to get upset like this. That was never my intention."
I nodded, believing him, tears on the brink of departing from my lashes. I wiped them away before they made contact with my skin.

"I know I haven't been there for you and it eats me up every day Lexi." I allowed myself a moment to let his words sink in before I spoke.

"Why now? Why do you want to know me now? After all these years?" I couldn't help the wavering in my voice.

"A few years ago, I had an accident. It was bad. I almost didn't survive it. Every night that I was in that hospital recovering, I had a recurring dream about you. I don't know why but I had an overwhelming urge to speak to you. It took me a year to get back on my feet and as soon as I had recovered, I contacted your mother. That's when she told me all about you, what a beautiful and intelligent girl you had turned out to be and all the wonderful things you had achieved. She forgave me. I had hoped that one day maybe you will too. I want to know you Lexi and get to be there for you. I know you're hurting and that your divorce has been hard but please believe me when I say that I want to make things up to you."

I stood and took in all the things he said. My heart and

mind were divided. I wanted so much to be able to let go of my anger and give in to the love that nature had placed in my heart for my absent father but I couldn't. All I could remember was my mother crying and my poor grandparents supporting us both through mums depression and how lost I have felt since.

I looked my father in his eyes, my heart hardening.

"You weren't there when I needed you. And now you're here, I don't want you in my life. I cannot work here anymore, I quit."

"Baby girl, wait," he pleaded, but the nickname that he used to use only for me made me feel the pain of the past even more.

"I am not your 'baby girl'." I tried to ignore the hurt in his eyes as I made my way out of the office, past my colleagues calling my name and onto the busy street. It was there that I let the dam break and my tears fall.

***

Having walked around the city aimlessly for an hour, I somehow ended up in front of Kade's building. It wasn't a conscious decision, somehow my heart and mind wanted me to seek out my friend even though we hadn't spoken in days.

Standing outside, I dialed his number on my phone. I half expected him not to answer but he did on the second ring.

"Alexa." Just hearing his voice saying my name brought me a little comfort.

"Hi."

"What's wrong? Have you been crying?" A sniffle escaped my lips and the tears started again.

"Um, are you home?"

"Yeah, I'm home. Are you hurt? What's happened? Talk to me baby." *Baby.* I couldn't think too much about his term of endearment.

"Can I come up? I'm outside your building."

"Of course. Come inside the lobby, I'll tell them to let you in."

The ride up the elevator to Kade's penthouse was quick and before I knew it the doors opened and he was out in his lobby waiting for me. He took one look at my tear streaked face and pulled me to him. I felt like it was the first time I had taken a breath that evening since I saw my father.

Kade just held me, not saying a word, not forcing me to talk until I was ready. After what seemed like an eternity of me sobbing into his pristine white shirt, I pulled away and he lead me into his home. He looked so concerned yet all I could think was how beautiful he looked, like a figure from a renaissance painting.

Papers were strewn all over his coffee table, evidence that he really did work hard judging by his scribbling in the margins and post it notes. He cleared some of the paper away and sat me down on the sofa while he made some coffee for himself and tea for me.

Once he sat down, he waited patiently for me to speak.

"I'm sorry to barge in on you like this. I can see you're busy."

"Don't be silly Alexa, you're welcome here any time. You actually saved me from reading some boring legal documents. Instead, I will be designating this work to William tomorrow morning. He just got married. I guess he will be staying at work late tomorrow night..." I looked at him, horrified.

"You can't do that! That's terrible!" Kade laughed.

"Don't feel too bad for him. William faked his grandma's death so he could take a week off to go skiing last winter. I have been slowly exacting revenge on him in honour of his very much alive and well grandmother for the past year in the form of these long legal contracts. Teaches him for putting Granny in the grave."

As usual he had made me laugh and it felt good. He smiled

at me and I felt even better. After a pause I knew I should open up.

"I met my boss today."

"Michael? He's a nice guy."

"You know him?" If he told me then that he knew he was my father, I'd have to kill him.

"Yeah, very few in my circle don't. He is well known and respected for his trade."

"Did you know that he is, in fact, my biological father?" Kade's surprise gave me comfort. *He didn't know, he didn't lie or conceal it.*

"What?" I took a deep breath.

"I stopped asking questions about my father when I was very young and realised he wasn't coming back. All I knew was that he was a businessman and lived in New York with his wife and kids. I didn't know that he's the owner of Atlantis Art and that he'd given me the job to get to do some kind of father daughter bonding by tricking me. And Jason knew Kade, he knew."

I started crying again. It hurt that Jason, of whom I had a high regard and the beginning of a good friendship with, had been part of the scheme. As for my mother...she had out done herself.

I told Kade what had happened, from the moment my father had walked into the gallery, to the moment I walked out and quit my job. He listened intently, rubbing my back in soothing circles as I spoke.

"Damn. Most people know and refer to Michael just by his first name and the gallery. I didn't know he was Michael *De Luca*. I'm so sorry Alexa. This isn't the best way to reconcile but maybe you should think about it? I know it's easy for me to say but maybe this elaborate idea of his was his desperation to get to you."

"I can't think about it right now. I know he's sorry but it's just not enough at the moment. I have too much going on in my life at this time that I can't cope with more complications. I just need some time."

Kade took my hand and began making circles into my palm with his thumb in a soothing gesture.

"Yeah, I get that. Just don't shut the door. You don't want to have those 'what if's' hanging over you like a dark cloud. You're a strong woman, you will be able to handle it when the time comes." I sighed and nodded.

"Right now, I'm an unemployed woman. It's back to the sucky job hunt again."

Kade looked thoughtful for a moment, quietly contemplative.

"Well, how good are you with administrative work?"

"Um, good, I guess. I worked as an administrator for a short time."

"I already know you are well articulated and people here dig the accent. How's your general coffee making?"

"Ok...I think."

"How are you under pressure? Scheduling? Taking meeting minutes."

"I can do all that. What are you getting at Kade?" He dropped my hand and leaned back into his seat.

"There's been a recent job vacancy in my department. One of the partners has a need for a PA. The only thing is that the asshole is very demanding but I know he will love you. You can come in tomorrow morning for a look around and interview if you want. Only if you're interested."

The smile on my face must have given him an indication of my thoughts.

"Seriously? That is amazing! I was so worried I would be sitting at home stuffing my face with cheetos and coke and wasting the days away in depression! This is brilliant!" I threw myself on him for a hug and he chuckled as he returned it.

"Ok, then you better report to this address tomorrow morning at 9am."

He took a business card out from the inside pocket of his

jacket draped over a chair and handed it to me. I was suddenly excited to see where this new path would take me.

Some of the job hunting related stress left me and I felt relief. Somehow, Kade Hamilton had become my knight in shining armour....again.

CHAPTER TWENTY ONE

Personal Assistant

I looked down at the address on the business card and then up at the looming skyscraper in front of me. Hamilton Towers was an impressive building, all steel and glass with high ceilings and all the mod cons of the age.

I entered the building wearing my best charcoal grey pencil skirt, white shirt and my black heels, heading straight to the reception in the main lobby to collect a security pass.

Before leaving Kade the night before, he had told me where to go and what to do when I arrived the next morning at his place of work. I was anxious to meet the man I'd be working for. From the way Kade painted him, he seemed to be a difficult guy. I was to meet with Lindsay first who would run through a few things with me.

I took my pass and made my way in the elevator to the 22nd Floor where the legal department was situated. The rush I felt when I stepped out and into a lobby with a view of the city through the floor to ceiling windows was a little overwhelming. Working in a place like this was something that most people could only dream of.

I walked over to the receptionist at the large desk in the

waiting area.

"Hello, I'm Alexa De Luca. I am here to meet with Lindsey Foster." The receptionist smiled politely and picked up the phone to call Lindsay.

A few moments later, Lindsay waddled over to me through the corridor, beaming, and embraced me.

"Oh my God! I'm so glad you're here! How have you been?"

"Good thanks Lindsay. How are you and baby?"

"Ugh, this thing is playing soccer with my bladder all the time. I can't wait until it's time to get him out, I'm so tired!"

"Aw bless you," I smiled at her and squeezed her hand.

Lindsay led me down the corridor she had come through whilst we chatted a bit and took on a tour of the department. I saw various offices of various important people and the conference room and the staff room and then she took me into a large office of the person I presumed I would be working for. It was a typical executive office with massive desk and leather chair for work facing two leather chairs on the other side for guests or colleagues and the leather single and two seater couches in an area slightly away from the desk for informal talks. There was a flat screen on one wall and a bookshelf full of books and files. The view of the New York City skyline was phenomenal.

"Is this where I'll be having my interview? The boss's office?" I asked, a little nervous for the lack of time I had for preparation the night before.

"Uh, yeah, but I think the job is pretty much yours. And your timing is brilliant Lexi. I'm so happy." I didn't have time to respond because the door opened just as I was about to speak and in walked Kade in all his suited glory. It took me a few seconds to work out what was going on.

"Are you kidding me?"

"Hello Alexa. So good to see you. Please take a seat." Kade's formal way of addressing me sobered me a little from the mouthful of words I may have had for him considering the situation and I took a seat as asked opposite him at his desk.

"Mr Hamilton," I replied through clenched teeth. He gave me a reproachful look which was supposed to mask his amusement. It failed miserably.

"I've asked you here for an interview. The vacancy is for a Personal Assistant, to replace Lindsay here whilst she is on her maternity leave. This is the contract, please read it carefully. Your salary and benefits are outlined in section three. If you have any questions, please do not hesitate to ask." He pushed an envelope in front of me and waited for everything he said to sink in. I stood up abruptly, pushing the chair out.

"I can't. Sorry." I turned to leave and noticed Lindsay was still in the room with us, sitting on the more comfortable looking couch.

"Alexa, please sit down. Let's discuss what is bothering you." Kade had never spoken to me in such a commanding way before and for some reason I found it...sexy. My body obeyed as if of its own accord and I turned to face him.

"Kade, I can't work for you. It will complicate our friendship. I appreciate the gesture of you helping me after everything but I can't do it."

Kade stood and walked around his desk and over to where Lindsay was sitting looking a bit sad. He placed his hands on her shoulders from behind her.

"It will not complicate anything. This is not a 'kind gesture.' I really do need a PA and Lindsay needs to go on her maternity leave. The person we had hired to take her place bailed on us. Linds needs to rest, I need help. You will be doing *me* the favour. And Linds. She doesn't think anyone is good enough and so when I mentioned you to her last night after you left, she was thrilled. You'd be perfect." Way to go for emotional blackmail.

I sighed and dropped my shoulders.

"I don't know. Seems complicated already."
Kade walked over to me and turned me by my shoulders
back towards the chair I had vacated and gently pushed me
down into it. Resuming his place in his seat he tapped the envelope in front of me.

"Please, Alexa. It's not that bad and Linds will train
you and handover before she leaves. Just trust me on this."
The long pause was deafening. I kept thinking of how de-
pressing it would be to not be working but then the prospect
of Kade being my boss as well as being my landlord already
felt like I'd been given an unfair advantage over others that
might deserve the position more than me. I gave myself a
mental shake. I didn't want to let them down, but I could always negotiate.

"Okay, here's the deal. Linds can train me and I will
work here until you find a permanent replacement. What do
you say?" He looked at Lindsay and they smiled at one another. I didn't like the way they looked conspiratorial when
they did that.

"Sound's fair enough. Have a look at the contract and
let me know if you find it to be satisfactory. I'll let you have
some time to read it. Linds and I have a short meeting to attend. I will be back within the hour. I'll have someone bring
you some tea." He shook my hand formally, not leaving me
any time to respond and left the room with Lindsay wad-
dling behind him.
Deciding that I didn't want to be sitting in a chair for an hour,
I walked over to the couch and sat as elegantly as I could in
a pencil skirt with the contract in my hand. The designer
clock on the wall read 10:03 am. I sighed as I opened the envelope and started to read.

**

It was 10:57 when I looked up from the page I was reading
upon hearing them enter the office. I heard Lindsay giggle

behind Kade as he stood there looking amused.

Some time after I started reading the dull contract pages, I had kicked off my uncomfortable heels and taken my hair out of the tight ponytail I had it in and had tucked my legs under myself comfortably on the couch after hiking my pencil skirt a little. The contract was pretty run of the mill apart from the part where it outlined the extremely generous salary and benefits. I finished reading it within ten minutes and felt bored until I saw a copy of Pride and Prejudice on one of Kade's shelves. I found it really funny that he would have the Austen Novel there amongst his law books, philosophy studies, autobiographies and binders. That was until I saw the dedication inside the limited edition. It read:

Blue eyes,
I see you here every Wednesday
and every time, you look at this book
and I can't stop looking at you.
I've tried to ignore the feeling I
get when I see you.
I SEE you.
I want to know you better.
Meet me at The Lake this afternoon
at 4pm if you feel the same.
Yours in hope, the guy in the green hat,
A.

After that, I just wanted to read my favourite Austen romance and see if there were any more clues as to who this book originally belonged to but got lost in the narrative.

At the moment, I felt highly unprofessional and hurried to straighten myself up in front of my new employer.

"I'm so sorry, I didn't think you would be back for some time," I hurried to say whilst putting on my heels and straightening my skirt and hair.

"Relax Alexa, in here we're not formal. Linds spends

most of her time on that couch pointing out my flaws and lecturing me. Only out there," he pointed towards the door, indicating to the world beyond, "do we do the formal thing. So don't stress."

"Still...I'm sorry. I just found this book on your shelf and it has the most intriguing dedication in it...also, sorry for snooping..." God, I was really not doing well on my first day.

"Lexi, seriously don't stress about it," Linds piped in, taking the book from my hands to examine it. "That book is a historical relic," she said with a smile, touching the cover tenderly.

"Well, it is a first edition," I replied matter of factly.

"What Mrs Foster means to say," Kade sighed as he carefully pried the book from Lindsay's hands, "is that this book is how my parents met."

I smiled at him, ready to pester for the story because I always was a sucker for a great romantic tale.

"You're expecting a story, aren't you?" Kade said with a knowing smile.

"Yup."

"Great. Another swooning romantic," he quipped but I could tell he enjoyed telling it just as much.

"Come on, tell me already!"

"Okay, okay!" He sat down on the couch and so did we.

"I've heard this story so many times but it always feels magical," Lindsay sighed. Once settled, he opened the book to the dedication, touching the words with reverence.

"My dad, back in the seventies, was a very privileged young man. Fresh out of college, he had the world at his feet and hadn't wanted for anything. Some would say he was spoilt but he always said he was bored and wealthy," Kade laughed at the memory.

"My grandfather was busy running his empire, my father was expected to join the family business but he asked for a year out so he could travel and find himself. Truth is, he never made it out of New York until six months later." He looked up and me and smiled.

"He met your mum," I smiled, loving the story so far.

"He met my mom. He was in this specialist bookstore looking for a gift for my grandmother. She was a poet back in those days. He was looking through the shop when he caught sight of my mother. She was about two rows away but he saw her through the gaps in the old wooden shelves. The way he describes that moment, he says she seemed like an angel that had suddenly appeared in front of him. He couldn't stop looking at her. And she was absorbed in this book. He kept trying to get a closer look at her but her face would be lowered so he would wait for however long it would take for her to finish reading her fill and then he would see her and her 'blue eyes.' He went to that bookstore everyday only to realise she would only visit on Wednesday',s when she had a day off from college and work. So he would be there, kinda like some hopeless Romeo, following her, spying on her, every Wednesday for four weeks. And she would always pick up this book, even if she didn't read it."

"Why didn't he just go up to her and talk to her?" I asked curiously.

"Funnily enough, for all his experience with women, he seemed to get nervous and tongue tied around her. He said he couldn't talk to her but at the same time he knew he couldn't let her go. He had to hold onto her." Our gazes met as a familiar fire burned and then blew out as he looked away and continued.

"He came up with this master plan. He bought the book, wrote the dedication and got his friend to ask the shop owner to give it her when she came the next Wednesday. He waited that day and when she came into the store, the owner handed her the package that was wrapped in ordinary brown paper. She was confused until she opened it. He says she gasped and her eyes lit up. And when she read the dedication she blushed." We laughed and aww'd at how cute that was.

"Dad said he didn't let her see him in the store as she looked around to try and understand who had just spent so much on a book for little ole her. So he waited with bated breath the whole afternoon, and she didn't show. He was about to leave, heartbroken, as it reached 6pm when he turned to see her standing there with her curly hair out, wearing a pretty dress and pearls. She had gotten late helping a friend out in an emergency. Turns out, she had been sneaking glances at him too all this time but was too shy to approach him. He took her to dinner that night, he treated her like a priceless porcelain doll - dad's words, not mine. He kissed her cheek goodnight with promises of tomorrow. Six months later, they married and the rest is history."

I looked and Lindsay and she looked at me as we sighed collectively.

"That is the most romantic thing I have ever heard! My husband asked me out whilst I was having a drink with my girlfriends at a sports bar. He proposed after beating the shit out of an opponent in the ring!" Linds pouted.

"Yeah, but he wouldn't be *him* if he didn't," I said, smiling at her.

"Yeah, you're right, he wouldn't." Her grin said it all.

"Your dad is an original romantic. I seriously need to get some more stories out of him."

He looked a bit peeved but there was humour in his eyes.

"Uh, I can be just as romantic, thank you."

"That remains to be seen, Romeo," I laughed, not quite sure what I meant by that.

He looked as confused as I felt. A knock on the door brought us back to business. Kade replaced the book carefully on his shelf and told Lindsay to show me the rest of the building whilst he talked to William, the granny killer.

***

"I can't believe Mr Hamilton is such a romantic," I said to Lindsay, as we made our way to another floor using the lift. So far I'd met a sea of new faces and seen a hundred different spaces in this huge building.

"Alastair is a sweetheart. And Kade is just like him. Andrea told me that when he was little, he would not let that book go. He was fascinated by books but especially attached to that one. So when he went off to join the army, she gave it to him. To remind him of her and his dad. He's a real softie at heart." She stopped talking as we stepped out into another lobby which happened to be where the staff canteen and cafeteria was. Once we sat down with a coffee and cake she put her hand on mine and gave me an appreciative smile.

"Thank you so much for agreeing to this. I know it makes you a little uncomfortable but I was so sure I'd be in labour and still looking for my replacement. Kade needs someone extra competent and capable of putting him straight and I believe you are all those things and more. And you're giving me the chance to get the rest Kade keeps telling me I need."
She looked emotional so I squeezed her hand.

"You're too kind Lindsay, I'm sure I can't measure up to you but I will do my best to fill your place until you come back."

"I don't know if I will come back, to be honest Lexi. I love working for Kade, he's an amazing friend and boss and he gives me way too much leeway at work because he cares for my health and happiness but I think I may just want to settle at home now and enjoy being a wife and mom for some time."

"I don't blame you. You're going to be an amazing mother."

"Truth be told, I'm petrified! I keep thinking, 'how will I do this?'"

"You're going to be a natural, as soon as you see that baby in your arms you will know exactly what to do." A pang of longing hit me square in my chest, causing me to physically want to rub it away. *Maybe. One day.*

"You say the best things Lexi. Thank you so much for being here. Kade's been telling me to go on my maternity leave for two months now but I wouldn't have been able to relax knowing he was stretched thin. You're going to love it here."

I smiled at her, believing her. This job was my big break, earning a lot more than I had hoped, working for a large international company and getting to spend almost every day with Kade. I didn't know why I had been so hesitant to say yes. Of course it would be amazing.

CHAPTER TWENTY TWO

I earned it

"Did you bring it?"

"Yes."

"No sugar?"

"No sugar."

"And one for yourself?"

"Yes. Would you mind telling me why you have me here in your castle at three in the morning with my passport and coffee? Don't you have a coffee machine?"

"Yeah I do but I like it better when someone makes me one instead." His eyes twinkled with mirth. I felt like punching his adorable fresh face as I yawned and frowned him down.

"Why have you got me up here at this godforsaken time, Hamilton?"

He put his coffee travel mug down and handed me an envelope.

"We have a business trip this morning. We're going to L.A. We'll be back in New York late tonight." My mouth dropped open.

"We're going to L.A? As in Los Angeles?! You could

have told me before I left home! I'd have worn something more appropriate!"

"You look fine to me. Besides, you need to be comfortable on the plane ride. When we get there, we'll get you an outfit when we land. Sorted! Now let's go. The car is waiting for us."

I didn't get a chance to argue, feeling like a loser in my black leggings and AC/DC band t-shirt that I threw on when I got Kade's phone call that morning. Luckily, I'd brought my bag along and not just my wallet like I usually would have. I didn't think Kade meant to take me on a business trip with him when he asked me to bring my passport. I was way too sleepy to see the obvious connection.

It had been two weeks since I'd started working for Kade at the Hamilton's head office, or fort, as I liked to call it. Lind's had shown me and taught me how to do everything. Everything except how not to wring his neck when he had ridiculous requests such as the day he got me running around town to find him a tie that was the exact shade of blue that he had seen in a magazine from Milan of a little known brand that was exclusive to only one store in the whole of New York City. The problem was, no one knew which store and it took me five hours to locate it, only for him to tell me that he wasn't going to wear it to the event he wanted it for after all. I had a whole week of this until I had enough and complained to Lindsay about it in a phone call one day after work when he'd decided to get me to take the entire legal departments coffee orders for the morning, lunch and afternoon.

"Oh my god...I'm so sorry I forgot to tell you," she giggled and then burst out laughing.

"What? what's so funny? I'm going to have a nervous breakdown and you're laughing?!"

"Oh god, I think I might have peed myself a little there. The baby is kicking the shit out of my bladder. Im so sorry Lexi."

"Sorry about what?" I knew I wasn't going to like

what she said next.

"So, Kade has this thing where he 'initiates' new team members into our department…"

"Go on."

"He's basically testing your mettle. Checking to see what you're made of. He's going to keep setting difficult tasks for you until you give up and then he'll let up. It's either that or you beat him at his own game."

"The bastard! I should have known!"

"Yeah…I forgot to warn you. Sorry about that. But you can always get your own back. So far, no one has had the guts to try…" That was all the motivation I needed.

The Monday of my second week, I arrived at work early. Kade would usually go jogging three mornings of the week from his home through Central park and then to work where he would shower in his office's attached bathroom and change into one of the suits he had in his closet there. I watched from behind a wall as he pulled off his shirt and grabbed his towel and the nearest suit bag that had been ready for him and headed in for his shower. Twenty minutes later, the shower turned off and then came his bellowing voice.

"WHAT THE ACTUAL FUCK?!"

I tried to contain my giggles as I sat down at my desk and picked up my gossip magazine to hide my face. No one else was in the office yet so when I heard an angry man cursing under his breath and coming towards me, I knew it was him. I didn't look up.

"Is there a problem Mr Hamilton?" I asked sweetly, as I continued pretending to read.

"Yes, there is a big fucking problem!"

"You sound stressed Mr Hamilton, you really should try some yoga to de-stress yourself."

"Yoga? Yog- Alexa, look at me!" And at that point I did. And I couldn't stop myself. I laughed so hard I thought I'd rupture an internal organ.

When I had come in earlier, I'd done a little makeover for Kade's entire collection of suits. Studs, feathers, ripped knees in the trousers, some slogans on his shirts. The current suit he was wearing had spikes in the jacket pockets. I had ripped off all the buttons on his shirt and cut massive squares into his trousers where you could see his muscular legs. His bare chest looked exquisite. He still looked yummy as he stood there glaring.

"You did this, didn't you?"

"I haven't the slightest idea what you're talking about." He grabbed me by the hand and pulled me inside his office towards his wardrobe with the five other suit bags. Each had their distinct Couture by Alexa design. It had taken me just an hour to destroy every one of his pristine and beautifully tailored, expensive suits. I felt guilty for a few seconds before I remembered him making me pick all the raisons out of his danish pastry and then not eating it, at which point I just went crazy.

He picked up one particular shirt and read the back of it out loud.

"'Alexa's bitch.' You sure you don't know what I'm talking about now?" I raised my hand slowly.

"Guilty."

"I swear to- Please tell me there is an undamaged suit here somewhere? I have an important meeting at 9am. I can't go to it dressed like this!" Of course, I knew this and had planned ahead but there was one thing he had to do first before I relented.

"Yeah there is. *Somewhere.* But first you need to give up with the crazy initiation pranks. Only then will you get your beautiful, blue, unscathed suit." His face looked like thunder. I knew he wouldn't want to admit defeat. He growled like an animal and I started to lose a bit of the confidence I had gained. He said only one word.

"Run." And then all hell broke loose.

He came at me as I tried to escape and although I managed

to side step a couple of times, he got ahead of me and managed to flip me onto his couch. Then he did the worst thing imaginable. He tickled me.

"Stop!"

"Tell me where the suit is Alexa."

"No way! Stop tickling me!"

"I'll stop if you tell me!"

"I'll tell you if you promise!"

"I'll never promise!"

"Then have fun being my bitch!" I started to cough because I couldn't stop laughing from him tickling me. Kade finally let up.

"You're a really stubborn woman Alexa," he breathed out, exasperated and still half on top of me.

"Thank you." My hair was a mess and he swept it aside from my face with his long fingers.

"Okay. I give up. You win. Now where is the suit?"

"Uh, you need to say the words."

"Christ! Okay. I promise I will stop with the pranks. Now please, pretty please, can I get some of my own clothes?" I pushed him off of me and he reluctantly got up and pulled me up with him. I chose to ignore the butterflies that constantly resided in my stomach when he was around. I walked to my desk and pulled out the suit bag I had kept under my desk. We turned to go back to his office when a flash startled us. I blinked several times before I saw Lindsay standing there with a camera taking pictures of Kade in his humiliation.

"What the hell are you doing here?" He said, more annoyed at her being in the office when she was supposed to be resting than her taking pictures of his defeat.

"I couldn't miss this for the world! When Alexa said she had a plan, I knew it would be epic. So I have filmed the whole thing. Who thought I would get to see the day Kade Hamilton was one upped by a woman!" She giggled cutely as he grumbled and slammed his door shut to go and change.

The next day, an email circulated all the departments in the building with a picture of Kade looking startled and me smiling in the background and the heading was 'The woman that has bigger balls than all of y'all!' Someone blew up the picture and stuck it in his office as a joke and his mood that day was tempestuous to say the least.

He kept his word and didn't harass me...much. And so far this past week had been plain sailing.

Now we were headed to L.A. on a private Jet with two of his security detail and the experience was eye opening. The luxury of how the other half lived was now more apparent than ever. I settled into the soft leather seat, big enough for two, and closed my eyes while Kade went over a document on his laptop. I fell asleep, dreaming of blue eyes and black coffee as the plane took off.

***

I jolted awake when I felt the plane land. I immediately saw Kade staring at me, deep in thought.

"Hey," I croaked from my sleepy voice.

"Hey."

"Did I really sleep through the whole journey?"

"Yeah you really did. Your boss is an ass, he shouldn't make you work all the hours of the day." I have him a nudge and he faked being hurt.

"My boss may be an ass but he's a big sweetheart on the inside." He raised his eyebrows.

"Sweetheart eh?"

"Yeah, sweetheart. Although that statement can easily be changed to 'arrogant.'" His laugh was deep and soul satisfying.

Getting off the plane, it was now almost midday and L.A was warm and slightly breezy on the bright August day.
Our first stop after getting in the waiting car was a department store where Kade made me pick out several dresses

and then didn't let me buy them.

"That's very inappropriate Kade. These are for me and you're my boss."

"I'm also the reason you left home without the appropriate clothes for our business trip. You can buy dinner, how about that?" There was never any arguing with Kade, he made every solution sound simple. The talents of a well educated Lawyer. I wondered if he would ever consider entering politics.

I dressed in a floral dress suitable for a smart casual day with heeled sandals and we headed to our first destination. This happened to be a visit to a police station. Apart from being a corporate lawyer, Kade often helped some celebrity 'friends' get out of trouble if they were stuck. It didn't happen often but sometimes damage control was needed, as Kade explained.

I waited outside the room and could hear the faint conversation. Someone said something about possession of Marjuana, Kade said something about evidence of it being in his clients possession. Something else was said about it being 'flushed' before the cops could get there. There was a lot of cursing from another party and then the reluctant release of the arrested person, who happened to be one of the Richardson twins.

Once they stepped out of the room, I got a good look at the bad boy twins just as the other twin walked down a grey lobby to hug his brother. They didn't notice me as they shook hands with Kade and walked towards the exit while I trailed behind.

"Thanks man. I thought he was done for that time. Stupid bastard doesn't know how to do discreet," the twin that hadn't been detained said, rubbing his two day old stubble and lighting up a cigarette as soon as we were outside.

The twins really were handsome in a rugged, unkempt sort of way. They were both in a rock band, constantly in the gossip pages. Dark eyes and dark hair, lean muscles and leather and denim mixed that made up their look. Almost 80's style but with a modern twist. Their hair was the only way to tell them apart, with Neil, the bad boy twin, styling his hair buzzed at the sides and long at the top, spilling into his eyes. Nate had longer hair down to his shoulders.

"You guys really need to get your shit together Nate. I could help this time because I'm here on business but they won't hesitate the next time he's caught in the possession of drugs. Keep it low key now, get out of town for a couple of weeks if you can. Are you recording at the moment?"

"Nah, on a break at the moment. I guess we could always go home for a bit." His brother grunted and he lit his own cigarette. Then he noticed me hovering on the outskirts, not quite sure what to do with myself.

"Who's the hot brunette?" Neil asked, taking a long drag and then blowing out smoke rings. Kade's jaw clenched.

"My Personal Assistant."

"I bet she's your 'personal' assistant," he laughed, which made Kade's eyes narrow,   "What's your name sweet thing?" Not wanting to seem rude, though I was offended, I stuck out my hand.

"I'm Alexa De Luca. Nice to meet you." Neil took my hand and gave me a smirk as he kissed it. I could feel the heat radiating off of Kade when he stared at Neil's lips on my hand. Neil didn't let go of my hand as he leaned in closer and whispered in my ear which made me laugh and I whispered back in his ear.

"I'll be seeing you, Alexa De Luca," he said with a wink before turning his attention to Kade as he walked backwards towards a waiting car, "thanks for today bro. I owe you one."

Nate said good bye to us both and they sped out of the parking lot just as paparazzi approached from the other side of the lot.

Kade took my hand and quickly led me to our car. Luckily, their attention was focused on the Richardson's and chasing them to notice us and so we left unscathed.

The quiet in the car was unsettling. Kade finally broke the silence, having been staring out of the window for the past half hour.

"What did Neil say to you?"

"When?"

"When he was hovering all over you just now, whispering in your ear. Must have been something interesting to make you laugh like that."

I didn't want to presume too much but it did seem like Kade was a little jealous again. *Puh-lease. If only he knew that no one measured up to him to me. Not that I would ever tell him...* Jack's words from a couple of weeks ago echoed in my mind. I wondered just how detrimental I could be in Kade's life.

"He told me that he wanted to try a little experiment. He wanted to see if Kade Hamilton could break his calm exterior and get jealous. I laughed because I told him that would never happen." He seemed a little startled by my revelation.

"Should've let the little bastard stew a little longer in there," he grumbled under his breath.

***

The rest of the day consisted of an actual business meeting to go over some contracts and new company policies. I took some meeting minutes for Kade and when we finished, we had time for dinner at a lovely cosy restaurant before our flight.

"This is nice," I told him as I took a sip of my drink.

"How so?" He'd been a little distracted since we left the police station.

"Getting to spend time with you like we did a couple of times in the beginning of our acquaintance. Back when you were just a normal guy to me, not the big shot celebrity slash Lawyer." He had a sad look in his eyes when he replied.

"This is all a part of me. I was born into it, I couldn't

escape it if I tried. So I have the choice to either hate it or embrace it and thats what I do. Just get on with life and hope that the constant interest in my public and private life doesn't interfere with all the important things in my life."

"I get that, I really do. Since coming to New York, I see your face plastered on a lot of magazines. Hell, I've even seen my own picture in the magazines." His expression was pained.

"I'm so sorry about that. I saw it and tried to get the whole rumour silenced. I try to keep my friends and important people in my life out of the limelight but obviously we're not invisible."

"It's okay Kade, really. I think it was initially a shock but I don't think anyone has found out who I am."

"They soon will though. As my PA, you're seen everywhere I go for business. I just want you to be aware in case it does happen. Usually they leave my staff out of photos." It was a lot to take on board. I decided to change the subject to lighten the mood.

"How's Bon Bon?" Instant happiness covered his face.

"She's fed up with being pregnant but she's got some time yet. I'm so excited to be an uncle again."

"I can tell. Gosh, another baby in the family! I heard you picked Annie's and Sophie's names. Will you get to pick this baby's?"

"I've been competing with Cameron for the honours. But I think Bonnie is going to let Cameron do it. Mainly because he's picked names she likes," he joked.

The conversation flowed easily as we ate and laughed. We hadn't realised how long we had been talking until Kade received a message from the driver that we needed to get a move on for the flight home.

"Thank you for a lovely evening Kade. You were sneaky giving your card to the waitress before we even sat down," I chastised him as he put my hand on his arm to escort me out of the restaurant.

"When we *restaurant*, I pay. When we *picnic*, you sort it. That's how it should be."

I stopped outside the car and scrunched up my nose.

"We haven't picnicked yet."

"Then you had better hurry up and arrange it."

"It would probably have to be at night, seeing as you're recognised everywhere you go," I joked.

"Hmmm. A picnic at midnight. Sounds like a plan."

We reached the plane in no time, took our seats and stowed the bags of shopping he had bought earlier. I reminded him that I owed him for wrecking his suits.

"They have already been replaced Alexa. Don't sweat it."

"Already? That was quick."

"You caused thousands of dollars worth of damage. Usually, such a crime wouldn't go unpunished Miss De Luca but I'll let you off with a warning. If you ever do that again however, the consequences will be dire."

"Dire?"

"Extremely dire."

"Noted."

The hostess that was on board our plane offered us some tea and coffee and placed the most delicious macarons on our tables. I ate mine and then pinched both of his.

"Hey, macaron thief!"

"What?" I said with a full mouth.

"You have such an innocent and sweet face, yet you do the most devious things."

"Listen here mate, I earned it." He thought about it for a second and then sighed. I popped another macaron in my mouth to take a bite and before I knew it, Kade leaned in and bit the other end, our lips touching briefly in the exchange and leaving me open mouthed at his audacity. He looked at me and shrugged as he pulled out a newspaper from his laptop bag.

"I earned that too."

CHAPTER TWENTY THREE

Letters of a madman

I was at work, typing an email when my phone rang again,. The name that popped up was of a person I was not yet ready to deal with. My father had been trying to speak to me for the past three weeks but to no avail. I couldn't answer the phone, I just didn't know how to win with the warring emotions I felt. There was the bitterness from his absence in my life, how high handed he had been in trying to trick me into speaking to him and then there was this silent joy that he cared and that maybe he was actually sincere and honest when he said he wanted to make up for lost time.

Another name that had constantly popped up on my phone messages was Jason's. He had sent me flowers every second day as an apology for two weeks until he finally cornered me at my favourite coffee shop near the Hamilton Fortress. He told me he didn't mean for me to feel like I'd been betrayed and that my father was only thinking of me when he asked him to help him. Since he'd been grovelling for some time and I'd seen the truth in his eyes as he apologised, I let him off the hook and we had coffee together. I was glad that we were talking, he was a good friend and I didn't want to lose that. He agreed to not talk about or advocate my father and I agreed that I'd talk to him when I was ready. Which could be never, but he didn't have to know that. I hadn't really spoken to my mother since the incident at the gallery and knew I couldn't avoid her for too long or she might threaten to come over.

I sat at my desk at work and was thinking about the drinks I would be having with my ex colleagues from the gallery after work in just half an hour as I finished typing. It was a Friday night and Kade had not been at the office for the past two days. He said he had some urgent business to attend to, which was weird because I had his diary of events and there was nothing scheduled, not even last minute. In fact, the past two days were just blocked off as 'out of office.' He had been acting strange the day before he took off and I couldn't quite place what had happened to make him switch like that. I decided that this could just be something personal, an appointment perhaps or rendezvous. The latter thought made me feel a spike of uneasiness.

Finishing up from work, I pushed the thought out of my mind as I made my way to the bar that was a block away from Atlantis Art.

***

"I'm getting the next round," I stated and got out of the booth to stand.

"I'll have a G&T," Mary said, already warmed by the alcohol.

"Vodka and Coke please baby," Clyde winked.

"Beer please," Denise asked sweetly.

"I'll have the same again," Skylar said, raising her empty cocktail glass.

"I'll come help you," Jason said, sliding out of the booth. We waited at the bar after giving the order, talking about how the month had passed so fast and Jason a.k.a Enzo was starting a new series of paintings but needed some inspiration.

"How about drawing pain from heartache," I suggested. He laughed without humour.

"Where do you think the 'Winged' series came from? I have used that particular emotion a lot in most of my work."

"You've had your heart broken," I stated more than questioned.

"Yeah. A few years back. It's ancient history now." He didn't elaborate and I didn't push.

"Then maybe you should pull something from the hope of new love? Something positive." He seemed to contemplate what I said.

"I suppose I could...I could call it the 'Flight' series. You're good for ideas Lexi. I'm going to see where this gets me." I gave him a side hug in support and heard my phone start to ring in my hand. I saw Kade's name and knowing that my work phone was in my bag, I picked up straight away, thinking there was more work that needed doing.

"Hello?"

"Hey." From his tone I could tell that something was wrong. He sounded distant, lost and alone. There was a deep sadness in that one syllable word. It hit me hard.

"What's wrong Kade?" He was silent for the longest five seconds. When he spoke, it was as if he had lost all his energy.

"I...uh...just wanted to know if everything went okay the last two days and if finance has signed off on those documents I had you type up." I knew this call wasn't really because of work and something was making me worry about the way he seemed so distant.

"Yeah, everything was finalised and filed. Are you okay?"

"Where are you at the moment?" he asked, changing the subject.

"I'm at Henley's around the corner from Atlantis with the guys from there. Why don't you join us? Jason is here." Again silence stretched in the void.

"Thanks for the invite. Just got some stuff to finish, so I'm at home for tonight. I'll see you Monday." The line disconnected without me having the chance to say goodbye. I got the feeling that he wanted to say more but couldn't quite get there.

I stared at my phone in my hand and saw an email alert from Lindsay sent earlier today that I had somehow missed. My heart sank when I read it.

Hey Lexi,

*I hope you're okay? Just wanted to give
you a heads up. Today, Kade went to
visit Marlon Bates, earlier than he usually does
every year. I don't know why it's happened, I
just got a call from the detective who didn't know
I was on maternity leave. It's a difficult time for him,
I know that you know all about what happened.
I only know about it all because I've worked with him for a
very long time.*

*Please, if he reaches out, help him. It's
really hard for him to ask for support from
anyone but he may just reach out to you.
Hope you don't think I'm being too presumptuous.
I just know that he means a lot to you too.*

Have a lovely weekend.

Linds xx

Now it all made sense. He had gone to visit the man who had murdered his best friend and had tried to murder him. The man who had killed so many and put Kade through the torture of seeing him so that he would release information about the identification and location of the bodies of the other victims that were still missing. Kade would sacrifice his sanity to meet that evil man. And something had happened to move that meeting up.

A sense of urgency came over me.

"Hey Jason," I called. He had been talking to a friend he had bumped into at the bar but headed my way when I called out.

"Whats up Lexi?"

"I need to head out. Something has come up. I'm so sorry."

"Everything ok?"

"Yeah, just need to sort something out before the weekend."

"Sure. Let's go take the drinks to the others and I'll walk you out."

I said my hasty goodbyes to my colleagues, conscious not to show my unease and worry.

Jason walked me out of the bar and hailed a cab for me, giving me a friendly hug before letting me go. The journey to Kade's place took less than ten minutes but it felt like an eternity to me. I just hoped that when I got there, he wouldn't close himself off.

***

"Good evening Miss De Luca," the night manager said as I passed him in the lobby of Kade's building.

"Good evening Duncan," I replied with a tired smile. He insisted on formality and I had stopped trying to get him to do otherwise.

Since becoming Kade's PA, I had been given the keys and full access to his home.

I took the lift up to the top floor and knocked softly on his front door. After a minute, I heard feet pad slowly across the floor on the other side as he opened the door. I wasn't prepared when I took in his appearance. His eyes looked hollow and sunken, a light stubble had made his usually clean shaven face look older. His casual shirt was creased, jeans hung low and hair disheveled from running his hands through it multiple times. In his hand was a tumbler full of amber liquor. From the looks of it, he had been hitting the bottle most of the evening. The moment he looked at me and I could tell he couldn't be left alone tonight.

"Hey. Can I come in?" I asked tentatively. He looked a little surprised but didn't answer and just opened the door wider for me to step inside. His home looked as neat and pristine as usual except for a cardboard box, mostly full of paper, placed on his coffee table as if it was unwanted yet important at the same time. He sat down and on the couch and stared at the box as he took a deep drink from his glass. I sat myself close to him, taking the glass out of his hand and placing it carefully on the coffee table. My feet were killing me so I slipped off my office heels and pulled my feet up behind me on the couch. He didn't stop staring at the box. I gave him a few seconds before I took one of his cold hands in mine. The moment I started to rub warmth into them, he broke his gaze away and looked down at me with his intense blue oceans.

"Why did you come?" I knew he wasn't being rude, wasn't accusatory. He meant something else and I felt a pang of sadness that someone who had so many friends and was constantly surrounded by people, could feel so alone.

"Why wouldn't I?" He looked away and rubbed his face with his free hand. He didn't want to break the connection of his hand in mine and neither did I.

We sat quietly for some time and that was fine, as long as he was still present in the here and now with me. I'd do anything to stop him dragging the past into the present to torture himself. I struggled with my emotions for this man. How had he come to mean so much to me in such a short amount of time?

I started to lean on his shoulder but he lifted his arm to bring me in close to his chest. His breathing was calm yet his heartbeat was erratic. It started to slow a little as I snuggled closer to him. I tried not to think of the fact that I was lounging in the arms of my boss. I'd deal with all that later. I just kept still and closed my eyes and when he spoke, his voice was hoarse.

"He's dead." My heart jumped at his words. The silence felt deafening. After I composed myself, I asked him to clarify.

"Bates?" He didn't look at me.

"Yeah. Marlon Bates is dead. Murdered by an inmate. He knew he was going to die when I saw him. He orchestrated it."

I shivered from the thought of how sick a person could be to set up his own murder. Kade pulled me closer to him and rubbed my arm for warmth when I was the one that should've been giving him comfort.

"How do you feel about it?" His jaw clenched and he finally looked down at me with cold eyes.

"I feel cheated. I feel like he shouldn't have been able to decide when he dies. He should have suffered like he made all those people suffer, how he made Scott suffer. The bastard got diagnosed with last stage prostate cancer. He somehow managed to coax the warden into allowing him an hour out in the yard a day away from his solitary confinement and thats where it happened. He got to put an end to his life the way he wanted it. They said he laughed as the man stabbed him repeatedly. Sick son of a bitch!"

He stood abruptly, careful not to hurt me and walked over to the floor to ceiling windows overlooking the city, hands in his hair. I worried what kind of damage he was doing to his beautiful locks of dark hair and, moreover, the damage being done to his soul. I remained seated where I was as he breathed through his anger and frustration. When he seemed to breath slower, I spoke.

"What did he say to you?" Kade sighed and came back to sit down next to me, leaving some space.

"Barely a few words. First, he told me he knew I wouldn't marry Giselle, like he told me the last time I saw him, because I wasn't the marrying type," he scoffed, "then he had a message for Sally, the woman he had tormented all those years, asking me to tell her that he will be watching her from beyond the grave, as if I would pass on his message onto her." I shuddered again at the thought. Kade moved a little closer.

"Did he give you anything on the missing people?"

"He said the map shows it all. God knows what fucking map that is. I have no idea. He gave this box with all of all his crazy ramblings from the past years to me the day I went to visit, the prison staff had checked it all out before handing it to me. It's basically all of his possessions, since the bastard knew he won't be needing them. The detective that had been heading the case from all those years ago is coming tomorrow and I will be voluntarily giving him this stuff as evidence. I have until the morning to look through this. Bates gave me this for a reason, probably to taunt me, but I can't make myself look at it."

"If I helped you, would it make it easier?" He looked weary.

"I can't ask that of you."

"Too bad, because I want to." I gave him a sad smile, knowing what this must have been doing to him.

"You're going to help me read through this transcript of evil? Are you sure you want to?"

"I'm sure. I want to help find some clues as to where these poor souls might be so their families can put them to rest."

"Alexa, you can't un-see what you read there," he pointed to the box, "I don't want that for you."

"If I can help in any way to put an end to the pain and suffering of so many families then it's of little consequence.

I can be selfless for today, just like you." He thought my words through, you could see the gears working. Finally he conceded.

"Okay, but the moment it gets too much, you leave it. Deal?"

"Deal. I wish I had brought more comfortable clothes though, this skirt doesn't allow much movement," I griped.

He held up his finger motioning for me to wait and retreated upstairs to where his room was while I waited. When he returned, he had changed into some jogging bottoms and a t-shirt and was holding a pair of new boxer shorts and a white t-shirt that looked clean but well worn. I took them gladly and changed in the downstairs bathroom, feeling bad for enjoying his scent on the t-shirt at a time like this. The ensemble was loose but comfortable.

I met Kade in his living room again where he had placed the contents of the box on the table and had made us both a fresh coffee. We took out the mass of papers and started to first order the letters and journal entries in chronological order. It was going to be a long night.

***

It was 2am when we had a breakthrough. We had been going around in circles reading all the letters and poems Bates had written for five hours. Some of his writing was just his boring day to day life in solitary confinement, thinking of his days in his cave. A lot of his writing seemed to be some sick romanticised version of his murders in poetry form. The majority was about his fantasies of Sally and the sick things he wanted to do to her. I skimmed most of those letters for fear of throwing up. Just when we were about to give up, I noticed a faint drawing on one of the pages I had placed face down because of feeling nauseous. Kade had been running his hands through his hair in frustration for some time. I showed him the outline.

"Doesn't this look a little like a piece of a map?" He looked closely, his eyes focussing a little more.

"Wait, there was another a bit like that here somewhere."

He searched the pile he was reading from and found it. We put the pages together and they seemed to match. After that we searched through the backs of all the pages that had poems written on just one side. By three am we had a big map laid out on the floor. Each poem on the other side was an indication to who was buried on that part of the map. It was upsetting just how many bodies lay hidden on this stretch of land in such a beautiful place. Kade and I stood, exhausted, and he held me to his side with one arm as he dialled the number of the detective.

"Kurt, sorry to wake you but we've found something. I mean, I've...found something. Come over. Ok. See you in a bit."

We waited twenty minutes after which Kade's buzzer alerted us to the arrival of the detective. Kade asked me to wait in his office while he talked to the detective, to avoid involving me any further. Unfortunately, Detective Anderson with his keen eye for detection and detail, noted the coffee cups and my heels at the side of the sofa and Kade called for me to come out.

"Am I in trouble detective?" I asked, a little self conscious wearing Kade's clothes. That too, what would be considered his underwear.

"How much do you know?" His voice was deep and he smelled of stale cigarettes. He had been a young detective when the case was first brought to him and now he looked old beyond his years. He had come out especially for the meeting Bates scheduled with Kade to try and gain more information on the missing victims.

"I skimmed through the letters...I didn't want to read, only to find something to help..." Detective Anderson rubbed his face but gave me a smile.

"Okay, I'm gonna get someone out here to process what you found. Should be done in an hour or two. I will need to take your finger prints for elimination and I will need a statement from you as to why you were here but you are not to mention a word of your involvement in this to anyone, Miss De Luca. Do you understand?" I nodded and quickly collected my things and put the cups away.

Everything seemed to move very quickly after that. I went into Kade's master bedroom after giving the detective a formal statement and washed my face in his luxurious bathroom, tempted to take a bath but knowing it would be seriously overstepping the boundaries. He had told me to just sleep in his room so I pulled back the covers of his massive bed and sunk into the softness. Thankfully, he had blackout curtains so whenever the sun rose, I would be none the wiser. I shot off a quick message to Allison and Sadie that I would be staying with a friend and didn't hear any of the voices downstairs as I drifted to sleep with the scent of Kade all around me.

Sometime later I felt the bed dip and the warmth of a body close to mine.

"Shhhh, it's just me. Sleep." He didn't have to tell me twice.

CHAPTER TWENTY FOUR

Just let go

I woke up with a start. My dreams had been infiltrated with the imagined voice of Marlon Bates, reading his gruesome poetry of romanticised rape, cannibalism and murders. With eyes wide open now, I felt unsure of where I was and my surroundings seemed foreign until I remembered what had happened earlier.

Kade was not there beside me and after walking to the curtains, I found that it was still a dark early morning, although the night sky had lightened somewhat. Checking the clock on the dresser, I read five am. I pulled on a robe I found on a chaise and carefully made my way around Kade's home looking for him. I didn't care how crazy I looked, I just knew that my dream had shaken me and I wanted his comfort. Door after door presented me with yet another beautifully designed room. His office, two guest rooms, another bathroom, a gym. I finally found some stairs leading up. At the top was a rooftop garden. Standing there watching the city below was Kade. I realised then that rooftop gardens were his 'thing.'

"Hey."

He turned around slowly, a sad smile on his face. He looked so tired, so defeated.

"Hey. Are you okay? Did I wake you?"

"No and no." Immediately, he took long steps towards me, holding me at arms length to look at me carefully.

"What happened?"

"Nothing Kade, it was just a bad dream." He cursed under his breath and looked away.

"This is why I didn't want you looking at those letters. I didn't want to bring this evil into your life as well."

"Oh shush, you. I had a bad dream because I was worried about you, it would have happened whether I read those letters or not. I was worried about you."

He looked at me with softer eyes, his smile easier.

"I'm okay, no need to worry yourself."

"No, you're not. But you will be." I place my hand on his heart, not realising that he was actually bare chested until the shock of his naked skin on my palm made me shiver. He thought that I was feeling cold and pulled me into him. His scent was intoxicating. He seemed to be breathing me in too. I sighed. This is what I needed to feel safe again, to feel happy.

"I don't know how I could have gotten through all those letters without you."

"I'm glad I could be there for you." He pulled back slightly to look me in my eyes.

"I'm glad you're still here."

"You just like keeping me trapped in your tower," I shot back.

"You have the most imaginative names for the places I frequent. 'Tower,' 'Fort.' Have you any other names for the brown stone house?"

"Yeah. That one is your 'home.'"

His smile was wide at my answer.

"Yeah, it is my home. It's where you are."

"You are so cheesy, Hamilton," I tried to laugh away

the shyness I felt. He made me feel like I was the only woman he could truly see.

"It's true. This isn't some chat up line Alexa."
Suddenly serious, he looked down at me, still holding me so close I could feel his heartbeat pick up.

"Well, it's been a long time since you've been home." I felt my breath hitch. It felt like something was about to shift, like something would happen any second.

"I intend to fix that."

His head bent closer, my eyes closed and then there was only the feel of his lips on mine. Soft yet demanding, his kisses stole my breath away. His tongue on mine, licking and teasing. His teeth nipping softly at my lips and then kissing them better. My hands found their way into his hair, his hands found their way through the open robe and under the t-shirt, onto the skin of my back. My head tried to make me see sense but my heart said *fuck it.*

As if he could hear my internal struggle, he simply said, *"Let it go, just let go."* And I did.

He lifted me so I could wrap my legs around him. I pushed his robe off of his shoulders and he did the same with mine. He started walking, carrying me back downstairs like an expert, all the while kissing me so deep that I could not see, hear, smell or taste anything but him. He bumped into a door frame and cursed and I laughed which earned me a growl as he reclaimed my lips with renewed purpose.

We reached his bedroom and I reached out trying to find the door handle, my hand catching an ornament on a table in the corridor that dropped and smashed to bits. I broke from his kiss, concerned for the damage but he wouldn't let me get away, instead kicking his door open and then shut, walking to his bed and almost throwing me onto it. He looked like a masterpiece standing there, beautifully sculptured.

My nipples puckered to attention as he prowled slowly and closer to me, first one knee making the bed dip, then his hands, crawling up over my body. I looked at his muscular body, feeling like a pervert for staring with so much lust in my eyes. He caught every look and when I finally looked up at him, the same hunger was reflected in his eyes. I pushed the remaining of my niggling doubts away from my mind as I reached out for his face so close to mine and bit his lip. That was enough to send him over the edge.

He lifted off the t-shirt I was wearing, and kissed my neck whilst he unclasped my bra. I helped him take it off and I gasped as he immediately closed his mouth around one nipple as his hand found the other. He suckled and licked each one and kissed around the curves as my hands travelled down his back to grip his firm ass under his boxers. His groan vibrated into my skin as he kissed me between my breasts.

Kissing my lips, he looked at me as he travelled down my body, taking off the rest of my clothes and baring me to him. I should have felt self conscious but in that moment I felt as if I was the only woman who could make him go crazy for me.

I felt his mouth on me *down there* and lost myself. Every movement from him stirred a reaction from me. I writhed and moaned beneath him, he was driving me crazy with his tongue. When he finally returned his lips to mine, I was desperate for him. Nothing about us was gentle, there was only an urgency to connect. No words spoken. Just primal carnal lust.

He removed the rest of his clothes swiftly and I felt him against my sensitive flesh, asking permission to enter with just a nudge. I shifted my hips to position him on me. My body said, 'I'm yours,' and his responded in much the same way.

My breath caught when he entered me with a thrust, his length thick and filling. His rhythm was never slow, just urgent. I met his actions with my own desperate need. I hadn't been with a man for so long now, and never with anyone so alpha male like him. He felt like an awakening, a different league to anyone I had ever been with. The sensations were intense as we ground into one another, his body against mine, sweat slicking the skin as he kissed me hard and fucked me deep. This wasn't us making love, this was us making sense.

When I let go and moaned his name, he got thicker and harder and poured into me with the most delicious sounds. And I had never known that I had wanted this so badly until I finally had it.

***

I felt the weight of an arm holding me close to a warm muscular body when I regained consciousness from sleep. Unlike the time before when I had awoken, I knew exactly where I was. And I panicked. *You just slept with your boss, your landlord, your friend!*

Funny how I had allowed those thoughts to just slip out of my mind when I was lusting after Kade and his body. I didn't have the mental energy to even start to think about my feelings for Kade in all of this.

I snuck a look at his peaceful face, a sliver of sunlight peeking in through the curtain that remained slightly open, illuminating his chiselled features. Long lashes kissed his cheeks and I tried not to sigh or even breathe as I slowly lifted his arm from the comfortable space it had been resting on over my naked torso. I felt the chill from being away from his body heat immediately. He stirred slightly, only to shift position and continue to sleep. I thanked my lucky stars as I quickly made my way to the bathroom to clean up and change. In the mirror by the vanity, I couldn't help but notice the difference in the way I looked. Completely naked, my skin looked flushed, there were a couple of love bites on my breasts and at the base of my neck, my eyes looked bright and my face rosy pink. I hadn't before realised that sex made you look incredibly refreshed. But this wasn't just sex. It was sex with Kade.

I pushed the thought out of my head while I quickly relieved myself, washed my face and then changed into my slightly rumpled clothes from the previous day and dug into my bag for a hair tie and brush. I didn't bother with make up, I just grabbed my bag and quietly left the bathroom. Kade was still dead to the world as I made my way to the discarded boxers, bra and t-shirt I had worn in the night. I grabbed the bra and, after a moment of hesitation, the t-shirt too and threw it into my bag. I could not find my knickers. I had one last look at him and then I quietly left the room, braless and knicker-less but thankful for my long blazer covering me and my abundant chest.

I made my way down and onto the street, aware that it was now 10am on a Saturday morning and the world was awake and on the move. I avoided looking at anyone I encountered for the irrational fear they may somehow find out what I had done and with whom.

I hailed a cab and sat inside gratefully. It was then that I let my calm leave me and the thoughts that I had quieted down earlier had returned. What the hell had I done?

**

"What's wrong?"

I had been inside the house for barely two minutes when I ran into Sadie and Allison in the kitchen eating breakfast as I reached for a glass to get some water. Allison picked up on my mood in an instant and looked at me suspiciously.

"Nothing."

"Don't bullshit me Lexi. I know you, somethings up. Where have you been all night?"

I looked at Sadie and she looked at me with questions in her eyes. I glanced down at my feet while I fidgeted and felt heat rise to my cheeks at the embarrassment of Allison finding out what had happened. Because she would. She was like a bloodhound and she never quit until she would know everything there was to know.

I wracked my brain for something to say but I took too long. Her eyes lit up as she figured it out.

"You slept with someone! Oh my God! This is great! I didn't know you were dating anyone! Oh no, wait, was he a one night stand?" Allison had the answer she needed when I finally found the courage to look her in the eyes.

"Wow, Lexi...look at you living wild! I'm so glad you're moving on. I just hope he was good to you. Is he anyone we know?" This entire time, I had only spoken one word. But when I looked at Sadie after hearing Allison's question, I knew I was caught. Sadie's eyes widened, she smiled at me and Allison took one look at her and I knew there was no damage control now.

"It was Kade? You slept with Kade?!"

"Fuck my life," I grumbled as I sat with my water at a kitchen stool and planted my face on my arms, unable to look at either of them. The excitement was palpable as they huddled around me looking for more information.

"Lexi, is everything okay?" Sadie asked, concerned at my behaviour.

"I don't know," my reply was muffled and I felt my stomach drop a little. Consequences were the darnedest of things.

"Did he hurt you? Did you fight? What's wrong hun?" Now Allison was worried. The best policy was the truth, but only enough without compromising Kade's trust.

I told them that Kade had been stressed about something and I had gone over. One thing led to another and we had ended up in bed together.

"So, what's the problem? He is completely into you, you're into him. It's simple," Allison said, placing buttered toast in front of me which I bit into gratefully.

"It's not. He's my boss *and* my landlord. This is overstepping so many boundaries."

"Lexi, we live in the twenty first century my love. No

one should judge you for liking him. And even if they did, why should it matter? Tell me, when do you think you will get the opportunity to find a guy like him? He's one of a kind, he won't be on the market forever you know."

She had a point, it shouldn't matter. But it did to me. I looked to Sadie for grounding and she looked at me with an understanding beyond her years. I wondered what she may have experienced to be so wise and weary.

We hadn't been chatting long when I heard the door bell and then a banging on the door. Sadie hopped off her stool and walked down the hallway to open the door. Allison and I followed slowly behind and by the time we reached the door, I could see a large hooded figure at the doorstep - a large *angry* looking hooded figure.

Sadie let him in and closed the door behind him. Allison looked a little excited and a little terrified all at once. She stood planted to her spot watching me and him with rapt attention until Sadie quietly pulled her away to the kitchen again. And then I was alone with him.

He started to stalk forward towards me and I walked cautiously backwards into the main living room. I only stopped when I bumped into a wall. He continued walking until he was just a centimetre away from me. I could feel his heat, anger, annoyance and lust all at once. He pulled his sweatshirts' hood away from his head and I was greeted with hard and questioning eyes, lips pressed into a thin line. He looked good enough to eat and his steely gaze was turning me on. My nipples betrayed me and he glanced lazily at them through my braless shirt situation, eyes growing stormier to a darker shade of blue.

"What the actual fuck, Alexa?" When he spoke in his deep voice, it vibrated through my body, doing funny things to my stomach. I opened my mouth to say something but he continued.

"I just woke up a short time ago, having had the best sex of my life, to find that the woman I have been fantasising about since I met her was gone without a word. No note, no call, no explanation."

He placed his hands and arms on the wall on either side of my shoulders, leaning his body into mine. My breath caught when I realised that under his hoodie and sweatpants, he was commando. His breathing was a little heavy and his chest sweaty through the halfway zipped sweatshirt.

"Did you just run all the way here?"

"Part of the way, traffic stopped the car from moving as fast as I wanted and I have a pressing matter of urgency, Alexa. Don't change the subject. Why did you just leave me like some dirty one night stand?"

"I..um..we..uh..."

"Yeah?"

"What we did..uh..." *This is new for me.*

"Sex. We had sex. Amazing sex. You're welcome. Now why did you run away Alexa? Did I hurt you? Is it because we didn't use protection? I need answers and my patience is running thin."

And boy did he look like he was annoyed. Which only made him look more appealing. There was something seriously wrong with me.

I took a deep breath and pushed him a little away from me with both my hands on his semi bare chest. Ignoring the warmth of his skin and tingles in my hands, I gathered the courage to look him straight in his eyes and answered truthfully.

"No, I'm sorted...protection wise. And clean, which I trust you are too. We, uh, got caught up in the moment. I was scared, you were emotionally exhausted. We sought one another for comfort. That's all it was. I came back home because I didn't want to face the awkwardness...and because I'm not particularly happy that less than two months into my new job, I've slept with my boss." I thought that maybe Kade would understand when I explained it like that but he looked madder.

"So that's why you left, because you care about what people might think? Or is it because you don't want to be anywhere near me?" He looked a little hurt but tried to hide it under that brooding, moody man facade.

"I didn't say that. I do like you. I just don't think it's a good idea for us to have…relations…when we work so closely together and you're my boss. Not to mention, you're my landlord!"

He inched closer slowly, my hands still pressed against his chest.

"So you would be happy just having an employee and employer relationship with me? Nothing more?"

"I want us to still be friends. I don't want things to be weird." He laughed humourlessly.

"Bit late for that, don't you think? If I had known this is how you'd react to something that happened so naturally, I wouldn't have touched you."

His words stung, I felt the rejection he was feeling in that instance and cursed myself. Why couldn't I be like him? Fearless of consequences and led by my heart?

"Please don't say that." My words were a whisper. He chose that moment to press all the way into me, pushing me against the wall and I let my hands find their way under his sweatshirt onto his bare skin and around his back. He kissed me softly, his lips soft and sweet. My body betrayed me as I kissed him back. When he pulled back, his eyes were softer, and pleading.

"Do you still want to back off? Do you want to stop this?" I wanted to say no but my mind was thinking of the practical reasons why I wanted to say yes.

"There's no other way Kade, I need to concentrate on myself and you need time, you said yourself. We're just getting caught up in the moment. Please try to understand."

I felt the immediate cold from the absence of his body against mine as he left my space abruptly and walked out towards the front door. I think I had expected much more of a fight from him and the way he just up and left hurt me. Now I was annoying myself with my mixed emotions.

I couldn't see his face as I struggled to keep up with him and called his name as he reached the door handle. He stopped but didn't turn around.

"Can't we still be friends?"

I selfishly didn't want to lose him. My internal conflict was killing me. When he finally turned to face me, his face was hard and blank. Emotionless. He put up the hood of his sweater low, covering his eyes from me with a baseball cap under it.

"I'll see you at work on Monday morning Alexa. Be there at 8am. The staff meeting will be at 10am, I will need everything set up and all the paperwork ready before then."

He didn't leave me time to respond as he turned and jogged down the steps to the waiting car that had caught up with him from the traffic. I stood, watching the car as it sped off, wondering how things had gone from easy to hard in an instant.

Sadie and Allison appeared by my side when I shut the door. I tried not to cry, to look strong. I made a decision but it may have been the wrong one.

"You guys heard?" They both nodded.

"I'm sorry honey," Allison said, pulling me to her for a hug. Sadie wrapped her arms around us both whilst I broke down in tears. I had made a decision to walk away, now I had to face the consequences.

CHAPTER TWENTY FIVE

Cold Shoulder

A month had passed since that night I had spent with Kade and all I was left feeling was empty. I would go to work everyday and Kade would treat me like another employee. Only, he wouldn't smile or joke like before and he was always serious, always stressed about something he was working on but would never want to talk about it, or much else, with me. My breath would catch every time he would look me in the eyes because he was excellent at wearing his mask of indifference. But every now and then there was a little fire. Like tonight, as I walked into the office wearing my dark red dress, ready for the social event we had to attend for the company, networking with others.

It was a Friday night in September and it had started to get a little chillier now that we were approaching the end of the month. Even though my dress was long length and long sleeved, it was backless and so I had a light jacket with me which Kade helped me on with, forever the gentleman. When his hand accidentally skimmed my back, I almost jumped out of my skin at the contact. He removed his hand quickly and looked annoyed with me.

"That was not intentional," he stated, taking a step back as he picked up his tie and started to knot it.

"I know."

I hadn't had time to go home and change for the event so I had used Kade's personal bathroom to get ready in his office. He seemed to struggle with his tie in his frustration so I removed his hands to stop him from strangling himself and undid the knot to start again. It was all so very domestic and strangely wasn't awkward. He started to relax while I carefully made the knot.

"You're quite good at this." These were the first conversational words I had heard him speak to me in weeks. I'd take what I could get.

"My Grandpa could never tie his tie properly. I was always the one doing it because he didn't like the way Granna did it. He said that she used the tie as an excuse to try to throttle him," I laughed at the memory, smoothing down his shirt collar. I glanced up at Kade and his eyes had softened a little, a small smile on his face making it more handsome than ever. He had been so serious and indifferent for so long that this change was a crack in the exterior. A miracle.

I didn't get to enjoy it for long because the elevator sounded and the noise of heels clacking on the marble floor made me visibly cringe, which didn't go unnoticed by Kade. He just moved to the side to greet the blonde bombshell with a kiss on her cheek and a smile. I didn't get any kisses on the cheek anymore, not even the smiles. But that smile he gave her didn't reach his eyes, I could see that.

Her name was Lisa Montgomery and she was a lawyer Kade and the company had hired to help with some of the extra workload he had recently been swamped by. She usually worked at the LA office but was currently based in New York where she was needed for the current case.

It had been two weeks since she had walked through his office door and I was introduced to her as she blatantly looked Kade up and down like he was something delicious to eat. She was good at her job but even better at digging her nails into him. He seemed to enjoy her company, maybe just to piss me off or maybe he actually found her conversation stimulating but I knew one thing for sure - I hated her.

She would spend hours with him in his office or the board room working late into the night as they ordered take outs so they could continue their work. And I would be on the outside during the day, at my desk with a view of his office through the glass. Sometimes the blinds were down and I would imagine what might be happening behind them and tried to push the thoughts out of my mind. Kade was too professional to do anything in his own office. *But does she go home with him?* It was none of my business. I had decided to walk away before anything real had started so now I would have to bear it. The women fawning over him, his coldness and the endless torture I acquired because of my own stupid thoughts.

Every day, I could still feel his hard body on my soft one from that night we had gotten entangled in this ridiculous situation. And every day I wanted him more. *It's your own fault,* that voice in my head would whisper and I would remind myself that I had to live with it.

It had only been a week after Lisa had joined that the papers and magazines caught scent of the new woman in Kade's life. From the rumours they had written about, Kade had found a replacement for Giselle. They had found out everything about her, pictures of her from her high school year book, her credentials. She was a stunner.

I couldn't be sure if Lisa and Kade were actually romantically involved because Kade was very professional with her at work but the pictures in the magazines told a different story. A couple were of them laughing, some of him walking into a building with his hand at the small of her back, a lot with her hand on his arm or chest when out in public. The pictures seemed to tell a story. I tried not to think too much about it, but then she was always around.

"You look rather handsome today," she cooed in her sugary voice. *Temptress.*

"And you look stunning Lisa, as always." *Ugh. Get me out of here!*

Lisa waved at me as an acknowledgement of my presence and I reciprocated with a forced smile. I noted that she was wearing an almost identical colour to the one I was wearing. Her dress was, however, short and tight with a low neck line which I would deem unsuitable for a high profile event such as the one we were about to attend.

Kade grabbed his suit jacket and held open the office door and we filed out. As we reached the elevators and Lisa was talking to Kade about revising some clause in one of the contracts they were working on, Travis O'Connor joined us and I felt relief flow through me.

Travis was a Chief Finance Officer and about Kade's age. He had, like Kade, achieved a lot at a young age and was very easy to get along with. He would have you in stitches in minutes at any given time and I had been told by a couple of the girls at work that he had a thing for me. He was a little too handsome for his own good, which made me giggle sometimes when he acted like an idiot despite his intelligence and looks. He had a huge grin on his face as he approached, which in turn made me smile because I knew that as awkward and difficult as it might be around Kade and Lisa tonight, I'd be able to get some respite in the form of Travis' company.

"Lexi, you look absolutely gorgeous. More than usual." I blushed and caught Kade looking at us through narrowed eyes.

"You scrub up well yourself, Travis."

Travis took my hand and kissed it. I didn't need to look at Kade to know he was getting worked up because he was paying no attention to what Lisa was saying now and as soon as the doors opened for the elevator he stepped in quickly and pressed the button for the ground floor.

"Good evening Kade, Lisa," Travis smiled. They reciprocated.

"Where are you off to?" Lisa asked in her faux sweet man trapping voice.

"Same place as you. Banks had a family emergency so he's asked me to step in for him. Luckily, tonight won't be so much of a drag, seeing as Lexi Lou is here with me." He winked and I giggled because he was a sweetie and I hadn't loosened up in ages.

"Lexi Lou? That's...new. I guess that's better than 'Lex Luther.'"

Lisa looked intrigued and asked what that was all about whilst Kade slipped his mask back on and pretended I didn't exist.

"Every time Travis here bumps into me, he has a new nickname. It's getting out of hand," I play punched his arm and he feigned being hurt.

"It's only because she looks so sad all the time. I can't live with looking at sad eyes, especially such pretty ones."

Travis was unknowingly exposing something I really didn't want mentioned in public, but he was unaware. I glanced at Kade and he was full on staring at me as if he was looking inside my soul. I didn't like the feeling and instead focussed my attention back on Travis as we exited the elevator. Travis pulled me into one of the waiting cars, insisting that we travel together rather than with the others so that we were more 'comfortable.' I didn't argue, I needed to get away from the annoyance Kade was radiating and the way in which Lisa kept pawing at him, using any excuse to touch him. It was going to be a long night.

***

Travis was a gentleman, getting out to open the car door, and any other door, for me. He paid attention to me and I couldn't deny that it felt good after four weeks of getting the cold shoulder from Kade. And there were so many laughs to be had.

I was meant to attend some of these events with Kade so that I would have exposure as to what was going on with different companies and clients, gather information on likes and dislikes and be his walking talking reminder.

Travis kept stealing me from Kade's side and because this didn't seem to bother my boss as he was too busy indulging Lisa and their other peers with shop talk, I let him.

We walked around the big room of the hotel, stopping as he talked to some important CEO or another and picked at some of the canapés being served. He told me stories about his escapades when he went backpacking through Europe and then his trips to the far east. He was an exciting guy, I could see his appeal but my thoughts always came back to *him.*

An hour into the event, Kade approached me as Travis was making me laugh about the way one of the bankers there was wearing his wig.

"Alexa, a *word.*"

His curt words and rude manner made my stomach drop and I excused myself from Travis to follow him to a quiet space a little way away. He didn't keep me waiting to hear what he had on his mind.

"Are you here to socialise?" He looked deceptively calm.

"Um, no?"

"Then I expect you to do your job." I felt my cheeks heat.

He had been cold and distant and had acted like my boss for all these weeks instead of my friend but he had never reprimanded me. I felt like a kid being told off in class. Considering that Kade was my boss, I had no choice but to suck it up.

"I'm sorry, I didn't realise-"

"You need to focus on the job at hand. I need you to

be alert and able to assist me when I need you. The last I checked, you work for me and not O'Connor."

Although he said it with practised calm, I could see his eyes turn steely blue when he mentioned Travis' name. I could hear Jack Mangle and Neil Richardson in my mind. *He's jealous.*

"I'm sorry, *Mr Hamilton*. I will make sure it doesn't happen again." He hated it when I addressed him formerly but since he had become a cold and distant being, I decided it suited him. I walked off towards Travis, conscious that Kade was watching.

"Uh oh, did you get into trouble with the boss because of me?" Travis looked concerned for me but also a little put out.

"He needs me to do my job and he's right. I'm sorry Trav, I'm gonna have to go endure all of those boring conversations about things I don't quite understand as yet." He took my hand and squeezed it.

"It's okay Lexi, you go and we'll catch up at the end. I wanted to talk to you about something anyway."

I smiled and assured him I would meet him later and then walked back to where Kade was standing. He led me with a hand on the small of my back to where Lisa was standing talking to an important looking man.

I ignored the heat I felt of the gentle brush of his hand on my bare skin of my back. Giving myself a mental shake, I focussed on my job as my boss steered us back into the world of media and business.

***

I was exhausted by the time we had finished with the event, having navigated and networked all the way around the room. My face hurt from all the smiling and pleasantries and pretending to take an interest. Luckily, I was able to assist and retain information for work. We already had three business meetings to set up on Monday.

I made my way slowly out of the hotel, following Lisa and Kade who were still talking about the last acquisition of a local newspaper under the Hamilton banner and the meeting scheduled for Tuesday morning to iron out the legal paperwork. Travis was waiting outside, just like he had promised he would.

"I'm glad that's over. Some people love the sound of their own voices in there," he joked. He helped me put on my jacket, brushing some of my hair out of my collar in a more than friendly gesture. I felt a little uncomfortable but that was mainly because I could feel *him* looking at us again.

"Thanks. Me too. Just need my nice warm bed now and to sleep through all of tomorrow." He laughed, his perfect white teeth shining in the lamplight of the night.

"Well, I hope you don't sleep through all of tomorrow because I'd like to take you out to dinner. If you're free."

I was not expecting that. Sure, we joked around and sometimes I allowed him more time in my space than other colleagues but I didn't think he would ask me out when there were many other women interested in him. And I didn't think of him that way because I only really thought of the guy who was standing there radiating a degree of anger and frustration that was making me uncomfortable. I surprised myself with the next words that came out of my mouth.

"Okay. I'm free tomorrow."

I had no idea why I said yes. It could have been because of the way Kade had behaved with me when we were inside. It could be because I was a sick person getting satisfaction from making him lose his mind. Either way, the words were out and I couldn't take them back because Travis gave me a genuine and happy smile and I felt the stab of guilt for being a complete cow.

"Wow, really? I thought you might blow me off."

"I doubt many women say no to you." *Great, now I sound like I'm flirting.*

"I was pretty sure you would but I'm happy you've said yes. How does 7pm tomorrow sound? I'll come pick you up."

"Sounds like a plan, I'll text you my address."

"Do you need a lift home?"

I was about to respond when Kade cut in from where he was standing about a couple of metres away.

"I need you to come with me Alexa. I have some urgent documents I need you to go through before you go home." His tone was authoritative and grated my nerves. I smiled apologetically at Travis.

He held both my hands and smiled before pulling me close for a hug and then a lingering kiss close to the corner of my mouth.

"See you tomorrow Lexi."

"Uh, see you tomorrow Trav." He got into the waiting car and drove off whilst I turned to find that Kade had sent Lisa off in another car. We waited as one pulled up for us and didn't speak all the way to the Fort.

Once we reached the building he walked fast, making it difficult for me to keep up in my heels, pressing on the elevator buttons and security codes hard. Once we were up in his office in the empty building, he pulled off his jacket and tie and threw them on the sofa. He paced like a caged animal for a few seconds before he looked at me. The look on his face made me want to cry. He looked so hurt.

Not knowing how to handle the situation, I settled on picking up his discarded jacket and tie and straightening them to hang in the hidden closet he had behind the desk. He followed.

"What are you doing Alexa?"

"I'm just hanging this up for you."

"No. *What are you doing?* Are you into O'Connor?" I turned to face him, my eyes betraying me.

"I'm just going out with him as a friend." He banged his fist hard on this desk beside him.

"He doesn't think of you as a *friend* Alexa. He *wants* you, I see it in his eyes and every time he touches you. And you *let him!* Was I such a bad experience that you just left me and go find someone like him? It's okay for you to have a relationship with him in the office but you can't even start a relationship with me when you know we have something special?!"

I tried to move past him, unable to explain any of what happened today. He grabbed me by my waist, pulling me closer to him. I placed my hands on his hard chest and pushed, anger consuming me all of a sudden.

"Kade, Travis is a friend and he's not my boss! I don't know why I said yes, okay? I wanted to say no but he was so nice to me. He has been a friend these past four weeks when you've taken your friendship away from me! You've been busy with *Lisa.* And she wants you but I don't see you pushing *her* away!" I expected him to retaliate again but instead he looked relieved.

"You're jealous of Lisa? Alexa, she's just a colleague. She's handsy with everyone."

"No, she *wants* you. She looks at you like you're a gourmet meal."

He laughed then, that beautiful sound lightened me a little but I was still annoyed. This time when he pulled me close, I let him. I missed the scent of him.

"Imagine how I feel when I see that man kissing the woman I want more than my next breath?" He looked down at me and the storm in his eyes seemed to pass and had settled into the deepest, bluest shade I'd ever seen.

"He's a friend and it's my business who I go out to dinner with."

In a split second, the softness was gone. He let go of me and turned around, leaning forward on his desk.

"So, you're still going?" The hard tone in his voice made me more determined.

"Yes." His jaw clenched.

365

"Then there's nothing else for me to say. You're free to go home Alexa. See you Monday morning." With that, he walked off into his bathroom and banged the door shut.

I walked out quietly, wondering how I could ever make things right and whether I could stay in this job when every moment I spent with him had me conflicted and on the edge.

CHAPTER TWENTY
SIX

Making amends

I spent most of the next morning tidying up my room and sorting out my closet. I had so many new clothes for work and the work events I'd had to attend that I needed to make space. Sadie was out with an old friend for the day, making the most of the last lot of good weather we were going to have for a while. Allison and Brent were home for a change, relaxing in the living room watching some romantic comedy. I passed them on my way to the basement with my basket of laundry but before I could reach the stairs, my phone in my back pocket started to ring.

Balancing the heavy basket on lifted knee as I reached for my phone was proving to be a task. I finally got my phone and answered, holding the basket at my hip with the other hand. I didn't recognise the number.

"Hello?"

"Am I speaking with Alexa?" It was a deep, male voice - one that I didn't recognise.

"Yes, this is Alexa. How can I help you?"

"Alexa I'm...this is Adam De Luca. I'm your brother."

My heart thudded in my chest. The first and only time I

had met my older brother, my fathers first born, was when they came to London when I was a child. He didn't seem to like me much back then but I suppose which boy would when he was five years older and meeting his fathers love child.

"Uh, hi." I couldn't manage anything more.

"Alexa, I know that you don't really want to hear from me or Dad, I don't blame you, but I need you to come down to the hospital. Dad's had a heart attack." I dropped the basket I was carrying and almost dropped the phone when Brent ran to steady me.

"Lexi? Alexa?! What's wrong?" Allison was shaking me as Brent took my phone to speak to Adam.

"Dad." That was the only word I could manage as Brent took details from Adam and helped me sit down on the couch in my daze.

"Lexi, Adam said that your dad had a big heart attack and they are trying to stabilise him. Can you hear me? He's in hospital and he's asking for you. Do you want me to take you there?" I managed a nod at Brent's question and tried to get up.

"No, just stay here for a minute okay? I'm going to make a couple of calls first." He motioned to Allison to stay with me as he went into the kitchen. I was still in shock. My dad was in pain, he could leave this earth at any given moment and I hadn't had the chance to make things right. I'd been stubborn, ignoring his calls, keeping hold of the past when all he wanted was to put things right.

"Hey, it's going to be okay Lexi. Brent's going to drive us to the hospital, we're going to be there in no time at all. Let's get your shoes on."

She was treating me with kid gloves but I was grateful for her. She was keeping it together for me. As soon as we stepped outside and Brent opened the car door, I looked at Allison.

"What if it's too late?" A big tear drop fell from my

eyes. Allison looked at me with tears in her eyes.

"He will be okay Lexi, I can feel it."

"I hope you're right." We sat in the car as she put a comforting arm around me. I watched the world go by outside of the window and prayed.

Please God, don't let it be too late.

***

From the moment the car stopped, up until the time I reached the door to the waiting room, it was all a blur. I just tried to concentrate on breathing. Why should I be surprised that I felt pain for someone who had not been in my life for ninety percent of it? Nature was cruel that way, placing love in our hearts for those who sometimes didn't deserve it. But somewhere in my heart, I knew that my dad wanted to make things right. He wanted to be in my life now. And It may have been too late. I heard a bit of commotion coming from the corridor we had just walked through and then from the double doors bursting open, stood Kade. He didn't say a word, just came up to me and pulled me into his arms and all my composure was lost. I cried like a child, gripping his shirt, wailing in pain. I didn't want to go into the room where my half brother and sister were waiting. I didn't want to hear that I took too long to forgive.

Kade let me cry into him and when my sobs died down, he stroked my hair and gave me courage. Our argument the night before was forgotten, the bitterness gone.

"Come, let's go in together."

He held me close to his side as Allison and Brent went through first and opened the door for us. Inside the room stood a man older than me who looked like a younger version of my dad. *Our* dad. He was standing holding two women at either side of him. One was an older woman, hair dyed red and dressed immaculately. She had been crying, gripping onto her sons shirt for comfort. To his other side was a woman who could have easily been mistaken for me, if she were shorter and if it weren't for her lighter coloured hair. They looked at me, equal measures of curiosity, fear and grief in their eyes. Adam let go of his sister and mother and came up to me. Kade loosened me from his side and held me in front of him by the shoulders in a protective way.

"Alexa, I'm so glad you came. He was asking about you before they took him into surgery."

"S-s-surgery?" I looked back at Kade. Kade squeezed my shoulders and I looked back at Adam.

"They needed to put stents in his heart. He should be out soon." He was tall, and handsome like our dad. He looked down at me, unsure as to how he should approach me. In the end, he took hold of one of my hands tentatively, trying to give me an encouraging smile.

"I wish we weren't having to meet like this in these circumstances," he said, rubbing his thumb over the back of my hand in a comforting gesture. I tried to smile at him.

"Me too."

"Hi Alexa, I'm Dana," the older woman said, smiling as much as the situation would allow her.

"Hi," was all I could muster as I let her take my other hand.

"I'm Annabelle," my older sister spoke.

She had kind eyes, I couldn't see any of the resentment she had shown when I met her so long ago. Oh, how we had grown. She gently pushed her brother and mother aside and surprised me by hugging me tight. We cried silently and I marvelled at how I felt the connection immediately. What was that saying? Blood is thicker than water?

Annabelle let me go gently and wiped tears from her face.

"He's going to be okay," she said, more as a way of re-assuring herself than anyone else. We sat quietly together on the chairs in the waiting room, Kade sitting on one side of me after I introduced my friends to them. They all seemed to know who he was and I could see the curiosity in their eyes but this was not the time nor the place for questions.

Allison and Brent brought us all teas and coffees as we waited, none of us wanting to talk any further with so much noise in our own heads. I leaned my head on Kade's shoulder while held me close to his side, every now and then comforting me with a squeeze. Forty five minutes later a doctor in scrubs entered the room and my heart skipped. Adam got up with Dana when he walked in closer.

"How is he?" The doctor had an infuriatingly unexpressive face and I couldn't read if what he had to say was negative or positive.

"Mr De Luca is out of surgery and is expected to make a full recovery. The procedure went well and without incident and he is now in the recovery suite. We are waiting for the anaesthesia to wear off and will soon be shifting him to his room after observation. You can wait for him in there if you want."

The collective relief we all felt was palpable. Adam shook hands with the doctor and we all talked between ourselves, happier than we had been just moments before. I looked up at Kade and he gave me his most heart melting smile. I reached up on my tiptoes, put my arms around his neck and kissed his cheek before hugging him, letting all my emotions flow through.

"Thank you," I whispered, "the whole way here, all I could think of was how much I needed you." He pulled back to look at me, seeming a little surprised by my words.

"I will always be there in a heartbeat, whenever you need me Alexa. As soon as Brent called, I left home."

I felt something warm in my heart, something I thought had died some time ago. I let myself enjoy this moment of comfort in his arms. I'd think about how I felt when I had time to process it.

***

We were all waiting in my dad's room on another floor to where we were before when they brought him in on his bed. He was still drowsy but smiled when he saw Dana, Adam and Annabelle. They all kissed and hugged him carefully, Dana cried a little and told him how scared she was as he soothed her. I was at the other side of the bed and he hadn't seen me yet. I felt a little envious that they had spent all their lives with him and I didn't even know him at all. Maybe I could change that, maybe that time was now.

When Adam indicated to me as he talked to our father, he finally turned his head and gave me a big smile. I felt myself crumble and Kade was there to hold me up. He was always there to hold me up.

"Hey, it's alright. I'm alright," dad said, reaching out for me. I took his big hand and he tugged gently to get me close enough for me to hug him gently. I cried softly into his shoulder. When I pulled back, I saw his own tears which he wiped away quickly.

"Way to get my attention dad. You could have just waited for me to call you," I joked. Everyone laughed.

"I'm glad you're here, baby girl. And I'm sorry I hurt you." I hugged him again, trying not to cry this time as the emotion welled up inside me.

"It's okay, I know you didn't mean to."

"I'm sorry for not being there. That is unforgivable. But I intend to make up for it for the rest of my life. I got a second chance." He pointed to his heart and we all knew what he meant.

Soon, a nurse ushered us out of the room so he could rest and Dana stayed with him. Adam gave me his and Annabelle's number and then seemed conflicted about something before he just threw his arms around me and gave me a tight hug.

"About what dad said, we intend to make up for it too." I was not expecting it but his words made me smile and when he pulled back he looked relieved.

We parted ways with promises of catching up the next day. I made my way outside with my friends and Kade led me to his car. It was the first time I had seen him drive. He usually was chauffeured everywhere for convenience and because of his security. He owned a couple of cars, from what I'd heard. Out of them all, this had to be the most beautiful by far - an Aston Martin DBS in black. I marvelled at its beauty and Kade smiled at me as we sat inside.

"Such beauty, such grace...." I purred as I pet the smooth interior.

"It's just a car," he said nonchalantly.

"No it's not."

"You're right, it's not." We both laughed as we shared our love for the beautiful machine and I felt the tension I'd held onto all day melt. We got back to the house in no time and I felt both emotionally and physically drained. When I looked at the time on my watch, I swore under my breath.

"What's wrong?" he asked as he parked outside the house.

"I'm supposed to meet Travis for dinner in half an hour! I forgot to call and cancel. I feel like a horrible person right now. I'm going to have to go because to cancel now would be rude."

Kade tried to look unaffected.

"If you want, I could arrange it so that he is suddenly busy." I looked at him suspiciously.

"Um, how would you do that?" Kade gave me a sneaky smile.

"I have ways Miss De Luca. I know a lot of people in a lot of places."

"That sounds scary and quite the bit mafioso..."

"I am half Italian you know."

"So am I."

"Then you understand that I have the means to make people disappear."

"I really hope you're joking."

"Relax Alexa," he laughed, "I can just set the deadline for something big he's working on with his team for Monday instead of Wednesday. They only have a days' worth of work to complete, so it won't be too tough on him and it will get you out of the obligation."

I thought about it. I felt really bad messing with Travis because he was a lovely man but I couldn't bear to go right now. I needed to be home and process everything that had happened today.

"Okay," I sighed. He tried to hide his relief and delight as he tapped out a message to someone. A reply came within a few seconds and a minute later I got a call from Travis.

"Hey Trav," I answered. Kade mouthed '*Trav?*' with a look of disgust and I smacked his arm.

"Hey Lexi Lou. I'm so sorry about this but I'm going to have to cancel our date. The deadline for a very important project has just been pushed up and I'm on my way down to the office now. Please forgive me and tell me you'll give me the chance to make it up to you?" I felt so guilty and I couldn't say no.

"Don't worry about it. In all honesty, its good you cancelled. My dad had a heart attack today and I just got back from the hospital."

"Christ, Lexi, is he okay? You should have called me, I could have been there for you."

It felt a bit weird that Travis would think he would be the first port of call for me.

"Um, he's okay now. He had a procedure done and regained consciousness well. I'll be seeing him tomorrow. And don't worry, I had a couple of friends with me...and Kade was there too." The line was quiet for a bit.

"I'm glad you had people there for you. Please let me know if you need anything. And let me know when you're okay for us to reschedule dinner, okay?"

I was conscious that Kade could hear the conversation

even though he was facing away from me and pretending he couldn't.

"Yeah I will. Probably next week, or the week after, since I'll be visiting dad a lot."

"Of course, I understand. I was really looking forward to seeing you tonight, you always brighten my day." I blushed a little and Kade's knuckles whitened from his grip on the steering wheel.

"You're too sweet Travis. Anyway, I got to go now. I'll speak to you later."

"Good bye Lexi. I'll be seeing you."

"Good bye Trav." I hung up. The air was a little thick with unsaid words. Kade turned to look at me, his expression unreadable but there was a sense that he was in deep thought.

"You have a lot of sway around this town Mr Hamilton."

"With great power comes great responsibility."

"Cute. Quoting Spiderman to me."

"I have in fact been told I am extremely cute. And knowledgable."

I smiled at him, getting that glimpse of how he used to be with me when we were friends.

"Yeah I'm sure. Are you coming home with me?" We looked at one another, knowing what I meant by 'home.' That house was a home. Our home. He didn't speak for a few seconds and then looked straight ahead.

"I can't tonight, got a few things to do. Take the next week off Alexa, you need to spend time with your dad and family. I'll check in on you from time to time."

"Really? Are you sure? I mean, there are those meetings on Monday and Wilcox Associates are coming in on Wednesday-"

"It's not as important as family. Plus I have Lisa and there are the others in the department to help out. Just concentrate on you and your family, okay?" He took my hand

and kissed it. I felt that kiss in my heart. I tried to ignore the sting from hearing that Lisa would be helping him out more.

"Thank you. You're amazing." I hugged him quickly before I could start to cry again and exited the car to return to the house.

I turned and waved to him from the top step, the tinted windows of his car too dark for me to see if he acknowledged. I took a deep breath and went in, seeing Brent and Allison sitting at the dining table with Sadie who had come home, cutting her time with her friend short when she heard about my dad, with take away Chinese food ready for us. I couldn't be more grateful for having the most amazing family of friends. I just wished Kade was with us too, right where he belonged.

CHAPTER TWENTY SEVEN

Caveman

I t's funny how things can change so drastically in just a moment. One minute your life and priorities lead you down one path but all of a sudden something occurs to open new pathways. That is how I felt the next week went along.

We were now feeling the autumnal weather, or 'Fall' as they called it in the states. The colours were beautiful as you walked through Central Park, crisp leaves in so many shades and the light breeze chilly enough for you to want to wear your scarf.

I went to the hospital every day to visit my dad and every time I saw him, he looked better and stronger and five days later they let him go home. During this time I learnt more about my brother and sister and my father and his wife.

Adam was a detective with NYPD and single and Annabelle was married with two kids. I got to meet my two nephews and their dad on the second day I went to visit my dad. Rory and Randall were intelligent but mischievous preteens and were constantly making us laugh in the quiet moments when unfamiliarity made us a little uncomfortable with one another.

My brother and sister were actually quite easy to get along with. Unlike Megan, who was quite a few years younger than me, they were both older and mature with real jobs and responsibilities. Annabelle was a restoration expert and Interior designer. I suppose we got our creativity from our father since he was an artist, mostly active in his younger years.

Once we broke the ice and started talking about everything that we had missed about one another over the years, it got easier to laugh and to be free.

When he got home, dad asked for some time alone with me which was both heart warming and gut wrenching. I didn't know what to expect or how I would feel but I was grateful for his time and I knew I had to let go of whatever resentment I had left if I wanted to move forward and have a relationship with my father.

We sat on his dark cherry leather chesterfield sofa in his beautiful house and he held a scrapbook he had asked me to pull off from a shelf in his study. All around us we were surrounded by beautiful pieces of art and there seemed to be a section for every kind that he loved in every room. It would have looked cluttered in a smaller house but his home was huge and apparently it had been in the family for many decades, passed down from one heir to another.

"This," he said, opening to the first page of the scrap book, "is how I've remembered you all these years."

I was surprised to see he had pictures of me from the day I was born, the few years that he was with my mother, all documented in picture perfect memories. In them, I was always smiling and he was my idol. What surprised me more were the pictures from my yearly school portraits and then my graduation. He had a picture of my wedding, one of Tom kissing me at the altar and another of us smiling at one another. Those pictures made my heart clench. The ones that I had were put away in my parents loft but whenever I saw them, I felt the lingering ghosts of nostalgia and the feelings I had when we were so happy and in love.

The most recent pictures were of me laughing into the camera. I remember these being taken by Jason on one of the days when we were all staying at work after hours to prepare for the soiree we had for his exhibition.

The last one was a picture I never knew had been taken. One of me standing close to Kade as we looked at one another. We weren't laughing but the chemistry was palpable even from the photo. It was from the exhibition because, I was wearing my lace dress. Must have been another picture Jason took.

This time the feeling I had was not nostalgia of a beautiful time that I couldn't get back. These feelings were of pure loss. I hadn't expected to react like that just looking at a picture.

"He's quite a man," my dad observed. I hadn't realised that my fingers were tentatively stroking the edges of the photograph.

"Yeah, he is." In an attempt to stop him from probing further, I changed the subject.

"You kept these all these years?" He lightly touched the picture of me and Tom.

"I was lucky that, despite what happened between me and your mother, she still sent me pictures and told me about how you were doing. It broke my heart when I found out what he did to you." He was referring to Tom. I looked at the happy picture.

"He was a good man, dad. He tried to keep me happy for a while, and I was. I just didn't know that he wasn't. What he did to me is inexcusable and the worst kind of betrayal. It hurt, sometimes it still hurts, but I am getting through it. I do feel stupid sometimes, like I'm not good enough and that maybe I'm better off alone. And then I have my angels here on Earth. All my friends and family with all their love and affection. I am truly blessed."

I couldn't believe how honest and open I was being with my dad who was still, for the better part, a stranger to me. His answering look made me smile. He looked happy that I could confide in him and that sliver of happiness transferred to me.

"Kade is a good man, baby girl. I couldn't think of a better person I know for you to be with."

"We're not together dad. Just friends." He looked at me as if he didn't believe it but graciously changed the subject.

The rest of the day was spent with him and then with my half brother and sister and step-mother as we ate together. Dad was on a strict diet now so he moaned a lot. I thanked my lucky stars again that I had another chance to make things work. This could have gone a whole different way.

I spoke to my mum later on the same day when I got home. I hadn't really brought up what I had been calling her 'betrayal' to her face, even though she knew what had happened from dad. We cleared the air about everything that had been on my mind after I told her about dad and his stint in the hospital. I felt so much better after we spoke. She told me that she was happy that I was getting to know my father and family as she gave me a teary smile on FaceTime and blew kisses. I missed her so much. I made sure I told her just as well.

Over the rest of the week I visited dad at home and got to spend more time alone with Adam and Annabelle. Jason popped in a few times and it was amusing to see how much of an almost father figure/friend relationship he shared with dad.

Kade was true to his word and checked in on me every day in the form of text messages and some funny pictures. One of the pictures was taken during a meeting he was having. He took a picture from under the table of a woman who had taken off her shoe and was cleaning out the crud from between her toes meticulously. It made me simultaneously laugh and want to puke. His caption was funny - 'Priorities in the conference room.'

It was friendly between us over our message exchange but I still felt like we would never be the same. That feeling of loss just seemed to linger and I found myself asking the same questions I had all those weeks ago - did I make a mistake? And most importantly, how could I fix this?

***

Weeks passed quickly and dad seemed to recover well. We met once a week for a coffee or for dinner, sometimes with Adam and Annabelle if they were around.

Work was bearable now that Lisa had been dispensed of to the office in LA. Kade was still the same only he wasn't as harsh with me at work and sometimes I would get a smile or a joke. When he thought I wasn't looking, I could still feel the heat of his gaze on me. I felt the loss of my friend keenly but I knew it was my fault that he held himself back.

I had managed to avoid Travis for a good few weeks due to all of his long term projects mysteriously receiving shorter deadlines. I quizzed Kade about it once out of curiosity and he just smirked at me. Smirked. Like it was a stupid question and his reaction was a good enough answer.

But his intervention didn't stop Travis from calling or texting me. He was a good friend and I realised that I was happy enough for him to remain that way. I told him as much when we happened to bump into one another.

"Has this got something to do with Kade Hamilton?"

"That obvious, huh?"

We were sitting in the staff cafe with coffee during an unusual lull in the day. I had dodged his requests to reschedule our date three times now and he had caught up with me and called me out on it.

"You would have to be blind not to see the tension there," he laughed humourlessly.

"I'm sorry Trav. I don't know what is going on with

me, myself. I think it's just not a good time for me to start a relationship." Even in my head I sounded like a cliched so and so.

"We don't have to start a relationship Lexi, it's just dinner between friends."

I sensed a '*for now,*' in there somewhere and although I didn't want to give him false hope, I agreed to dinner 'as friends' so as not to be rude and I could hear Granna's voice in my head telling me to stop being so English. It was hardly a hardship going to dinner with Travis since he was great company.

I should have known that the little spies in the building would get word back to Mr Hamilton Jr.

***

"This chicken is so tender. Oh my God, I'm in love."

Travis chuckled as he cut into his steak.

"That good, huh?"

"This is now my new favourite restaurant in New York City."

He smiled at me and that smile was infectious, though it didn't make me tingle inside like Kade's smile did, I noted. I pushed the thought aside as I continued with my meal. It was the last week of October and we were in a lovely family run restaurant in Tribeca. We had finally managed to make a plan to go for dinner and I was enjoying the good food and company. Friday night was always a busy night but it was a little quieter than usual tonight which gave us space to enjoy our food and talk without loud noises interrupting us.

Unfortunately, there was something else interrupting us now, as I finished my main course. My phone buzzed and I looked at the screen to see a message from Kade.

Kade: There's been an emergency, need you for work.

I text back immediately, worried what had happened.

*Me: Everything ok? Give me half an hour, I can
get to the office by then.*

Within seconds I got a reply.

*Kade: I'm coming to get you in five. Just stay
there and wait for me.
Will explain on the way.*

I looked up at Travis and my expression must have said it all.

"Work?" he enquired with raised eyebrows.

'Yup. I'm so sorry Trav." He smiled with understanding.

'It's okay Lexi, I can relate. It's what you sign up for. Come on, let me get the cheque and I'll walk you out."

As I waited outside with Travis, something occurred to me.

He wouldn't...would he? The answer was yes. Yes, *he would.*

I managed to school my reaction as I saw Kade's driver pull up and I knew he was in the back seat watching as I stood on tip toes and kissed Travis good night on his cheek, a little close to the corner of his mouth. Travis smirked at me, aware that I may have just used him.

Saying good night, I quickly got into the car as Luke opened the door for me. I didn't dare look at Kade when Luke drove us away. After a few seconds I took calming breath.

"What is the emergency Mr Hamilton?" I chanced a look at him then and his tense jaw relaxed a little when he peered down at me. I realised then that he was wearing a tux and looked extra hot and groomed. Definitely lickable.

"I've been roped into going to a musical as favour for a friend that cannot attend, as a special guest. I need you to accompany me." I tried not to lose my cool.

"That was the emergency? A musical you could have

asked absolutely anyone to? And how is it that you knew exactly where I was just now?" His smile as he looked straight forward was all the proof I needed.

"You sabotaged my dinner with Travis on purpose, didn't you?"

That smile turned cool, as he looked me over, head to toe in slow perusal that made me shiver with lust. I knew what it felt like to have his hands on my body. I knew what it felt like to have him inside me and the ache started all over again.

"Why would I do that?" There was no remorse in his expression, only the aura of a man who had just won the game.

"Well played Hamilton," I muttered to myself as I turned my head away to hide the shiver of excitement at the thought that I had once again unknowingly activated the caveman in him.

CHAPTER TWENTY EIGHT

Iris

Halloween arrived and I got my first taste of just how big they celebrated it in the States. Our street was lined with houses decorated to the max. Skeletons and pumpkins, ghouls and mummies - there was little that was left out.

As it was, Allison had arranged a big party at our house so naturally our place had to be the best decorated. And by best decorated, I meant absurdly over the top. Brent chuckled as his Bride of Frankenstein explained that she had a reputation to uphold. He was obviously dressed as her counter part - Frankensteins monster. I had been roped into wearing a fancy dress of Allison's choice. Tonight I was Princess Jasmine. Allison had sent a supposedly random character to every invitee of our party - there would be his and her outfits to make the group into couples. I complained to Brent that Allison was trying to turn Halloween into a mass hook up event with her terrible penchant for matchmaking.

I groaned as I looked at my abundance of cleavage and naked belly in my harem trousers and top that might as well have been a glorified bra. Since I had left it quite late to get my costume, the more modest Jasmine costumes had already been sold or hired out.

I kept self-consciously covering myself as I made my way past Gomez and Morticia Adams who had found each other in the crowd of misfits. I hated to admit it but some of the coerced couples looked like they were hitting it off. Some, not so much. I caught Batman and Wonder Woman shouting at one another in the kitchen and in the basement Han Solo and Princess Leia couldn't have been sitting further away from one another if they tried. It made me wonder why we all got trapped in Allison's coaxing and crazy ideas.

Sadie was Harley Quinn and she looked HOT. And by that, I mean she was stunning. I had grown so used to her casual daily wear that without her usual jeans and converse and dressed as a character, she seemed to have gained more confidence. She was wearing hot pants after all. I thanked the stars that Allison hadn't given me that character at least, claiming 'random selection.'

I was seriously doubting her selection of the character couples was 'random' and I was proved right when I saw who my characters other half was.

Wearing nothing but the baggy Aladdin pants, waistcoat, fez hat and shoes, Kade stood at the other end of the room bare chested and jaw dropped as he took me in. The feeling was mutual and I was vaguely aware that a lot of the women in the room were lusting for a touch of his golden skin.

We made our way to one another as if we were magnetically attracted to the other. I returned his look of appreciation when we came to a stop just a couple of inches apart.

"You're the sexiest Jasmine I have ever seen."
His eyes were dark with a promise I wish I had the guts to take him up on.

"Not too bad yourself, Aladdin."
The tension was too much to handle and after the initial unbearable few seconds, I started to turn away to defuse the situation when I felt him pull me back towards him by my

waist. His hands on my bare skin pressing that skin to *his* bare skin. Shivers ran through both of us.

"Tonight, I'm not your boss Alexa. We're going to enjoy this as much as we can. Agreed?"

I nodded, stunned by his words.

We swayed to whatever music was playing, unconscious of much else but the feel of one another. I leaned my head on his shoulder and we fell into an easy silence in the crowd.

I had missed the feel of him. The strength of his embrace, the way it felt almost possessive yet liberating. I couldn't help but bask in his attention as we danced to the ever changing music playing on the stereo.

At some point, Kade had to go mingle with some guests and I was pleasantly surprised to see that my brother had turned up too. Allison had made a point of inviting both of my half siblings but Annabelle had a kids party she couldn't avoid and Adam had said he would try and now he was here. His costume, as 'randomly' chosen by Allison, was a cop outfit. Original. I laughed when I saw him find me in the crowd and make his way over.

"You made it!" I said loudly over the music. He gave me a quick hug and grinned, proving he was a good sport. His tight shirt revealed a lot of muscle and I could see he had turned a few heads. I didn't think that I'd feel a sense of pride that my brother was getting checked out by a lot of the females there, but I did.

"I decided it was time for me to stop being a hermit."

"I love the costume," I giggled. He twirled for me and tipped his policeman's hat.

"Couldn't resist. It's been a while since I've been in uniform." We sat down on the sofa that had been pushed to one side to make room for the makeshift dance floor and enjoyed the companionable silence. Suddenly a song started playing on the iPod's randomly selected playlist that felt like it hit me right in my heart. This song had no place at a party in full swing but no one seemed to notice or mind.

I hadn't thought of Tom in weeks, almost months with all my distractions in life but this song got to me.

You know how sometimes certain smells, sights and sounds trigger memories of different times or people? This song was *us* - Tom and me. This song was our's. He played it for me right after he first told me he loved me and we danced to it on our wedding. Adam noticed the change in my demeanour as I frowned, confused as to why now, of all the time I'd had apart from him, I was feeling this way. He squeezed my arm.

"Are you okay?"

I smiled sadly up at him, trusting him for the first time.

"This song was mine and my ex's song. It just brings back memories of him to me." He nodded in understanding and gave me a sad smile.

"I know that feeling."

He didn't elaborate and I didn't push. He had that look of pain behind his green eyes. We sat quietly, his hand on my arm in comfort.

Kade approached me through the crowd, smiling, but his smile vanished and was replaced by a frown when he took in my watery one. Without a word, he pulled me up into his arms into a slow dance I couldn't even refuse. He didn't question, didn't judge. He just sang words into my ear as we swayed.

"...*And I don't want the world to see me, 'cause I don't think that they'd understand. When everything's made to be broken, I just want you to know who I am.*"

And even though this song caused me an anguish of memories of me and Tom, the lyrics rang true for me and Kade.

***

"Have you seen Adam?" I was looking around the masses of people in our house for my brother, worried that I had abandoned him.

"Oh don't worry about your brother. He's found his

jailbird. Just caught them flirting." Allison was right - there he was standing on the stairs with a woman in a striped jail suit laughing and talking. I was relieved and thanked Allison as I made my way to the kitchen for some water. I'd seen Sadie talking with her Joker counterpart earlier. Both of them had so much face paint on for their costume, I wondered if they would ever know one another out of it.

I bumped into some of my old colleagues from Atlantis and was happy to see them enjoying the party and hospitality courtesy of the overload of buffet nibbles and alcohol that Allison had arranged for.

Kade was leaning against the kitchen sink in the empty kitchen when I entered.

"Hey," I smiled, reaching past him to fill the glass at the sink.

"Hey."

"Your head pounding from the loud musical shenanigans too?"

He smirked at my choice of words.

"Nah, just taking some time to breathe."

"Everything okay?"

"Yeah, just busy with work."

I took a sip from my water as I assessed him.

"You work too hard Kade."

"Someones got to do it. I knew what I was signing up for when I took over so I can't complain."

"Still, shouldn't you take some time out? For a holiday?" He raised his eyebrows at that.

"I'd love to but I can't before February. You know my schedule like the back of your hand, it's impossible at the moment." I sighed, knowing he was right.

"Yeah, I know. But still."

His slow cheery smile made an appearance. I missed that smile these days.

"Worried about me, are you?"

"I'm allowed to worry about my boss, aren't I?"

"You keep telling yourself that, sweetheart."

I hid my reaction to his endearment and continued rinsing out the glass I'd just used. He chuckled and placed his hands gently on my upper arms after I set the glass down to bring me in front of him so he had my attention. I didn't feel a shiver of delight at all. *Liar.*

"I'm glad I got you alone, I've been meaning to talk to you about my trip to London in November. I want you to come with me."

"You want me to come with you?" I parroted. I couldn't hide my surprise and then the seed of excitement at the possibility.

"I could use some help and you would get some time to spend with your family."

"You mean I get to go *home?*"

I am sure my eyes were sparkling with happiness at the prospect. Kade gave me an adoring smile.

"Of course. I knew it would make you happy. I heard you saying you missed home the other day when you were on the phone to Linds. I need some assistance whilst there anyway and you can have a few days to spend time with your family. Win-win." He said it like it wasn't a big deal when it totally was.

I felt extremely grateful, my heart swelling with his thoughtfulness. I knew his entire schedule, like he had pointed out, and I knew he didn't really need me in London with him. He was allowing me a free trip home. I wanted to squeeze the life out of him with gratitude. I opted instead to squeal in delight and kiss his cheek tenderly.

"Thank you Kade, you're amazing."

He looked amused but the fire in his eyes and his hand on the bare skin of my waist made me shiver.

"Don't mention it. Come on, lets see this party to the end." He dropped his hand from my waist to grab my hand and led me back into he main room where we laughed and danced all night, forgetting ex's and complications and decided to live in the present, for once.

CHAPTER TWENTY
NINE

The Pursuit

The weeks leading up to our mid November trip to London were pivotal. To say something had changed in my life was an understatement. I spent more time with my father, learning more about him, his life and his family. I was introduced to his Older brother Gianni and younger sister Guilia along with their families at a family dinner. It was overwhelming but I was grateful and endeared by Annabelle and Adam's protective natures as they acted as buffers for every conversation I entered with family members. Soon, I was able to relax and enjoy the company of my father and his children. They made an effort and although I knew there was a part of me that was withholding myself to see how consistent they would be as the weeks turned into months and years, I found my walls chipping away slowly and a warmth start to fill the cavities of my heart.

"I want you to come back to Atlantis, Lexi," dad said one evening.

I had come to see him after work and had made the mistake of complaining about my work load as I took off my irritating heels and settled in a comfy position next to him in his study. He had been reading a newspaper at his desk when I walked into his room and my heart squeezed at his delighted expression when I walked over and kissed his cheek. We sat together on his chesterfield when he dropped his latest request.

"Papa," I said in a stern tone.

Initially, I had found it strange when he asked me to call him what I used to call him when I was little. Annabelle still called him 'Papa' too although Adam only used the term occasionally. But once I said it, it felt right. I mean, I'd been calling my step father 'Dad' for a whole lot longer and I felt like I was betraying him at times when I called Michael dad. This way, the man that brought me up remained my 'dad' and the man that gave me life became 'papa.'

"Lexi, you were excellent at your job. I wanted you to handle PR and events for the gallery. The Enzo exhibition was a huge success. We were in the Arts news again, they are still talking about it."

I gave him a big smile, happy that something I helped with was successful.

"Papa, I can't leave Hamilton's. I have been busy, yes, but I like it there for the most part. I can't let Kade down and just leave to return to Atlantis."

He looked disappointed but tried to hide it with a smile.

"Okay but you said that the job was temporary. When you decide to leave, give it a thought okay? I will be the happiest when at least one of my children actually shows an interest in the family business." I laughed at him and his sagely countenance as he said this.

"Nice try papa."

"Can't blame a man," he laughed and winked.

"I will consider it. Only if I decide to leave Hamilton's. Any other item for emotional blackmail that you'd like to discuss on the agenda for todays meeting?"

We laughed when he rolled his eyes at me. I was thankful we got this chance to work things out because life kept moving down different paths and although some were scary to walk down, I realised that when I put my heart into it, the outcome was usually in my favour.

***

Work, in the lead up to our trip, was intense. This had less to do with the work load, although I was crazy busy, and more to do with the fact that things had changed between Kade and I.

Ever since our argument and then unspoken making up after Papa's heart attack, we had started to ease back into a comfortable sort of relationship that had no label. We weren't friends, we weren't lovers. We just *were.* Nothing made sense and sometimes it did and no one was confusing me more than my subconscious.

I marked the major shift in our relationship as being from the morning after the Halloween party when I woke up flustered and frustrated. The reason being a very vivid and realistic dream that I'd had about the gentleman occupying most of my thoughts.

I had taken a colder shower than normal that morning and tried to occupy my mind with images of stepping on hot coals and broken glass. Once I was dressed for work and in the kitchen where my housemates and I were usually in transit before departure for work, Allison made a comment about me looking flustered. I told her that I didn't get a lot of sleep following the late party and subsequent clean up after. She blew me and Sadie a kiss and said she loved us both for letting her get carried away with the party and we all went our separate ways.

I'd been at work for five minutes when I'd bumped into Travis' PA, Jenny. She started chattering away about how much she enjoyed the party and thanked me for extending an invite to her. We had a giggle on the subject until I saw Kade pass by from the corner of my eye.

"Good morning ladies," he smiled as he walked over to the coffee station in our lobby wearing his sharp fitted charcoal grey suit. I blushed and immediately turned away, the dream lingering in my mind. The thing is, the dream I had about Kade was no ordinary dream. It was perhaps the first ever sex dream I'd had in my life and it was causing me no end of embarrassment despite no one being aware of it but me.

"You okay Lexi?" Jenny asked, smiling curiously.

"I'm okay, I just didn't sleep very well." Jenny's eyes grew wide as she turned to look at Kade's retreating back and then me.

"You didn't?! Did you?" *Oh shit.*

"NO! No we didn't."

"I have to say, you guys looked pretty hot last night. You were dancing quite close too you know..." Her insinuation and mere presence at the party could cause me a lot of problems at work, despite the fact that I had, in reality, already slept with my boss. I winced at the reminder.

"No. We were friends before I started working here."

"Lexi, you're blushing bright red. Somethings up."

Damn Jenny and her bloody nosiness!

"I just had a dream about him, okay! Thats all." As soon as I blurted the words out, I regretted them because Jenny broke into a huge grin and then started giggling. And the woman only had the loudest fucking giggle in the world.

"Jenny! Shut up!" I hissed. She was attracting quite a lot of attraction from others in the department from her noise and I wanted so very badly to squeeze her windpipe to shut her the hell up. As my luck would have it, Kade stopped on his way back to his office, an amused but questioning smile on his face.

"Everything okay Jenny?"

Jenny took a breath from her hyena hysterics and looked up at her superior only to burst out laughing again.

"Oh, Lexi was just telling me about her dream," she

said when she had recovered somewhat. At my glare in her direction, she quickly excused herself and took her still laughter trembling self back to her department.

I couldn't look Kade in the eye as I made my own way back to my desk ahead of him, avoiding his questioning eyes.

Once I'd sat down, I made myself look busy as he lingered by the door to his office, obviously wanting to ask me something but soon he carried on inside. I let out a breath I didn't know I'd been holding and sat back in my chair, letting my head drop back, closing my eyes. I couldn't help the flashback that hit me full force of the dirty dream...

It's a hot night and I'm in my Jasmine costume in a Sahara palace. Only, it's not a costume, I'm actually Jasmine and I'm laying in a luscious four poster bed lower than the one I have at home which is draped with beautiful colourful chiffons and rich silks in a room filled with marble floors and pillars and open balconies. The air is so stifling that I can't sleep as I toss and turn when I try. Suddenly the voile curtains to my balcony part open and he's there, climbing in like the thief he's supposed to be. Only he's not looking for treasures. He's looking for me. The look in his eyes is so hungry, I gasp for breath when I realise his intention. He stalks slowly towards me as I sink further into the bed.

Climbing up onto the bed, he places one of his hands on the naked skin of my stomach, sending a gasp out of my lips. He presses a finger to his lips as a warning for me to be silent, his hand wanders down into the waistband of the loose chiffon trousers and into my soft flesh while I try to contain the moan escaping my lips. I find I don't need to when his lips cover mine hungrily. I kiss him back with urgency and find his other hand grasping the material of my top as the need to have me overcomes him and he rips it right through the middle to expose my generous breasts.

I feel his hard length against me and his hand leaves my pulsing core to pull down the obstructing trousers, his hot wet mouth finding my nipples to suck hard and lick while I writhe in an un-

controllable mess of sensations. I can't stand it, I need him.

"More," I whisper and he smiles wickedly at me as his mouth leaves my nipple with a 'pop.'

In seconds he is kneeling and pulling off his clothes with lightening speed and before I know it, our naked bodies are pressed flush together and he's guiding his length teasingly up and around my opening.

"You want this?" he asks, teasingly.

"Yes," I answer breathlessly.

"How much do you want it?" His blue eyes dilate when I lick my lips.

"More than my next breath."

He growls and thrusts himself inside me, clamping his hand over my mouth to muffle my scream of pleasure. He thrusts and pumps in and out of me, attacking my mouth with passion, gripping my thighs for purchase to go even deeper and extract the innermost pleasure trapped inside me. I feel it build up to a pressure I can no longer resist and bite his shoulder as I let go and contain the sound of my release and he does the same with his face buried in my neck.

Panting, we stay interlocked and intertwined for what seems like an age until he pulls out and pulls back to look into my eyes, resting his weight on his forearms.

"I want to do that to you for forever," he whispers.

"I want you to do that to me for forever," I retort. His eyes darken once more.

"I'm going to fuck you into oblivion." I feel him lengthen and harden against me.

"Again?"

He smirks at me and grinds into me.

"Hold tight, Alexa."

"Alexa? Alexa?"

I was jolted from my meanderings into dangerous territory by the man of the moment himself, who was now standing way too close to my desk for comfort. I swallowed nervously, feeling the heat return to its position on my cheeks.

"Sorry," I mumbled and stood up.

"You okay? I called your name a few times but you were somewhere else." *Yeah, with you buried deep inside me.* Shit, I needed to collect myself. Throwing a mental bucket of water over myself, I made my way around my desk and followed him into his office watching as he sat back down at his desk.

"I'm sorry Kade, I'm still recovering from last night." I plonked myself as gracefully as I could in the chair opposite him. He looked thoughtful and I felt a little nervous. I didn't think he would probe what Jenny had said.

"So, you had a dream?" Okay, so he just did. *Fuck my life.*

"Yeah, it was silly...nothing really." I prayed he would drop the subject as I kept my pinkish red face bent forward, suddenly really interested in my bracelet. The silence stretched longer than I anticipated and when I looked up, I could tell that he knew. He wore the biggest knowing grin on his face and I felt mortified.

"You had a dirty dream didn't you?" His eyes sparkled with mischief.

"I don't think it's entirely appropriate to talk about this matter in the office, Mr Hamilton." My reply seemed to turn up the mischief.

"Judging by the way you cant look me in my face without turning beet red, I'm guessing it was about me. Am I right?" I may have started to feel more for this man but in that moment I really wanted to punch him hard.

"Kade!"

"Alexa," he grinned.

We stared at each other, with me glaring and him chuckling. After a few seconds his eyes went from pleased to heated and that look was so similar to his look in my dream that it made my breath hitch. He stood slowly from his chair and walked around to lean on the desk right in front of me, never breaking eye contact with me. He was so close, I could smell his delicious scent. He leaned down to look me in my eyes, so close I could smell the mint from his toothpaste.

"I've given you space, Alexa. I've been your friend, I've tried to only be your boss and I'm trying to be just your friend again. All of this only because you asked me to. I am fighting whats in my nature to do this for you but I can't do that anymore. I'm not going to fight what I want, I'm going to fight *for* what I want. Enough with the just friends bullshit."

I felt like the breath had been knocked out of me. I could only stare back at him, open mouthed, as he continued.

"Just in case you didn't get that, this is me giving you fair warning that I am now going to be pursuing you, no holds barred. I am not going to care what issue you find with it. Because the only way I'll stop is if you tell me yourself that you don't want anything to do with me."

He lifted my chin with the tips of his fingers and smirked. "Nod if you understand."

I nodded, too in shock and hypnotised by his words.

"Good. I'm dying to know about this dream but I know you're never going to be able to tell me about it *yet*. That's fine, for now. You *will* tell me one day. Now, let's get down to work Princess."

I gasped at his choice of word for me and immediately regretted it. He was as sharp as a tack that man, picking up on anything and everything straight away.

"Interesting..." he mumbled with a knowing smile. I wanted to hide under my desk for the rest of the day. Unfortunately and yet fortunately, Kade Hamilton the professional returned to the forefront and I was able to make it through a short meeting with him before returning to my desk and cursing my red face. Why hadn't I refuted what he said? *Because you want him and you're ready to stop fighting it,* said the voice inside my soul.

***

The days following Kade's declaration of full out pursuit were exactly that. He started with subtle gifts on my desk with cards that made me either smile, giggle or blush. The first was a bar of chocolate in the shape of a man's well defined torso, pecs, abs and all. I glanced at the note:

I modelled for this myself. Now you can lick these abs...until you get the real thing.
X

I almost spat out my morning coffee and took a peek up to his office door to see it wide open and him staring at me with an amused smile and an eyebrow raised from his desk. I shook my head, hoping this was just a one off. It wasn't. Avoiding him was out of the question because he was everywhere, so I sat there looking thoughtfully into his eyes over the few metres that separated his office and my desk. And to my own shock I smiled and held the chocolate up to my mouth...and *licked* the abs like the brazen hussy I was becoming whilst maintaining eye contact, aware that at any moment someone could walk around the corner and wonder what the hell was going on.

Kade's eyes darkened and I saw him pick up his phone and start tapping on it whilst watching me. My phone beeped with a message alert and I broke from his hypnotic gaze to read the message.

Kade: Why don't you get yourself over here and demonstrate on the real thing?

I shivered, ducking to hide my pink cheeks from his gaze and replied.

Me: I'm sorry, I'm very busy. My boss has given me a shed load of work.

I chanced a peek up to see him smiling at his phone and tapping a reply. My phone beeped.

Kade: Sounds like your boss wants to work you real hard...

I felt my heart rate pick up, my face get redder and my body start to tingle in all my naughty places. He was playing dirty and I'll be damned if I said it didn't turn me on. Looking up at him there at his desk, sitting back casually in his chair, eyes twinkling with promise and mischief, I wanted us to be alone in his bedroom, in his office, anywhere at all so that I could take my time licking his abs and other delectable parts of his body. No one had ever made me feel so wanton before.

I ignored my temptation to reply and bit into the chocolate instead, well aware that is was too early in the day to eat chocolate and that my boss was watching me intently as I closed my mouth over the most delicious confectionary I'd ever let pass my lips. That is, second to a certain man's deliciously soft lips.

The next day, I received a beautiful bouquet of flowers in deep pink autumnal Orchids with greenery spread in between. They made me smile instantly as I walked towards my desk. I looked around and couldn't see my boss anywhere inside his office. I plucked the card from the arrangement and read.

These remind me of that beautiful colour you
turn when you blush.
X

And so the blush appeared on cue as I softly touched the petals and felt my heart squeeze.
Jenny popped her head around the corner and immediately saw the flowers.

"Ooooo! Who are these from?"

I looked at her and wished she would just stop talking so loudly because it attracted the attention of a few passers by, including Travis, whom I had been avoiding. I saw him start to walk over at the same time that I felt *his* presence behind me. I don't know how I always knew, I only know that the hairs on the back of my neck would stand up and I could feel his heat from even meters away. He came to stand next to me just as Travis reached my desk with a slight frown on his handsome face.

"Looks like Alexa has an admirer," my annoyingly handsome boss remarked. I finally turned to the side to look at him and saw the humour in his eyes as well as the heat.

"Really? And who might he be Lexi?"

I saw Kade tense slightly as Travis addressed me.

"Well, it's a secret admirer by the looks of it," I mumbled and sat down, wishing my audience would disappear.

"I'm sure he'll make himself known soon enough." I looked up with shock at Kade and narrowed my eyes at him. He wouldn't dare! Travis looked a little put out, gave me a small smile and walked away to his office at the other end of the Fort. Jenny followed soon enough after giving me a wink and a smile.

"Do you like them?" I jumped at the sudden closeness of his voice, acknowledging that he was also now standing behind my chair with his arms on either side of me on my desk, effectively caging me in. To the outside world it may have looked like he was showing me something on my computer screen but I knew differently. He was breathing me in, just as much as I was breathing him in.

"You can't keep sending me things like this at work, Kade. People will notice." He seemed to tense and suddenly my chair was swivelled so that I was facing him and his serious expression.

"When I told you that I am not going to fight my natural instincts anymore, I meant it. I don't mean for you to feel uncomfortable Alexa, but I will not stop letting you know just how much I want you. You deserve to know how precious you are. Now, tell me, do you like your flowers?"

He took my breath away with his words. *Precious.* No one had ever called me precious. I smiled and willed all my gratitude into my voice when I replied.

"They are beautiful, I love them. Thank you."

He gave me his happy smile, one that I saw more often when he was with me and it was heart melting. I felt the tips of his fingers brush against my cheek before he walked back into his office.

Day three of 'operation pursuit' involved a key in a box. I looked at it in puzzlement and then at the card.

The elusive key to the Man Cave. This is a little surprise for when you get home.

x

I felt my heart beat faster. What could this possibly mean? I couldn't even ask him because he was away for the whole day for meetings across town. I pulled out my phone and sent him a message instead.

Me: Why do I have a key to the 'Man Cave'?

He replied straight away.

Kade: Good morning to you too, beautiful.

I let out a frustrated growl that had Freddie, our latest intern, jump a bit as he scurried away with the latest batch of photocopying to be done. I smiled apologetically and returned to my phone.

Me: Good morning Mr Hamilton. Why do I have a key to the 'Man Cave'?

Kade: Because I have a surprise for you lady.

Me: What surprise?

Kade: It wouldn't be a surprise if I told you now, would it?

Me: But I don't like surprises!

That was a lie. I loved surprises. I was just impatient to wait until I got home.

Kade: A little bit of patience will go a long way
baby. Just trust me. I miss you.

I sucked in a deep breath. He called me *baby*. He said he *missed* me. I willed it to stop but the anxiety started to creep up. I felt like I was suffocating. I scrambled to get into the nearest toilets, which happened to be Kade's private ensuite.

I slammed the door shut and willed my erratic breathing to calm down, whilst I fumbled to turn the cold water tap on. I splashed water on my face and started a mantra. *Inhale....exhale...inhale....exhale.* I felt my heart rate slow and breathing even out and after a few minutes I was able to tidy up my appearance and leave the restroom looking as normal as possible.

The rest of my working day was spent trying to finish half completed work whilst worrying about my panic attack. I needed to understand what was happening to me. I hadn't had a panic attack for a very long time. Why now? I tried to keep busy until it was time to go home. I didn't know what awaited me there but I tried not to think about Kade's surprise until I got there.

Walking out of The Fort, I put in my ear buds and pressed play on my phone as Trouble by Coldplay filled my ears and my soul.

CHAPTER THIRTY

I need you

I got home to find a note left on the side board in the hall.

Proceed to the Man Cave!

It didn't look like Kade's writing. I begrudgingly made my way to my bedroom and dumped my bag, shoes and coat on my bed and pulled out the key I had from the box. I wondered why the hell he gave me a key when we all knew where the spares were but then I noticed that the key was engraved with 'Alexa' at it's head. My butterflies mixed with trepidation as I made my way to the door that led to Kade's private quarters within the house. When I reached the first floor of his apartment, I couldn't help the gasp escaping my lips.

"Surprise!" Sadie and Allison said in unison.

The open plan living area of Kade's Man Cave had been set up for what looked like a girly night in. I saw bean bags and cushions all scattered over the floor, which I knew Kade did not own, snacks and take out at the kitchen counter and coffee table, a few bottles of wine and what looked like the beginning of "The Wedding Singer," on the large suspended flatscreen.

"Oh my god. Did you guys do all of this?"

Allison put her arm around my shoulders to guide me

to one of the massive comfy looking bean bags and Sadie handed me a glass of wine as I settled on the softness and placed the glass down on the coffee table.

"We just took delivery and direction. Kade organised all of this," Sadie piped up. I felt tears prick at my eyes.

"He said that you've had a rough few weeks what with your dad and his recovery and that we all needed a girls night. So he organised all of this. We came home early from work, we've taken the morning off work tomorrow so we can have a midweek treat!" Allison's eyes sparkled.

I couldn't believe he had done all this for us, for me. I felt myself admitting something I'd known for some time. I was falling for him and it had been gradually building up. I ignored the slight panic from that little revelation and concentrated on the faces of my two friends that I hadn't had enough time to catch up with.

"I love you guys," I said, pulling them both in for a hug and squealing when we toppled over the huge bean bag.

"We need to have a big catch up, lady," Allison said once she gathered herself and plonked back on a beanbag of her own.

"I'll get the food. Don't start anything until I'm back!" Sadie shouted from the other end of the apartment.

I looked around and noticed the candles and some of the British snacks that weren't always available easily in NYC. I smiled to myself and caught Allison looking at me with a knowing look.

"Boy did good huh?" I retuned her smile.

"Yeah, boy did good."

***

"You set the wedding date and you didn't tell us?!" I screeched at Allison.

We'd finished most of the movie but abandoned the ending for the catch up that was clearly needed.

"We haven't had the chance to sit down together for five minutes these past two weeks, what with work and all. I didn't want to tell you girls over the phone!" She huffed, looking adorable with all her blonde hair about her shoulders. Sadie giggled at her.

"I suppose you're right. So when is the big day?"

The excitement was palpable now because we all had something beautiful to look forward to. Two of our dear friends coming together, vowing to spend the rest of their lives with one another. For a woman scorned, I was a sucker for weddings and happy endings. I only had an issue with my own.

"I know it's so freaking cliche and typical but...February 14th!" It *was* unoriginal but none of us cared about that.

"Oh my God I can't wait!" Sadie said hugging Allison as I did the same.

"I'm going to need so much help, I don't know where to start! It's Just over three months away! Brent doesn't want to wait any longer because he thinks I'm going to take forever deciding on a date and place, which he's right about, so he's booked the hotel we stayed at in the Bahamas already and given me this limited time to sort everything out. It's a beach wedding. I'm stressing out!"

"Don't panic, we've got you," I reassured her, even as I thought, *we don't have long*.

"That's why I love you girls! Anyway, enough about me, Sadie...who was Mr Joker you were talking to at the party?"

Sadie's face turned a little red.

"You should know Allison, you invited everyone!" Allison looked at me confused and then thought about it before turning back to Sadie.

"I did invite one of Brent's colleagues as Joker but he RSVP'd 'no.' Must have changed his mind, unless we had a party crasher. Anywaaay...stop avoiding me Sadie! Did you get jiggy with the Joker?" Judging by the increasing colour on

Sadie's beautiful face, she had and both Allison and I giggled like school girls.

"Oh stop it you two! It was just a bit of fun, no names were exchanged and we both agreed to something with no strings. Two consenting adults!" I was seeing mellow and sensible Sadie in a whole new light, not just the quiet and shy red head I'd initially met.

"Well that's great for you Sadie but if you *want* a name, I can get it for you...."

Sadie whacked Allison lightly with a magazine on the coffee table and laughed.

"No thank you. That was part of the allure - no strings. I'm happy without complications thank you!"

We found ourselves talking some more about the party until they eventually got around the subject of me and a certain blue eyed, sexy fiend.

"You and Kade, eh?" Allison wiggled her eyebrows at me suggestively. There was no need to beat about the bush. They already knew I'd slept with him.

"He's vowed to pursue me."

"No way! Good on him," Sadie said approvingly.

"He's sent me chocolates and flowers so far and now everything that he planned this evening. He plans to reduce me to a pile of mush I think," I snorted, trying to look unaffected.

"I think he's head over heels for you Lexi, or at least he's well on his way to being," Allison nudged me.

"I don't know what to expect. He's like this super intense person, so unashamed of his feelings and how the world perceives him. I envy him that and I don't know how to handle it when I'm still not sure if I'm completely recovered from Tom."

I could see the empathy in Sadie's eyes and understanding in Allison's.

"I don't think he expects you to just jump into something with him without caution Lexi, maybe he just needs you to acknowledge the chemistry between you both so you can give yourselves a start. I know it sounds stupid but I think you guys need to just get together for it all to fall into place."

Sadie's words seemed to connect with something in my mind. She was right. Maybe we just needed to 'fall into place' to make sense.

We joked and laughed all night, snacking and drinking and just unwinding. I smiled at my friends and thanked my lucky stars. Kade was going to get major brownie points for this tomorrow. I messaged Kade at one point during the evening.

Me: Thank you. You're wonderful x

The reply came instantly.

Kade: You're always welcome baby. Now don't let me see your beautiful face at work before midday x

***

I hadn't been in work for longer than five minutes the next afternoon, as directed, when I saw Kade hurry out of his office and take me gently by the elbow back towards the exit. He looked worried.

"What's wrong?" I asked, trepidation creeping up.

"Bonnie has gone into labour early and the baby is in distress, I need to go to the hospital. I need you." Without a second thought I followed him to his waiting Aston outside The Fort. He had been driving in to work himself this week, getting in early.

The drive to the hospital didn't take long, Kade drove with an urgency and I could see his brow creased as he worried his bottom lip. It was endearing that he cared so much for his sister. I knew he didn't need words right then, just contact, so I let my hand rest on his thigh and he covered it with his.

Once we reached the hospital and found Andrea and David waiting patiently in the waiting room, Kade asked for an update. David wore hospital scrubs and looked like he had the weight of the world on his shoulders.

"They are going to perform an emergency C-section now. I'm going back in there now. Just wanted to let you know. Thank you for coming Kade. Nice to see you again Alexa." He left the room and Kade moved to his mothers side. She hugged him tight, worry evident on her face, and Kade sat her down on the chair whilst taking the seat next to her with his arm still around her shoulders. I moved to take the seat opposite but Kade grabbed my hand and pulled me down next to him, keeping my hand in his.

Andrea noticed the exchange and gave me a small smile, grabbing my free hand.

"Thank you for coming Alexa. My boy can be erratic when he's stressed, I think you're helping keep him grounded right now."

I didn't know what to say to that so I just smiled. Kade pulled me into him with his other arm now around me and I let him. I rested my head on his chest and felt him kiss my head.

Twenty minutes later James arrived looking just as distressed as his mother and younger brother. I found out that their father was in Italy for business. The boys seemed to love their sister a lot, evidently. I felt my heart melt further.

Kade's grip on my hand didn't seem to escape James either but he just gave his brother a knowing smirk that was scarily identical to Kade's.

Finally, when almost an hour had passed, a tired looking David reentered to waiting room with a smile.

"It's a girl! She's well, they are just checking her over. Bonnie is fine - tired but well. They didn't get time for the cesarean because my baby girl decided she wanted to come out naturally. Impatient, just like her mother," he laughed proudly and with relief.

Everyone exhaled relief and took turns to hug and congratulate David. Even I got a hug from David. After Bonnie was moved with her little bundle to her room, Andrea and James went in first to meet the new arrival and I waited with Kade in the waiting room. I stood up to get some water when I felt a tug on my hand. I turned to find his eyes gleaming with a new emotion that felt like an electric shock to my system.

"Thank you for being here today," he said in his deep voice.

"I wouldn't have wanted to be anywhere else Kade. That's what friends are for." I saw a little flicker of annoyance at the word 'friends' but it disappeared just as quickly.

"You went above and beyond Alexa. Having you here made me feel optimistic that everything would be okay."

He looked a little embarrassed admitting he needed reassurance but it did nothing to stop my heart from warming. I turned to fully face him, looking down at him as he looked up at me from his seated position. From that angle, it looked look like a vulnerable position for him to be in but I knew better. He was allowing me to absorb the quiet power that emanated from his body to mine as he gently gripped my waist and pulled me closer to him to stand between his legs. I didn't fight it because I really didn't want to.

"I feel the same about you. When papa was in hospital, you were there every day for me." He shakes his head with a small smile.

"Alexa, I think I'm addicted to you. I can't seem to get enough and I don't want to stop feeling like that. Is that crazy?" He said it quietly but the impact of his words were loud to my ears. I tried to tamp down the two conflicting emotions building inside me - the soaring exhilaration and the overwhelming anxiety. Taking a deep breath, looking into his eyes I replied honestly.

"No. Because I feel it too."

The breath he released made me feel some ease. He was just as nervous as me about the way he felt. He pushed his face to my stomach and pressed an innocent kiss there before leaning his forehead against it and breathing me in. Butterflies were wreaking havoc in my belly right under his pressed head at the intimate gesture. My hands instinctually went to his head and my fingers weaved into his dark silky hair. We remained silent like this for a few minutes while I massaged his head with my fingers, playing to my hearts content with his luscious locks.

We broke from our trance when James walked into the waiting room with a big smile on his face that just got bigger, if that were possible, when he caught us in our intimate embrace. I scrambled to remove myself from Kade but his grip on my waist got tighter and he actually growled in annoyance, holding me still.

"Kade!" I whispered loudly to get his attention, pulling slightly on his chin to get him to look up. He grumbled but moved his head and gaze up until his confused face looked past me to his brother standing with a now amused expression on his face, leaning against the door frame. But there was no embarrassment in Kade's expression, he actually looked smug as he exchanged a knowing look with his brother.

"Whenever you two lovebirds are ready, you can go visit with Bonnie and the baby. Mom's gone to call dad so she's outside." I pulled away from Kade and ducked my blushing face while he led me out of there, after clapping his brother on his shoulder, towards Bonnie's room.

We entered the private room and immediately saw Bonnie and David, him with his arms around his wife and baby daughter looking lovingly at her while he whispered words of pride and adoration to his wife. I felt like an intruder, looking into a private moment of unmasked emotion but as soon as they heard us they looked up and gave us huge smiles that I couldn't help but return.

While Kade and David man-hugged again, I sat down by Bonnie's side and gave her a gentle hug, mindful of her little bundle. And what a little beauty she was. A tiny button nose, rosy chubby cheeks, a head full of dark hair and when she opened her sleepy eyes a little, I could see a glimpse of the bluest blue. Kade's blue.

"I'm in love," I sighed, stroking her tiny little hand. Bonnie reached out and squeezed my hand which made me look up at her.

"Thank you for being there Alexa." The emotion in her eyes made me feel like crying. I didn't know why they all kept thanking me.

"It was no bother at all Bonnie, you don't need to thank me." She gave me a soft and knowing smile.

"Kade may act like he's a tough caveman but inside he's just a guy that has dealt with so much heartache and loss. It makes a difference that he has someone who he can share his good and hard times with. I'm so glad it's you," she said in a quiet voice so that only I could hear her.

My heart started to beat faster and for once I didn't correct her and tell her that we weren't together. Instead I returned her smile and then looked up as Kade ventured over with the most breath taking joy evident on his face.

"You've enjoyed enough time with my niece, now it's my turn," he complained and came close to Bonnie with his arms stretched out wide.

"I've barely had her for an hour!" Bonnie swatted him away playfully but then she carefully placed the adorable bundle in his arms and I felt like my heart would burst.

He was a natural, he held her like the precious little thing she was and the loving way in which he looked at her just made me melt and my mind went places I wished it wouldn't.

I'm standing in our kitchen at the Brownstone, looking out of the window and Kade comes up behind me to put his hands over where mine are resting on my huge belly. I see the rings on my left hand glinting in the light as well as his wedding band. I lean my head back against his chest and look up at

413

him and he smiles at me as if I were the most precious per-
son in the world and then kisses me softly on my lips.
"I love you Mrs Hamilton." And I feel my heart clench
every time he says those words so I tell him the truth that
I know will always remain, even when we are gone.
"I love you too."

I gasped for air. Lucky no one had noticed since David had gone to call his sister to bring the kids to meet their new sibling and Kade was perched on the edge of Bonnie's bed where he was telling her how amazing she was and how proud he was of her.

I edged myself back towards the door, struggling to breathe through the rising panic. I almost made it unnoticed when I knocked into a chair that screeched a little as it displaced from it's position. Kade and Bonnie looked up immediately and noting my expression Kade calmly stood up, placed the baby back into Bonnie's arms and kissed her on her head.

"I'll call you later Bon," he said calmly, never taking his eyes off of me as if to say, *stay there.* I could see Bonnie's concerned face from the corner of my eye but I couldn't find the words to speak as I struggled with my breathing and felt the pain in my chest and the sweat beads on my forehead build.

He took a few strides to reach me with his tall legs and before I knew it, I was ushered out of the room gently, my hand in his as he walked. I followed as if my legs had a mind of their own, starting to shake a little now until I felt him squeeze my hand. He led me into a courtyard with seating out in the open. He sat me down then crouched before my trembling body. He squeezed my hands and it was then that I realised I had my eyes clenched shut. I opened them to look down on concerned but calm blue eyes. That gave me a little comfort and as Kade tapped my knees apart and gently pressed me on my back to place me in a position so that my head was between my legs, he talked me through a breathing exercise. With my concentration on his voice through the sound of the blood rushing in my ears, I managed to focus on my breathing to calm down enough for the blood rush to disappear. When all my other senses seemed to calm too, I pulled myself up slowly, forearms resting on my knees and my eyes finally met his where he had stayed sitting on his haunches. If it was uncomfortable, he didn't seem to show it. All I could see was the worry in his eyes for me. It made me want to cry.

"I'm sorry," I whispered shakily. He took my hands and rubbed his thumbs on the backs of them.

"Don't apologise. What's going on angel?" *Angel.* I almost wished he wasn't so perfect.

Maybe it was because I felt exhausted from all the emotion and the panic attack or maybe I was just tired of having to withhold my feelings to not complicate things, that I decided to tell him.

"I've been having panic attacks." Admitting it out aloud and to him of all people, made me feel bare and vulnerable. I was unable to look at him and wouldn't until I felt him tip my chin up with his fingers.

"How long for?" The concern in his eyes I understood, but I also saw empathy and that made it easier for the words to come out of my mouth.

"Initially, I had them just after I found Tom cheating...after that it was during the divorce but I haven't had one for a long time. Not until yesterday when you arranged the girls night for me in your apartment." He listened and I saw the moment he put two and two together when he gave me a small smile.

"You're feeling overwhelmed."

"I freaked out," I replied, feeling the blush of embarrassment on my face.

"You freaked out."

"I'm sorry." I felt terrible, turning a beautiful moment

sour.

"What did I tell you about saying sorry?" He finally got up from his crouching position, which was making my legs seize up from watching, and sat down close to me on the bench. We sat in silence for a while and I knew he was waiting for me to be ready to explain. I questioned what good would come from bringing up my past to my present, possibly *my future.* And then I realised that there wasn't a damn thing that I wanted to keep from him anymore. I took a fortifying breath and opened up my most painful scar for him to see.

"My relationship with Tom ended badly because he cheated but it was something worse than his cheating that initially broke us."

"Worse than *that?*"

"Yeah. I had a miscarriage at 18 weeks while we were still married," my hands started to shake as I said the words and I willed the emotions welling up inside me to calm down. Kade took hold of my hands again and rubbed soothing circles over the backs again and I couldn't meet his eyes so I stared at my hands in his and carried on.

"When I walked in on Tom and Rebecca, he told me he had been seeing her for four months. I had miscarried our baby three months previously at that point. I found out he was screwing her while I was desperately trying to call him, bleeding and in pain."

"God Alexa..."

"Theres more." His eyes widened at my words.

"*More?*"

"Oh yes," I laughed humourlessly, "When he informed me he was leaving me, Rebecca quite smugly proclaimed that she was two months pregnant with his baby." No sooner were the words out of my mouth than Kade had pulled me up and onto his lap in the tightest embrace I've ever had. Tighter than the ones Granna gave me, and she was a strong woman.

My arms went around his back as if it was the most natural thing for me to do, heart racing and mind exhausted from, well, everything. When he released me, I barely had time to take a breath as his lips met with mine in a soul searing kiss, deep and passionate and enough to make me forget whatever the hell had been tearing me apart.

"Wow." That was about all I could manage to say when he pulled back, lips red and face a little flush which made me feel joyful that he looked like *that* because of kissing *me.*

"You know what Alexa?" he said, cupping my right cheek with his hand, looking deep into my eyes.

"What?" I answered breathlessly.
"Fuck them. He lost you because he was blind to the precious gift he had right in front of him. It's his loss. The only thing I'm sorry for is you having to go through all that on your own."

The anger that flashed through his eyes softened as he removed his hand from my cheek and placed it gently on my stomach. My breath hitched at the tenderness of his actions and I couldn't stop the waterfall of tears. I buried my face into his neck and he held me as I cried softly while the world carried on about it's way around us.

CHAPTER THIRTY
ONE

NYC - LDN

I had been counting down the days until our trip to London. Three days were left and we would be landing on the morning of my birthday. My family was ecstatic and I had a long list of things to get for my sister and younger cousins.

It had been a week since the night at the hospital where I'd cried myself out in Kade's arms. Every day since, Kade had made sure to spend time with me.

Lindsay had her baby boy, who was late making an appearance, just a couple of days after Bonnie had her delivery and although I was a little apprehensive of having another panic attack, I insisted on going with Kade to see her and the baby. Turned out that I was perfectly fine but glad for his reassuring presence and I even managed to hold the little handsome man.

The gifts from him kept coming in the form of delicacies from around the city and hilarious and inappropriate cards. We had lunch together every day and even when I'd sneak out to avoid the inevitable office gossip, he would somehow show up at the bistro or the restaurant where some of our coworkers would also be. Talk was rife of our 'special friendship' at work and although it did make me a little uncomfortable at times, the joy of spending time with him out weighed it. I still got all my work done so it didn't affect my abilities as his PA. That's what I told myself anyway as I sat across him whilst eating my big slice of pizza and he ate all of the dishes on one side of the menu.

"Seriously dude, you can eat for all of England." Kade just grinned like he was super proud of that fact.

"And you sound like a New Yorker." I tried not to but couldn't help the giggle that escaped.

"Whatever!" The secret smiles between us made my belly flip in the most delicious of ways.

When we finally came to the day of our departure, I brought my suitcase with me to The Fort in the morning since we were to leave together from work that evening. By the evening, when everyone had left, I packed up my workstation and gathered the important documents needed for the meeting Kade had in London. Turned out to be the only meeting and apart from one other public event, we basically had a free week in London. I knew that Kade had done this for me and I adored him for it. Getting to see my family and friends and celebrate my birthday with them was the biggest gift he could give me.

We left for the airport and I was relieved to see that instead of the private plane, we were on a regular plane. And by regular, I mean first class but at least it wasn't the overbearing luxury of the private jet. Still...first class was just 'wow.'

I sat in a seat big enough to fit two of me comfortably, being offered beautifully presented food and drinks every half an hour. I fell asleep for most of the flight and when we were about to land, Kade woke me up so I could look out of the window. My city was visible in the early morning light, sleepy but dominant. I felt a flutter in my heart. I was coming home and I wasn't alone. I was coming home with *Kade* and that made it all the more special.

I'd stopped hiding the truth from myself ever since he held me tight and let me cry out my sadness into him. I could admit that I had serious feelings for Kade Hamilton and I wanted to explore them. Even if he hadn't kissed me again since then.

I wasn't going to lie, that had stung me a little because I had hoped he would do it again but I got a feeling that the ball was in my court now and he was letting me get accustomed to the idea of there being an 'us'. I hadn't had another panic attack since that last time but he was careful with me - attentive but not overwhelming and forever paying me those compliments on a daily basis.

As soon as we were off the plane and out through baggage claim, I breathed in the cold air and wrapped my arms around myself. Kade stepped beside me and put an arm around me, rubbing me for warmth. Standing there with him, waiting for our driver to bring the car to us, I felt the biggest sense of contentment. I was excited to have Kade here with me in my city and our trip was about to commence with a stop at my parents' house. The schedule had us with a free day today, a meeting tomorrow, three days free and then a formal event for the London office thrown by the Hamilton's for which Kade was making his dutiful appearance on behalf of his father after which we would return home. *Home.* Since when had New York become home for me? I felt myself feel happily split between the two cities - a natural love for my birth city and falling in love with the city I had adopted as my own. It may have also had something to do with the blue eyed man who was just now smiling down at me as he ushered me into the car that pulled up while he helped place our luggage in the back.

When planning the trip, we had decided that I would spend the first two nights at the hotel due to work, the next two at home and the last two back at the hotel. When we broached the subject of what was happening in the free time we had, Kade said he didn't want to intrude on my time with my family. I assured him that my family would love to meet him and that I would love for him to meet some of my friends too.

He seemed a little nervous now, sitting in the car twiddling his thumbs. I don't think I had ever seen him like this and enjoyed the fact that the formidable celebrity/lawyer/ businessman could ever feel nervous. But then again, knowing my family, maybe he had a right to be. I reached over and gave his hand a squeeze for comfort and he threw me a tired smile. We spent the rest of the ride to the hotel in a comfortable silence.

***

"We're here princess, wake up."

I had fallen asleep at some point of the journey, my head resting against the window. I opened my eyes to find my breathtakingly handsome man in front of me looking like he was about to make a court appearance judging from his apprehension. I gave him my biggest smile because I'd just looked out of the window and seen my childhood home and he was here with me. That seemed to ease him a bit. We had gone straight from the airport to the lavish hotel in Mayfair to freshen up, eat and rest before the afternoon trip to my parents' house.

"Happy birthday Alexa," he whispered.

I had thought that maybe he hadn't remembered. I had felt downhearted about it when he failed to mention it on the plane and then at the hotel but then mentally scolded myself for being so self absorbed and sensitive, telling myself he was a busy man with way too much going on to remember something so trivial. Now, looking at the warm expression on his face, the tenderness took my breath away.

God, I could love this man. I could actually let myself fall head over heels, arms stretched wide in love with him. And hell if that didn't scare the shit out of me.

"Thank you," I managed to say, feeling shy again. My heart was beating like crazy right then.

"I didn't forget sweetheart." Add telepathy to his list of skills please.

He swiftly exited the car to come over to my side and open my door for me to get out. He held out his arm to me and led me over to my parents' home.

I saw the curtain twitch before I reached the front door, someone shouting "She's here! She's got some bloke with her!" I wanted to bury my head in the ground and chanced an embarrassed look at Kade to see him trying to stifle his amusement. He just winked at me and went to ring the bell.

It took half a second before the door was thrown open, as if mum was waiting there for us to knock before she felt it was the right time to politely open the door.

"My baby!" she exclaimed and grabbed me away from Kade into her warm embrace, almost suffocating me with her bosom.

Wow, she was a sight for sore eyes. I felt a wave of emotion hit me as she pulled back with tears in her eyes, holding my face with her hands. We both stood there, tears welling and laughing at our silliness.

"Oi, stop hogging her!" I heard dad say from behind mum.

I was engulfed in another big hug, and then there was Megs. I almost forgot about Kade. I say almost because I could never fully forget him. If I couldn't already feel his eyes on me or his presence then he was always somewhere there in my subconscious. I was herded into the house just as I looked back to find him being pulled into a hug by mum. I giggled at his amused but incredulous face as he looked at me from over mums shoulder whilst being hugged out of breath. Soon I was pushed into the living room by my sister...to a room full of my family and friends.

"SURPRISE!"

"HAPPY BIRTHDAY!"

"Oh my god, who is that hot guy?"

"Lickable Abs!"

I was elated, aptly surprised and then embarrassed in close succession. I could hear Kade chuckling beside me. My sister, cousins, uncle and aunts took turns to hug and smother me with their affection, questions and curiosity towards the fine American specimen standing just behind me, possibly using me as a shield against the ogling public in the room. After my family cleared, I got to finally see Ash standing there with a small baby bump making me tear up as we hugged tight.

"You're glowing!" I gushed. She wiped the tears from her face and smiled widely at me.

"I'm a bloody nightmare at the moment. Ask Imran." And as if summoned by forces unknown, he appeared beside her and squeezed the life out of me.

"She's a bag of raging hormones, I tell you. One minute she wants to throttle me and the next she can't keep her hands off of me!"

I giggled when he put me down and I realised I hadn't introduced Kade. His amused expression met my beaming one.

"Everyone, this is Kade Hamilton. My boss...and friend," I added. I saw the mixed reactions form over the sea of people in the room.

Some of my friends in the back just stared in awe. Hannah and Brian (who had taken a flight out to see his parents), Ash and Imran looked at me knowingly. My aunts and mother looked like they might swoon. They started to introduce themselves and I took that moment to notice that I couldn't see Granna anywhere. The person I wanted to see and wanted Kade to meet the most.

"Mum, where's Granna?" Mum looked at me with a warmth only your mother could look at you with.

"She's in the kitchen putting the finishing touches to your favourite pecan pie."

I left Kade at the mercy of the women and went in search

423

for her.

In the kitchen, I could hear her humming before I saw her. Wearing her apron, putting away her ingredients and wiping the surface, she was my whole childhood personified. I went up behind her and hugged her tight.

"My Alli girl is finally home," she laughed. When she turned she laughed and wiped the tears that I hadn't known I had shed. I couldn't believe I hadn't seen her in over four months. That was a long time for us.

"I missed you so much Granna," my muffled voice came out as I lost my face in her embrace.

"I know honey, I missed you too."

We stayed in the kitchen for a few minutes as I told her about the sites I had visited in New York City and my work and new friends. I was so engrossed in laughing at her witty comments and enjoying her company that I didn't hear Kade come in. I only noticed when Granna looked over my shoulder and raised her eyebrow.

I turned to see Kade looking a little harassed. I covered my mouth to try to control my giggles. I really should not have left him to the feeding frenzy out there. I could just imagine how the Spanish Inquisition had started.

"Uh, Alexa, they are asking where you got to."

I walked over to him and tried to stifle my smile but he narrowed his eyes on me; nothing escaped him. Taking his hand, I brought him closer and introduced him to Granna.

"Granna this is Kade." I didn't need to tell her who he was to me. She knew because I had told her about him once. Not in the detail I would tell Ash but enough that she knew he was important to me. He had to be important for me to even mention him to Granna in the first place.

"Nice to meet you ma'am," Kade said, extending his hand. Granna took it and smiled.

"No need for the formalities boy, you can call me Granna," and the she turned to me and added, "now he's quite the looker. My Alli did good."

I actually saw him blush a little which was super rare. Instead of getting embarrassed this time, I only returned her smile and looked at him. I hoped that he saw the affection in my eyes because I was pouring it all into that one look. His face morphed into one of wonder. It was probably the first time I hadn't denied out loud that we had something more than a friendship.

"Well, let's get back out there into the circus. Your mother made such a fuss, I won't be surprised if she has a piñata strung up in the garden." We laughed and made our way back out into the living room to be engulfed by all the people I cared about.

***

"You're telling me that not only did you meet Jack Mangle, you spent the entire evening with him?" Hannah and Ash stared at me in awe.

I laughed at their expressions because I could imagine that was how I looked when I was introduced to him that first time.

"I actually seriously hate you right now." Ash pouted and looked adorable.

"I would sell my left kidney to spend an evening with him," Hannah sighed. We laughed at the dreamy look in her eyes.

I felt him before I saw him, unashamedly putting his hand on my lower back. I think I heard the girls actually sigh when they looked up at his beautifulness. I couldn't blame them when that was how I felt every time he was near.

"Hello ladies," his deep voice vibrated through the atmosphere. Add one knicker melting smile to the equation and they were all goners.

"Ash, Hannah, this is Kade Hamilton. Kade this is my best friend Ash and my cousin Hannah. She's Brian's twin."

He shook hands with Hannah and Ash stood up steadily

from where she sat, wobbling a little and spilling her water on Kade's shirt before she could shake his hand. *Was that an accident?*

"Oops! I'm so sorry! Crazy pregnant lady clumsiness!" Kade shrugged it off and took the napkins Hannah offered him.

"It's fine, don't worry about it."

He pulled his shirt out of his trousers to dry the material which allowed the girls to get a good look at a sliver of his tight abdominal muscles. Ash turned her wide eyes to me.

"Definitely lickable," she smiled widely, saying it out loud and making me wish that the ground would swallow me up. *And that was definitely not an accident...*

Kade looked up from wiping his shirt dry, his confusion turning slowly into a knowing smirk.

"Ah. You're the friend encouraging Alexa to eat food from off of my body."

If he had thought he would embarrass Ash by calling her out, he would be sadly mistaken. My fiery friend was far from shy. I could see how impressed Kade was by Ash as she gave him the biggest cheekiest eye sparkling smile I'd ever seen her give.

"In the flesh." Kade took her hand and planted a kiss on it, giving her that wink he knew made ladies melt. With *that,* he did get a blush from her. No one was immune.

"It's lovely to meet you ladies, Alexa talks about you all the time." And then they both went and fell in love with him too.

We spent the next few hours laughing and catching up. Imran, dad and Brian accosted Kade and soon a group of the men were typically sitting in the back room watching football on telly. To be honest, I would have loved to go and watch with them but the ladies were having way too much fun relaying the events of the past five months to me. I had missed them all so much and was happy to finally do this earlier than I had planned.

Kade seemed as engrossed as the other men in the events of the match on the screen, shouting at the referee, telling him he was blind while the other men agreed with his statement when their favourite player got yellow carded. I smiled at the familiarity, at how at home he looked here amongst my family and friends.

When he looked up to notice me ogling at him, he gave me a warm smile and wink before his attention was commandeered by Brian again.

Another two hours, a cake and buffet later, we were saying goodbye at the door with me promising to be back to stay a day after the business meeting we had to attend. As we were driven off to the hotel, Kade pulled out an iPad that was lying on the seat between us and handed it to me.

"What's this?"

"Open it and see."

I opened the cover of the tablet and unlocked the screen with a swipe. On the screen I saw a painting that Jason - Enzo - had sold at our exhibition at Atlantis. It was the one that I was in love with - of the fairylike fire haired creature sitting on the edge of the world looking out to a blazing sun that had it's own fantastical landscape. It was incidentally also the painting in the private room where I broke the champagne glass and where we almost kissed.

"You bought the Enzo piece?" Of course he had. It was beautiful and had only cost two hundred and fifty thousand dollars. I remember the prices of each piece but then again, they were stunning works. I had been told by Mary that a private collector had acquired it and she was handling this particular transaction. Obviously, I now knew it was Kade.

"Yeah I did, for you. Happy birthday Alexa."

Speechless didn't quite cover what I was feeling. I sat with my mouth agape for a few seconds, trying to process. When my mind felt like it was about to burst, I managed a reply.

"That painting was two hundred and fifty thousand

dollars, a quarter of a million dollars," I whispered. Kade looked amused.

"Is that what you're worrying about right now?"

I nodded, still in shock. He sighed, taking my hands in his and looked me straight in the eyes as he spoke sincerely.

"I need you to know that I was not thinking of the monetary value this painting has when I bought it. All I thought about, all I could think about, was how you looked at it in wonder as if this beautiful piece held all the answers to the questions you had in your mind. That innocence, that wonder, is why I bought it. Not to flaunt my wealth or make you feel uncomfortable. If it makes you feel any better, I would have bought something from the exhibition just because it is an Enzo piece. Buying this for you is more meaningful."

Fair enough. I gave him all of my gratitude at his thoughtfulness in a tight and lingering hug.

"Thank you Kade, I love it. It's now one of my prized possessions." He looked relieved.

"I'm glad. I've scheduled to have it delivered to the house when we return and they will install it wherever you want it."

We spent the rest of the journey in a comfortable but thought filled silence. I couldn't believe he had bought me such a meaningful gift but spent so much on it. How could I possibly make him take it back?

Once at the hotel, we said goodnight and went our separate ways to our rooms at the opposite ends of the floor.

That night, I dreamt I was sitting on the edge of the world gazing out to the sun but instead of being alone, he sat there next to me. Giving me my freedom to dream and protecting me from getting burnt.

CHAPTER THIRTY TWO

A night without 'adulting'

T he meeting the next day was held near Kings Cross and then the executives decided to go for an informal late lunch together in the Southbank area. I politely declined the invitation, instead telling Kade I would meet him once he was finished and decided to go and visit the Tate Modern instead.

Getting off at Southwark station, I walked to the looming iconic building, a sense of belonging filling me as I recalled all the memories I had as a student and then after of visiting the art gallery for various exhibitions. Entering the great Turbine Hall, I admired the latest installation and took a seat to observe my surroundings. Tourists and Londoners alike wandered the vast space and different floors that were visible from where I was sitting.

After an hour of exploring, I made my way to a cafe to buy a sandwich and then took a walk onto the Millennium Bridge. This bridge held a lot of memories for me. As well as once being my favourite spot in London, it was the place where Tom had proposed to me. I felt the nostalgia creep in but surprisingly, along with the sadness that often accompanied the feeling, I felt a sense of freedom that I had never felt before.

My phone buzzed with a message from Kade asking where he should meet me and I sent him the location. Twenty minutes later I could see him walking towards where I was standing still in the middle of the relatively busy pedestrian bridge.

"Hey," he said softly, sensing the mood I was in.

"Hey," I replied with a small smile and then continued to stand, eyes closed, breathing in deep and exhaling deeper.

"What are you doing here?"

I turned to look him, feeling my adoration for him and the way he could read the situation correctly - that I was having one of those rare life altering clarity filled moments.

"I'm taking my city back."

I didn't need to explain because he simply nodded and joined me in my quiet reverie. We stood there, side by side and I felt my sadness become part of the fabric of my soul but didn't let it rule my whole being. I allowed myself that feeling but a bigger part of me accepted that it was okay to still love everything that had reminded me of a happier time now lost, and be able to enjoy it with new meaning.

When I felt that I could peel myself from the view, I quietly slipped my hand into Kade's, looking him in his eyes to find him pleasantly surprised and pulling him towards St Paul's Cathedral on the other side of the Thames.

We quietly walked through the courtyard and then I told him about this part of London and how much I loved coming here. He told me about his visits to London during his university days and otherwise and that he had always been fond of the Tate and loved the tranquility of the cathedral.

"I'm glad you love my city as much as I do."

"Ditto. Although another positive point about London is that I'm not so widely recognised here. I don't have a constant barrage of paparazzi harassing me so it is as normal as it could get for me here."

"I never thought of that. It must be a relief."

"It is. I get to walk with a beautiful woman, holding her hand and enjoying the sights without the gossips getting every single bit of information on what is happening. This way, I get to have you all to myself."

I was quiet for a second or two before I looked at him with the sincerity I felt before answering.

"I'm glad that I get to have this time with you too."

The afternoon blended into the evening as we walked for ages and then had a light dinner before returning to the hotel to retire for the evening. My heart felt heavy as I said goodnight, my hand lingering in his. Our hands had been held together for the majority of the evening and mine felt empty as soon as I reclaimed it. It felt natural to be holding onto Kade. He felt like he was mine and I felt like I was his. Yet I hesitated, unsure exactly where we stood. He was giving me the space and time I needed without the pressure of being labelled as one thing or another, yet he had made his intentions clear. I was standing on the precipice of something monumental and my heart just said, 'hold on.'

I went to bed that night confused yet excited to see what the next day would hold for us. I was going to be staying at my parents house for the next couple of days and Kade was busy catching up with his own friends and work from London office but we had planned to meet the day I was due to return to the hotel so we could have drinks with both his friends and mine. Yet just a day and a half without him seemed like an eternity.

I laughed at my silliness and made myself comfortable in the massive bed. I was in deep and I had no intention of pulling myself out.

*****

"He's dishy, isn't he mum?" My mother was looking all goo goo eyed at Granna.

"Oh, he's far too handsome for his own good," chuckled Granna.

I had been at my parents house for just ten minutes before they had started on me.

That morning, I was disappointed to find Kade had left the hotel early to go meet an old friend. He had left a note under my door that made me smile like an idiot:

Beautiful,
Parting is such sweet sorrow...
Make sure you miss me.
K x

As if *not* missing him was an option. Right now, I sighed into my cup of real English tea made with my favourite Tetley tea bags and two sneaky spoons of sugar while two of my favourite women in the world sat opposite me at the kitchen table. The sun shone in through the patio doors on the crisp November morning and I soaked in the atmosphere.

"See! She's smitten! Missing him already, are you love?" Mum was giving me a teasing look and I gave her the same one back.

"Maybe."

"Oh he's just perfect for you! And you deserve someone who looks at you the way he does."

I could see mum welling up and felt a jolt of warning. I didn't want to make another mistake, I didn't want to break more hearts than just my own if things didn't work out.

But wasn't that just what any relationship was in the beginning? A gamble? There was never a full guarantee that all your feelings would be reciprocated all the time. You just had to take the plunge and put yourself out there, hoping for the best, building trust and breaking down walls. You would never be able to control the feelings and emotions of others and that was something we all had to accept in life. *Humans really are the strangest of creatures.*

I spent my day basking in the attention from my family, Hannah and Brian popping in to see me in the evening for family dinner.

"I've seen you more here than when we've been in New York," I joked whilst elbowing Brian who was trying to inhale his large piece of pie.

"I know, I'm sorry Lexi. My job is demanding as fuck - ow! Granna!" Brian rubbed the back of his head where he'd been whacked.

"No swearing," Granna scolded him.

"Say's the woman who swears like a sailor," he quipped.

" - at the dinner table," she added with a smirk which was returned with an equal amount of affection from Brian.

"I know it's demanding Bri, just wish we could make more time. I will try when we get back."

"Well, it's going to be a lot easier when we get back because I have accepted a partnership in a practice. No more ER for me!"

"Oh my God! That's amazing!" I hugged him tight and mum, Megan and Granna took their turn to squeeze the life out of him.

"Congratulations Brian! Very proud of you son," dad said from the head of the table.

We spent the evening grilling Brian on his new job and then we were both asked a lot of questions about life in NYC. My aunts and uncle joined us later for coffee and we stayed up until just after midnight before everyone left.

As I got comfortable in my bed that night, I was disappointed that I hadn't received a message from Kade. I did however receive a message ten minutes later from Ash:

Ash: Are you asleep?

I smiled, still awake from my evening coffee.

Me: Yup.

A second later she replied.

Ash: Well, open your door then!

I ran downstairs and laughed when I saw a disgruntled looking Imran dropping Ash, who was dressed in a cute but ridiculous onesie with her bump sticking out. Slamming the car door shut, we waved at Imran and hugged one another.

"Old habits, eh?" I smiled down at my best friend.

"Babe, we will be doing this shit when we're sixty and over when our boobs touch the floor."

After a reluctant Imran left his pregnant wife, who assured him she would be fine without him, I sat on my bed in my childhood room with Ash leaning out of my window.

"So many memories in this room."

"Yeah, like sneaking out for those parties we were forbidden to go to," I snorted.

"Until your mum found out and had that tree outside trimmed down," she laughed.

"God, we were so bad," I chuckled.

For a few seconds there, I could see the silhouettes of our youth dance around the room to some Backstreet Boys song that was all the rage in those days. It wasn't that we were that old in years, it was more that those times seemed so far from our now more responsible lives.

"I just realised that we are proper 'adulting' right now," I thought out loud.

Ash turned around to face me, thinking about what I had just said for a few seconds. She then walked over to my bed, grabbed a pillow and threw it in my face.

"I refuse to adult tonight." That statement started a short but giggle inducing pillow fight in which I was tricked, twice, by Ash using the pregnant woman card.

Lying side by side on my bed, we stared up at the glow in the dark stars that I had stuck on my ceiling when I was eight years old. *That's some strong adhesive.*

"You're falling in love with Kade Hamilton." Trust Ash not to beat around the bush. Hearing her say it out aloud was a little scary, yet I couldn't deny it.

"Do you think I'm making a mistake?" I watched Ash in profile until she turned fully to look at me, the sweetest smile on her face.

"No. One hundred percent no. He adores you, you deserve a man that worships the ground you walk on, who looks at you the way *he* does and just *gets* you. Did you ever think you would be here? Lying here and exploring the possibility that you could fall in love once again? Because babe, you are. After everything you went through, after losing the baby, losing Tom to his betrayal and moving thousands of miles away to forget and rebuild. You're here, smiling, happy and alive again."

"I'm scared Ash, I'm so fucking scared that one of us will mess this whole thing up. I can't go through that again."

Ash sat up and took my hand in a squeeze.

"You're the strongest woman I know, and I know a lot of strong women. There is nothing you can't get through but let me just say this. I don't think that man is capable of hurting you the way Tom did, I don't think he could do that. You would be taking a chance with anyone you met Lexi but I've seen you two together and it's so different to you and Tom. It's on a different level, the intensity is palpable. Just trust your heart once more. Do it for that future you want for yourself so that a year from now you can sit with me and say, 'I knew I'd make it."

I blinked back tears and hugged my best friend who always knew the right thing to say to make everything feel right again.

"I'm going to tell him how I feel," I said with confidence as I pulled away.

"Atta girl."

CHAPTER THIRTY THREE

Echoes of the past

The pub was busy on the Saturday afternoon but not too loud for us not to be able to talk to one another. A few of my friends had turned up and so had a few of Kade's. Of course, Kade's friends circle was little more glamorous in the sense that all his friends were some kind of celebrity. I was introduced to a couple of friends of his from University, one that happened to be a popular young politician and member of parliament and another who was a relation to the royal family. Another was a celebrity chef and one was a news anchor. Unsurprisingly, all of them were humble and easy going people that made us laugh with their stories.

My friends included Hannah and some of my ex colleagues from the boutique I used to work for. Somehow the mix of personalities just about worked out as we laughed and had a few drinks.

Kade was in his element, more relaxed than I had seen him in days and I had to admit to myself that the minute I saw him walk into the pub with his friends, I couldn't stop the smile on my face that I saw mirrored in him. I felt guilty that he had been stressed for months because of the tension between us and excited that I was going to end that confusion by finally letting him in.

Right now, I was going to enjoy his company, his thigh brushing mine under the table and the way he would look over at me every now and then. A wink here and a gentle hand squeeze there. I revelled in it, wanting much more and knowing that soon enough I may just get that.

Waving good bye to our friends, we made our way back to the hotel in a black cab whilst drinking in the sights and talking about everything we had been up to whist we had been apart. Which felt like an eternity but was really just a day and a half.

"So we ended up sitting on Brian and tickling him until he gave me back my phone," I laughed, remembering how Hannah and I thwarted his plans to dig out embarrassing photos of me and post them on Facebook. It was a lifelong habit that I had, unfortunately, not always been lucky enough to stop from occurring.

"Man, Brian is lucky you guys didn't break something," he laughed, sitting so close yet feeling so far away.

"Actually, one time he had taken Hannah's phone and sent her boyfriend a picture of her with her retainer in and toothpaste on her spots and she punched him so hard in the gut, he fell and hit his face on the corner of a table. Had to have his front two teeth fixed *and* wear a retainer. True story."

"Now thats what I call poetic justice," he laughed again, this time taking my hand in his and kissing it, almost as if he couldn't help himself.

He was quiet until we reached the hotel. Holding out his hand for me to step out of the cab, he paid the fare and led us to the lifts. Inside, he let out a sigh.

"Are you okay to attend the event with me tonight? It is being held here in the ballroom, you can leave any time you wish."

"Of course, I'm not tired. Slightly buzzed but not tired. And I got a dress especially for this evening," I beamed up at him. I could tell this was important to him.

Reaching our floor, he walked me to the door of my room and left to get ready while I stared after him like a lovesick puppy. I felt the nervousness creep in. *You're going to tell him tonight.* The voice deep in my soul was growing restless and making me feel a little unwell. I walked into my room to get ready and steady myself for the big evening ahead.

***

"Wow."

I stood in front of Kade, eyes cast down and feeling extremely shy around him all of a sudden. My champagne pink dress was form fitting silk, off the shoulder bardot style coming down to just under my knees. My satin silk heels matched as well as my clutch. You could tell I had bought this ensemble especially for the occasion. I had attended many events and parties with Kade and worn one of my many formal dresses but tonight was different because this was for him.

"You look beautiful beyond words," he continued once he had taken a few seconds to look me over.

"Thank you," I said to my shoes and felt him lift my chin to meet his appreciating eyes.

"Don't hide that beautiful face from me Alexa." I nodded, dumbstruck whenever I saw him in one of his formal dinner suits.

We entered the big ballroom to a sea of bodies walking around and schmoozing already. Kade picked up two champagne flutes from a passing waiter and passed me one.

I looked around to see if there was anyone familiar from our business clientele when I saw something that I hadn't expected.

"Um, Kade?"

"Yeah?"

"What is this event for, exactly?"

"Oh right. I forgot to tell you since our visit was so last minute. This is an event held by Hamilton's for our London office employees and our associates here. We've also got the architects designing our new London based office here tonight. It's basically the unveiling of the model and plans etcetera. The company decided to host this fancy event for it - dinner and dance. Any excuse for a party huh?"

Noting that I remained still and quiet, he took my elbow and led me to the side of the room.

"What's wrong?"

"Nothing, it's silly." Inside I was shaking just a little.

"It's not nothing when you've turned pale and look like you don't want to be here." His concerned eyes bore into mine and I felt the panic ease a little.

"You know the company that designed your new Fort?"

"Yeah, Reid and Clarkson. What about them?" His brow creased with confusion.

"Thats the firm I used to work for. That Tom still works for. I saw the stand at the side with their poster. It freaked me out a little is all."

Understanding washed over his handsome face and he soothed me with gentle rubs on my back.

"He may not be here."

How strange was it that my current love interest was soothing me about my past one. If I wasn't in the situation myself, I would laugh.

"I know, I'm just a little taken aback thats all."

I knew there was a good chance he would be there. Tom was a senior architect, he had worked hard for his position. This event was a good opportunity for the company and networking was his forte.

"I really should have looked at your resume properly. Then I would have known about this little nugget."

"Do you mean to tell me that you hired me without actually looking at my credentials?"

"I already knew you'd be perfect for the job," he joked. When my smile dropped, he took my hand and squeezed it.

"We don't have to stay Alexa, let's go get dinner somewhere and leave this for today."

He said it so kindly but I knew that if I didn't face this situation now, I would just prolong the inevitable. I may never be ready for it but at least I could try and then maybe I could finally let go of that last part of me holding onto Tom, making the whole of me ready for whatever came next.

I squeezed his hand reassuringly in return and smiled the best I could.

"No. Thank you, but no. I need to face the situation if he is here. I have nothing to run away from. And I have you here. I will be okay."

"Of course you will. I'll always be here. And for the record, I did look at your resume."

His words warmed my heart. We worked our way through the room and various business associates that knew the Hamilton's and sipped on drinks, eating the delicious canapés being brought out to us in the foyer.

The people here had respect for Kade but apart from that, they were at ease around him. It made my heart happy to see how well he had earned that kind of adoration.

Once dinner was announced, we were led into he dinning hall where sparkling chandeliers shone upon the lavishly dressed tables and the settings upon them. We found the table with our names on the place cards and sat down. I wasn't paying attention to anything or anyone around me whilst Kade told me about the time he and his brother Jared had wrecked a model his father had installed in the old office building of the then newly proposed present day Fort. I was struggling to contain my belly laugh as he got me giggling with his impressions of his father, when I felt a hand on my bare shoulder.

Maybe a lot of time had passed that I had forgotten what his touch felt like or maybe I had been sufficiently distracted enough that it took me a bit of time to feel the contact on my skin. I think it was seeing Kade's face morph from jovial to granite in seconds that finally got me to acknowledge something was happening.

"Lexi?"

I felt my body freeze upon hearing the very familiar voice from behind me. A voice that I used to love the sound of. A voice that had hurt me with words that I had never thought I'd ever hear.

I felt Kade's strong and steady hand move to rest on my knee as I slowly turned around in my seat. There he stood, in his crisp black suit, brown hair neatly combed, a clean shaven face. Slight lines had appeared by the corners of his warm brown eyes and even though he looked handsome and sharp in his suit, I couldn't help but notice a tiredness in him. So much time had passed yet the familiarity was there between us and it felt like a betrayal to Kade. I was hyper aware of him next me, of his gaze and possessive energy.

"Tom. How have you been?" My voice sounded alien to me. I sounded a lot calmer than I felt.

"I'm well, thanks. What are you doing in town? I thought you were in New York?"

The calm that I had previously thought I possessed seemed to melt a little as I felt myself grow irritated.

"I am allowed to come visit my family and friends, you know." My voice came out icier than I wanted it to and I felt Kade's hand squeeze my knee in support. Tom looked taken aback but quickly composed himself and cleared his throat.

"That's not what I meant Lexi. I just didn't think I would see you for a very long time, let alone at an event like this."

I took a stabilising breath and managed a small smile.

"I work for Hamilton's. This is Kade Hamilton." Tom's reaction told me that he knew exactly who Kade was, his only confusion was what I was doing with him.

"It's a pleasure to meet you Mr Hamilton. Tom Mills." Tom extended his hand to Kade who in turn shook his hand more firmly than required.

"Please, call me Kade." You could tell that this was his automatic response to new business associates.

"I am the lead Architect for the design of your London offices."

I turned to look at Kade. Gone was his earlier boyish Softness. Now, l could solely see the businessman, only he had a stony look in his eyes. I watched as Tom's eyes travelled from where I sat to where Kade was sitting close to me. I cringed the moment I realised he had noticed Kade's hand on my knee. Add that to the way we had been sitting closely together and laughing, I could see him connecting the dots and his eyes lost their softness too. When he turned to look at me, there was judgement there. I felt my hackles rise but calmed myself down. *He has no right!*

"It's an impressive design Tom. My father is very pleased with the plans and he is glad that we chose your firm for it. You are very talented."

He sounded genuine when he said it and my confused heart almost burst with pride that the man I was almost completely certain I was falling madly in love with had complimented the man I used to be madly in love with. I was proud of them both and it was starting to make me feel nauseous. My past and future were colliding and tilting my world off its axis. I took a few deep breaths to abate the panic that was threatening to set in. How had I gone from a relaxing and much anticipated evening to feeling like I was in the twilight zone?

Tom gave Kade a small smile.

"Thank you. We made sure we remained as close

to the design specification as possible. The plans have been approved and we are all set to start construction in the next month or so."

"I'm glad to hear it, the staff will be pleased with their new premises." Kade politely nodded and I took it as a sign that he was done talking to Tom. Only, Tom was still standing over me, looking gingerly at the table.

"I guess you had better take your seat, they're serving the starters now," I said with a small smile, hoping he got the hint and would leave. Tom gave me a cheeky look, one that used to make me giggle but was now making me feel more than a little off kilter.

"Uh, yeah. Which is why I'm here. My place setting is next to you." He picked up the place card on the setting next to mine and sure enough it read, 'Tom Mills.' I silently cursed the events management and Tom. Ever the ambitious man, I was certain he had pulled a few strings to be seated at the table where Kade Hamilton would be. Little did he know, he would get an added bonus. Or booby prize, depending on how he looked at it.

I placed the card neatly on the table and returned my gaze to him where he stood, slightly smug at having caught me in an awkward position. I wasn't going to let it bother me. That's what I kept telling myself as I gave him a curt nod and shuffled a little more into Kade's side to avoid any part of me touching any part of Tom.

Once an amused Tom had taken his seat, I turned my attention back to Kade, avoiding the burn I felt from Tom's gaze on me. Kade looked calm but I knew a man restraining himself when I was sitting next to a heated body of pure muscle that was so tense, I was scared he'd give himself a muscle cramp or an aneurysm. I placed my hand on his thigh, fully aware of how intimate a thing it was to do and how it looked in front of Tom, who seemed to be watching my every move. I didn't want to lose the playfulness we had been enthralled in today over my ex husband showing up at this event.

"I can have us moved and seated elsewhere if you prefer," he finally whispered in my ear, his arm splayed protectively and possessively behind my chair. The action brought him closer to me, letting me breathe in his delicious scent.

"No, I'm not letting him chase me off. I'm okay. Let's eat."

For the first part of the dinner, I sat there with my body turned towards Kade whilst fully aware of Tom. It was agony and made me feel like an adolescent ignoring him but I needed to prepare myself to even be able to acknowledge him again. I could hear Tom speaking with people at the table, forever the smooth talker.

Kade was constantly accosted by people coming up to him as he tried to get a spoonful of the specially catered food into his mouth. He refused to leave his seat beside me throughout the badgering. It made me happy internally that he didn't want to leave me alone with my ex but I know a lot of that was also to do with he fact that he was asserting his presence in my life in front of said ex.

Eventually, he had to leave me at the table to go and make a speech at the podium at the front of the hall. He was charming, made the crowd laugh and then unveiled the model and plans for the new London HQ with my old boss Mr Jenkins standing beside him.

I ignored Tom, who was staring at me the whole time I was staring at Kade making his speech. A couple of times his thigh brushed mine and made me jump a little and move myself which seemed to amuse him because I swear I heard a chuckle.

Once the speeches were over, they announced the informal 'party' they had held in the hall next door. Guests started to filter into the adjoining room where music had started being played by a live band as the dinner service was cleared from the dining hall. I took Kade's hand as soon as he approached me and didn't bother looking back as we moved into the other room.

"We can leave any time you like Alexa," he reminded me as he slipped his hand to my lower back, guiding me.

"I'm okay Kade, really. Had to face him one day and that one day just happened to be today. Let's at least stay for a little bit. I haven't had the chance to dance with you for some time."

I felt some of his tension ease the further we got away from the dining room and with it, so did mine. I felt myself relax as I smiled up at his handsome face and let him lead me into the room. God knows that I would go anywhere with him.

***

The music soothed my soul as the singers sang Frank Sinatra hits and people either stood around talking, swayed to the music or took to the dance floor in partners.

Kade wouldn't take 'no' for an answer as we got closer to the dance floor. Kade's natural ability to just be at home wherever he went was enviable. And, of course, he was a good dancer. Sensing my awkwardness, possibly by my 'fish out of the bowl' look, he gently pulled me close to him and whispered for me to follow his lead as we slow danced.

He whispered things in my ear that made me giggle and then he'd pull back to look at me, a pleased expression on his face. I should have known it wouldn't last.

I could feel eyes watching me from the moment we entered the hall. I knew he had followed us in before I had even seen him. Kade had noticed and I guess that was the reason he had been distracting me, although being pulled so close to his body was distraction enough. Especially when I still had daydreams about that body.

"Mr Hamilton, I am sorry to interrupt but may I cut in?"

I think I stopped breathing. The actual nerve of this guy

was unbelievable and he definitely didn't look sorry. We turned to look at Tom who stood a few inches shorter than Kade. I felt Kade's hand tense on my waist as he held me protectively close to him. He looked down at me and then towards Tom, frowning and jaw clenched, indecisive as to what to do. I didn't want Tom to cause a scene but I also didn't want to spend any time alone with him. I didn't want to hurt Kade but I knew I had to handle the situation that could look bad for him in front of all these important people should things go awry.

I turned to face Kade, placing my hand on his chest to get him to look at me. The storm that was brewing was clear and I needed to calm him somehow.

"Hey, it's okay. Tom can have until this song is over and then you and I are leaving."

I could see that he didn't like the sound of that, in fact he even looked angry but I stood on tiptoe and whispered in his ear, "...and when we leave, we're going back to your room..."

This time when I pulled back, he could see the intentions I had and that ignited a fire in him that was so palpable, I almost blushed as he squeezed my waist. I heard a throat clearing and turned to see Tom looking irritated. Kade, slowly let go of me and towered over Tom.

"One dance." The finality of those words and the delivery of them were not lost on him. Tom had the audacity to smirk as Kade walked away and disappeared into a crowd of people, some of whom were waiting to get a moment alone with him to discuss business. I felt so proud of him for being so gracious about the situation, for trusting me to handle this when it was clear it bothered him that Tom would be dancing with me. I felt the loss of his security too because now I was facing Tom, after a long time, alone.

He didn't waste any time in stepping into my personal space, putting his hand on my waist and taking my hand in his other one. I took a half step away from him, already uncomfortable with the familiarity of him, his body and his scent that used to haunt me for so long after his betrayal.

"I won't bite Lexi, unless you want me to." I used to find his little jokes hilarious but now I was just annoyed. I forced myself to look into his eyes.

"What do you want Tom? What's your play here?"

"Play? Wow, you sound like one of those yanks already." I rolled my eyes like the child I am.

"Why are you doing this?"

He looked taken aback by my attitude. I guess he had always been used to me being so compliant with him when we were together, that my abruptness was new to him.

"I just wanted to see how you are Lexi, that's all. I still care about you, that doesn't stop with a piece of paper."

He looked hurt and I felt bad for being so abrupt. I guess a woman scorned is not one to forget so easily, and the bitterness of what he had done still made me feel hostile towards him.

"I'm fine Tom. Shouldn't you be with Rebecca?"

This time, there was no hiding the contempt in my voice. He looked a little uncomfortable.

"She's not here. We're no longer together." I felt a pang of satisfaction at that.

"I can't say I'm surprised."

"Yeah, you always were a good judge of character," he laughed bitterly.

"Well, obviously I'm not always right. Got it completely wrong with you." *Meow.*

"Ouch. Okay, maybe I deserved that but you think dating your boss is a good idea?" he shot back, anger simmering in his brown eyes.

That axe swung both ways.

"I beg your pardon? My personal life has nothing to do with you! And for your information, Kade and I were friends *before* I started working for him!"

I was trying my best to keep my voice hushed, conscious of the people around us. He was getting me riled up.

"So you're fucking him huh? Jumping into bed with the billionaire lawyer?"

I felt my face heat up. I pulled out of his hold, putting on a sickly sweet smile and talking as calmly as I could.

"I wouldn't be the first woman to jump into bed with my boss, Tom. Or did you forget about that when you were fucking your baby mama?"

He stood quietly fuming, fists balled at his sides. Taking another step back, I smoothed my dress down.

"The song is over. Good bye Tom."

With that I walked away, not looking back.

CHAPTER THIRTY FOUR

Nothing good happens after 3am

I looked around for Kade to no avail until a security guard approached me with a note from him.

"I came back to my suite. I'll see you up here when you're ready."

I rushed to the elevators, avoiding people and staff and pressed furiously on the button to get me to him. The closer I got to the floor he was on, to him, the calmer I felt. I couldn't wait to be in his arms, I craved that like an addict.

As soon as I reached the door, I knocked furiously. The door opened nearly as soon as I had stared knocking. I threw myself into the room and almost forgot how to breathe. Kade was standing in front of me wearing only his dress pants, chest and feet bare and hands in his pockets. His hair looked like he'd run his hands through it a million times. His beautiful body called for me to explore it and I had to scold myself for thinking of sex when I should be appeasing my man. *My man.*

"You okay?" He sounded tense, concern was written on his face but I knew he was agitated.

"I'm okay. I just wanted to be here with you."

He turned and walked slowly to the couch and I watched the muscles in his back the whole way as I followed him. He sat down, running his hands through his hair again.

"Those were the longest few minutes of my life."

I felt relief in his admission.

"Mine too. All I could think about was getting back to you."

He suddenly reached out and pulled me to him, his face pressed against my stomach in his seated position. My hands automatically went to his hair, running my finger through it, causing him to look up at me with unbelievable intensity.

"Please tell me you've made up your mind about us?"

"Yes," I whispered, without hesitation.

"What do you want?" he asked.

"You."

"Thank fuck."

In one smooth movement, he was stood up, walking me back against the closest wall and putting his lips on me.

He was everywhere, his lips on my shoulders, my neck, before finding my lips that were thirsty for him. Our hands desperately sought one another, the urgency apparent in every move. I felt his muscles greedily and vowed to explore more later. For now, I wanted this man under me, over me and inside me.

Kade bit my bottom lip and then licked it, causing me to shiver.

"I want you," I said wantonly.

He answered by hitching my dress up and lifting me off the ground, leaving me no choice but to wrap my legs around his waist. Pushing me against the wall, I felt his bulge against me, right where I wanted him.

"Can you feel how much I want you?" he said seductively in my ear, his hot breath making me pant with anticipation as I nodded my answer.

"I'm too wired right now to be gentle Alexa. If you don't want me taking you hard, right here against this wall, then you had better tell me now because once I start I won't be able to stop. Not with you."

"I need you Kade."

I kissed him deeply, my tongue meeting his, making him growl which just turned me on even more. Before I knew what was happening, he'd hiked my dress up further and pulled the shoulders of my dress down with the cups of my bra to reveal my breasts, nipples standing to attention. Ripping my knickers off with precision, he unzipped his trousers that I had already pulled the buttons off of. Taking his hard length in his hand, he guided it to my entrance and slid into me slowly and purposefully, keeping eye contact, teeth gritted as he hissed. I moaned as he filled me up, deliciously stretching me. My eyes closed at the sensation.

"Look at me Alexa." I did as he asked, sharing his intensity. "Now hold on tight."

I tightened my grip around his neck and my legs around his waist and he started to thrust punishingly into me. I swear I saw fireworks as he relentlessly worked us into a frenzy of moans and pleas of more. I never thought that the sound of skin slapping against skin would turn me on but the harder he fucked me, the more it brought me closer to the edge. I said his name over and over again like a mantra, and he said mine like a prayer. When he could tell that I was getting closer to the brink of my orgasm, he took my nipple into his mouth and sucked hard, causing me to shatter into a million pieces on a loud scream of ecstasy and soon after he was growling out his own release with my name on his lips.

Panting and spent, he wiped the hair away from my sweaty forehead and sweetly kissed my forehead.

"Fuck."

"I believe we just did, but I don't mind going again," he smirked, wiggling his eyebrows suggestively.

"You're insatiable Mr Hamilton," I giggled, revelling in

his touch and the fact that we were still joined together in the most intimate of ways with his trousers around his ankles and my dress hiked up.

"Only with you baby."

I felt my heart soar like a kite and kissed his sexy lips. He kicked off his pants from his ankles walked with me hanging onto him into the bedroom, placing me gently on my back onto the giant bed and stood back, completely and gloriously naked. I propped myself up on my elbow on my side, thinking about just how content I would be to just look at his masculine beauty all night long. Amongst doing other things.

"Are you just going to keep staring at me?" he smirked, making me want him more.

"Yup. Why? Did you have something else planned?"

He stalked closer to me, leaning over my body, his arms caging me in. I could smell his scent mixed with mine and our sweat. It just turned me on even more. I felt him grow against my exposed thigh, as if he caught the scent too.

"I have a lot planned to do with you, Alexa. I'm gonna take my time with you this time."

"You are?" I sounded like a breathless wanton woman.

"Yeah baby, I am going to map every inch on your body with my lips and hands. Only problem is, one of us is a little over dressed."

My breath hitched when his eyes hooded with lust and he nipped my lip like I had done to him earlier. I pushed him off of me gently and sat up. Forcing him back against the headboard, I stood at the foot of the bed on shaky legs from anticipation. I'd just had him yet I already craved him again. Summoning my confidence, I pulled my zip down my back as far as I could and slipped off the dress slowly. Standing in my heels and bra, my knickers already discarded somewhere in the front room, I reached back to unclasp my bra. I saw his eyes hood further and the real evidence of how he liked what he saw when he got bigger and harder, taking himself in hand. Lord, the sight of him doing that almost had me panting.

Leaving my heels on, I stalked purposefully back to him letting him pull me by the hand, as soon as I was close enough, onto the bed and astride him.

"You're beautiful."

I saw him wait for me to deny it, to deflect his compliment that I could tell was so sincere. Instead I smiled and leaned into him as my breasts brushed his chest to whisper, "So are you." In that moment, I knew I was exactly where I was supposed to be.

**

The sound of my phone beeping and buzzing faintly next to me woke me up. I rubbed my eyes, aware that my body felt deliciously sore when I stretched it out. I turned my head to side to make sure I hadn't made all of what had happened up in my sex starved mind. Lo and behold, there lay my adonis in all his naked glory, a sheet barely covering his impressive bulge, one arm over his head revealing his muscular biceps and the other hand possessively on my hip. I could cry at how lucky I felt at that exact moment.

Hearing my phone chime again, I tore my eyes away from him to my clutch bag that Kade must have brought into the bedroom for me at some point after he'd knocked me out with his sexletics.

I opened my bag to see there were twelve missed calls and five messages from Tom. I wondered for a minute how he had my number before I realised that I was using my old UK sim card in my phone. I felt angry that he was trying to intrude in my life, trying to get my attention and distracting me from my dream man lying next to me in bed.

The time on my phone read 2:43am. I pressed on the message icon and read.

11:56 pm - "I need to speak with you. Pick up your phone."

00:09am - "For fucks sake Lexi! Pick up your damn phone!"

00:38am - "Lexi, please answer me."

01:50 am - "I'm srry."

02:41am - "Im stil at tha hotl. I knw yur stayin her. I wil cum up and bng on evry door til u answr if yu don call me bck rite nw."

The last message woke me up for good. Tom was drunk. I could always tell when he was drunk and texting me when his spelling was, well, like a drunk man trying to type a message out. And drunk Tom was relentless. He would cause a scene right here at this respected five star hotel just to get what he wanted. And for some reason, that was to talk to me. I looked over at Kade who was sleeping like the dead.

What should I do? Let Tom embarrass me and get Kade mad or give into his request? God knew I didn't want to cause a scene. Kade was still my boss and this was his business trip. There were important CEO's and directors staying at the hotel who had come from the European division of the Hamilton empire to attend the event we had been at.

I ran a hand through my hair, exasperated and decided to make an executive decision.

Pulling on my clothes quietly, I left the bedroom with my bag and phone and made my way to the living area of the suite. I dialled Tom's number while I pulled on my heels. He picked up straight away.

"Lexi." Shit. He was slurring a bit and was well on his way to being shit faced.

"What do you want Tom?" I wanted to sound stern but instead I heard the worry in my own voice.

"I need to talk to you babe. We need to talk."

"So talk." There was a pause and the sound of a

clink of a glass.

"Face to face. I need to see you." I let out an exasperated sigh.

"You know that can't happen."

"Why? Your *boyfriend* won't let you?" The sneering voice was grating on my nerves but I didn't want to push him to do something stupid.

"My relationship with Kade is nothing to do with you Tom." He was quiet for a few seconds.

"I just need to see you Lexi. Everything is so shit right now and I just wanted you."

He sounded so distraught, I felt my traitor heart pinch at the thought of him being hurt. Fucking typical. I pulled the phone away from my ear to curse the ceiling in frustration.

Putting the phone back to my ear, I heard myself say words I never thought I'd say.

"Fine. I'll meet you but you need to sober up some. Get a cup of coffee or two and then I'll come meet you at the bar or wherever you are."

"Okay, I will do that right now, definitely. Thank you."

I hung up and crept into the bedroom to see Kade still passed out. I wasn't about to wake him up to tell him I was meeting my ex. I'd tell him in the morning when Tom would be way out of the way and he wouldn't be able to do anything about it. I left his suite quietly to go to my room to clean up, shower and change.

I had managed to slip on my underwear when I heard a knock on my door. The bedside clock read 3:35am. Throwing on a bathrobe, I made my way to the door. I was convinced it was Kade who had probably woken up and come looking for me. When I looked out of the peep hole, I swore out aloud. Seeing no other choice but to go with it, I opened the door to Tom standing there, tie undone, jacket draped over his arm and eyes bloodshot. His usually neatly styled hair was messed up, his shirt half tucked into his trousers and crumpled like it had been chewed on by a goat. He looked awful and I didn't feel anything but pity for him.

"I thought we said we'd meet downstairs?"

"I, uh, didn't want to speak down there. Some of the guys from work stuck around for more drinks. They are pretty generous with closing time down there."

I wondered if they had seen his erratic behaviour while he was furiously calling and texting me. I thanked God again that I had disabled my voicemail. I cringed at the thought of him leaving me voicemails in front of all those people.

"How did you find out which room was mine?"
He scratched his head sheepishly.

"I may have bribed one of the young wait staff to find out for me..."

Letting out another exasperated sigh, I stepped aside for him to come in.

He stepped inside, walking straight to the sofa in the large room and sitting down heavily, dumping his jacket on the armrest and leaning his forearms on his knees, head down.

I followed and sat as far as I could from him at the other end of the sofa. The silence was heavy and I felt myself getting impatient. I finally stopped tapping my foot on the carpet and turned to face him, sitting forward slightly to get his attention.

"You wanted to meet to talk at this ungodly hour, Tom. So talk."

He chuckled and turned his face towards me.

"Yeah, I did. I'd forgotten how feisty you are."

"Well, time, distance and divorce can do that to a person. Also, fucking someone who isn't your wife is an indication that you don't think much about her at all."

I could feel the cat claws wanting to come out to play but reeled it in as much as I could. I suddenly wasn't sure if it was a good idea to be having a conversation in close proximity to my cheating ex husband.

"Touché."

He was silent again for a few seconds and each one was agony. He stood suddenly, hands in his hair, pulling in exasperation.

"Maybe this isn't such a good idea Tom-"

"I wanted to apologise Lexi. I was out of order, I'm sorry."

He had stunned me silent. Tom wasn't really the kind of guy that apologised often.

"What exactly are you apologising for? How you behaved tonight? Or for breaking my heart?"

The hurt was still there, the feeling of betrayal creeping in. I may not have had the same feelings I had for him when we were married but that didn't make things easier. I had enough years with this man as my partner, my best friend. I never expected an apology face to face after everything.

"All of the above, Lexi. I was out of order tonight, I shouldn't have said the things I said. I know I don't deserve forgiveness from you for everything else I put you through but I hope one day you will forgive me."

"So you drank yourself stupid and have come up here at close to four in the morning to ask for my forgiveness?" Now it was my turn to let out an exasperated sigh. "Tom, I can't say that I forgive you because it's still raw for me. It's hard for me to accept anything from you at the moment. It's not easy to trust anyone again after something like this, it's not easy to let go of the memories and the pain that is linked to it. I will always have that insecurity in any relationship I'm in, that he may leave me the way you did."

I hadn't realised the tears were running down my face until Tom sat down again, closer to me, and wiped one away with his thumb.

"I hate that I did that to you. You have no idea how much I hate myself. I know it's hard for you to accept that right now, you're right, but I beat myself up about this everyday."

"You can't take it all back." He looked like he was

suffering but instead of feeling happy, I felt sad for him.

"I know. But I was hoping...I just wanted to see if..."

This was a first, Tom Mills speechless.

"See what?" He took my reluctant hands into his, making me automatically weary.

"I wanted to see if I could make it up to you. If we could be together again. If not right now, then maybe some-time in the near future."

"Tom-"

"Hear me out Lexi. I know you don't trust me right now and I expect that but I want to try."

"I really think-"

"Lexi, please. Everything would be at your pace. I won't rush you. Come back to London. We can work this out babe, I love you so much and it's taken losing you to realise just how much and seeing you here today makes me feel like it's my last chance to try."

He looked so hopeful, it made me almost feel like a bitch but enough was enough. I couldn't let this carry on. I pulled my hands out of his.

"It's never going to happen Tom. I could never do that and although the obvious reason why is me not being able to trust you, the bigger reason is that I don't love you anymore. I'm sorry but you need to forget that idea. I won't ever be getting back with you."

He looked crushed, standing up again and pacing in front of me as he made a mess of his hair with his hands

"So you think your rebound guy is going to last? The billionaire's son?"

I felt my defences rise again.

"Kade is a successful, Oxford graduated Lawyer. He happens to be the son of a billionaire but that doesn't de-fine him. He's a good, kind and hard working man."

Tom looked at me with his hurt puppy dog eyes again.

"There was a time when you said the same about

me."

I gave him a small smile.

"You still are Tom. It's just that I found those qualities and more in someone else."

"You think he will stick around?"

He was egging me on, hoping I would reveal a weakness in my relationship with Kade. What he got instead shocked him speechless.

"Yes. Because I love him. He's the one."

This time, he sat down and leaned back as if the wind had been knocked out of him. I felt the same. I never thought that the first time I would admit it out aloud, that it would be in front of my ex husband.

"I came here in the hopes of a reconciliation. I hadn't expected you to say that," he said, swallowing hard as if he'd taken a bitter pill.

"I hadn't planned on it happening, it just did. You can't expect that I'd always love you Tom, after all this time. After *everything*. I'm still hurt, yes, and I feel angry about what you did but I don't have that kind of love for you anymore. It belongs to someone else. I still care for you because I can't just switch that off but I'd prefer for my past to be far away from my life right now. I'm in a good place now, I've come to terms with a lot of things and I've built a new life for myself. You're not a part of it but you're a lesson that I've learnt from."

He took in my words and I knew the moment they had sunk in when his shoulders slumped and he shifted forward in his seat again, head down in defeat.

"I shouldn't have let you go."

It was a statement full of pain but there was no satisfaction in it for me. I thought I would feel delighted in his misery but I didn't. The reason I could feel this way was Kade Hamilton. The moment I had let go of Tom and had opened my heart to Kade, was the moment I was able to breathe again. Now all I could think of was getting back to him but I wasn't cruel enough to just kick Tom out when he clearly wasn't ready to leave.

I got up to get us some water and returned to the sofa, handing him a bottle and taking a sip of my own.

"I'm happy now Tom. I've moved on, found something good and positive and *real.* I hope you find that again too. What we had was special but it is over, for good. You're a big part of my story, I will forever be grateful for you. You did me wrong, it's hurt me for so long that I'm finally ready to let it go. Not for you, but for me, because I have a second chance at happily ever after. Or close to it anyway."

Tom smiled at me, sadness and pride emanating from it.

"You're always going to be the best woman I have ever known and loved, Lexi. I want nothing more than for you to be happy, even if I don't get to be in your life."

We sat together for another hour and he told me about his parents and his new projects at work whilst I told him all about reconnecting with my father and life in New York. I had forgotten how important his friendship had been to me and in that moment I missed my friend because I knew I probably wouldn't see him again after this morning.

"Tell me about your little boy."

His smile was no longer sad but bright as he pulled out his phone to show me hundreds of pictures of a gorgeous little brown haired boy. He looked just like his daddy and it made my heart ache even thinking about what our baby would have been like. Sensing my sadness, he took my hand and squeezed.

"I think about our baby all the time. I know you think I didn't care because I was so caught up in the…affair… but when you left and everything broke apart…I thought a lot about the baby. I didn't support you, I should have been there and I will never be able to take that time back." I looked away as I felt the tears creep in.

"Yeah."

I heard him curse under his breath as a fat tear drop fell

on the skin of my bare knee peeping out through the long bathrobe. I felt him hesitate as if he was having an internal battle with himself before I felt him shift and gather me in his arms. There was a strange familiarity and security there that brought me some comfort that I felt myself let go of the pain I had been carrying for so long and I sobbed into his chest. His smell was like the scent of the past eight years of my life all bottled and sprayed on this man. I knew it was nostalgia the moment I thought how his arms didn't feel as strong or secure as that of the man I now loved. It was that thought that allowed me to pull away and wipe the tears, laughing awkwardly at the situation. Tom laughed too, looking just as confused.

"I'm okay Tom. I think I needed to hear you say that, to acknowledge it and our lost child. What you just said means a lot to me." He nodded, looking deep into my eyes for a few seconds before nodding again and standing up abruptly.

"I had better go, I have to pick Matt in the early after-noon from his mothers so I can take him to the park. You going to be okay Lexi?" His brow creased like it used to when he was genuinely concerned about something.

"I will be, Tom. I'm going to be great and so are you."

"In time."

He walked to the door, pulling it open and stepping out into the hallway.

"Oh, you forgot your jacket," I reminded him, fetching it from the arm of the sofa. Handing it to him out in the hallway, I felt his hand brush mine as he took it. There was a sadness hanging around us, both of us knowing that this was the part where we said good bye for the last time.

Standing there facing one another, I was caught up in the emotions. So caught up that, when Tom closed the half step separating us and put his hands on my face, I didn't stop him. Neither did I stop him putting his lips on mine for the last time, pressing softly but long enough for him to pour out his feelings into the motion. It was intimate, familiar and sweet. When he pulled back slightly, resting his forehead against mine, eyes closed and hands still on my cheeks, I stood still against him. And then his hands were gone and he had taken a step back to give us space. He looked at me, the bittersweet smile on his face as he said the last words.

"Good bye Lexi."

"Good bye Tom." He turned and left and my eyes followed his retreating back until I couldn't see him anymore. I breathed in deeply and exhaled slowly. I felt an overwhelming sadness.

It had been an intense night and morning and I could do with a bit of sleep before I'd have to get up again.

I turned towards my door when I caught a figure standing a few metres away from the corner of my eye. When I focused completely on the person, my stomach dropped.

Kade was standing there in his boxer briefs, danger radiating off of him in waves, body shaking with anger and the vein in his neck throbbing from the way he was gritting his teeth. *Oh shit.*

CHAPTER THIRTY
FIVE

If I could turn back time

"**K**ade?" I asked tentatively, afraid of what his reaction was going to be. He was silent and thats when I noticed he was staring at the space where Tom had disappeared, towards the stairs and back to the hotel lobby before he must have headed out. When he finally looked at me, my heart felt like it was breaking. There was so much pain in those oceanic eyes. I started to realise exactly what he must have seen and exactly how he must have taken it. I had just spent time with my ex husband in my hotel room and then let him kiss me good bye. This was not good.

"Oh no, no no. This is definitely not what you think it is Kade."

He was still deathly quiet. I felt myself tremble in fear. Not of him but of what could happen next and of how I might lose him.

I started to walk towards him slowly as if I was approaching a frightened bird and cautiously as if I were about to tackle a raging bull. He remained silent when I reached him and I could feel the heat radiating off him even before I

464

pressed my hands to his chest.

He jerked away as if I had shocked him with a live wire. I felt hurt by his reaction, my hands still in the air where he had been standing. I dropped them slowly, looking him in his blue eyes when I approached him again. He turned and walked back to his suite so fast that I had to run to keep up before he could slam the door in my face. I reached the door just in time and pushed it open, following him into his bedroom.

"Kade. Talk to me," I pleaded.

He shoved past me, ignoring my plea and pulled his suitcase from the closet then proceeded to pull clothes from the hangers in there.

"Kade will you stop and just look at me?!"

He went into the bathroom and shoved his shaving kit and cologne into the case with such force, it was a miracle it hadn't broken.

"Kade please, just talk to me! Let me explain-"

"EXPLAIN WHAT?! That you just fucked your ex husband after you slept with me?!"

My body was trembling so much that it took me a couple of seconds to respond. I felt torn between anger and that absolute fear of losing him.

"I did *not* sleep with him! He came to talk to me! Kade-"

"You're in your *underwear,* Alexa! You were *kissing* him! Are you telling me I made that up?"

The heat rolling off of him turned up a notch, the vein at his temple throbbing from his anger. Any one else would have steered clear of him but I just couldn't. I needed him to calm down.

"Kade, please listen - "

"No."

"Please," I pleaded, trying to grab his hand. He pulled out of my grip and my heart felt like it was breaking.

"I would like for you to leave."

I gasped, shocked that he would do this to me.

"I'm not going until you let me explain, until you understand."

I was scrambling around trying to get him to look at me. At my words he turned to face me with thunderous eyes.

"YOU LET HIM KISS YOU!"

I felt the tears fall onto my cheeks, feeling pathetic and feeble when I said the words that were equally pathetic to my ears.

"It meant nothing to me, Kade. It was just good bye."

The anger and hurt in his eyes ignited to a new level for a second before I saw him mentally shut it down. The fire died, his face slackened from the anger that was evidently there just a few moments before. I knew what he was doing, I'd done it before many times myself. It was self preservation and I'd done this to him because I was 'too nice' to say no to Tom and stuck in some misplaced nostalgia of what we had before.

"Alexa, I would like for you to leave my room now. I think you should stay in London for as long as you like. I will make sure your severance is generous and you are free to leave Hamilton's without notice and look for new employment. I will be happy to provide you with a good reference."

With his mask of indifference firmly in place, he walked into his bathroom and shut the door in my face.

I sat down and tried to process everything he had said. It was taking some time to sink in but once it did, it was too late to bang my fists against his door. He wanted me out of his life and it was all my fault. I held onto the tears and the emotion as I stood up shakily from his bed that was still unmade. I couldn't bear to look at it for the reminder that we had been intimately entwined on there just a few hours ago. Before I made a stupid decision, the biggest mistake I could have made.

I heard the shower start up and realised that I couldn't be

there like a psycho stalker when he came out. I slowly left the suite, shutting the door behind be, holding my head up as I made my way back to my room. Once I had closed the door, I slid down against it and cried while my world crumbled around me once again at the loss of a man that I loved.

***

BEEP BEEP BEEP BEEP BEEP BEEP BEEP BEEP BEEP BEEP BEEP BEEP BEEP!

I felt around on my side table for my phone to turn off my alarm. The bedside clock read 8:30am. It was the time we were meant to get up to get ready for our departure. Kade had arranged it so that I could see my family for breakfast at home and then we would leave from there for the airport but I doubted that plan remained in place. My head was pounding from crying and from barely two hours of sleep.

I had cried until I had fallen asleep and now when I looked in the bathroom mirror, I looked like hell. My eyes were red and puffy, my hair looked like a nest of birds had abandoned it and my body bore remnants of the previous night when Kade had left love bites over my breasts in the height of passion. The sight of them was making the devastation more palpable and I quickly threw myself into the shower to keep busy from thoughts of what happened earlier this morning with us.

I needed a plan, I needed to get him to talk to me. But I knew, even as I devised plan after plan, speech after speech, that he wasn't going to listen. If there was something I had learnt about him after all this time being around him so much, it was that he was a stubborn, pig headed man.

I changed, packed my bags and left the hotel room to go and knock on his door, summoning up as much courage as I could to face him again. As I approached the door, I noticed it was open with the housekeepers trolley outside. There was a woman inside, stripping the bedsheets down. I felt dread start to build up inside me.

"Um, excuse me? Do you know where the gentle-man staying in this room is?" The woman turned around and gave me a polite smile.

"He checked out earlier than he was supposed to madam, I'm just getting the room ready for the next guests."

My heart sunk. Thanking the woman, I made my way to the lobby downstairs, hardly paying any attention to my surroundings. I looked around, eventually, to see if he was in the lobby waiting for me but only a few guests were milling around.

Reaching the reception, I approached the woman who had been keen to check us in and eye up Kade in the process when we had first arrived.

"Hi, I'm Alexa De Luca, Mr Hamilton's PA. I just found out he has checked out early. Do you know if he has left for the airport already?"

The woman, whose name tag read 'Karen' gave me her fake sweet smile and looked on her system after I gave her his details.

"Mr Hamilton left earlier this morning, Miss De Luca. He asked for us to contact the airport to charter a private jet for as soon as possible and then left promptly. I believe he said it was urgent business in New York that made him have to leave so early. He must be halfway across the Atlantic by now."

I felt like I couldn't breathe. I had to keep it together for now, long enough to get home to my parents. I thanked Karen and checked out as quickly as I could. I hailed a black cab from outside the hotel, holding onto the tears. He had meant it when he told me to stay in London. Maybe he didn't want for me to come back to New York at all. He had already dismissed me from my job. Despite how I had come to work for him, I loved my job. I loved working with him, being close to him and watching him kick ass as a brilliant legal mind. Now, I was jobless and possibly homeless. I had no idea if Kade would let me stay in the brownstone anymore. I had no idea what to do. All I knew right now was that I needed to see the one person who could give me comfort at this time where I had once again felt cheated of my happily ever after.

I told the cabbie the address and took a deep breath.

***

"What's wrong?" were the first words out of my grandmothers mouth.

Granna stood at the front door with her little apron on, white hair in it's immaculate curled style, red lipstick on and wearing her pretty sixties style skirt and top with a frown on her face as she reached out to me. I dropped my bags and ran down the path into Granna's arms. I had messaged her in the cab to make sure she was home and not already at the club where she was meeting her friends this morning for their charity bake sale.

As soon as her arms engulfed me into her bosom, I broke down. She held me and rocked me quietly in her arms as I bawled like a baby right within earshot of her neighbours and passers by. When enough time had passed and I had somewhat calmed down, she ordered me to bring my bags into the house and sit down at the kitchen table.

"Okay, spill."

I had forgotten how much my New York born and raised grandmother was my personification of home. As soon as she placed a steaming mug of hot cocoa in front of me, I told her about what had happened from the start. She listened quietly as I told her about our evening with friends and then getting ready for the event last night. She only made a sound when I mentioned Tom turning up and that was to curse under her breath. I told her about leaving with Kade, about us 'being together' without going into too much detail and then my catastrophic mistake of meeting with Tom and what happened after.

Granna looked lost for words but when she did speak, she was both sad for me and angry.

"That two timing son of a bitch Tom just had to be there to ruin a perfect evening! Why that boy has any hold on you, I don't know but he is the most undeserving little prick I have ever known!"

She continued to berate Tom, I didn't dare to stop her, until she sat down quietly and took my trembling cold hand.

"Alli girl, look at me. You have always been a good natured girl, right from when you were a little-un. You have so much empathy inside of you, so much goodness. I know why you let Tom see you. I may not like that you did it but I know *why* you did it. I know you have a beautiful heart sweetheart. He knew it, he wanted to exploit it but that handsome young lawyer has got into you. You love him."

I nodded, not needing to pretend anymore, even though the subject in question had no clue how I felt.

"I've messed up Granna, big time. He's never going to forgive me. He thinks I *slept* with Tom. The fact that I didn't doesn't register with him because I let Tom kiss me and he saw that happen! I'm such an idiot!"

The despair I felt was overwhelming. I let Granna comfort me until I felt like a selfish bitch for making her miss her bake sale.

"I'll be fine here Granna, please go. It's just started so you haven't missed much." Granna looked at me sceptically.

"Nonsense! I'll have Steve pick up the cakes and take them. I don't want to leave you alone." I felt myself smile a little despite my current turmoil. Steve was Granna's new "friend.' We had been teasing her about him because he seemed to love giving her lifts and offering to help her with things whilst knowing full well she had a car and was more than capable of running her own errands. It was cute that Granna got prickly when we questioned or teased her. I wanted for her to have someone too, after all these years without grandpa.

"No, I want you to go. You look too sexy to be sat at home playing babysitter to your moping granddaughter. Get Steve to pick you up and I'll catch up with you later. No arguing!" She looked torn but eventually gave in with strict instructions for me to call if I needed her.

Steve offered to drop me to my parents house on their way to the club. Thats where I found myself half an hour later. I felt exhausted and so when I told my mother that I needed to get some sleep and then I would explain why I was staying in London longer than expected, she didn't argue and let me have my way. It was going to be a long evening when I woke up.

***

Ever have those moments when you feel like you've stepped outside of your skin and are watching everything happening to you from another perspective? That's how I felt these days. I didn't want to believe this was all happening to me and the only way I could justify the pain was from viewing things as a bystander in my life. That is when the questions would crowd my mind. *Could I have stopped this from happening? Should I have told Tom 'no'? Did I set myself up to fail? Will he ever talk to me again?* The last question always hurt the most. I spent almost four weeks like this, moping then crying then getting angry at myself and then at Kade.

When I eventually told my mother what had happened, I couldn't stop crying as she held me close and gave me the comfort only a mother can provide. She didn't tell me what I should or shouldn't have done, she just held me and soothed me as much as she could. My sister even spent time trying to get me to go outside but I refused. I just wanted to be miserable and let the misery consume me. Every night, when I'd finally fall asleep, I would dream of stormy blue eyes telling me they never wanted to see me again.

My family tried many ploys to get me to talk, go out and try to heal, but they failed. So they brought out the big guns. I'm only surprised that it took so long.

In all honesty, I should have known it would come to this when I didn't respond to the messages she had sent but at the end of my fourth week of my self induced hibernation I awoke to my bedroom door bursting open and a furious looking pregnant woman standing at the end of my bed.

"Wake up!" Ash screamed, pulling off the duvet that I then scrambled to pull back on.

"ASH!"

"Get the fuck up, De Luca. Don't make me say it again. I'm on maternity now so I got all the time in the fucking world to make this morning hell for you if you don't WAKE. THE. FUCK. UP!"

There were a couple of seconds of the duvet being pulled to and fro until I gave up and covered my eyes with my arms whilst growling.

"OKAY! You are one crazy possessed pregnant lady!"

Ash just smiled at me.

"Oh yes I am. Get your arse out of this bed and make me breakfast." I pulled my arms from my face and watched Ash's smug face turn to one of horror.

"What the hell happened to you?! You look like Freddie fucking Kruger!"

In the weeks since Kade left me, I had cried until my nose was red, my eyes were swollen red and well the rest of my face -

"IS THAT A UNI-BROW?!"

Yep, I'd let my brows suffer and now I wouldn't hear the end of it.

"It's not that bad!" I argued, knowing it was futile.

"Get your clothes on, wash up and lets go. I don't even want to look at you, let alone talk to you when you have that thing on your face. Now, Lexi, move it!"

I groaned, knowing she would not let this go and got moving. Ash sat on my bed and watched me run around getting ready.

"You are getting more and more difficult with each pregnant day," I grumbled again, "More than usual." Ash looked proud.

"I know. But you love me so you'll just have to deal with it." I felt myself smile for the first time in weeks.

We left my house within half an hour, my mother looking on with hope that I'd finally broken my own exile.

Ash drove, not even mentioning Kade and I was grateful. I knew we would talk about him at some point but my best friend always knew when the right time was and what I needed. I squeezed her hand in thank you as she chattered away. I got a squeeze and beautiful smile back. I realised in that moment again just how lucky I was.

***

"Ouch!"

The pain usually was something I could bear with ease but today, as the women waxed my nether regions with precision, I was just not prepared for it. Ash had dragged me to her local beauty salon and ordered the ladies to get to work on me as soon as possible. Two hours later with three women working on me, I was hairless, polished and looking a lot better than my former self. She had even made me get a hair trim and blow dry. And I did feel better. It was something only my best friend could achieve.

Once we were done, Ash took me to our favourite Italian restaurant and ordered the most calorific pasta she could find on the menu.

"You better eat Lexi because I am not putting up with you getting skinnier and losing your Beyonce butt."

That was an exaggeration, it wasn't that big. But I had

lost a noticeable amount weight in the month following the drama that was my life.

"I could never leave any of Dante's pasta uneaten, Ash," I laughed. She had ordered a pasta *and* a pizza, claiming that that baby was turning her into a heifer.

"So...Kade, huh?" Ash was not known for her subtlety. She had waited until I had eaten all of the carbs placed in front of me and after my desert was given to me before she approached the subject that had been giving me relentless pain.

"Yeah." We were quiet for a breath as I mushed a little bit of my Tiramisu with my spoon.

"Have you tried to contact him?"

"I called and messaged endlessly like an obsessed teenager for the first two weeks and he just cut my calls and ignored my messages." It was embarrassing and hurtful but he was hurting too. I had to keep reminding myself of that.

"But he didn't block your number...interesting." Ash had a scheming look on her face.

"Ash, I don't think that means anything. He hates me right now."

"There's a very thin line between hate and love Lexi." Her wisdom knew no bounds.

"At the moment, I'm pretty certain he hates me."

"Have you heard from the girls?" She meant Allison and Sadie.

"I speak with them every couple of days. They say that Kade has gone MIA. Not in the media, not at work, probably bolted up in his tower. They keep asking when I'm coming back."

Ash looked up from her desert and sat back with a spoon in her mouth.

"When are you planning to go back?"

"I don't know if I should." The devastation I felt when Kade told me to stay in London was too much to bear.

"Just because of something he said when he was

upset? Lexi, you know that people say a lot of things they don't mean when they are hurting. He didn't mean it. You need to go back and sort out your life. Sort things out with him, make it right. He loves you!" Something ached in my chest at her words.

"You don't know that," I whispered, feeling the tears creep up.

"Babe, I know he does. Theres no way that a man who is that confident, that self assured and that delicious can look like a man scared to death of losing you when you're right in front of him. I've seen that look in his eyes, like if he blinks, you'll turn out to be a figment of his imagination. And that's with you in the room with him! If he wasn't in love with you Lexi, he wouldn't be hurting as much as he is right now. It wouldn't matter as much."

The tears slipped and I wiped at them with a napkin. Ash squeezed my hand.

"What should I do?" I knew what she would say before she said it but I still needed to hear it.

"Go home, Lexi. Go back to New York, get him to see sense and you live your happily ever after. We take so much for granted Lexi. Didn't you convince me to take Imran back? Didn't he grovel like hell for the chance to have me back? Now look at us, we're together stronger than ever and we have this little miracle in our lives." She rubbed her bump lovingly and I couldn't resist a little rub of her belly too.

Just then my phone decided to ring and I pulled it out of my bag to see a number I definitely didn't expect to receive a call from. I showed Ash the screen and she whisper shouted at me to answer it.

"Bonnie?"

"Hey Lexi," Bonnie's voice came from the other end of the phone. Her voice sounded strained, worried even.

"What's wrong? What happened? Are you and the kids okay?"

Ash noted my look of concern and leaned in closer to support me with a hand on mine.

"We're fine hon, everything is good. It's Kade."

I nearly dropped the phone and then held onto it for dear life. My heart plummeted to my stomach and I fought the urge to be sick.

"Is he okay?" My voice sounded so weak and afraid and I had to force myself to soften my death grip on the phone, afraid I'd crack it.

"He had an accident. He'd been cooped up in his apartment for weeks and decided to go for an early morning jog. He didn't see the cab coming as he crossed the road. It hit him head on." My throat went dry, heart beating faster and the dread started to consume me.

"Is he hurt?"

"Nothing major, apart from his pride. He broke his leg but they expect that to heal with the plaster cast within six to eight weeks. Some cuts and bruises but he will heal. It's his heart I'm more concerned with."

I breathed in a sigh of relief but then I realised she'd mentioned his heart. Oh crap.

"I'm glad he's okay," was all I could manage.

"Lexi, I know my brother. He won't tell me much about what happened with you guys but I knew the moment I saw him that his pain was soul deep and he wouldn't tell me what had happened to him. Then I did what most sisters would do in my situation. I looked at his phone while he was sleeping."

Any other day, I would have laughed but right now, I didn't like the fact that Bonnie would think of me being the slut Kade obviously thought I was, and worse, disloyal.

"I know it was wrong but I can't stand seeing my brother being like this. His pain makes me sad. I saw your calls and some of the messages. You seem to want to explain something to him, you're always apologising and pleading. I'm guessing you guys got together and then something fucked it up?" Hearing the 'F' word from Bonnie was unusual given that she was so careful around her kids.

"Yes." I couldn't deny it but I really didn't want to explain what happened to her.

"Look, he's a stubborn ass. Everyone knows that. Whatever happened between you guys, it's not too late to save your relationship. I know that he isn't listening right now but he will."

"Bonnie, he hates me. He won't listen." I refused to cry on the phone to Kade's sister but still my voice sounded wobbly.

"Honey, he can't hate anyone, let alone someone he loves so much."

"You think he loves me?" The hope in my voice was palpable.

"I know he does. I just need you back here asap. This month of misery and separation bullshit isn't good for you both. I'm gonna get you booked on the next available flight so get your stuff packed." Her tone left no room for argument but one still escaped my lips.

"But Kade won't-"

"You leave Kade to me. I have a plan and I am not going to let him wallow in self pity and the same goes for you. Now get started on the packing and bring me back some Cadbury's whole nut chocolate!"

We disconnected the call after she said she would send me flight details as soon as she booked it and seeing as she wouldn't listen to a word I said when I told her I thought she was mad to think Kade would let me near him right now, I had no choice but to comply. I looked over to find Ash beaming from ear to ear.

"I want to be introduced to this woman as soon as possible. That is my kind of girl!"

"Yeah, Bonnie is a live wire when she wants to be."

"So, you're going back to New York, huh?" Her eyes twinkled at the possibilities but I wished I felt just as

hopeful and sighed in surrender.
       "I guess so."

CHAPTER THIRTY SIX

Homecoming

New York was a sight for sore eyes. I felt the cold winter air as keenly as London's. I had left my family before celebrating Christmas with them but they urged me to go. Granna made sure I got on the plane and I could never forget her words.

"If I hadn't have left my family all those years ago to follow your grandfather here, we wouldn't have had so many wondrous years full of love and adventure together. I almost didn't go Alli. I almost turned back but I regret nothing. Don't let yourself regret not trying. We can celebrate Christmas together another year. If you leave anymore time and distance between you both, it will be irreparable."

So here I was, standing outside Kade's apartment building - the tower of celebrities. The town car that Bonnie had arranged to pick me up had just left. I went up to the concierge and told them to notify Bonnie that I was here. I got into the elevator and took a deep breath. I was preparing for battle.

Reaching Kade's penthouse took less time than I wanted it to and before I knew it, I was at the front door that was slightly ajar. Bonnie had left it open for me and I heard their voices when I entered the hall way.

"I don't need fussing over, Bonnie. I'm fine. Giselle

has brought me some soup and magazines and I got all the security detail acting like fucking babysitters."

The sound of him heated my aching bones. I couldn't see him yet and it made me tremble in fear and anticipation until a realisation hit me.

Wait. Giselle had been here? I felt a pang of jealousy. He had allowed her back into his life, she who had slept with his friend. Yet I was kicked out of his life for an innocent kiss? Ok, maybe it wasn't innocent on Tom's part, and maybe I shouldn't have let him do it, but still! Rationality wasn't winning here.

"I'm sure Kade will be fine Bonnie, he's got a lot of support around here."

My jealousy went from double to triple to fucking quadruple in seconds. *Giselle was in there with him!* I felt like I could just turn around and walk out and was about to do just that when I heard Bonnie's next words.

"That's very well *Giselle* but *I* decide what my brother needs when he's clearly not capable to see it. That is why I have brought in extra help. Someone known to our family, reliable and already under Kade's employ who is discreet and will be staying here in the guest room so she can attend to his every need."

I heard her footsteps come into the hall as Kade started protesting from his living room that he didn't need help. Bonnie appeared in the hall and gave me a look that would scare any grown man or woman. It said, *Don't you back out because if you do, I will mess you up.* I knew better than to argue and now realised why her kids and younger siblings didn't push her too far. She extended her hand and pulled me by the arm, half forcing me into the living room.

Kade was sprawled on his sofa with his right leg in a cast and propped up on an extra cushion whilst the left was planted on the floor and his crutches were by his side. He wore a pair of loose marl grey shorts and no shirt, displaying his beautiful torso to all and sundry. Sat across from him was the stunning blonde Giselle, looking polished in her cream shift dress and nude heels. Bracelets sparkled from her wrists and something else on her ring finger that must have cost a fortune. The diamond was ridiculously huge. For a split second I thought the worst, that she was back with Kade but really if I knew him at all, he would never do such a thing. No, that diamond must have been from her new fiance.

In my diamond glaring, I hadn't noticed how quiet the room had gotten. When I looked up at Kade, he was doing some glaring of his own. Straight at me. I don't know why but the expression made me smile quite wickedly back at him. I could feel the tension between us and I got the feeling that the other two people in the room could too.

"What is *she* doing here?" Kade bit out to his sister through gritted teeth. His face was the scruffiest I had ever seen, beard growing a couple of centimetres past his jaw. It made him look strangely more caveman. My Heart skipped many beats. My eyes had been hungry for him and now I felt the thrill of being in front of him tinged with the weighty sadness of our separation.

"Hello to you too, Kade."

I was poking the bear, I knew it, but it actually felt good. It was better than crying and begging for him to listen to me. He needed me to force him to see me every day (Bonnie's plan) and that was exactly what was going to happen.

"Bonnie, explain." He sounded angry but it only made me smile wider.

"Lexi is going to be staying here to look after you. After all, it says in her contract that she is to be at your beck and call as your PA. So here she is."

Bonnie was also smiling. I swear I could see steam coming out of Kade's ears.

"She was relieved from her post a month ago," he bit out, shifting in his reclined position which only made his muscles look more delicious with the movement.

"Well, Mr Hamilton," I piped up, addressing him directly, "according to my contract, I have a two months notice to work through. You wrote the contract, you should know."

"Well, I will allow you to leave before that period and compensate you accordingly." He looked like he was going to burst a vein.

"Unfortunately, as you are now on extended leave of absence due to your injuries, you don't have the power to decide that. Miss De Luca is now under dads instructions to stay as he sees fit."

Bonnie's glinting eyes of triumph said it all. No-one went up against the senior Mr Hamilton. A small cough reminded us that we were not alone.

Giselle stood up and smiled cautiously at me.

"Hi, I'm Giselle," she said politely. I couldn't sense anything catty about her although I took her outstretched hand and shook it with a forced smile. I guess she knew Kade wouldn't be introducing me to her.

"Alexa," I said, sneaking a look at Kade who now looked like he wanted to scream at Bonnie by the way he was staring at her.

"Well, I uh, should be going. Chris is picking me up before dinner with his parents. I'll check on you another time Kade. Nice meeting you Alexa. Bye Bonnie." She didn't wait for us to respond and whizzed out of the penthouse in a blur.

Once she had gone, Bonnie got to fussing over Kade and propping his pillow and he grunted at her, still shooting daggers intermittently at both me and her.

"Stop with the fluffing, woman!" he finally said, letting out some of his frustration.

Bonnie was undeterred for a few more minutes until she straightened up and faced us both. I was still standing on the outskirts of the living room, taking it all in. *Alone with Kade and his stubborn ass angriness 24/7, serving his every need.* It was a daunting task ahead indeed.

"I'm only going to say this once Kade. Play nice or dad will find out and I won't be responsible for what happens next. Any complaints from Lexi that you're not complying and you're going to be in trouble, got it?"

He didn't answer and I just grinned at him making his expression stormier. Bonnie grabbed her coat from the arm of one of the seats and patted his head like he was a puppy, gave me a kiss on the cheek and then left the apartment whilst humming a tune.

The air between us was thick with tension, his jaw tight as he unashamedly looked me up and down. I took the liberty to do the same to him. I noticed the sharper muscles on his body, no doubt he noticed I had lost some weight too. We were both suffering because of a stupid mistake. After a long stare down, he finally spoke.

"Let's get one thing straight here, Alexa. I don't want to hear your apologies or any explanations. You're here against my will because my sister is playing some sick game with my life. You're here to do a job but I don't care if you stay in the guest room all day for a month. I don't need anybodies help, let alone yours." His words stung me but I knew the only way to fight fire was with fire, in this case.

I walked over to the edge of the sofa that he was lying on, careful not to press against it. This close, I could smell that intoxicating scent of him that always had me wanting to draw closer.

"Let's get one thing straight here Mr Hamilton. I am here to help you in every capacity I can. If you don't comply, I am well within my rights to report any 'misbehaviour' on your part."

He wanted to lash out, I could see it in his eyes but he was controlling himself well.

Before he could respond I walked to the suitcase one of the concierge had helped bring up for me and proceeded to get the heavy bugger up the stairs to the guest bedroom. I could hear a snicker of laughter from Kade in spite of himself as I struggled. *Bastard,* I thought, smiling to myself.

***

The exhaustion from the past twenty-four hours had resulted in me conking out as soon as I sat on the bed in the guest room. I was vaguely aware that although Kade had been less than welcoming, I had gotten the best sleep ever in a month and it was because he was under the same roof as me.

I awoke to a noise coming from downstairs. I hadn't come down since leaving Kade snickering at my attempt to get my luggage up his winding stairs. I checked the bedside clock that told me it had been two hours. That was a long nap. I freshened up, changing into my pyjama shorts and top, and made my way down.

Kade was not in the living room but in the kitchen, attempting to pick up a pot he had dropped on the floor with water spilled everywhere. He was heavily cursing the pot to hell. I found it really cute and amusing. He didn't. Hopping on one foot to stop the plaster cast from getting wet, he had been trying to pick up the dropped pot. I watched him for a few seconds longer than I should have, enjoying his discomfort because when he looked up to glare at me, we both realised the truth - he needed my help.

Walking slowly into the centre of his palatial kitchen, I made a show of looking over his mess. A packet of pasta, mushrooms, chicken and other items were strewn around haphazardly on the granite counter top and it was evident that he had been trying to get the pot full of water from the kitchen sink all the way across to his cooking hob with crutches and hopping on one leg. *Stubborn arse.*

"Could have just asked for help, Mr Hamilton." I made sure to make an annoying 'tsk-ing' sound whilst walking the rest of the way to him, avoiding the spreading puddle of water.

"I can manage just fine, thanks," he ground out through his gritted teeth. It seemed like this would be his normal way to converse going forward. I smirked at him, earning a growl that just made me want to kiss it right off his mouth.

"Obviously you can't," I gestured with my hands to the mess. Deciding that it was better to get on with cleaning up than the endless to and fro between His Royal Stubbornness and myself, I got to work and he made his way slowly to a chair and sat down. Despite his effort to look like he was well, I could tell he was in pain. It killed me that I couldn't comfort him, that I knew he wouldn't *allow* me to comfort him. I was so close to him, standing there and feeling the heat of his stare but he was so far away. Out of reach. *For now,* I told myself, until I could make him come around.

I moved the pot out of the way and then spent a useless amount of time looking for his mop. He just sat back, enjoying the fact that I couldn't find it and not helping me in locating it either. Giving up, I found a discarded, expensive looking T-shirt of his on the sofa he was lounging on earlier and started to mop up the water on the kitchen floor. It gave me some satisfaction to know that I'd got my own back on him, as childish as it was. I alternated between wiping and then wringing out the material in the sink. Every now and then I would hear Kade shuffle in his seat until he got so restless, I eventually had to turn around to see what was going on and felt myself blush.

Kade Hamilton wasn't in discomfort because of his leg right now, he was in discomfort for a completely different reason. He was currently trying to hide his giant, um, *issue down below.* I couldn't understand why until I realised his low lidded eyes were trained on my pyjama short clad arse currently in the air from my position on all fours on his kitchen floor. He was getting an uninterrupted view of my bum, thrust out while I mopped up his mess.

Even though I could feel the heat rising in my cheeks, I managed a smirk.

"See something you like, Mr Hamilton?" Kade met my eyes unashamedly and smirked right back, throwing me off guard.

"I'm a man after all, I can't not look. It's a natural *human* reaction."

His smugness just made me want to slap that smirk off his face but I dutifully returned to my cleaning, making sure that I scrubbed hard enough to make my bottom jiggle in retaliation of his pig headedness.

Once the mess was cleared, I set about making a version of chicken and mushroom pasta that seemed edible, conscious of Kade glaring at me while I pretended to be unaffected, humming as I got to work.

I set the dining table for two and asked Kade as sweetly as I could to sit at the table as I piled on most of the pasta onto his plate and a more moderate amount on mine, placing it on the table with the salad and garlic bread.

Kade tucked in wordlessly and although he never complimented me on the food, which actually turned out to be tasty, his silent glaring-slash-devouring of the food pleased me to no end. I was smiling to myself when I caught him glaring harder at me over my fork.

"This is nice," I said, trying to diffuse the tension.

"Why are you here Alexa?"

The harshness of his tone almost made me flinch. Almost, because I had expected him to be hostile towards me but it didn't hurt any less.

"I'm here to help you while you recover." His jaw tensed, his eyes glinting dangerously but I didn't feel fear, just a deep longing to make him believe me. To tell him I was sorry.

"You know what I mean Alexa, quit playing games. Why are you here?" I took a deep breath, looking anywhere but in his eyes.

"I'm here for you. For us."

He was quiet for a few seconds and when I looked up, I wish I hadn't. There was such a solid look of anger and pain and determination on his face that it made me want to cry.

"There is no *us* and the sooner you accept that the better. Just because I can't tell you to leave because Bonnie has some stupid ass idea in her head that she will get us back together and she's using our father to implement it, doesn't mean I want you here. As far as I'm concerned, you're just here doing a job and I'm being forced to put up with it. Don't mistake this *arrangement* for something else."

His words cut like a knife. Without another word, he got up, pulling his crutches from the chair next to him and left the dining table.

I knew he wouldn't listen to me right now, but given some time maybe he would soften and this situation that had been forced upon him would turn out to be a blessing for us, to bring us back together. I could only hope and pray.

***

"Fuck!" I could hear him curse at the bottom of the stairs. It had been three days since I had been stationed in Kade's sky fortress, enduring the bitter freezing temperature of his cold shoulder and now it was Christmas Eve. He would scarce speak more that a few words to me, that too only when absolutely necessary. I kept thinking, could he really be so cold? Could he really be so unfeeling when he could see that it hurt when he ignored or brushed me aside? It seemed that Kade's pain ran deeper than I could imagine which in turn gave me hope. *That kind of pain can only be caused by someone you truly love.* I remembered what Bonnie had said to me when she called me in London, that she knew he loved me. I felt hope bloom in my chest, supplemented by words from chats with Ash and my mother. I could do this. I would make him see that I am in this for the long haul, that I am his.

Walking to the top of the stairs, I had to hold back from bursting out laughing. For the past three days, Kade had refused to ask for help up the stairs to his bedroom and had knocked me back when I had offered. He had made the sofa his make shift bed and although the expensive seating looked comfortable to sit on, I doubt it had made a good bed for the past few nights. I had been leaving clothes for him downstairs, without him requesting them, because I knew he would do anything not to ask. Stubborn as he is, he would not let it be otherwise and now he seemed to be struggling to get himself upstairs.

"Um, what are you doing?" I asked, aware that my needling would make him angrier. On cue, I got a full force glare. I'd gotten used to those.

"I need a shower."

That was probably all the answer I would get. Although there was a nice sized restroom downstairs, it didn't have a shower. And he did need a shower and a shave come to think of it. His beard had grown quite a bit, the longest I'd ever seen it and though I found it kind of sexy, I missed his clean cut look too.

Cursing some more, he attempted again to jump up on his good leg whilst leaning on his casted one with his crutches in hand and keeled over in pain again.

"Let me help," I said, skipping down the stairs in a hurry.

"No."

I was getting used to his shortness with me, it reminded me of the time when he was all Mr Business at work when I refused to take our relationship further. I wished for those days when he wanted me, I'd do anything to get those back. Now, I felt my long abated frustration reach my limit and smacked his hard bicep with moderate force, earning a sharp look my way.

"Now you listen to me, Hamilton. I've had it up to here," I indicated with my hand up to the top of my head, "with your stubborn arse! You are behaving like a child! Your nieces and nephews are better behaved than you! You need to get up these stairs, I can help you. Bonnie is not coming, your father and mother are not coming. None of your friends are around at the moment. *Giselle* is not here. So you got me. I am here to help you get your stupid self up these stupid stairs and if you can't see the logic behind that then you are an asshole!" I screamed the last words at him, not realising how close I had gotten until I felt his breath in my hair and his heat radiating from his body.

I took a step back up from him on the stairs, giving me some room to calm down. I saw a flicker of fire in his eyes and the slightest of smiles on his lips before he blinked and donned his mask of indifference again.

"Fine."

It was one word, but it gave me relief. He was going to allow me to help him.

I slowly stepped down and to his side, gently placing my arm on his waist and felt him tense to my touch. *Still affected by me,* I smiled to myself at the knowledge. Placing his left arm around my shoulders, he leaned some of his weight on me and some on his arm at the hand rail as we began a painstakingly slow ascent up the stairs and into his bedroom. When we finally reached his bedroom, we were both sweating from exertion. Kade wasn't exactly light with all of his muscles and tallness. Inwardly I sighed at the loss of his warmth and being close to his body.

I fetched his crutches from below and found him in his bathroom with his shirt thrown off, leaning against the counter, puzzling over his plaster cast.

"We need to cover it with a bag. Luckily, I got one for you." I set about the task of pulling a bin bag over his cast, taping it up over his muscular legs to make sure no water could get through. Once finished, I caught his confused look.

"I broke my leg when I was fourteen. Jumped off the roof of the garage." He seemed to absorb the information and then look at me expectantly.

"I am not leaving because I need to make sure you don't slip and crack your skull open. I won't watch but I'll be here." He opened his mouth to say something but I just pushed him gently towards the shower.

"Do it, or I'll come give you a sponge bath." He seemed to muse over the idea and smiled to himself as he turned and did as he was told for once. *Dirty man.*

I turned around to allow him privacy to take off his shorts and boxers and heard him get into the shower. Turns out Kade Hamilton is a great bathroom singer. I heard him sing quietly and hum a tune I couldn't quite place as he showered and dared a peek at him. His back was to me, the steam not quite rising to cover up the glass shower door entirely, giving me a delicious view of his muscled back and delicious derrière. I could see the bruises from the accident more clearly there, allowing myself to absorb the fact that I could have lost the man that I love in an accident. I hadn't thought about it properly until now and the implication sobered me.

I faced away when I saw him turn the shower off and handed him a towel without turning back when I heard him open the door. He took it with a quiet thanks, quickly drying off and wrapping it around himself. When I was sure he had covered himself up I faced him, careful not to look at his bare torso and the 'v' of his muscles going down, and pointed to the chair I had dragged into he bathroom.

"You need a shave," I said, before he could ask why. Frowning he sat down and watched as I arranged his shaving kit out on the vanity.

"I'm perfectly capable of shaving myself," he quipped from his seat, looking at me sternly in the reflection of his mirror.

"If you stand and shave, you'll risk losing balance and slitting your own throat. If you do it from the chair... well you wont be able to reach anything from that angle. So your best bet is to let me do it." I smiled smugly as he glowered, knowing I was right. I didn't wait for a response and squirted the shaving foam into my palm. I hesitated for a second before putting my hands on his face, aware that his eyes followed every motion, aware that we were intimately close.

His beard felt soft under my fingers and I knew I was lingering on a little longer than necessary as I softy spread the foam over his cheeks, jaw and chin, carefully applying to his upper lip. Taking a shuddering breath I pulled away, feeling emotions well up inside of me that I had been afraid of for so long. *Hold it together, Lexi.*

I pulled out his razor and thought I would see trepidation in his eyes. Instead, I saw something strange flicker in his expression. It felt like pride and want.

I took a tentative step towards him again and smiled sadly at a memory of the last time I had done something like this.

"I think I told you about my Grandpa who had a heart attack close to four years ago," I started telling Kade the story he hadn't asked to hear as I mowed a neat line with the razor through his beard and shook it out into the basin of water. I felt his hands hold onto my waist to steady me as I leaned over and urged my heartbeat to slow and my body not to shiver at the achingly familiar touch.

"He didn't have the strength to shave in his last few weeks on Earth but he always wanted to look his best. Mostly for Granna," I laughed softly at the memory of how he would make me hold up the mirror so he could admire my handiwork.

"I wasn't so great at it in the beginning but towards the end, he told me I was an expert. He trusted me enough with a sharp instrument in my hand close to his face. He said I was his little angel, that I always knew how to brighten up his day. He was truly the best man I ever knew."

I hadn't realised I'd finished shaving him, just like I hadn't felt the tear fall until it dropped on Kade's chest. This whole time, he had been looking at me in quiet contemplation and now a sliver of warmth was pulsing through those deep blue eyes I loved so much. My hands on his cheeks, leaning over him so close as he held my waist to stop me losing my balance. It was so natural, so intimate that for a second, we could forget everything that had passed before between us.

In a flash, that moment was gone with the ringing of his phone. In came the cold indifference and he pushed me away gently, letting his hands drop from my waist, and got up as steadily as he could from the chair to take his crutches and hobble over to his bedroom and take his call.

By the time I had cleared everything away, quietly cursing his phone to hell, he had changed into a smart pair of trousers and a dress shirt, hair that had grown longer than usual brushed in his casual manner. He looked delicious but he was also back to looking unaffected again.

"There is going to be a small party here tonight, mostly my family and some friends." His tone was cold as usual, lacking emotion or indication of any emotion he might be feeling apart from indifferent.

"Bonnie mentioned it." Bonnie had told me that since Kade refused to be 'carted around in a wheelchair' for the world to see, they were all coming to him for Christmas Eve but would be spending Christmas Day with their parents whilst 'misery guts' stayed home (her words, not mine).

He fastened the buttons at the cuffs of his shirt and sat down to put on a sock on his left foot. His cast was expertly covered by his loose trouser leg. He looked up at me after checking a message on his phone.

"I have called in for some supplies," I continued. "They should be arriving within the next hour. I didn't think I'd find anyone willing to work on a holiday."

Kade gave me a pointed look.

"*You're* working through the holiday." It was true but I didn't like the reminder that I was there as an employee rather than his friend or his lover. I had gotten used to the sting of his words these days but it didn't hurt any less.

"I shall go and prepare for them Mr Hamilton," I replied formally, straightening and moving out of the room. For now, I guess I needed to remember my place and position as his employee.

CHAPTER THIRTY
SEVEN

Merry Christmas

T he caterers, designers and wait staff all filed in roughly in ten minute intervals of one another. I directed the interior designers, helping them with the decorations, namely hanging the ornaments on the large Christmas tree now dominating Kade's living room. I had chosen the festive decor myself, remembering christmas time back home in London as inspiration. I missed my family.

The living room now looked like a real home, with green, red and gold on the tree, stockings at the fire place, crystal snowflakes hanging from the ceiling and soft christmas carols playing on the sound system. To top it off, it had started to snow outside for real. It looked like it would be a white Christmas after all.

The food smelled delicious and I instructed the staff on the order of events for the evening. I thanked my lucky stars that I had done all of my Christmas shopping in London for everyone here and that all the gifts had been wrapped earlier for me to place now under the tree. Kade was still in his room, wrestling with the wrapping of his own gifts and making calls to work associates.

I got changed into my dark red velvet swing dress, reserved for festive occasions. I put on my little snowman earrings mum had given me last christmas and slipped my black heels on my black tights clad feet. I brushed my long hair, leaving it out and put on make up with black eyeliner and red lips. I felt happy looking at my reflection. It had been some time since I looked well put together. Even though I had dark circles, now well concealed with make up, and had lost weight, I looked like I was in the festive spirit.

I left my room and immediately saw Kade attempting to get himself down the stairs. I rushed to his side, quietly scolding him for being so stubborn with asking for help and took my position with my arm around his back and waist with his arm over my shoulders as we made our way down slowly. It took less time going down. Reaching the bottom, he took the crutches I held out and took his time looking me up and down.

"You look nice," he managed to finally say. The heat in his eyes said something else but I'd take what I could get.

"Thank you, so do you."

The awkwardness of the moment passed when he noticed the transformation of his home. For a moment, I thought he would scold me like a child for having Christmas vomit all over his living space. Instead, an almost content look passed over his features and I felt proud of myself for achieving that, regardless of his lack of vocalised praise.

Soon we were receiving guests, Bonnie and her brood arriving first, Allison and Sadie arriving last. In between, the large space was filled with Kade's parents, siblings, friends and some work colleagues. I was surprised to find Travis there too. He came up to me with a flirty grin on his face, handing me a cup of mulled wine which I accepted gratefully.

"Man, you are a sight for sore eyes."

I rolled my eyes at him, laughing off his blatant chat up line. Even though I no longer desired his attention, it felt good to feel wanted and I found myself laughing for the first time in what seemed like a long while.

"Trav, you need to stop with the compliments, I'll get a big head."

His sandy hair was combed to perfection and his dark eyes were perceptive as always, never missing a thing.

"You have those sad eyes again, Lexi Lou."

My smile died on my face. I looked away, lest I start crying with all my built up frustration and hurt.

"It's been a tough few weeks." There was no point denying anything.

"I noticed that you hadn't come back from London with Kade. Kinda put two and two together when everyone was steering clear of him at work the few times he managed to come into the office, especially when he would bite their heads off for asking where you were." That was so unlike Kade, that it shocked me to hear it.

"I'm sorry he's been like that."

"You don't need to apologise for him being a dick, Lexi," Travis huffed out a laugh.

"I do. It's my fault and now he won't speak more than a few words to me, and that too when it's absolutely necessary."

Travis looked thoughtful and took a sip of his drink before he spoke.

"Well, whatever happened between the two of you, it doesn't change how he feels about you. He's crazy about you. He will forgive whatever it is, he's just being stubborn about it."

"How can you be so sure?" I asked with so much hope in my voice. Travis grinned at me wickedly.

"You haven't seen the way he is looking at me right now like he could pull my intestines out through my mouth."

496

I should have known the burning sensation at the back of my head was instinctively Kade's molten gaze. I refused to look back. Instead, Travis' grin turned mischievous and he leaned in to whisper in my ear.

"Let's put him to the test. I give until the count of ten that he comes here and rips you away from me."

I had no time to protest as Travis' arm slipped around my waist for an embrace and I sucked in a breath of anticipation. Not because of Travis' action, but because of what Travis thought he would achieve. He whispered a countdown in my ear, drawing me closer.

"One....two...three...four..." I felt stupid for letting him play this game but the longer he counted, the sicker I felt. What if he no longer cared?

"Five...six...seven-"

"Alexa, I need you to check that the staff have everything in place for dinner."

The relief of hearing his voice made me turn immediately to see him standing so close, jaw ticking in undisguised anger as he looked at Travis. So hostile, where Travis just looked to me and winked whist mouthing the number 'seven.'

"Uh, yes, Mr Hamilton." I left as quick as I could, my heart racing. *He's jealous,* said the many familiar voices in my head. Affirmation that I could possibly turn this all around, make him see how sorry I was for messing things up.

The catering staff had, of course, already gotten everything prepared and needed no further direction. Soon the buffet was out and after meeting with all of Kade's family and familiar friends, I sat down with Allison, Brent and Sadie at one of the tables that had been set up for dinner. Jason had been invited but was away in the Hamptons with his family.

It was nice to catch up with my friends, although they seemed concerned for me.

"So, you gonna stay here with his royal highness until he comes to his senses?" Allison quizzed.

"I guess I'm here until his family say otherwise."

"He's got this hot 'wounded animal' thing going for him right now. I see why you're still hanging around even though he's fucking brooding as hell."

"I'm right here, you know," Brent piped up.

"Oh shush. You know you're the only one that makes my corn pop." *Bleurgh.* Sadie and I exchanged disgusted glances as Brent laughed, used to Allison's lewdness and she grinned at us wickedly.

The doorbell rang and I looked to the door, not expecting anyone I knew since everyone I thought had been invited seemed to be in the room. Someone opened the door and in walked Lisa Montgomery wearing the shortest black dress she could have found in her closet. I felt my mood plummet. Even more so when I saw her scurry towards Kade and push herself, and her fake tits, into him as she squealed 'Merry Christmas.'

He seemed to be standing there awkwardly as she fussed over him and talked of how she had just got in from LA and had to come see him. He smiled politely but he let her man handle him as others around us pretended not to watch and I silently fumed. Allison squeezed my hand and Sadie shook her head at the spectacle. Their disgust grew when Kade caught my eye, no doubt noting my expression, and smirked as he sat down on the sofa with her tucking herself close into his side.

"Sexy bastard is playing you at your own game," Allison muttered.

"I wasn't flirting with Travis, Allison. He was flirting with me." She wrinkled her nose.

"You didn't stop him though. Thats what *he's* doing now. That fake tit bitch may as well be slobbering all over him."

"She's horrid," Sadie agreed. Thank god for girlfriends who would have your back and make you feel better, no matter what.

"Soon she'll be trying to hump his leg," Allison whispered. Sadie nearly spat out her drink and we laughed so much that my sides hurt.

The girls plied me with drinks for the rest of the evening, just enough to get me tipsy but not drunk. I ignored the way Lisa kept touching Kade's chest and the way he just smiled down at her as if it was normal. Even his mother looked at them disapprovingly when Lisa edged so close to Kade that she may as well have been sitting on his lap.

Bonnie joined us out on the balcony where us girls had taken our drinks to sit out in the cold air with shawls. Brent was talking to some friends inside and I had had enough of witnessing the show Lisa was putting on and Kade was allowing.

"That whore is all up in Kade's grill and he's pissing me off. If I stayed in there a minute longer, I would have pulled her fucking hair out." We all nodded in agreement.

"Where are the kids?" I asked, having only seen them long enough for them to grab their christmas presents from their uncle and hide out in the games room.

"David took Tyler and Annie home and he'll come pick me up later. Mom's got Chloe. Jared called it a night and took his family home. For now, I'm stuck sipping on apple juice while y'all get to drink wine. At least the company is good."

We made space for Bonnie to sit and talked into the evening. I was glad for the distraction.

Soon, people started to leave and we went back in to bid them farewell.

"Thank you for a lovely evening, Alexa," Kade's mother said to me as she kissed me on my cheek.

"I didn't do anything," I smiled, confused as to why I was getting thanks for her son's dinner.

"I know it was you that brought Christmas to this cold place. Kade's never really home to decorate and usually all the kids end up at home with us during the holidays but

499

this feels right, being able to see him in his home surrounded by warmth. I'm glad you're here for him." I didn't know how to respond and hugged her instead.

Bonnie handed little Chloe to me as she put on her coat. I smiled at the little baby in my arms, remembering how I had submitted to a panic attack the first time I saw her. I didn't feel any of those things now, holding this little life in my arms. I caught Kade looking at me with something akin to pride before he shut off again with his emotions and hobbled over with his crutches to kiss Chloe on her forehead while she snoozed. Bonnie took her from me carefully, pecking me on the cheek and hitting Kade on his shoulder, which was as far as she could reach.

"Ow! What was that for?!" He scowled, rubbing his shoulder.

"You know what that was for." Her scowl was scarier.

Soon all the guests had left after wishing us a Merry Christmas and only Lisa remained as the staff cleared out.

"Oh, I've drank waaaay too much tonight," she giggled, hanging off of him in a way that made me cringe. The woman needed to get some self respect.

"I can have someone drive you home," Kade offered, looking a little impatient now to get rid of her.

"I came here straight from the airport. I haven't had a chance to find a place to stay." *In a mini dress?* Figures she would try to find her way into a sleepover.

"Of course. You can stay in the spare guest room. Alexa is in the room across the hall from mine, you can take the one at the end."

Lisa looked at me as if she had just realised I was standing there and wasn't happy about that little nugget of information. I smiled sweetly and walked toward the stairs, saying good night.

"Uh, Alexa? Would you mind helping me-"

"Oh, I'm sure Lisa can help you get up all these

stairs," I replied before he could finish.

I turned on my heel and hurried up the stairs but not before catching his glare. I chuckled to myself. *He's gotten himself into this mess, he can get himself out of it.*

***

Christmas morning in my household was always a loud affair. Mum would be up early getting the food prepared for our family christmas lunch and then the desert we would take over to Granna's where we'd all congregate in the evening and dad would be up watching old re-runs of Only Fools and Horses. Megs would come and bug the hell out of me before I'd relent and get out of bed to trudge down the stairs to the presents under the tree and we'd tear through the presents together as a family.

When I had gotten married, the only difference was that we would wake up later and I would take something I had made to contribute to mums lunch and then onto Tom's parents' house before we joined the rabble back at Granna's for dessert.

This Christmas morning, my first away from home, I felt like I was truly alone.

The night before, I couldn't sleep, tossing and turning in my bed. Lisa had taken a fair amount of time helping Kade up the stairs, no doubt using her excuse of being inebriated to touch him anywhere and everywhere. Her giggles travelled through my shut bedroom door and lasted a good deal longer than they should have. I wondered if Kade would succumb to the temptation of an easy lay but my heart told me *no.* I refused to believe that he would do that, even if Lisa was making it clear what *her* intentions were.

When I finally fell asleep, it was three in the morning and now I was up again, dressed in my favourite black skinny jeans and a deep green sweater, pulling on my boots and putting my hair up in a high pony. I had a bag full of presents for my family in New York. It would be my first Christmas with my papa, albeit for a few hours over lunch. I'd already exchanged presents last night with my friends but there was one present I had yet to deliver. Stepping out of my room, I saw that Kade's door was closed. The spare guest room where Lisa was sleeping was at the end of the hall and the door was wide open, no doubt as a ploy to get Kade to see Lisa lying there, fast asleep in her bra and nonexistent knickers.

Shaking my head, I descended the steps quietly and placed the present in my hands under the tree. Taking ahold of my bag, I left the tower for my fathers home, hailing a cab to get me there in time to help Dana and Annabelle with the cooking. The snow fell lightly around us as we drove through the quiet streets, New York City slowly waking up to a snowy Christmas morning.

***

"I got it!" I laughed, taking the hat and plastic ring out of the christmas cracker I had just pulled with Adam. The wine was flowing and the conversation was light, having eaten a delicious meal. I found that the more time I spent with them, the more I felt like a part of my fathers family.

"Why was the snowman looking through the carrots?" I asked, reading out the joke written on a little piece of paper from the cracker.

"Oh God, I know this one," Annabelle said, rolling her eyes.

"Because he was picking his nose!" I laughed, throwing the paper onto the growing pile of discarded things in the middle of the dining table.

We sat together in easy conversation with Papa insisting that I sit next to him. He wanted me to be a part of his family and that helped fill some of the emptiness I had been feeling lately.

Annabelle's twin twelve year old boys, Rory and Randall, were excused from the table and went to play their newly acquired nintendo game and her husband Rick was treating us all to some more of his delicious Christmas pie. Perks of having a Michelin star chef as a brother-in-law.

Papa leaned in to me whilst the others chattered away.

"What's on your mind baby girl? Sometimes you slip into a daze. Is everything okay?"

I smiled at him. He was really trying and it made me feel lucky for the chance.

"I'm a little wobbly right now but I will be okay, Papa. Missing home." I could see he wasn't convinced but he let it slide.

When I got up to leave, I received hugs and kisses all around with requests to meet up soon. I felt my phone vibrate in my bag and waited until I was in the cab before I checked it. Three missed calls from Kade and two messages.

08:03am - Where are you?

14:56pm - Are you okay?

I took a deep breath and pressed call. He answered on the second ring.

"Where were you?" He was trying not to sound worried but it didn't work. I felt my heart warming.

"I was visiting with my father and family." I heard him let out an exasperated sigh.

"You could have told me."

"Why? Did you miss me?"

"I thought you might have done something stupid."

"What, like go home? Or go meet people that actually want me around?" The following silence spoke volumes.

"I just didn't want you to be alone on Christmas day." I remained quiet for a few seconds. I didn't know what to say to that. I wasn't alone but I felt it. But he was alone, or possibly not depending on where Lisa was.

"I'm on my way back to you now anyway. No need to send out a search party."

"Fine." The line went dead and I stared at my phone thinking that it being Christmas didn't really make a difference - he was still rude and unbending.

Once I reached his highness' tower and stepped out of the elevator to the penthouse level, I found him standing waiting for me at the door with a look of anger about him.

"Afternoon," I mumbled, trying to move past him in his tight white t-shirt and navy board shorts.

Right now, it annoyed me that he looked this good when he was treating me like shit. I was not in the mood for his moods. Unfortunately, getting past him meant brushing my body against his as he only gave me so much space to get past. The electricity that passed though me made me shiver and I got satisfaction knowing he was not so unaffected as he tried to make out when I felt his body tense.

I walked into the living area that was still looking beautiful and cosy, the tree lights were on and Kade had turned on his fireplace. I decided that rather than sulk around in the guest room upstairs, I would sit in front of Kade's giant television with some popcorn and watch whatever festive movie was showing. Might as well make the most of the holidays.

"Lisa gone home?" I asked, trying not to sound like I cared as Kade hobbled into the room, anger still radiating from him. I looked over my shoulder from the sofa I had sat down on in front of the TV. I didn't bother taking my bag and the presents I had been given upstairs, instead just leaving them on the side by the sofa. Kade's quiet anger was puzzling.

He narrowed his eyes at me and came closer to where I was sitting, placing his hands either side of the back of the couch to lean into my face.

"You left me with that woman! She wasn't even thinking of leaving!" His anger and the agitation rolling off of him in rivulets of frustration made me laugh. And laugh I did, which in turn made him look angrier.

"It's not funny, Alexa! I had to practically spell it out to her that I had plans and she needed to leave!" I calmed down when I remembered her display from the night before and Kade's reaction which started to piss me off again.

"Serves you right Mr Hamilton. Maybe you shouldn't have let her think that you are into her." The steel in my voice made his angry face morph into a smirking one.

"I'm not *into* her. Sounds like someones got a case of the green eyed monster."

He was an arrogant arsehole and the hurt I felt when he allowed Lisa into his space the night before just made me feel like crying but I held onto it. Instead, I knelt up on the sofa, leaning into the back of it and closer into his space.

"Your behaviour last night said otherwise, *Kade.* She was practically in your lap, touching you and pushing her fake breasts up against you and you didn't push her away. So if you're not into her, what was *that* all about? Huh?"
His face was screwed up in a scowl now but I didn't care. He did not get to play with my feelings like that, so I continued.

"You want to know if I was jealous? Yes, I felt jealous. I wanted to rip her away from you and tell her to keep her claws out of you. In reality, you should have been the one discouraging her because she now thinks that she has a chance with you and I feel like...it doesn't matter how I feel. You should have not done that, in front of all those people, your mother included."

Kade's jaw twitched. I didn't realise I'd gotten so close to him in my tirade. I saw his eyes flicker to my lips, my breathing hard from just being tired of this already when it had only just begun. Slowly, he pulled himself away, giving me his back as he leant on his crutches to come around the couch and sit at the other end.

Once he had sat down he looked over at me, the anger having dissipated to what now looked like wariness. I looked away, my eyes catching the two presents under the tree. It was the perfect change of subject so I got up slowly and went to pick them up. One was the present I had wrapped, the other was a small gift bag with my name written on it. I frowned, recognising Kade's handwriting on the tag and brought them back to the couch.

I handed Kade the gift I had picked up.

"I got you this when we were in London before... before you left. I intended for it to be your Christmas present. I hope you like it."

At first he just stared at it, not sure what to do. I could see the cogs in his brain spinning with *should I? Should I not?* In the end, curiosity won. He unwrapped the gift - it was obviously a book. When I saw the emotion on his face, I knew I picked the right gift.

"On one of the days when we were in London and you were in a meeting, I went exploring. I came across this little old bookshop in Kings Cross. I started looking through these lovely old books, pre owned and pre loved books with so much history and when I saw this, I just thought of you and what you had told me when we first met about your mum reading the stories to you all as children. I had to get it."

He held the very old book titled "The Tale of Peter Rabbit" by Enid Blyton. It wasn't a first edition but it was an early edition that had been well read and loved so some of it was a little worse for wear but the illustrations inside were beautiful and the little notes written in the book gave it character. It was still a bit pricey because of its antique nature but I couldn't resist it. Kade opened the first page and read my own little note:

Dear Kade,
For the first Christmas since our acquaintance.

Love from Alexa
XX

He stared at it for some time until I was sure he might just get up and leave because he didn't want to say anything. He surprised me but looking up suddenly into my eyes and when he spoke his voice was sincere.

"Thank you Alexa, it is a thoughtful gift."

I sighed. That was probably the best I would get out of him. He wasn't going to apologise for the spectacle with Lisa but at least he acknowledged the gift with politeness.

I stared at the gift with my name on it. I hesitated, not knowing what I would find. Kade cleared his throat and I looked up at him. His eyes were on the gift in my hand.

"I also bought this gift when we were in London. Didn't know if I'd get to give it to you but you're here now."

I think that was his way of saying he wanted me to have it despite what had happened between us. I slowly pulled out the little wrapped box inside and carefully unwrapped it. Inside the box was a necklace joined by two thick rings in the middle, one silver and one gold. There were numbers engraved on each one that looked like coordinates.

"The gold ring has the coordinates of your home in London, the silver has the ones for home here. I wanted you to have both reminders close to you wherever you go," he explained without looking at me, almost in a bored tone like he hadn't just given me a beautiful and thoughtful gift that brought me to the verge of tears.

"I don't know what to say. This is the best gift ever. Thank you." I wanted to hug him and kiss him but all I could do was look at his face in profile and pray for the ice to melt between us.

"Merry Christmas Alexa," he said quietly, looking down at the book I had given him, his thumb caressing the cover reverently.

"Merry Christmas Kade."

CHAPTER THIRTY EIGHT

You only hurt the ones you love

T he days after Christmas passed by with us being busy making up for lost time...in terms of work. Kade was quiet for the rest of Christmas day and we sat in a somewhat agreed upon silence watching "The Nightmare before Christmas" on some channel.

The days that followed, I found myself useful again, helping sort through piles of work that had caught up with Kade whilst he was recovering from his injuries, both emotional and physical. I didn't mind being busy with him, it made me feel like we were in our old routine. Even his distance and coldness towards me was familiar, reminiscent of the time when he was mad at me for not wanting a relationship with him. The irony didn't escape me.

We got into a routine during the day where we would wake a little later than normal work hours due to everyone being away or off work for the holidays. It gave us a more relaxed work day although we worked until a little later without the restriction of work hours and being at home.

We were the most professional people around one another but the moment it came to getting close to Kade to help him up the stairs or having dinner together, the gulf between us was achingly obvious. I didn't want to force myself on him but I just couldn't stand the distance between us.

New Years eve consisted of Brent, Allison and Sadie coming over and even they could feel the tension. Our original plan a couple of months ago had been to go to a nightclub but seeing as so much had happened between that time and now, and because of Kade's injuries we opted to have a quiet night in with dinner and a few bottles of wine whilst we listened to Brent and Allison talk about their wedding preparations for Valentines day.

"How do you put up with it Lexi?" Allison said once she joined me in the kitchen with some plates from the dinner table. Brent and Kade had cleared up most of the stuff and only a few things were left. Sadie wandered in with a couple of empty bottles of beer.

"Put up with what?" She questioned innocently.

"Allison is talking about the unforgiving Arctic freeze emanating from our host tonight that is only directed towards me."

"Ohhhhh," Sadie replied, looking immediately sorry about it.

"When we're working from his office here, I can pretend that it's just another day at work but when we switch off with work…it's been really difficult, I'm not going to lie. I miss him." I felt some of my control break in those last three words. One tear let slip down my cheek and I was surrounded by four arms in the most comforting of hugs.

"Oh sweetie, I'm so sorry he's being an ass," Sadie said, her voice sounding so sad for me.

"I hope he will come around, but if he doesn't Lexi, promise me you will try and let go. Don't do this to yourself. You've lost too much weight, you don't smile as much as you used to and you two don't talk at all. It's not healthy for you. I worry about you."

Allison was right of course and I had been thinking about

it. Sure, it had only been a couple of weeks since I'd been back and with Kade in this apartment, under duress for him. It had changed nothing between us. He just withdrew more, got quieter and at times his anger would return again. I felt him watching me sometimes and I ignored it because the few times that I would catch his gaze, he would look cold and like he was barely controlling his emotions. I couldn't stand to be in his sights and for him to think that for much longer.

"I promise," I whispered to them.

Back in the living room, Kade gave us a questioning look when Allison returned Kade's smile with a scowl and Sadie just shook her head. I decided not to even look at him and felt my hackles rise with the news that some work colleagues and other acquaintances would be coming by to bring in the new year with us.

Soon the penthouse had another ten guests seated, one of whom was Lisa. Travis was another. It felt like some kind of sick game. Lisa trying to corner Kade, this time with him discouraging her and Travis just being himself and flirting, albeit heavily, with me and me laughing it off whilst Kade shot daggers at him. And yet we weren't together. It was all exhausting.

Just five minutes before the countdown to the New Year, I escaped quietly and undetected into the kitchen. Travis had warned me he was going to plant a smooch on my lips in front of everyone just to piss off the Boss Man because he thought he was being ridiculous. I think he was joking but one could never be too sure around him. I shut the door behind me and relaxed, looking out of the floor to ceiling window overlooking the city. There would be fireworks soon out around the city and I had one of the best views. I felt so lonely surrounded by so many.

I heard the kitchen door open and immediately cursed myself for being careless in finding the kitchen, and not a closet, to hide in. I turned to see Kade sneaking in. Why he would sneak around his own home, I wouldn't know.

"Why aren't you inside?" he asked before I could say anything, avoiding my eyes.

"I'm kinda hiding. From Travis." I didn't bother to explain more because his eyes finally caught mine and he looked beyond irritated, bordering on angry again.

"If he's troubling you, I can ask him to leave." I gave him a small smile.

"He's just being a friend. I just don't need the smothering at the moment. How come you're here?"

He looked around, trying to avoid my eyes again.

"Lisa." There was no need to explain there either. I huffed a laugh and turned towards the windows again.

"I'm just going to watch the fireworks from here," I explained, not wanting to look at his beautiful face anymore. It hurt too much. I thought about what the girls were saying earlier and wondered when I would reach my limit and finally give up.

"You know you can go out onto the balcony there. I just keep it locked because I usually use the doors in the main room."

He gently moved pass me, eliciting sparks of awareness as his body brushed mine. He unlocked a door hidden behind a curtain that I hadn't paid much attention to which opened up to a smaller, more private balcony. There were no seats but the view was just amazing. He gestured for me to go first and I felt surprised that he was being so nice to me.

"Thanks," I muttered and stepped outside. From this height, you could feel dizzy looking down but the view was mind-blowing. Kade came to stand just a couple of steps behind me and from inside I heard the television and the guests start the countdown. With every number counted down, I felt his warmth get closer to me as my heart beat faster.

"FIVE!"

Fingers touched the skin on my back.

"FOUR!"

Big hands followed a path down my back to engulf my waist.

"THREE!"

I felt a sob catch in my throat and tears escape as I closed my eyes.

"TWO!"

He turned me around to face him telling me to open my eyes as I shook my head.

"ONE! HAPPY NEW YEAR!"

He pulled me closed so fast that I had no choice but to open my eyes and then close them again at the feel of his lips smashing against mine in a wild hunger. After the initial shock, I felt myself react, pulling at his dress shirt whilst he grabbed my ass as if he couldn't stand even a millimetre of separation. Our tongues danced in a frenzy, my hands found his hair and his found my breasts, squeezing with desperation. We were like animals, going at it, not even thinking about what had happened between us.

But like all good things, reality soon set in. The kisses slowed, his lips sliding to my neck as he caught his breath, holding my nape with one hand and balancing with his arm on the rail and his good leg supporting him. I could scarcely breathe myself, taking this opportunity to take in as much of his scent as I could while he was there in my arms.

He slowly pulled back, eyes searing into my soul. His fingers traced my lips, now swollen from his kisses, in reverence before he dropped his hand from me entirely. I felt the loss worse than the cold air around us. My hands were still gripping his shirt. He tugged them gently away. I saw the wall go back up again. He was closing off, he was breaking me again.

I debated later if it would have been worse if he had said something before he had left me standing there alone but I decided that his silence made it ten times crueler. I stepped back inside only a few seconds after he had left me to find

Sadie in the kitchen. One look at her and I knew she had seen us and her expression made me fall to my knees. She comforted me on the cold tiled floor. As the people inside and around the city celebrated their new year, I couldn't help but feel that the night marked the start of the end of me trying anymore.

***

He pretended the kiss had never happened. The day the holidays ended, Kade Hamilton decided he had enough of being cooped up at home and suggested we return to the office. The sterile environment of the work space at The Fort was just what he needed and surprisingly it was good to be back in the familiarity of the space. It was easier to breathe being away from him, being around colleagues and strangers meeting for business. Kade suddenly didn't seem to mind that he needed the crutches in public - he still looked commanding enough. Of course, when the media reported the accident he had had, they were disappointed that for a good three weeks, he was out of sight. Now that he was back to work, they were all up in his grill for the first week until the Richardson brothers took the front page headlines again.

I was still living with him, helping out as much as I could. I don't know why I stayed and why he hadn't told me to leave, since he was getting about a lot better with little or no help from me. Two more weeks and he would be out of the cast, he was told by the doctor. I told myself that I was a masochist for living there still. I hadn't been home to the brownstone since I had come back to New York. Sadie or Allison would bring around some clothes for me and the more I though about it, the more I felt like I should go home. Only the thought of him being alone in his tower stopped me. *Why should I care when he couldn't give a shit?*

Those were my thoughts as I made my way back into The

Fort with the sandwiches I had bought from my favourite deli, waving at Bill the security guy at the ground level and getting into the elevator. Once I got to my desk, I dropped my lunch on it and took a plate and a tray to place Kade's on before walking to his office door. The door was ajar and because my hands were full I didn't bother knocking, pushing it open with a foot.

What I saw when I got inside almost made my heart stop. Kade was stood in front of his desk, his crutches forgotten and leaning at the side of it. His top few shirt buttons were undone, tie discarded at his desk and shirt sleeves rolled up over his corded forearms. He was looking down at a tall blonde with such intensity that they didn't hear me come in. She had her hands on his chest and he had his hands on her waist in a way that suggested an intimate connection. Like the way he had held me on New Year's Eve. *They know one another intimately.* It took me a few seconds to realise it was Giselle.

What happened next almost stopped me breathing. Giselle stood on her toes, eyes closed and kissed Kade on his lips. It wasn't a long kiss but it may well have been from the emotion radiating from them both behind it. It was soft, full of longing and it made me want to cry from the pain I felt seeing the man I loved, and had been trying to be patient for, let his ex fiancee kiss him. I hadn't realised that the strangled gasp had come out of my lips until they both turned to look at me. Giselle looked horrified and guilty, quickly grabbing her bag and making a beeline for the door behind me. Kade looked worried as he frowned.

I felt my hands shake and the tray rattle with the plate on it. Giselle was long gone once I told myself to keep it together, keep it professional and walk with one step after the other towards the desk to place his food there. Once I had shakily placed it down, I turned to leave when he called my name. I was struggling with all my strength to keep my emotions in.

"Alexa, that was not what it looked like." His voice was soft, which made me angry.

"You don't have to explain yourself to me. We're not in a relationship."

I didn't bother to look back but I knew he was behind me within seconds before I could leave, surprisingly fast for a man with a leg in a cast, grabbing my arm to turn me towards him.

"Stop pretending Alexa! You need to listen to me. Giselle came to see how I was doing. It is Scott's birthday today. We got emotional. There's no romantic-"

"I don't want to hear it!" I screamed at him. Tears were running down my face angrily.

"Alexa-"

"NO! For *weeks*, you've not spoken more than a few words to me, you've ignored me and shut me out of your life so completely because of what happened in London with Tom and now you expect for me to hear the same explanation you didn't let me give you?! How dare you!" I took a step back from him, not wanting to be close again. I didn't get why he looked so angry now, until he spoke.

"Hurts, doesn't it? Seeing someone you're crazy about kiss the last person you would ever think they could kiss?" I looked at him in disbelief.

"So, what? Is this payback? Is it tit for tat? Do you know how fucking stupid that sounds!" He grabbed me by my shoulders, forcing me to look up into his blazing blue eyes.

"You think that just because I didn't love Giselle enough, her betrayal didn't hurt? I'm not exacting revenge, Alexa, if thats how petty you think I am. I didn't plan for this to happen and it certainly doesn't mean a thing to me. I didn't know you were here!"

I looked into his beautiful eyes and felt the anger melt into pain. I could see him register it when his anger slipped too.

"That doesn't mean you should have let it happen," I said quietly, "what happened in London with me and Tom? That shouldn't have happened, but it did. I learned my lesson then and have been paying the price for it. What happened between you and Giselle? That should not have happened because of *that* lesson."

I pulled myself out of his hold and walked slowly over to the door that was still ajar, no doubt with a hundred spectators outside from all the shouting. I was suddenly so tired of it all. I wanted out.

"Alexa, stop," he pleaded, his voice soft but tinged with a fear I recognised. I looked at him over my shoulder.

"I quit. I am not going to work out my notice, I think I have earned that much having lived with you these past four weeks. I will clear out my desk and the room at your home today. If you will allow me some time to look for a new apartment, I will leave the house in due course."

I didn't wait for his response. I left his office, aware of the people around that had heard the commotion, despite the massive space and private offices. Some were poking their head out or pretending to be in the staff kitchen. I grabbed the few things I had at my desk and in the drawers and put them in a tote shopper I kept folded in one of the drawers. Aware of the time and how close Kade still was in his office, I left many things in hurry, grabbing my hand bag and making my way to the elevators as fast as I could. Tears were still running down my face and the harder I tried to stop them, the faster they came.

As the elevator stopped and the doors opened for me to step in, Travis stepped out. One look at my face and he stepped back in, pulling me gently beside him.

"What happened?" For once, he was serious and his usually handsome smiling face was darkened with worry and a frown.

"Could you give me a lift?" I stuttered in my misery.

"Of course, anywhere." He didn't question me any

further and let me have my space.

Travis drove me to the first place on my list - Kade's tower. I packed up my belongings as fast as I could, not lingering around to think of all the time we had spent here recently. I left his keys with his concierge and hopped back into Travis' Porche.

He drove me home and in that time I explained briefly what had happened with us in London, the time apart, me coming back to New York and then today, without mentioning Giselle's name.

"I'm sorry Lexi. This is the shittiest thing to happen and I wish I could do something to help."

I gave him a sad smile.

"Me too."

"You're one of the smartest, bravest and most beautiful of women I know. You will get through this."

I huffed a humourless laugh but felt grateful for his words.

"Thank you Trav. I just need to sort my life out. I don't know what I'm going to do."

"You're thinking of moving back to London?" He didn't look too happy about the idea.

"Nah. The thought had crossed my mind but I don't think I'm done with New York yet."

"I'm glad. Don't let a man run you out of town," he smiled.

"I won't. I'm so grateful for your help."

"Any time you need me, just call. Okay?" He kissed my hand and let me go into the house.

No one was home when I got in and I was glad. I hadn't been here for weeks and every room here had memories of a happier time.

As I got up the stairs, I saw that the painting Kade had bought me was hanging on the wall. I remember him telling me it was too big for my room. It made my breath catch just looking at the painting I loved so much with memories of the night at the gallery. I sat down on the landing and buried my face in my hands. I had finally reached my limit. It was time to let go. I just wished my brain would get that message through to my heart.

CHAPTER THIRTY NINE

Destination wedding

"**O**kay, everybody got their passports? Bags packed? Shoes? Booze? My sanity?" came Allison's voice from the foyer as we hurried to get down for the taxi coming to pick us up.

It had been two weeks since I left Kade in his office, left his life and his company for the last time. I felt empty for the most part. I cried and then got angry at myself for crying for most of the days but soon enough I realised that I had a great distraction to the shit storm that was my life - Allison and Brent's wedding.

When I had gone back home and found that Sadie and Allison had both rushed back from work to be by my side, I had broken down. When I found out that Kade had called them, I shattered. Why he cared at all was beyond me but I was grateful not to be alone. I'd felt alone for too long in this and now I just wanted to let that all go.

The girls had stayed with me all the while, never letting me be alone with my thoughts and by day three, I had had enough. I threw back my covers, made Sadie go to work and told Allison that this was the last day she was 'working from home' and that I was going to be okay. That and I was going to stop being a shit friend and help her with the last minute details for her wedding.

It was a great distraction indeed and had almost worked. I say 'almost' because one thing kept pinching at the hurt. Kade had not once called or messaged me in all this time. It hurt afresh every time I remembered that little nugget, like a healing wound that was constantly being picked at. There was also the whole mystery over whether or not he would be making an appearance at the wedding. I told myself I didn't care. I was going to the Bahamas to my friends wedding and I was going to enjoy myself so *screw him*. But I knew I cared, I still cared and I still wanted him even though he had pulverised my heart.

In that first week, I allowed myself to cry and be hurt but I had honestly done so much of that when he left me in London the first time, this time I wanted to try to be stronger and protect myself from the harsh reality. I was on autopilot and the less time I had to think about intense blue eyes, the better. It didn't stop him coming to me in my dreams, so very real and beautiful.

I decided fairly quickly that I was allowed to feel crappy, to hurt and to feel his loss but I was not going to stop living. I had to remember why I came to this city in the first place. I didn't want to be driven away from London because of one man and then returning because of another. I was going to embrace my fresh start. Or my fresher, fresh start. It didn't stop the pain but it helped me focus.

I started looking for a new place to live by the end of that week, determined to get away from the house that screamed his presence. Finding a place of my own in New York City was difficult and expensive. Kade was a generous landlord. I found that out the hard way as I looked for places close to work. In the end, it looked like I might have to move further afield, even with a decent salary and my savings for the deposit but I found a studio apartment in the Upper East Side eventually and had to give the landlord an answer in a couple of weeks' time. I hadn't told the girls yet, especially not Sadie, and I felt horrible about leaving so soon after Allison would.

Next, I had called up Papa and asked him if my old job offer was still there to which he had happily and hastily said yes before I could change my mind. He had asked me if I was okay and when I said nothing, he correctly guessed that it was to do with Kade Hamilton. I was grateful when he didn't push it but I knew he was disappointed. I told him I was available to start after Allison's wedding and then I got to sorting out the last details left for her big day.

I enjoyed this part, the event planning. It consumed so much of my time and although she had been reluctant to get me involved since my own romantic entanglement had ended badly, Allison was happy once I took over. And now we were standing waiting for the taxi as we left the house for the long weekend.

"You excited?" I smiled at Allison, grasping her hands.

"I'm so bloody nervous! I need a large G and T as soon as we get on that plane!"

"I'm on it, captain," I laughed back.

Sadie rolled her small suitcase out first as the cab stopped in the front. I felt sadness creep in as Allison took a look around the house before closing and locking the door. The sadness was always around me these days but today it was more for my friend, who would be leaving this house to live with her husband when we returned. I, too, was planning to leave. It made my chest hurt just thinking about it.

Turning around to catch the look on my face, Allison pulled me into a big hug that had Sadie joining us and telling us quietly that we needed to move to catch the flight.

"I'll never be too far," Allison promised tearily.

"I should hope not," I laughed lightly, wiping my

own tears away.

***

The resort was beautiful and I couldn't help but wonder at the natural beauty around us. The weather was warm but I was told that this was mild compared to the heat tourists normally sought out.

The luggage got taken from us by porters to store and we were informed that we were a little early so we were sent to the bar while the rooms were made up.

"Brent just sent me a message. They just reached the airport now. Should be on their way soon," Allison muttered with a straw in her mouth.

She was drinking some blue coloured cocktail that was quickly going to her head. I signalled to the bar tender not to give her anymore. She was not going to be a hungover bride on her wedding weekend, not on my watch. The barman didn't seem to think I was serious until I had him quietly pull back the fresh cocktail he had placed in front of Allison when he saw the look of thunder on my face.

"Okay, time to go get some beauty sleep, princess," I sighed heavily as I put one of Allison's arms over my shoulder and Sadie took the other, trying to haul her out of the chair and walked her slowly through the bar.

"I wuv you girls...I weally dooo," she slurred a little drunkenly. The giggles were starting as well. This was bad. She had only had a few cocktails but there must have been some strong liquor in them to get her drunk so quick. I threw a prolonged glare back at the barman who looked a little sheepish. I was still glaring as I turned back to face forward to the reception and concierge area when I came face to face with the object of my torment.

"Alexa."

That deep voice made my body shiver, remembering the way he'd said my name countless times before. I looked away from his painfully beautiful face before I could answer shortly.

"Kade."

Although I had looked away from him, that one initial look at his tall frame was already seared into my brain. Wearing tan coloured chinos and a baby blue shirt that was unbuttoned at the top and navy Derby shoes. His hair had been freshly cut, styled somewhat shorter and more modern than before with a parting to the side that just highlighted how sexy he was. He had grown his stubble into a closely trimmed beard. He looked well. It sucked.

Here I was, using a shit tonne of concealer on my dark circle craters and he looked fresh and like he'd just stepped off the catwalk from the New York Fashion Week. Gone were the crutches and the plaster cast. I let the anger simmer in me, allowing me to put on that facade of indifference he had once used on me, when all I wanted to do was run into his arms.

"Allison? Honey?"

It took me a few seconds to remember that Kade was not alone. We were joined by a group of good looking groomsmen and Brent who looked like he wanted to laugh but was holding it in. From the fond grins all around from the six other men there, including kade, who I refused to look at again, they were used to this version of Allison that got too happy after a few drinks in her.

"Sorry Brent. The bartender went a little heavy on the liquor in her cocktails," Sadie explained with an apologetic smile.

"Don't worry about it. I'll take over from here. Come on party girl."

Brent scooped Allison up in his arms as if she weighed nothing and went in for a light peck on her lips when Allison pulled his face to hers with ungodly strength and planted a dirty, inappropriate kiss on him.

"Take me to bed, lover," she whispered loudly.

Brent didn't waste time getting away from his teasing mates who were loudly cheering them on all the way until the lift doors closed on the couple.

While we were standing there watching them leave, some more members of the wedding party had arrived - Allison's parents, brother and sister (who had thankfully missed the show) and Brent's parents as well as more family and some of Allison's girlfriends. We stood around introducing ourselves, and I could feel the heat of his eyes as I ignored his presence the best I could. Slowly everyone got checked in and I tugged on Sadie's arm to get her attention.

"I'm just gonna head up to my room. I think I need to freshen up before dinner. Meet you later?"

"Sure hon. I'll see you at the restaurant," she smiled and turned back to the guy she was speaking with after I waved them goodbye, careful not to run into Kade who was talking to some red head pin up from Brent's family. I pushed down the jealousy. Even with his eyes trained on me, I wouldn't let myself look directly at him. I smoothed my sweaty palms down my navy and white striped maxi dress as I reached the bank of elevators and pressed the call button for the lift. Once it arrived, I shot inside with relief and was almost home free when a hand stopped the already closing doors before they shut completely. In a whirlwind of motion, I found myself pushed up into the corner of the otherwise empty lift, the doors closing and me staring into deep blue eyes.

"What are you doing?" I said breathlessly, doing a terrible job of relaying my annoyance. It was pathetic. He looked at me with an intensity that I knew. A determination that only spelt trouble to me. My heart rate picked up.

"You weren't looking at me Alexa. Why wouldn't you look at me?"

I felt my breath hitch and struggled to keep my eyes focussed as I felt myself tear up.

"You know why."

His body was so close to mine, his arms braced either side of my head, his forehead almost touching mine as he exhaled as if he had just run to get here. He probably had.

"Alexa-"

"Don't, okay? Just don't," I managed to say, my voice breaking as I looked away. He grabbed my chin and forced me gently to look at him.

"Which room?" he asked, now that we had reached the fifth floor where I was staying.

I just shook my head in reply. The lift door opened and then slowly closed, the lift staying stationary as his gaze burned into me.

"Which room, Alexa? Don't make me ask again." His tone brokered no argument but I couldn't care less.

I moved to go towards the doors but he pulled me by my waist and flush against his hard body. And then kissed me hard. At first it was just his lips on me, his tongue seeking and pleading with me until I felt my arms involuntarily snake around his neck while I returned the kiss with equal desperation and urgency. His hands roamed my body as mine trailed down his chest and abdomen. I finally came to my senses when I felt the bulge in his pants against me and broke the kiss.

"WHICH. ROOM?" He growled, breathing hard from desire.

"512," I whispered, wondering why I let that information out.

I saw the sly, smug grin start to spread across his face when I scrambled to hit the door 'open' button before fleeing that cursed lift and the man who was pulling all my strings, besides all my strong woman power talks to myself.

I reached my room and hurriedly shut the door, despite knowing that he hadn't followed. I threw myself on the big sized bed, not even getting a chance to enjoy the beautiful suite I had treated myself to, and I growled my frustration into the pillow. One passionate kiss, and I was already putty in his hands.

**

"You sure you're not up to dinner tonight?" Sadie's voice came through the phone.

"Yeah hun, I think I've exhausted myself today, I'm just going to order in and I'll see you tomorrow morning."

I felt bad cancelling on Sadie but I was not up to mingling with the wedding party guests. I told her I was tired, which wasn't a complete lie. Allison was not going to make it to dinner and Brent had crashed in early with her, no doubt exhausted himself.

"You're not bailing because of a certain brooding man are you?" I was quiet for a second too long.

"Is he there?" I couldn't help myself. I was a glutton for punishment.

"Yep, and he looks kinda pissed off. You sure you don't wanna come down? They have the most amazing deserts." Her tempting offer wasn't enough to coax me.

"I'll catch up with you tomorrow," I laughed and we said good bye.

Yes, I was a chicken shit because I didn't want to look at the man with whom I'd fallen in love. His kiss was still burning on my lips. Seeing him was like being able to breathe for the first time in so long. Even when he was mad at me, I'd had the relief that he was near and not seeing him when I was in London and then these past two weeks, I felt the jolt of excitement again and it pissed me the hell off. I couldn't forget the way he had hurt me, knowing how it had felt when I had made that same mistake. The image of Gisele kissing him was burned in my brain, making me angry and jealous all over again. The rational part of me reasoned that he let it happen, just like I had with Tom, because of our history and because it was a goodbye but the jealous monster in me wanted to rip Gisele limb for limb because she had her disgusting hands and lips on my man. God I needed help.

After some time, I ordered a stupid amount of food to get me through the night and then lay back with the remote for the TV and flicked channels.

There was a knock on the door fifteen minutes later and I jumped off the bed to get it, surprised the food had come so quick. When I opened the door, I saw a man holding a massive bouquet of beautiful mixed orchids and folliage. Before I could ask who they were from, the man handed them to me with a curt bow and left. I went back into the room, still wondering who they were from when setting them down on the table and I saw the card tucked in neatly in the bouquet.

"I missed you at dinner. I miss you
all the time.

K."

I felt my heart melt a little as an involuntary smile spread across my lips and I traced the shape of one of the orchids with my fingers. I hated that he was so smooth. So charming and thoughtful. *This is all temporary,* the voice in my head said in warning, *you need something real.* What I needed was to stay away from him.

CHAPTER FORTY

I've got you, baby

"**I** know you want so badly to leave right now Lexi, but you really need to ride this out. Just relax, enjoy the sun," Allison whispered whilst smiling at my scowling face.

"Why does your cousin have to be the biggest whore on this planet?" I asked her for the fifth time since we had come down to the private beach the resort offered, to find Kade being accosted by a petite brunette who just happened to be Allison's first cousin. The redhead pin up from the night before wasn't put off either, stalking her prey from afar whilst talking to another handsome looking man, waiting for Allison's cousin to leave her spoils for her chance to pounce.

For his part, Kade seemed to be politely answering her questions and accommodating her but in my jealous mind they were already doing the dirty to spite me. Every now and then he would look from his sun lounger to where I was and I hated that I couldn't see his eyes with his sunglasses covering them. That was usually the best way to gauge his real emotions. Part of me thought he was happier with the mask in front of him - it left him less vulnerable.

He was about five loungers away from me and that was good enough distance for me to not hear their conversation or see too much of his beautifully defined and tanned body, although I would have to be blind not to notice it.

"Tara is always going to be a ho bag. We've all accepted it, even her parents have just given up," Allison scowled over at Tara, earning major best friend points.

It could have also had something to do with the fact that Tara had been trying to flirt with Brent earlier, earning herself a very loud talking to by Allison in a very public place. Thats why I loved Allison, I thought, smiling fondly at her. *She is not afraid to be herself and show her emotions.*

"Currently, Tara has her hand on Kade's chest," I said bitterly, noticing that she had no concept of what a persons personal space was. Luckily, Kade seemed to be scowling at her and gently moved her hand away, which she took as an invitation to pull him towards the beach. *Wearing an itsy bitsy string bikini with her arse hanging out.*

"That's it, I've had enough," I grumbled, getting up from the lounger, disturbing a dozing Sadie next to me and pulled off my sun dress to reveal my 1940's inspired black high waisted bikini bottoms and black and white polka dot halter neck bikini top.

When I dropped the dress, I got a few cat calls from the boys we had met yesterday and their appreciative looks made me smile and blush. I saw Kade turn around from where he was being dragged by a determined Tara into the sea to look to the noise. When he saw me, I could see his frown lines return and nostrils flare a little.

Allison gave me a huge grin as she dumped her magazine on the loungers table and stood up, stretching her long limbs whilst Sadie rubbed her eyes and got up too. I had my girls with me, it was time to actually enjoy this vacation.

We walked into the sand, all the while getting cheers and whistles when we waved back. A couple of the guys joined us, as well as Brent looking predatorily at Allison, who naturally looked like a knockout in her red bikini.

Sadie's white one piece sculpted to her body perfectly and set off her already tanned skin and beautiful red hair. I think we all looked like a commercial waiting to be filmed for the Bahamas and one of the guys unexpectedly lifted me up and ran into the sea, dumping me into the cool water as I squealed and tried not to swallow water. When I came up for air, I could see his laughing dark eyes assess the situation.

His name was Hayden and he was one of Brent's good friends. Body built lean like a surfers with sizeable biceps and sun kissed skin, he had dark dirty blonde hair. He was probably hot. Not that I noticed men in that way anymore. Kade had ruined me forever.

"You. Are. TOAST!" I screamed at him and put my hands on his shoulder to hoist myself up against him and take him under water with me. I had a feeling he let me do it to him as there was little resistance, seeing as he was a tall and built guy who was definitely heavier than me. We were soon joined by the others in the water and had fun being carefree, completely ignoring the infuriating man who had finally shaken off Tara and looked so sexy in his dark blue trunks hanging low on his hips.

Half an hour passed quickly and I was playfully splashing Brent back when I felt a warm body press behind me, a familiar warmth envelop me and a voice that vibrated in my very soul took my breath away.

"She's coming with me."

His voice brooked no argument and Brent simply nodded at the towering figure behind me then gave me a sheepish smile and shrugged his shoulders. I hardly had time enough to give Brent the full force of my glare before I was whipped out of the water and looked up into the face of an angry looking Kade who had lost his sunglasses and had his darkened eyes concentrated forward to the shore whilst he carried me in his arms to the beach. I had no choice but to hold onto him as I looked over his shoulder at the stunned or smiling party of friends we left behind us. I opened my mouth to say something but one sharp look from Kade made the words die before they could leave my mouth.

He returned his focus to the task at hand and I saw us pass the loungers and walk past the hotel and into a grove of palm trees where he slowly set me down on my feet but pushed me up against a tree with his body, anger and frustration radiating off of him.

When I felt brave enough to look up at his face, water still dripping off his body, his hair mussed where it was slightly longer than the rest and his hands tight on my hips, I just wanted the world to melt away and for it to be just us there. We stared at one another for some time until I couldn't bear to look at him without saying something.

"Why did you just man-handle me?" My words came out as a whisper but with an undercurrent of desire I knew he noticed when his eyes darkened a little more.

"Why did you let that dickhead man-handle you into the sea?" His voice sounded rough, hoarse and so much like how it was when we made love.

"We were just playing around," I replied, my breath hitching when he growled.

"I don't like any one touching what is mine."

If any other person had said that to me, I would have laughed in their face. Kade Hamilton saying this to me, made my knees weak and made me want to jump on him.

"Well, I don't like other women touching you," I countered back aggressively, unaware that the anger brewing inside of me was so severe.

"Jealous, are we?" He sneered, pressing impossibly closer into me so that I could feel the bulge in his trunks and the rough bark of the palm tree at my back.

"Yes," I answered truthfully and breathlessly added, "aren't you?"

"Yes." We breathed one another in, absorbing all

that yearning, all that passion until it built into emotions I couldn't control and it got hard to breathe.

"What's wrong?" he asked, passion turning into deep concern at my shift in mood.

"I can't do this right now," I said quietly, trying to breathe through it. I pushed him away gently and moved to walk past him and back to the hotel.

"Alexa-"

"No! Just please, leave me be."

I didn't look back at him and he didn't follow. In my room, I walked into the shower and wondered when my life had become so complicated.

Drying off, I lay my head down on the bed but tears didn't come. Instead, exhaustion took me by surprise and I fell into a deep sleep.

***

A loud banging on the door jolted me from my deep sleep.

"LEXI!"

"Alexa De Luca, you had better open this mother-fucking door!"

"Do you think we should get security?"

I scrambled from my bed, realising I was still in my towel from my shower and my hair looking like a birds nest. I opened the door to a startled looking Allison and Sadie who were dressed in pastel coloured semi formal dresses.

"What the hell happened to you?" Allison demanded, pushing me aside and coming into the room.

"I fell asleep. What time is it?"

"It's a quarter to eight," Sadie piped up, giving my dress that was draped over the armchair a pointed look.

"Oh shit! The wedding rehearsal!"

"Yes, the wedding rehearsal! Everyone is waiting for us! Get your sexy arse into that bloody dress and sort out your face. I'll do your hair. Jesus!"

Allison assumed the role of commander and directed us to get me ready collectively.

"I'm sorry Allison, I didn't realise I'd been knocked out for so long."

I felt so bad. It was her big day tomorrow and this weekend was about her and all I'd done was play hide and freaking seek with Kade.

"It's okay," she said sighing, "the things I do in the name of friendship. How I suffer!"

We groaned as we were subjected to a ten minute monologue about her sacrifices for friendship and by the time we were finally out of the door and bundled into the elevator and going down to the restaurant, we had a little group hug.

"I know you're going through some crazy shit right now Lexi, but he's going through some shit too," Allison said supportively.

"He was going out of his mind when you didn't show on time. We had to stop him from coming up himself," Sadie concurred.

"I'm sorry guys. It's just been a hard time. I think we just aren't supposed to be around one another."

"I think that's exactly the *opposite* of what you guys need," Allison replied with a raised eyebrow.

I let her words sink in but had no real time to process as we hurried out of the elevator and into the restaurant an hour late.

I made my apologies to Brent and everyone. Turns out that the officiant had only arrived fifteen minutes ago so we were not too far behind schedule. I saw Kade make his way determinedly to the front as best man and I took my place as maid of honour. We were to walk in together, ahead of the rest of the procession of bridesmaids and groomsmen. He smelled amazing and was wearing a light pink dress shirt and navy trousers. It seemed to coincidentally match my pastel pink chiffon dress. I could see our reflection in the foyer mirror and we looked good together. Kade looked back at me in that reflection, his face contemplative.

Quietly, we walked to the instruction of the officiant and were reminded that we would be doing this on the beach tomorrow so we would need to make sure we knew what we were doing. I had to put my hand on the crook of Kade's muscled arm and felt him tense as we walked out first into the private function room in the restaurant from the foyer where we had been waiting. Not a single word was spoken between us and we walked in sync to the soft music playing. We went through the motions, separated to either side of the bride and groom, moving when told, sitting when asked to. It was a blur but we made it through and when dinner was served an hour later, we sat side by side and ate in silence as everyone talked around us. I felt his thigh against mine in the closely set table spacing and relished in the comfort it afforded me. Once we'd eaten desert, a group of the girls decided to take a walk for the last night of Allison's freedom. I could tell she was nervous, she had always been fiercely independent and now having a husband meant sharing so much more than just their time. As I stood to leave, Kade stood in his gentlemanly manner as did a few other men as the ladies left. He pulled out the chair for me and stood aside.

"Thank you," I muttered and avoided eye contact before escaping to the beach.

Outside, the air had chilled somewhat. Gone was the tolerably warm weather and now the crispier air made me shiver and curse myself for not bringing a shawl like some of the other better prepared women in our group.

"So, how you feeling? Or is that a stupid question?" I looked at Allison and she actually looked a little pale.

"I think I'm making the right decision, right?" She spoke quietly to me and Sadie, careful that the other girls trailing behind were out of earshot.

"Bones," Allison scowled at the old nickname,

"you're the most sensible person I know, bar when you drink, " I added laughing.

"Yeah, but am I doing the right thing? You don't think that I've rushed into this?" Sadie and I looked warily at one another but there was only one way to solve this.

"Could you see Brent with someone else?" I asked.

"No," she replied with a frown.

"Would you ever want to be without him for a long period of time?" asked Sadie.

"No I wouldn't."

"Would you ever be able to live without him in your life?" I asked her, suddenly asking myself the same question.

"I wouldn't be able to breathe without him," Allison smiled tearily.

We hugged her together.

"Thats how you know you're ready," I whispered, feeling just as teary all of a sudden.

"Thank you. I don't know how I could ever get through life without you girls," she laughed, wiping the tears away.

"You better not disappear on us when you're on Brent Cloud Nine," Sadie warned with a grin.

"Never!"

We walked a little further along the beach until we got to the gazebo that had been set up for the wedding the next day. Some of Allison's friends were gushing about how amazing it was to get married on a beach and we looked in awe at the candles that they had lit to add to the romantic atmosphere around it. The light fabric draped through the arches flew delicately in the wind as I wandered around it.

When I turned around, the girls had walked some way along the beach back toward the hotel, Sadie and Allison waving at me. Not to join them but as a good bye which confused the hell out of me.

"I asked them to bring you here."

I jumped at the sound of his voice and turned again to see Kade appear as if by magic. *Traitorous bitches.* My heart beat fast, partly from the suddenness of his appearance and partly from him being near me.

"What are you doing here?" I asked breathlessly.

"We need to talk Alexa," he said, hands in his pockets. He was wearing a navy blazer to match his trousers.

"Then talk." I was tired of avoiding him all the time, it was exhausting. Maybe we just needed to hash this out, one last time.

I shivered and he took off his blazer to put around my shoulders. I was not about to decline the much needed warmth and the scent of him any time soon. I wasn't sure I'd be giving him the blazer back at all.

"I've been thinking about my behaviour towards you these past few months," he began but stopped to my annoyance.

"And?" I asked impatiently. His eyes sparked with mischief when he heard my tone of annoyance.

"I wanted to figure out why I behave the way I did with you, why I said things I wouldn't normally say. And I came to a conclusion."

"And what was that," I asked, shivering now from anticipation of his answer.

He stepped closer to me, the lights around the gazebo and the candles in the covered lanterns casting a warm glow on his face. His hand reached up to cup my chin, his thumb tracing the path of my cheekbone.

"That I am unequivocally, madly and deeply in love with you and it scares the shit out of me."

His hand trembled a little as he said the words, sincere and with fear and hope.

"Then why did you hurt me?" I asked quietly, tears choking me.

"I'm so sorry baby. I knew that I was falling in love with you that first night we had together. It was confirmed the night I saw Tom kiss you. I felt like I could rip him apart, I couldn't see past the jealousy and I didn't deal with it properly. And I hurt you. I'm sorry baby, please forgive me." His expression was so tender, eyes so expressive that I couldn't look away and he continued.

"I will never do that to you again, I can't bear the thought of hurting you. I've been selfish in my own pain, I didn't think what you were going through." He slipped his arms around my waist, pulling me closer to him.

"You're everything I could have ever dreamed of having. I have never been a jealous man in a relationship until now, it's very new to me Alexa. I hate the way I become, I just can't see you with any man but me. I can't." His fierce emotion was searing. It floored me.

"Kade-"

"But I promise to trust you, to think before I act. Or try, at least. I can do that because I love you and need you more than my next breath."

"Kade listen-"

"Please don't walk away from me again, I'll go crazy. You don't know how agonising these past two weeks have been without seeing you. Bonnie made me stay away from you. She said I had done enough damage and nearly kicked my ass."

He huffed a laugh and for the first time ever he seemed nervous.

"Kade, will you let me finish before you start talking again?" He opened his mouth to speak but closed it quickly to nod for me to proceed.

"I know how it feels to be that scared of loving someone, to feel jealousy that was never there before because thats how I felt when I saw Giselle put her filthy lips on you. I wanted to cut the bitch."

Kade's lips twitched in a smile he was trying to hide but he remained quiet while I continued.

"And that Lisa being all over you? And Tara today?

Kade I have to compete with so many women for you," I sighed, letting him kiss my forehead as he frowned.

"Not one of those women compare to you. I care for no one but you baby. I want you in my life for every single day I have left on Earth. You're the strongest, most beautiful woman I have ever known."

I felt teary again and looked up at him as I uttered the words I had wanted to say to him for so long.

"I've known I've loved you for so long, I can't remember when it started."

I saw him close his eyes and swallow a pain I hadn't seen before. When he opened them there was relief and unmistaken love shining out just for me.

"Say it again."

"I love you, Kade Hamilton. I don't think I'll ever be able to stop."

I squealed when he suddenly picked me up and twirled me around.

"I love you, Alexa De Luca. And we're going to make up for lost time starting from right now."

He scooped me up like he had earlier on the beach. He leaned into me and kissed me long and softly on my lips and started the walk back to the hotel. As we neared it, I ran my hand over his neatly cut shorter hair, getting his attention.

"I am able to walk, you know," I teased and he took that as an opportunity to bite my lip hungrily.

"I know, smartass. I just like to have you in my arms, and this is way quicker. You'll just slow us down."

"Charming!"

"Hey, I've not been inside you for a long time now. Can you blame a man?"

He whispered as we drew close to nosy spectators standing outside on the terrace of the hotel, enjoying the crisp evening air after dinner. He let me stand on my feet, holding me steady by my hips and I placed my arms around his shoulders.

"No, I can't," I shivered in anticipation. Something still niggled at the back of my mind and I had to say it.

"What's on your mind beautiful, just tell me," he said, reading me like a book. I guess I wasn't the only one with a talent for reading expressions.

"What happens if I'm not strong enough for what is to come? What if who you are gets in the way of things and they tear us apart?"
I didn't know how I would survive that.

"Then I will be strong for both of us and when I can't handle it, *you* will be strong for both of us. I'm not giving up on us ever again. Trust me when I say that in time, you and I will never have to fear being *with* or *without* one other. I got you, baby."

As we stood there on the terrace outside the hotel, l felt the tide change in my favour. I felt free at last from all the doubt that had surrounded me. I didn't feel so lost anymore, I felt like he was my home.

***

The sound of the ocean and feeling the warmth of the suns rays on my naked body woke me up. Eyes still closed, I recalled all of the ways in which Kade affirmed his love for me throughout the night and how I reciprocated. My body was delightfully sore in all the right places.

He had brought me back to his suite and my word, what a suite it was. Apart from the usual luxurious fixtures and hot tub, the view was spectacular. Ceiling to floor windows facing the private beach afforded us the best view on the island of the beauty surrounding us and we made love through the night with the beautiful calm surrounding us.

A smile spread across my face and I stretched myself languidly only to meet resistance and hear the clanging of metal when I tried to bring my arms down from above my head.

"What the...? Kade? Kade!" A few moments later, Kade appeared from the bathroom, toothbrush in his mouth and wearing just his boxers. His slow and sexy smile spreading across his face softened my scowl a little and I looked up pointedly at the two pairs of handcuffs attaching me to the rail on the bed.

"Good morning baby," he said after taking his brush out of his mouth and giving me a toothpaste covered peck on my lips that had me scowling more with the taste of mint.

"Cute. Now tell me why I'm handcuffed?" He chuckled, shaking his head at me in amusement.

"So demanding. No please, 'no thank you for rocking my world last night.'"

"Seriously? Are we in high school?" I huffed in disbelief. He just shrugged and got up to leave for the bathroom again.

"I'll come back to you when you're in a better mood for conversation." He winked at me, enjoying my growing discomfort in not knowing why he had me chained to his bed.

"Wait! Kade! Don't go!" After a few seconds of silence after he had disappeared, I added, "PLEASE!"

He reappeared again, wiping his face with a towel, his muscles on display flexing at the motion and making me lick my lips. I had kissed and licked my way all over him last night. The memory made me press my legs together trying to relieve the sensation building in the place between them.

"Yes baby?" he asked me innocently. I pulled at the restraints and raised an eyebrow in question. The action had made my breast jiggle and it was hard not to notice his eyes darkening as he watched my naked body on display for him.

"Ah, the handcuffs. You'd be surprised what you can get the concierge to procure for you at short notice and with great discretion. However, they only got me one pair.

The other I borrowed from Allison. Don't ask. She offered."

Now I had an image of Allison and Brent in my mind that I really didn't want to see.

"Okaaaay...why?" He smiled and I rolled my eyes in frustration.

Finally putting me out of my misery, he lay down next to me and placed a hand on my stomach.

"Because I wasn't going to wake up without you in my bed, again. The two times you've been with me before, you left before morning. This time, I'm making sure you stay. Third time lucky." I softened at his reasoning. I *had* run out on him after those times and didn't realise how much it must have hurt him.

"I'm sorry baby," I whispered when he came closer and kissed my forehead, "I didn't mean to. Just so you know, I will never leave you like that again. So you can take these off now, please."

"I'm not sure I want to, I like the idea of you tied up and at my mercy," he whispered with eyes full of intent. He moved down and licked and then sucked my nipple, causing me to arch off the bed with a moan.

"As much as I like that idea too, we have a wedding to get ready for and I need to pee."

He stood up, faking disgust and muttering about how he gets no appreciation while he fished out the keys to the handcuffs from the side table drawer and unlocked them. He massaged my wrists and then I stood in front of him, pulling him down to whisper in his ear.

"Meet me in the bathroom in ten minutes, lover, and I'll give you some appreciation."

With that I walked away with an exaggerated sway of my hips, earning a groan from behind me. When I looked over my shoulder to wink at him, he looked like he was restraining himself from lunging at me. This was going to be fun.

***

After spending way too much time in the shower 'appreciating' one another, we finally got dressed for breakfast and made our way down. Brent was not allowed to see Allison before the wedding at the request of her old fashioned and superstitious mother so he was made to have breakfast in his room but the rest of the wedding guests were there eating and turned to see us approach with mixed reactions because Kade refused to keep our relationship, as new as it was, under wraps. He held tightly onto my hand, never letting go and made a show of pulling out my seat at the breakfast table and then being super attentive to me, even stealing kisses when he could.

I loved this side of Kade, it was new to me. We hadn't had the chance of having this before and now he was mine. I let that thought sink in as the realisation made the butterflies dance around again in my stomach. There was no comparison to Kade in my past. His place was so far elevated than any other man had ever been and I made a promise to show him that every day we were together now.

I took pleasure in seeing the disappointment and disapproval in Tara and the redheads stares. Allison and Sadie beamed at us and the guys seemed to be passing Kade knowing smiles. It seems like a lot of them were aware of the tension between us than I could have guessed.

After breakfast, Kade wouldn't let me leave with Allison until he had taken his time planting the sexiest and almost inappropriate kiss on me, thankfully in a more private setting.

Once we were in Allison's room, the make up artist and hair stylist she had hired worked their magic and we helped her get into the beautiful light ivory gown she had selected for her wedding. The strapless dress was stunning in its simplicity and it's shape and Allison looked like a princess with her hair piled up in a wispy up do with flowers twisted in. Our bridesmaids dresses were baby blue, thin strapped dresses that had a dipped hem. We picked up our bouquets and kissed Allison while getting emotional.

"This is it," she said, looking tearily at us and her mother.

"Let's go make an honest woman out of you," Sadie laughed as we made out way to the beach and to our positions.

Kade looked so handsome in his white linen shirt and trousers, a blue flower pinned to the linen blazer to match my dress and the flowers Allison had ordered for us all.

"Beautiful, as always," he whispered.

I smiled up at him, remembering a time when I found it hard to accept his compliments. Now, I embraced and coveted them.

The ceremony was beautiful, we all cried a little at their personally written vows and when the speeches were made at the reception, they had us all in stitches.

For me, every sensation and experience was amplified because of the knowledge that we loved one another and cheering on my two friends now married and laughing happily on their special day was an even happier memory to keep.

"I spoke with your papa," Kade suddenly said, approaching me with two glasses of champagne and handing me one whilst we stood around the reception room as people danced or mingled.

"Okay...why?" I asked, already confused.

"I called him because I heard you are going back to work for him when we get back," he replied as if it was quite normal for him to interfere in my work life now that he was no longer my boss.

"I wonder which of the two little birdies told you that?" I looked over at Sadie and Allison, both of whom were blissfully unaware of my death glare directed at them.

"They were concerned and looking out for you, thats all," he said soothingly as he pulled me into his side and kissed me softly.

"And you thought it was okay to call my papa to thwart my efforts of escaping your fort?" He grinned at the annoyance in my tone.

"No, I know how much you enjoyed working at Atlantis but I wanted to spend some time with you since you can't seem to keep your hands off of me," he sighed, as if he was put out by it.

"Oh yeah? Because that was me pinning you against the shower wall when we were supposed to be getting ready for the wedding, huh?" I teased, earning a sexy smile in return.

"I didn't see you complaining."

"I'm just pointing out the fact that *you're* the one unable to keep your hands off of *me*."

"Which is why Michael agreed to let you have a couple of weeks before you start back at Atlantis. Before you say anything," he continued, cutting off my retort, "you do have to find your replacement for me at work. And I need you with me on a business trip."

"What kind of business trip?" I looked at him sceptically.

"One that involves me having you all to myself in Greece for a week?"

"You are absolutely abusing your power here, Mr Hamilton," I sighed, unable to be angry when I was going to be spending a week with his undivided attention and in a beautiful place, no less.

"Damn right I am," he almost growled placing our glasses on a nearby table and taking me into his arms.

"And you're sure Papa is okay about this?"

"Your father is one scary man. He gave me the third degree about everything, you know. I had to *earn* the right to have that time with you. He went Italian on me."

I laughed at his consternated look, kissing him softly with reverence.

"I adore you."

He beamed at me, kissing me for longer before he looked me in the eyes and let all his affection show.

"And I love you."

EPILOGUE

About fourteen months later...

"**O**h my God, he is going to want to skip the ceremony and start the honeymoon as soon as he sees you!" Ash squealed, clapping her hands like a cheerleader as she jumped on the spot.

Her daughter, little Aliyah, sat on the floor of my hotel room whilst chewing on a biscuit and giving me a big goofy grin.

Sadie sat on the bed, changing a setting on her camera and then taking a few shots of me getting ready for my big day as Allison rested against the dresser, rubbing her small but visible baby bump.

Mum and Megan rushed about putting the final touches to my dress, making me put on my shoes and generally fussing about. I let them do whatever they wanted because I was busy being nervous and excited about becoming Mrs Kade Hamilton.

The first two weeks after we finally got our act together and started our relationship for real, Kade had coaxed me into staying with him. It was really only for a week as we left for an amazing holiday in Greece after I extensively interviewed for my replacement.

Kade didn't like any of the candidates and I think he was

secretly hoping I would change my mind until I found John, a young graduate that had super potential. He was smart, had a good sense of humour and was very organised. Best of all, he could handle the moody Hamilton who was still looking for an excuse to not hire him.

Eventually even Kade couldn't fault him and he was now working for the boss man for the past year. In that time, I would fill in at the Fort when John would take his vacation time, which usually meant Kade would find excuses to get me alone and fulfil his work related sexual fantasies.

I refused to move in with him, even though we spent most of our time at his penthouse and sometimes at the house. I wasn't ready to give up the comfort of the house, even though Kade promised that he would eventually move into it when he figured a way to bump up the security as discreetly as possible.

The media got a whiff of the elusive Hamilton being in a relationship soon after we left for Greece. We got word of some paparazzo's waiting outside of the hotel we were staying at on Mykonos and Kade's answer to that was to leave the hotel holding my hand and then giving the Paparazzi something to take pictures of when he dipped me and kissed me full on my mouth in public. After that, my life was very much a public affair which was difficult to handle at times but true to his word, Kade stuck by me and helped me through every step of the transition. His father controlled most of the leaks the press had about my former life and marriage and eventually we were old news, although there were always photographers looking for scraps from us every now and then.

Life moved on into a routine and I felt like I was walking on cloud nine with everything in order and finally going the way I wanted. I had a job I enjoyed, friends who were amazing and a man that I loved who would do anything for me. I had to pinch myself to believe it was all real.

When Kade proposed the first time, we had only been officially together for a month and he had planned an elaborate and beautiful proposal. When I turned him down, he didn't speak to me for a couple of days. I eventually explained to him that I was not ready for marriage again, maybe one day but also maybe never. He, of course, didn't back down and saw it as a challenge. He proposed a total of six times, once a month - each proposal new and exciting and different but every time I gave the same answer.

Things changed one night when I awoke crying from a nightmare. I saw that all trace of him had vanished from my life and I was alone. The feeling of emptiness wouldn't leave me alone and I called him. He came over within half an hour, comforting me as I poured out all my fears about life and not being with him and even fears about not being able to have children. He listened through everything with patience, gave me empathy and restored my faith that everything would be okay. It was then, in the early hours of the morning, curled into his body and warmth, that I told him I would marry him.

Everything seemed to happen so fast after that. He told me that he didn't want to give me time to change my mind. Before long, he had recruited mum into organising a lavish London wedding with all our friends and family and quite a few close celebrity friends of the Hamilton's.

And now here I was, standing in front of the mirror taking in my full sleeved lace wedding gown with trail and button up detail. It was so beautiful, just what I had envisioned for this wedding. The boat neck detailed with lace, the veil secured to my pinned up hair that had twists and braids running through it, beautifully finishing off the look I had aimed for.

My engagement ring sparkled in the light, a rare oval cut yellow diamond set with white diamonds on either side of it. He knew me so well.

All I remember from my wedding was walking down the aisle with Dad, looking up to see Kade with eyes shining bright with the exact emotions I was feeling and him reading vows he wrote for me with fierce sincerity. I remember his sweet kiss as we were pronounced husband and wife and then his words that made me smile wider.

"Thank you for making me the happiest man alive, Mrs Hamilton."

In that moment, I thanked the stars, divine providence and fate for everything that I had been so fortunate to have.

"Thank you for being mine, Mr Hamilton."

The End

ACKNOWLEDGE-MENTS

Thank you for reading my debut novel - the first in the 'In time' series!

This is the tricky part, because this book took me the better part of six years to write and another year to have the courage to put out there for the world to see. Therefore, you can appreciate that there are quite a few people I want to thank.

To give you a little context, I started writing this book shortly after I got divorced. I was a young, newly single mother with a 16 month old child that needed medical care and as with a lot of people struggling to deal with loss and stress, I fell into depression.
I started writing whilst working in a boutique in Kensington, between the lull in customers, on little index cards I found behind the cash register. And so my writing journey began. Three other jobs and seven-ish years later, I'm putting my labor of love out there, sharing my (second) baby with you, the readers. It was a journey of self discovery, hardship and acceptance. And now, I have reached this point where I can express my gratitude in full.

Firstly, I would like to thank my wonderful supportive parents and family who have been with me through all the ups and downs these past few years.
Mum, there truly is no one as amazing as you are on this

planet and I am forever grateful that God gave me you. You are the one that sees the brighter future for me, when all I can see is fogginess. You're my heart.

My little sister, Nizia, you've always encouraged me to keep on going and that encouragement and support means everything to me. Love you to the moon and back.

To the many friends, colleagues and cousins that kept pushing and prompting me to finish (in the most loving way) - you are all absolute DIAMONDS.

To the girls at Yacco, you were there for the start of my journey and saw it through with me for two years - thank you for asking me questions about my plot and the characters and for encouraging me with your interest. Laura, Inma, Emma, Abi, Ayaan and even our elusive Tatiana - thank you, with all my heart.

For my wonderful friends Sana, Nuria, Reena, Lula, Madiha, Jasvin, Aziza, Farha, Zabeen, Aamna, Sundus, and Anjli. The school mums - Mishal, Reba, Simona, Mariam, Shahida, and their respective family and friends. There has been so much support and love - I can't thank you enough. This is the family that I got to choose for myself and I'm forever grateful. This book is dedicated to you, just as much.

Gareth (Gazza) and Juliet (me Julie!) - you guys are truly my soulmates. I am so glad you just burst into my life in an explosion of colours, right when I needed it the most. I've never laughed so much in my life, than in my time with you. So glad you're both in my life and thank you for those Costa coffee's and shortbread for when I was having a crappy day.

To my cousins and extended family - thank you for your patience whenever I spoke of my book these past years. I know everyone has been waiting for me to finish this book (ta-dah!) Again, your encouragement and support is invaluable.

Thank you to Milan and Mila for allowing me to use the

beautiful image on the front cover when designing something meaningful that felt right to me. I am extremely grateful and thankful for your talents.

To all the men I met these past few years whilst looking for a new beginning (on the off chance you find this book), thank you for the good and (mostly) bad experiences. Without those eye opening experiences, I may have never learnt to never settle for just anything. So cheers!

To Mr S - you're the first man I trusted completely and although it didn't work out, I'm a better person for the lessons that I learned from us and a broken heart. Thank you for the good memories, that I forgot for so long, we had shared.

I want to thank my little angel, Inaya. You probably won't know until much later how much you helped me through the very difficult days and nights when it seemed like nothing would work out right. I'm here, and whole, because of you. I love you unconditionally and more than anything on God's green planet. I hope you never read this novel...

Lastly, thank you again to whomever is reading this book. I put my heart and soul into it over the long time it took to complete. Please forgive any errors I may have made, this is my first rodeo after all!

I hope you enjoy reading it and, if possible, please do leave feedback/a review.

If I forgot anyone, I apologise in advance - there are just too many people to thank!

The next story will be Sadie and Jason's - stay tuned and follow me on instagram!

Forever grateful,

Nida

ABOUT THE AUTHOR

Nida is a Medical PA who lives in one of the greatest cities on Earth - London - where she was born and raised. A true Londoner at heart, she enjoys the rainy days, walks thorugh parks with her daughter and creative projects.

When she's not writing, she's reading. Or re-watching BBC's Pride and Prejudice (yes, the one with Colin Firth in it) or Persuasion, because who doesn't love Captain Wentworth? She obviously has her priorities set right.

She hopes her next book doesn't take six years to write and publish. Here's hoping...

Follow En Bee on Instagram: @en_bee_

Printed in Great Britain
by Amazon